WITHIN THE HAUNT
OF THE
UNSEELIE COURT

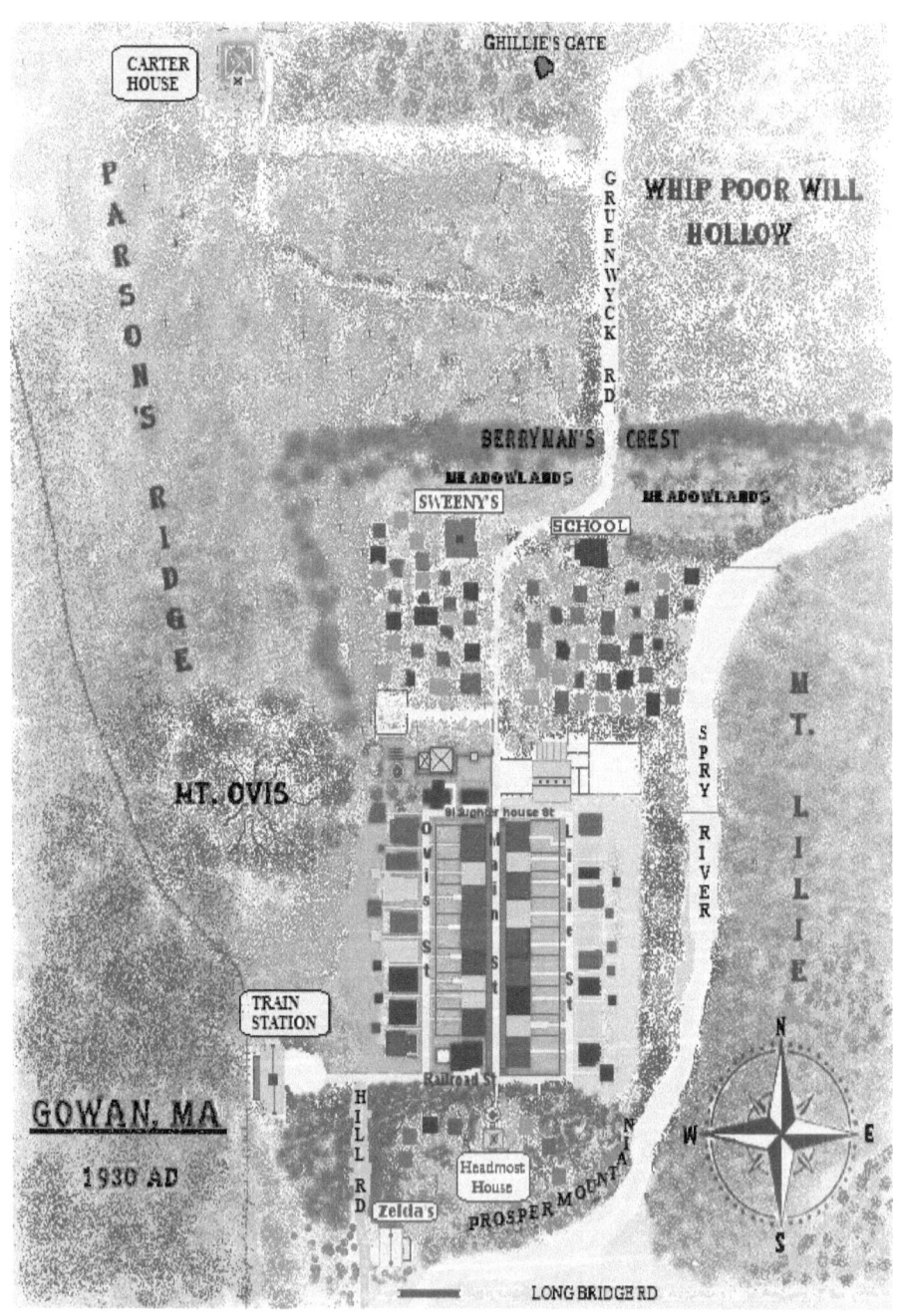

CARTER HOUSE

GHILLIE'S GATE

PARSON'S RIDGE

GRUENWYCK RD

WHIP POOR WILL HOLLOW

BERRYMAN'S CREST

MEADOWLANDS

SWEENY'S

SCHOOL

MEADOWLANDS

MT. OVIS

Slaughter house St

Ovis St

Main St

Lilie St

SPRY RIVER

MT. LILIE

TRAIN STATION

Railroad St

HILL RD

Zelda's

Headmost House

PROSPER MOUNTAIN

GOWAN, MA

1930 AD

LONG BRIDGE RD

N
W E
S

WITHIN THE HAUNT OF THE UNSEELIE COURT

BY

R.C. DAVIS

FOR
MALIKAI

CHAPTER ONE

JANEY

1

~

1

Janette 'Janey' Emery Carter rode in the back seat of the 1928 Cadillac, the breeze through the open windows whipping her short, blonde bob. Annoying as it was, it still felt good on that hot Thursday in July. 1935 was already shaping up to be a strange year. There was a burgeoning foreboding in her gut; the usual harbinger of something dark coming her way. She couldn't shake it, and the only thing that brought her any degree of relief was that, like with all of life's difficulties, she would tackle it head on. Taking the bull by the horns was standard procedure for Janey Carter.

Percy Snoaks hardly said a word as he fought to control the Cadillac on the rough surface of the roadway, sweat beading on the dark skin of his forehead. Janey began to feel pity for the old man who occasionally threw her a nervous smile from the rearview mirror. She could have easily taken the train and walked the breadth of Gowan to Headmost House. But her mother wouldn't have it. So, she sent Percy.

Janey's sympathy for the man had its limits though. It was his fault for choosing the route. Instead of driving south out of Bournemouth to Arkham, and then west on the Aylesbury Pike to turn south on the road leading from Princeton to Grunewyck, Percy had chosen the older, less traveled roads. Working his way down to the Old Turnpike, he turned west on Long Bridge Road so they could enter Gowan from the lower end of town. Janey suspected he was trying to avoid the precarious mess that was Whip-poor-will Hollow, with its mud and treacherous fishhook turns. But mostly; it's spooky atmosphere.

Janey fell into reflecting on her two years at Thayer College for Women. She had never once returned home during the time that she was away pursuing her education in teaching. She had simply written letters and received them in return.

Upon the receipt of one particularly distressing correspondence from her mother, she fought the overwhelming desire to abandon school and return home immediately. Included within the envelope was a copy of a letter received by her mother but meant for the both of them. It had been postmarked, 'Kelso, Scotland'. It was from her father and was dated several weeks before. The bulk of his words had been those of abandonment. Janey knew he had been abroad on business and could only assume it was for land speculation.

Benjamin Edrick Carter had met another woman. He had banished Janey and her mother, plain and simple. They were to be out of Carter House by the time he returned to Massachusetts. Every one of the Carter House servants was to go, except the groundskeeper, Kaleb Knight.

Janey and her mother were to take up residence at Headmost House, Benjamin's deceased brother's place in the village. It had been years since Janey had set a foot in that mansion where it sat vigilantly on the north slope of Prosper Mountain.

Uncle Bart had resided there until his death, which occurred a little over a year prior to her going off to Thayer. He and aunt Trudy were buried in the family plot just outside the brick wall that surrounded the backyard. There were others buried there, assorted cousins, an orphaned niece, and an adopted child that had died from the so called 'Spanish Flu'. Even Sissy and Elijah Koontz, the household help, had been given a corner of the tiny cemetery because they had been so much like family to the Carters.

The old Victorian had been closed up and the furniture covered. Percy and his wife, Janey's much beloved, Tabitha, had been charged with tending to it. Janey would visit with Tabby and Percy whenever she came to call on her aunt and uncle. It wasn't the same, though. Now, they would all be back under the same roof, the prospect of a shared happiness looming before them.

The letter cautioned that they were all to give Carter House a wide berth. No unexpected visits. Janey had been born there, though. She had lived her entire childhood in her parent's dream house overlooking the village from Nixie's Bluff.

Janey imagined her mother, Constance, pacing the rooms at Headmost, occasionally stopping at one of the two bay windows to look down on Gowan, brooding, a glass of claret in her hand.

A goal formulated in Janey's head. She would go to Carter House and give her father a piece of her mind. She would come in the backway through the apple orchard, walk right through the kitchen and go straight into Benjamin's study without announcement. She would confront him about his adulterous ways. They never had much of a relationship. It was an association based on patriarchy. He had been the master and had lorded over the manor—and her life.

2

The Cadillac soon rolled to a stop at a T-intersection. Janey read the worse for wear road sign, a white painted pine board, tacked to a post, proclaiming in black letters:

GOWAN-NORTH-1.5 M →
BRIMFIELD-SOUTH-13 M ←

The bumpy ride was over. Janey smiled to herself as Percy turned north, passing Zelda's Roadhouse on their right. It stood alone out there on the edge of town. It's massive, two-story bulk of arcade porches and bargeboard, was quietly awaiting the influx of working men, barflies, and ruffians that would start arriving within a few hours. The activity would go until the wee hours of the morning, giving Tip Thomas, the proprietor, just enough time to get things cleaned up before the next onslaught of drunken men and dubious women. Janey was glad it was out on the edge of town. Brenner's tavern on the main street was bad enough on a Friday night; Gowan didn't need any more boozy mayhem.

Percy appeared to relax and the car picked up speed. Hill Road (or just 'The Hill') was in much better shape where it cut through the western slope of Prosper Mountain on its way down to Railroad Street. They would take a right-hand turn at the bottom and after about a block, another right into the lane leading up to Headmost House.

"Almost there, Miss Janey," Percy said, glancing back, the relief apparent on his face.

"Yes, I see, Percy. Long Bridge Road is such a terrible excuse for a road. Don't know why you chose it, but… you got us through."

"Better'n that Whip-poor-will Hollow, can't abide that place. Gives me the heebie-geebies, if you know what I'm meaning."

"I know all too well. You did a fabulous job on that beat up ol' road, Percy, but you know, I could have taken the train home and saved everybody the trouble."

"Yes, Miss Janey, but the Missus were dead set on you getting a car and I don't dare argue with the Missus. Besides, I got to be the first to see you. Been over two years, as you know. Ain't been the same without you, specially at Headmost. Which, you know… ain't really home."

"Thank you, Percy, it's good to see you, too. I can hardly wait to see Tabby. Been so long since she and I have talked." He gave Janey a quick grin and returned his focus to the road.

Percy and Tabby had been with Janey since the day she was born, having been largely responsible for her care. Then, her uncle's housemaid, Sissy, had to go and die on the back porch at Headmost, keeling over her washboard and tub with suspected heart failure. Her husband, Elijah, the gardener, fled the property out of grief and was never to be found. It's been said he had drowned himself in the Spry River; but that was pure speculation. So, Janey's father sent the Snoaks to Headmost and Janey was left to fend for herself. Soon after, Kaleb Knight was hired for Carter House and brought his wife. Josephine Knight took over for Tabitha, but a year later was found dead under the clothes lines where she had been hanging the washing. Apparently, she had met the same fate as Sissy, except Doc Bolen mentioned that there was evidence Josephine had been literally frightened to death. Whatever she had been witness to, proved too much for her heart. Kaleb, having heard her scream from the stable, was first on the scene. He refused to ever talk about it.

Upon reaching the stop sign at Railroad Street, Percy brought the car to a halt. The train depot came into view on her left and Janey could see it had a new coat of blue-grey paint with chocolate brown trim. She wasn't surprised. Gil Carson had always been attentive as Gowan's Station Agent. His assistant, Danny Billings, had probably done the work with Gil waving and pointing at the spots that the agent-in-training had missed while perched precariously on a ladder.

Percy got the Cadillac moving again and they were soon rolling up the lane to Headmost House. At one point, they cleared the dense canopy of trees and Janey could look back to see Gowan's sister town of Grunewick off in the distance. Her eyes soon strayed over to the tiny visage that was Carter House perched high above the town to the northwest, its windows reflecting the light of the late afternoon sun. Janey felt her ire rising. That's where she should be going, the house where she was born. She had a right to be there. Turning away, she huffed and her mind filled with visions of what might be going on up there.

Benjamin and his new wife were probably behaving as if Janey and Constance never existed. Acting as if there had never been a lively family in that home, living a vibrant life as pillars of the Gowan community.

Yes, Janey was going up there whether Benjamin liked it or not. She would confront him and put her eyes on this person—this woman. She was most likely some sly, cunning, seductress like one of the characters out of Hopwood's play, *The Gold-Diggers.*

The Cadillac finally reached the large, brown granite fountain centered in the turn-around. Janey could see that Percy couldn't keep up with the groundskeeping. It was a two-man job and Janey supposed he was probably just doing the minimum. But there was no one to care anymore. With her uncle gone and Benjamin Carter keeping his distance, her mother could only expect so much from a life-worn, old man, like Percy.

The car circled the fountain and stopped in front of the house's portico. Percy scrambled to get out of his door to open Janey's. She cast her eyes to the floor and sighed. Not being a lover of chivalry, she would allow it for Percy's sake. Stepping out, she thanked him and going to the back of the car she stopped and looked up at the old Victorian. The windows in its cupola reflected the retreating sun as if sending a signal to Carter House that Gowan's princess had returned.

The heavily varnished oaken front door with its ornate glass, swung open and Constance shuffled out of the vestibule. She was weeping and patting at her eyes with a dark, lace trimmed handkerchief. Dressed in black from toe to crown, a mourner's veil draped her head. The image of Queen Victoria in mourning, as seen in a framed photograph in Headmost's library, ran through Janey's mind. Constance had adopted the fashion of her friend and partner in gossip, the widow, Beulah McKay, both mourning the loss of a husband; one to death, the other to circumstance. Constance always did have a flare for the dramatic. She had also gained a considerable amount of weight since Janey saw her last, her shape as round as an apple below her ill-fitting corset

"Janey! Oh, Janey! I am so relieved that you are finally home! The house has been so quiet."

"Mother! I'm so happy to see you."

They embraced and looking over Constance's shoulder, Janey grinned at Tabby who stood on the top step, wiping at her eyes. Percy opened the Cadillac's trunk and removed Janey's small suitcase. Carrying it up into the house, he gave his wife a quick peck on the cheek as he passed.

"I hope you had a pleasant ride," Constance said.

"I could have easily taken the train and walked up from the station, you know?"

"Oh, but that's such a distance. Better that Percy drive you."

"Very well, it's over now. So... good to see you."

Her mother stepped back and ran her moist eyes up and down Janey's frame, obviously searching for something to nag her about. Things like, "Janey, my dear, you are too thin," or "Your hair, Janey, do you honestly like that bob? Nothing womanly about that."

She had been Constance Arabella Whitney of Springfield, Massachusetts. Her family had been well to do and her father had been involved with numerous partners in the manufacturing of rifles.

Benjamin Carter had been involved in transporting goods, something his family had been engaged in for nearly two centuries. As the story goes, it was during the late portion of the 'Gilded Age' that a young

Benjamin spent an evening with Janey's grandfather and the visiting, Colonel Mordecai, in the family's library, smoking cigars, and drinking bourbon.

They had been talking transportation methods and delivery, when Constance entered the room to bring fresh tumblers and to empty ash trays. For Benjamin, it was love at first sight. The rest was history. Janey came along late in their marriage and was only three years old when the influenza pandemic began taking its toll on the world.

As a little girl, Janey rarely ever saw Benjamin. When she did, it was only on occasions like suppertime in the great dining room or when spying through the crack in the door of his study. She hadn't spent that much more time with Constance, who had frittered away her days in the master bedroom with the door shut, moping, and sipping claret.

Constance had grown somewhat melancholic after Janey's birth. The girl overheard the servants say it was because the lady of the house blamed Janey for stealing her 'grand existence', a social butterfly whose life had been spoiled by pregnancy.

It wasn't until Janey's seventeenth year that her and Constance started coming together. Then Janey was off for Thayer and contact was limited to the occasional letter. Now that she was back, they would have to learn to live with each other in a house that wasn't theirs. Percy and Tabby would make the transition more bearable for Janey.

Her mother wrapped her arm in Janey's and they walked into the house, chatting about everything under the sun except for the separation. That would come later, when Constance would open a fresh bottle of claret and they would toast the bond created from their most recent discontent.

Janey would be expected to sit in the parlor while Constance lamented about their forced move, all the things she had to leave behind, and the trivial amount of money given her monthly by her ex-husband through their attorney, Philip Shannon. It was most likely a substantial amount but would never seem to be enough to the matriarch after having lived most of her life so high on the hog.

As a dutiful daughter, Janey would sit and listen, sipping her wine, unable to get a word in edgewise. She could live without the wealth. Constance, on the other hand, had been blindsided. She lamented on how unfair it was that this event had come so late in her life.

When her mother had fallen asleep in her chair, Janey rescued the goblet dangling precariously from her fingers. Taking it and hers to the kitchen, she walked in to see the dark skin of her adopted mother's arms powdered to the elbows with flour as she manipulated the dough for a long list of baked goods that Stewart's Bakery didn't produce.

Tabby took the glasses from Janey and set them on the little kitchen table. Then apologizing for the trace of flour she would leave behind on her dress, she took Janey in her arms.

Janey could care less about the mess. Two years had passed since the last time she had received such a substantial hug and she practically melted in the older woman's arms. Janey felt the relief that came with a true embrace and fought the unexpected tears that stung her eyes. A slight sob escaped her lips and Tabby soothed her with soft words, repeating the phrase that Janey had heard so many, many, times before, "Everything gonna be alright, sugar-pie. Everything gonna be alright."

CHAPTER TWO

TOM

1

~

1

Janey was early to bed, early to rise, and out the door with just toast and a cup of tea in her belly. Constance slept in. A quick kiss on Tabby's hollowing cheek and she was gone. The sun was just ready to break the peak of Prosper Mountain, half a mile up the wooded slope behind the house. Janey could already feel the air heating up this Friday morning.

On the long ride from Bournemouth, Percy had told Janey that Miss Durnell had quit her position as the local school teacher. He had seen the notice hanging on the board outside of the townhall when he stopped to drop off a basket of Tabby's famous molasses cookies for the clerk, the mayor, and the chief of police. There was benefit in staying on the good side of Gowan's civil servants.

Crossing Railroad Street, she chose the west side of Main so as to keep the sun on her as she walked. Passing Jones' blacksmith shop on the corner, she moved north on one of the two boardwalks that lined both sides of the street. She stopped and turned to take in the view as the sun broke the mountain top behind her. Two years was a long time to be away and she wondered how people were going to react to her return. Janey hoped they would see the change in her and not treat her like the spoiled tomboy they had grown to know; the untouchable,

Janette Carter of the Spry River Valley.

Passing Sally's clothing store, she smiled and waved at Sally who was in the window rearranging the display. Sally's eyes went wide and she grinned. Waving frantically, she turned to speak to someone at the back of the store. Janey presumed it was her assistant, Bessie LaVern.

Constance had told her in a letter that Bessie had taken the job. The news had come to her mother through the grapevine (Beulah), along with a mention of 'Sally and Bessie's unholy alliance," whatever that was supposed to mean. Janey returned the wave and continued on down the street.

Passing the Telephone House, Jeramiah's Gun Shop, and Blanchet's (the village tailor), Janey stopped to watch Silas McCarthy roll down the awning in front of his general store. He had to do a double take before it dawned on him who she was. Grinning in disbelief, he said, "Well, Janey Carter, look at you! Back home now, are you? Mary! Mary! Come out here." Janey stood fast, smiling, feeling like what she thought a specimen under a microscope might feel like.

Mary McCarthy poked her head out and with a smile wide enough to show all her teeth, the old woman moved out onto the boardwalk. Several bulky sacks of cornmill filled her arms. "Well, I declare, look at you! Janey Carter... all grown up now. We sure missed you around here."

Janey felt nervous under their scrutiny even though they had always been nice to her, probably because she never stole fruit or vegetables from the produce boxes out front; a common practice in Gowan. Wealthy kids didn't need to steal apples when their fathers could simply purchase the whole damn store.

"Sorry, have to get to the townhall before Maddie goes for lunch. Good to see you both."

"Going for Durnell's old job, hey, Janey? Well, you couldn't have come home at a better time. Gowan needs a teacher... real bad like. People up Grunewyck way have been talking about building another school, but it will be years before that'll happen. It was looking like Gregory Bly may have to substitute here in Gowan until they can find someone with the learning for such a job. But now that you're back, well..."

10

"Gregory's a good teacher."

Silas and Mary threw each other a look, the doubt apparent.

"Well, stop in when you have the time, Janey. We're always here," Silas said with Mary grinning and nodding her head.

"Certainly will."

Janey walked away and glancing back with the smile still on her face, she saw they hadn't moved, their eyes still on her. She threw them a little wave and they abruptly returned to their tasks.

Gregory Bly had tutored Janey several times as a child and other than his somewhat creepy appearance, he was thorough in his methods and a pleasant conversationalist. She liked him and never failed to rise up to defend his reputation when people maligned him in her presence.

Biddy Tomes was placing the sidewalk sandwich board chalked with 'Specials' out front of Boots' A Walk Inn café across the street. She gave Janey a wave and returned inside, her actions indifferent as if, "That Carter girl..." had never been away.

Janey had no doubt that as soon as everybody felt it was the right time, they would all switch from their surprise over her return, to asking personal questions like: "Why'd your folks split, Janey? Wouldn't think Gowan's wealthiest would want to weather the slings and arrows of a sinful separation. So sad." She would blame it all on her father and his gold-digging bride.

She passed Brenner's Tavern before moving down a short set of steps to the cobblestone walk that would take her past Philip Shannon-Attorney At Law and Loeffler's Butcher Shop. Coming to Slaughter House Road, she crossed, making a slight deviation to the right to get around Doc Bolen's office.

Gowan's only municipal building sat two-thirds of the way back from the street, a large two story of the Italianate style with its wide overhangs, roof brackets, and classically trimmed windows. It stood without the typical cupola centering it's nearly flat roof. Shrouded by ancient maples, it housed the mayor's office, the school superintendent, the clerk's office, and several small meeting rooms. The Gowan police department, a holding cell, and Judge Benson's office and court room occupied the second floor.

The cobblestone walk turned left there and passed through the base of the small belltower. Its bold clock face told her that it was about to peal the tenth hour. It's mammoth Revolution Era bell (that someone had donated back during Reconstruction), began its clamor. Janey covered her ears and hurried away.

Upon reaching the community bulletin board outside the front door, Janey saw the water marked notice behind the glass. As she expected, a new 'School Marm' was being sought. Janey caught her reflection in the dusty glass and grinned at herself. Her appearance exuded confidence, something some people often misconstrued as arrogance. She let them think what they wished. Folks around Gowan, like most places, had trouble accepting a woman who stood her ground.

The front door squeaked when she opened it. Maddie Clemens, the town clerk, turned to look, only her head visible above the high counter. The woman actually smiled. Her chestnut brown hair had gone from low curls with a single victory roll at the top, two years before, to low curls with bangs. Janey had feared she would get an earful for wearing a bob, but Maddie had no room to talk. Bangs on a woman Maddie's age looked ridiculous.

"Well, if it isn't Janey Carter. Where have you been these last few years?" she said, obviously teasing.

"Just home from Thayer, you know, the Teacher's College up in Bournemouth? Which is why I'm here. I see you're looking for a teacher and I…"

"So, you want the job? Well… you can just have it. I'm fed up with trying to fill that position. You ought to see the likes of those who've been coming in here trying to make it theirs. They were just not worth looking at twice. Gregory Bly was one of them. There's just no way a man that ugly is going to teach school here in Gowan. Scare the children half to death, he will. As far as I'm concerned, it's yours. If I wait much longer, it'll be me down there teaching those little hooligans, and you know darn well my other job is playing nursemaid to Mayor Wilton's kids. Can't do all three. I 'spect Mayor Wilton would love it if I would take it, though. That man has always thought I wasn't worth my wage. You got your diploma with you?"

"Well, no, it's up at the house, uh… Headmost, and… well… we are at Headmost House, now."

"Well, that's real nice. You just bring it around and show me so I can say I saw it. I should have you all signed up by then and don't you worry about Superintendent Pike. He might be in charge of the school, but I shouldn't have any problem convincing him that you're the one. Put an end to this nonsense, once and for all. Been hanging over my head like a dark cloud ever since Miss Durnell sprang it on us that she was quitting. I won't be coming back at the end of summer break, she said. Nearly thirty years and she just waltzes right in here and says she's going to leave us, and then waltzes right out. Leave us high and dry, is what I'd say. You'll have to go before the board sometime soon, young lady, but don't worry, they're just as desperate as I."

Janey listened to Maddie prattle on, unable to get a word in. She thought it might take some convincing but, here they were, handing her the job on a silver platter. So, she just smiled a lot and nodded yes to everything Maddie said.

"Here, you take this," she said, opening a drawer and taking out a key tied to an old wooden ruler. "You go on down there anytime you wish. The place is going to need a good cleaning, and when you come back with your diploma, maybe you can bring a lesson plan to present to Mr. Pike. We can talk about your pay at that time, and maybe a few rules that the board would like for you to follow. Sound good to you, Miss Carter?"

"Well, yes. Thank you very much," Janey said, bewildered.

Maddie handed her the ruler. The same ruler Miss Durnell had used to slap her palms ten times a day when she misbehaved. The old clerk's grin oozed with relief. "You come back on Monday. As you know, this office won't be open over the weekend. That should give you two days to get set up at the school house, do some dusting, maybe fix up the place a little. You can live in the room in the back, it's got an inside toilet now; Durnell saw to that. Oh! and it's also got a new bedframe and mattress. You can offer summer school if you want, or we can just skip it for this year. Special circumstances, you know? Okay, see you on Monday."

Janey took the grime-covered ruler with the large skeleton key dangling from one end, eyed its nearly indiscernible markings, looked into Maddie's smiling face and said, "Thank you very much. I'll have you know that I'm going to do my best."

"Three years ago, I wouldn't have believed a word of it, Miss Janey Carter. But I suspect you are not the same little scamp you were before buckling down and getting through Thayer. I've heard that place is no picnic. Yes, you're finally a grown woman. Well… you have a pleasant weekend and we'll see you in a couple days," Maddie said, seemingly anxious to get rid of Janey.

Janey nodded again, smiled, and turned away. A certain excitement stirred her gut as she closed the door behind her, saying to herself, "Yes, my dear Tabby, you were correct, everything is going to be alright."

Returning the way she had come, Janey thought to cross Main Street and walk up the other side so she could peek in the window of the newspaper office. Before crossing, she took the ruler in one hand and gave the key a jerk, snapping the string. Placing the key in the one pocket on her dress, she smiled defiantly as she broke the ruler over a knee and tossed its pieces into the narrow space between the butcher shop and Philip Shannon's office.

"Hey! What are you doing there!"

Janey's stomach tried to climb up into her throat. Looking around in distress, she saw no one. The tone was familiar, though. A voice from her past. She caught movement up on the balcony of Brenner's Tavern. The sun was in her eyes, making it difficult to see the man leaning over the railing.

"What business is it of yours, mister?"

"Well, it's not. But I couldn't resist teasing you… Janette Janey Carter. Emery? It's just been too long," he said and laughed. "Don't look so surprised, you'd think you'd seen a ghost."

Her brain raced. She thought maybe he was just a drunken stranger who had somehow weaseled her name out of one of the locals. "How do you know me, Mister? Come clean now if you don't want trouble," she said.

The words were just out of her lips when the memory rolled panoramic across her mind's eye. Summer days at Carter House spent in the stable where Kaleb Knight worked caring for the equestrian stock, and—his nephew, who came to help in the summers. That one kid who she couldn't help but grow fond of. It was a grown-up Tom Lynn.

14

2

"Tom Lynn," she said as if thinking aloud.

"Janette Carter," he replied, mockingly.

"Janey… whether you mind or not."

"Why of course, how forgetful of me."

"Why are you up there?"

"It's summer, don't you remember…"

"Of course, I remember, but it's been years."

"You've been away, Janey. Much has changed."

"Thayer… I was at Thayer."

"Yes, I know, and your father was off to Scotland. All the help has been let go and my uncle's last letter was an urgent request to come and lend him a hand. I am a week early. So, I've taken a room."

Janey said nothing. Tom would be able to offer a little insight into what was going on up at Carter House. Any information he offered would better prepare her for her coming confrontation.

"Come down here, Tom Lynn, my neck is hurting."

"Say, please."

"Oh, my giddy aunt!" Janey said with frustration. "Please!"

Some things never change. Tom was still annoying. Coming out the front door of the tavern, he grinned at her. "Sorry about that. I was testing you. Still have that quick temper, I see."

"Still have that annoying as hell attitude, I see."

"Okay, I apologize."

"Very well, I accept—this time."

"I promise I will work harder at not letting that kid I used to be intrude upon us becoming fast friends—again. That suit you?"

"I'll do the same… in all fairness."

Tom smiled and stuck out his hand, "Deal?"

Janey took it and gave it a shake. She studied his face. There was a sincerity in his eyes that she had never seen there before. They could have easily gotten off on the wrong foot. She wasn't going to let that happen. Smiling back, she released his hand.

"There it is," he said, "I've missed that smile—as rare as it was. Shall we walk? Got a bit of catching up to do."

"Why certainly, I have the whole day, now that I've accomplished

15

my goal."

"And that was?"

"I went for the teaching job and they gave it up without a fight."

"School teacher? Janey Carter, a school teacher? Never thought I'd see the day."

"Yes, what do you think I was doing at Thayer? Learning to keep a house, cook, and raise children?"

"No, actually… that would not be the Janey I recall."

"And you, what are you doing these days?"

"Clerking down in Salem, teaching a little horseback riding, and trying to write a book."

"A book? The other two I can understand, but a book? What kind of a book? What's the title?"

"Don't laugh… Folklore Of Massachusetts. I thought of writing fiction, but I wanted to write what I knew. Not much on story telling."

"Well, you told some whoppers back when we were kids."

"Yes, so… trying to move away from that."

"You're a folklorist, are you?"

"Actually, yes. Spent some time at Amherst."

"Tom Lynn… a student?"

"Believe it or not. Four years. Graduated the same year you left Gowan for Thayer. When I returned and came looking for you, your mother told me you had gone off to college to make something of yourself. Wouldn't let me in the house, though… she still doesn't like me. All those years I spent at Carter House took their toll, I guess."

"Well, I'm sure she would think differently of you now. She might even be impressed. I have to admit… I am."

The look that came over Tom's face was one of pure gratitude. Janey found his smile somewhat endearing and chastised herself internally for feeling like she was already surrendering to his charm.

"I don't know, Janey. I suspect she hasn't. Not Constance Carter, the matriarch of Nixie's Bluff."

"Uh… not anymore," she said and smiled, trying to distract herself from what she knew was a returning infatuation. "I think I'll stop at the school house and try to determine what may need my attention." She thought he might leave her then and she could be alone with her

16

thoughts.

"I'll walk with you; you might need some assistance."

So much for that.

"Are you sure? It's a ways out."

"I know where it is, and… I'd be more than happy to."

He smiled that smile again and his green eyes, framed by his unruly dark hair, twinkled.

"Very well, have it your way."

Janey decided not to fight it. She would just keep her eyes off him for the rest of the day.

They never made it to the school house. Reminiscing got in the way and they stopped to sit on a bench placed for the students where the path from the school met the street. When the sun had reached its zenith, Janey decided she had all she could bear of Tom Lynn for one day. She couldn't believe how enamored she was. It had been a long time since she had made love with a man, and she feared she would say something stupid.

"Well, Tom, I think I'll head home to tell my mother the news of my new job."

"I thought you… we, were going up to the school house?"

"It can wait, I still have a couple weeks to get things ready. Got to get a teaching plan in place. It will be a tough year. I've never taught before."

"You'll catch on quick. You always were a smart girl, Janey."

She smiled and turned to look back at the distant Headmost House up on the hillside. Something was changing—or had already. Tom wasn't that pigtail pulling imp that he used to be. She now felt at ease with him, perhaps… too at ease.

Tom had never really been a serious love interest because of Sully Albright. Janey and Sully at thirteen years of age, holding hands, lots of kissing. He was her first kiss. There was never anything solid, though. Puppy love, followed by a curiosity that drove them toward the forbidden. She let Sully fondle her breasts when they had grown big enough for such a thing. Then came the coercing to let him have a peek under her dress. It only got worse after that. She was constantly fighting to keep him out of her panties. One day she'd had enough and punched him in the nose. She ran away as he stood screaming and crying, blood dripping down his lips. From then on, it was just rude gestures back and forth until Sully hooked up with Becky Haines. Rumor had it, she let Sully do anything he wanted. That lasted until she got pregnant and the Haines family fled Gowan.

Jumping up from the bench, Janey began her trek home. Tom followed. Leaving him on the street outside of Brenner's, Janey said, "Good bye, Tom, nice to see you again. Good luck up at Carter Hou… my house. Hope Kaleb doesn't work you too hard."

"Janey," Tom said with a pleading tone.

She turned and studied him. There was a feeling that she wasn't picking up on something. Had she not been reading him correctly? Tom looked miserable standing there in his tieless white shirt open at the throat, the dark suit of European cut, and the black wing tipped shoes now coated in dust. He looked attractive in a rough sort of way. Janey trembled. Their eyes met and he said, "Can I see you again?" His words were beseeching.

"Well, I'm coming up to 'my house' to give my father a piece of my mind. If you're there, you'll see me."

"Might not be until next Friday. I don't know. As I said, I came to Gowan earlier than expected. Thought maybe… oh, hell! I was hoping to spend some time with you, Janey. There, I said it!"

"I do like you, Tom, and I know where I can find you," Janey said and turned away. "So… we'll see."

Tom stood scratching his head as he watched her go. Sighing, he said to himself, "Always has to be your way, huh, Janey?"

3

Nealy Garret exited the front door of the townhall and stopping to stand on the steps, he looked across the green toward Main Street. It wasn't proper for an officer of the law to tease the town clerk, but Maddie Clemens could hold her own, and even though she might complain to Chief Cobb, Nealy knew the chief did his share of tormenting the clerk.

Merlyn Cobb soon joined Nealy, using the front door instead of the official Gowan Police Department entrance at the back.

"You see that, Chief?" Nealy said, pointing. "That's Janey Carter, but… who's she with?"

"Looks like Tom Lynn," Merlyn said, rolling a toothpick back and forth across his lips.

"Now, wasn't he that troublemaker you were going on about?"

"Yeah, he was."

"Suppose I should keep an eye on him?"

"Naw, that was years ago."

"But people don't change. Bet he's the same ol' scalawag he was."

"Well, Janey Carter wasn't much better. You didn't dare cross her, not unless you wanted to come out and find your tires flattened… or something worse."

"Well, maybe we should keep an eye on the both of 'em?"

"They're grown folks, now, Nealy. Both been off to college and all. 'Spect they're not looking to make any trouble nowadays."

"Well, what's he doing in Gowan? He don't live here."

"Working up at Carter House, I s'pose. That's why he's always been here."

"What's he doing up there?"

"Helping Kaleb, I'm guessing. Ben Carter fired all his help ever since he came back with that woman. Hell, even kicked Constance and Janey out. Sent them packing to Headmost. I imagine Kaleb needs Tom coming around to help out. I know I wouldn't want to be wearing Kaleb's shoes right now, no way, no how. He sure got his work cut out for him. That woman, the one Ben Carter married and brought back, well, she brought others with her, but they just girls. I don't think they do a lick of work, except to wait on her."

"Who's her? You mean Carter's new wife? She some kind of princess?"

"You'd think so by the way ol' Gil Carson talks. They came in on the last train for the day. All secret like. Kaleb met them at the station in that big Pierce Arrow of Ben's. Had Gil deliver the luggage up to the house afterwards. They didn't want to wait around for him and Danny Billings to load the car. You know that slow poke that helps Gil out o'er at the station? Had to take a horse and wagon up there… to Carter House, that is. Those three girls stayed just out of sight around the corner, giggling and snickering, while Danny brought their luggage into the kitchen."

"So… Chief, you suppose I should keep an eye on that Tom?"

"Naw, like I said, you don't make no trouble, he don't make no trouble. Got me?"

Spitting the toothpick from his lips, Merlyn walked down the steps, leaving Nealy to watch him go. Half way to the street, he stopped and turning back, said, "And stop badgering Maddie, she don't like it."

"But…" was all Nealy got out before Merlyn turned away and headed toward Boots'. Nealy's stubborn streak wouldn't let him leave it alone. Taking a cigarette from a pack in his shirt pocket, he lit it with a match struck on the clapboard siding of the building, and then taking a long drag he exhaled the smoke, saying to himself, "We'll see who's going to make trouble."

ᛡ

Angus McGowan, a dubious business man, fled Boston in 1812 because like most, he was against another confrontation with the British. But that's only what he told people, though. It had more to do with the small fortune he had swindled from some very prominent people.

He went looking for a place where no one would know him and settled on Grunewyck. His idea was to start a basket factory. Everybody used baskets and the only other thing that was used as much were, buckets. But those could come later. Once the factory was in full swing, he switched his sights to buying up property, his focus—the land just south of the village.

Angus soon owned all of the land from the Spry River, west to the farm fields on the sunset side of Parson's Ridge, and from the Davidson's farm all the way south to the base of Prosper Mountain. This included Whippoorwill Hollow, the Meadowlands, and the vast woods beyond where Angus built his mansion. The large, two-story late colonial era house had a cupola, something that was unusual for the design. His house was the biggest in the county.

Angus began selling off plots of land in the woods south of his home for cheap. Mostly to the employees at his factory in Grunewyck. Within a few years, a cottage village had sprung up in the trees around his home. His oldest son, Lachlan, returning from Andover, convinced his father to build a church across the road from the mansion where he could minister to the cottage community. Angus gave in to his sons wishes with the condition that Lachlan turn over half of the weekly collections; it was, Angus's building after all.

Mount Lillie, Prosper Mountain, and Mount Ovis formed a Shepard's Crook around the southern half of that great woods, Parson's Ridge forming the handle on the western side. That would be where Angus would establish Gowan's coming business district. A mill was built, the trees felled, and cheap lumber became available to anyone who wanted to build a shop there. Soon a line of buildings sprang up on each side of the stagecoach trail that would become Main Street.

The village began to prosper, and by 1820, Angus felt it was time to incorporate. Petitioning the state, he established the town of Gowan, dropping the 'Mc' in honor of his father. Soon, a village green was created, a townhall built, and Angus's wife, Adeline, would become the first town clerk. To finalize it all, a belltower with a bronze plaque was erected to honor Domhnall, Angus's grandfather. A clock and a bell soon followed.

When the store owners began to prosper and their mortgages were paid off (to Angus), most of them built large Victorian houses of different styles out behind their shops at the base of Mount Lillie, to the east, and Mount Ovis, to the west. Moving their families out of the upper floors of their businesses, they took up residence in their new abodes to dwell in nineteenth century luxury.

Soon, four new streets were added. They formed a square (dissected by Main Street) around the business district to allow direct access to the new homes. The prominent folks wouldn't have to leave their Cadillac's, Pierces, or Duesenberg's parked in front of their places of business anymore, not when a carriage house awaited their prize automobiles.

The majority of the poorer folk resided in the cottage filled woods, families who had resided there since the beginning of Gowan itself. The village offered little in the way of employment, so most toiled away their days over in Grunewyck.

They were servants in the big houses, drivers, mechanics, low wage help in bakeries, grocery stores, butcher shops, and slaughter houses.

There were tinkers, blacksmiths helpers, furriers, tanners, saddle and leather workers, food servers, tellers, clerks, housekeepers, a school teacher or two, and several committed civil servants. There were hunters and trappers who resided on the slopes of the mountainsides, folks who transformed into fishermen in the summer months to keep the villages supplied with game, fur, and fish.

It was just prior to the onset of the War Between the States, that certain business dealings brought Uriah Ezra Carter to Gowan. Angus owned a log cabin up on Nixie's Bluff that he used for hunting. Uriah, looking for an inexpensive place to roost, decided he wanted that cabin. They shook hands on the deal and the Carters moved in.

Uriah soon found himself unhappy with the isolation and his family's constant complaints of the annoying, 'little folks' who were supposed to inhabit the woods around their new home. True or not, he grew tired of their laments. His business dealings had begun bringing in much needed revenue and he could now afford a bigger home. He sought to purchase land; real estate that Angus McGowan didn't own. Namely, Prosper Mountain, which was thought by many to be worthless for anything other than hunting and firewood gathering.

The mountain had been owned by Harlan Prosper, sawmill owner, and eventual nemesis of McGowan. The man who had provided the lumber to build the village no longer resided there. Harlan had found the conveniences of Boston more conducive to a rich man's life.

Uriah tracked him down and made him a deal he couldn't refuse. Within a week, Angus's soon to be rival, began to build his massive house on the south slope of the mountain. Designated 'Headmost House', the design mimicked the Italianate style of the townhall, but only larger, and with a roof top cupola which allowed Uriah to keep an eye on the village.

The deal had been done without Angus McGowan's knowledge, and the quasi-oligarch suspected nothing until the day the workman began to clear trees and brush a third of the way up the slope.

This created a rift between the two men and hostility ensued. Benjamin Carter, Uriah's oldest son, being of a clever nature and something of a hardcase, took it upon himself (possibly goaded by his father) to make life difficult for Angus. It was a year or so after the end of the war that Angus McGowan conveyed his wishes to benefit from Reconstruction.

Heading south out of the village on something of a reconnaissance mission, he rode in his rather elegant horse drawn carriage with his wife and son. The vehicle lost a wheel at high speed on Long Bridge Road. Angus was thrown from the carriage and killed instantly. His son, Lachlan, was crushed to death within the vehicle, along with his mother, Adeline. The driver and the footman were severely injured but survived.

At a later time, if anyone of the residents had chosen to examine documents or deeds indicating ownership of McGowan's properties (those still thought to be in his name, anyway) would have discovered Uriah's signature at the bottom of the page; not Angus McGowan. Winslow Pike, the man who quickly stepped in to replace Adeline, had been the Notary Public to every one of them. Historical record shows Winslow had amassed enough wealth to move him and his family to Springfield, but only after resigning his pen to Lydia Clemens, Maddie's mother.

Gowan thrived under the Carters. They brought the railroad to the village a short time after the McGowan family's demise, and with it came the appropriate train station. The building was erected five hundred yards south of the point where the railroad navvies curved the tracks around the foot of Mount Ovis to run along the western base of Parson's Ridge, which adjoined the mountain on the north side and ran all the way to Tilson's Furrow.

The Carter's became the railroad moguls of the Spry River Valley, bringing freight and passenger service to the village, Grunewyck, and all the other little towns between Gowan and Kingsport.

Gil Carson had always been the station master there. Arriving Gowan the morning of the ribbon cutting, he took charge of the facility and settled in for the long haul. Gil, now in his nineties, was one of the oldest members of the community. When he decided he could no longer do the hard labor required for some tasks, he hired Danny Billings to apprentice.

Danny's family had lived in Gowan since day one. Grandfather Billings had been a good friend of Gil's before Billings fell sick and died in 1919. Danny would take over when Gil decided to fill his days with fishing and bouncing his grandchildren on his knee. That time was close at hand.

Headmost House was offered to Benjamin upon Uriah's death, but he refused it. Benjamin had big plans that involved Nixie's Bluff. So, his younger brother, Bartholomew, was bequeathed the property as well as the basket factory. Their two sisters married and moved away to Salem, but Sarah died in childbirth; her husband committing suicide soon after. Natalie and her husband both perished from Cholera while touring Mecca.

Benjamin soon became acquainted with Constance, and wishing to marry, he built their future home next to the cabin on Nixie's Bluff. It was to be of the same design as Headmost, but last-minute thoughts and two architects later, a French Mansard roof was added to make it three floors instead of two. A centralized tower was soon added to the front wall and then topped with a rather decorative belvedere. Benjamin told people, jokingly, that he wanted to 'one up' his younger brother, Bart. The cabin was soon converted and then expanded to become the stable and Benjamin began to purchase prime equestrian stock.

He courted Constance a reasonable amount of time before she accepted his proposal. Despite the somewhat annoying behavior of the supposed 'fair folk' up on Nixie's Bluff, they made a home at Carter House.

The Carters ruled Gowan, but not in a manner that was too displeasing to the population. Benjamin Carter was a fair man—most of the time. Constance ran the house, Ben took care of business, and local people were hired to act as servants in the mansion and on the grounds. The only outsider being—Kaleb Knight.

Constance gave birth to Janette Emery Carter on a stormy night in 1915. The world was at war, and the United States would soon be suffering the ravages of a pandemic, but Gowan—not so much. The isolation of such a place would keep the virus at a reasonable distance. Otherwise, Gowan was your typical New England town. The residents were quite familiar with each other and found a great deal of comfort in that. When strangers came to Gowan, very few if any of the citizens wouldn't be aware. Merlyn Cobb was expected to do his job. If those strangers stayed to make the village their home, they would eventually be welcomed in.

Over time, the McGowan mansion became a funeral home run by the Sweeny family and the church became a school. Gowan, as a whole, was not much on religion. The few church goers that did reside there, took their beliefs to Grunewyck on a Sunday, pious folk who never got over the town father's decision to convert their meeting place into a school. When Grunewyck's forty-something year old school house burned to the ground in 1932, all the families interested in having their children attend school, sent them to Gowan. This action filled the large room to capacity. Some of the young scholars had to seat themselves on benches in the coat room at the back and peer through the door to see the chalkboard. Miss Harriet Opal Durnell had her hands full. Her ruler descended on tender palms twice as much than ever before.

When the town fathers of Grunewyck announced they would not be building a new school because of some difficulties with the state of Massachusetts, involving eminent domain and the seizure of property for future projects, Miss Durnell up and quit. In her opinion. Thirty something years of teaching, what she referred to as "...children of the backwater variety," was enough.

There were the typical holiday celebrations. Picnics on the village green, the Gowan Band playing from the gazebo. There was no shortage of banners and confetti on all of the appropriate dates. Fisherman lined the banks of the Spry River on hot summer days and lovers strolled Main Street in the evenings, maybe going as far out as Berryman's Crest to stop, gawk, and exclaim about the strange, but wonderful, Whip-poor-will Hollow, the closest thing to a swamp Hantescree County had to offer.

The cool autumn months were the favorites of Gowan's denizens as the trees in the valley and on the mountainsides seemed to explode with breathtaking reds, yellows, and oranges. Hunters would fill the woods as the reticent gobbler was sought for the Thanksgiving meal. Business at Loeffler's butcher shop would increase twofold for a week or more.

In the winter, children sledded the slopes, skated over the frozen river, built snowmen, and had snowball fights. Wreaths were hung on doors, garland was woven through the numerous balustrades, and candles lit the windows late into the cold evenings. It wasn't unusual for carolers to stroll the streets on Christmas eve with Brenner's offering hot cider to the carolers before they retired to their homes and beds to await Saint Nick. Gowan was a prospering place, a good place to live, but… even good places go bad.

🜓

Janey was back at Headmost by lunchtime and joined Constance in the front parlor. Tabby was setting up the table in the dining room for their afternoon meal. She could be heard humming to herself.

"Well, I got the job, mother. I'm going to be the new school teacher for Gowan."

"That's wonderful, darling, but you know you don't need to work. You're a Carter, we don't labor. Leave that up to the other folks. How is that going to look, you working for a living… being who you are?"

Janey felt her temper flare and struggled to keep her tone civil when she said, "I do need to work. I went to Thayer for just this very thing. I want this job. I don't want to go around like I'm highfalutin' or something. If you want to sit around up here like… like some dowager queen, that's fine, but I want to teach school, and now I'm going to, and… you don't have a say."

Constance said nothing and just sat sipping her wine, studying the patterns on the curtains. Janey could see Tabby through the open door of the dining room and wished she hadn't heard Constance say what she did about working folks. Tabby smiled at her in a sympathetic manner and moved back into the kitchen.

"Saw Tom Lynn today," Janey said, knowing it would trigger a response. Constance's glass froze half way to her lips. Her eyes went to a squint and setting down her goblet, she took a deep breath and put her eyes on Janey.

"Did you talk to him? He was working with Kaleb last year, came up to the house asking for you. Your father was still off to Scotland. I'd be damned if I'd let him inside. Janey, you know how I feel about that boy."

"He isn't a boy anymore, mother."

"Always will be to me. Making trouble around the house, pulling pranks, chasing you around like a wild Indian."

"That was years ago, and if I recall, I did my share of chasing. He

26

had a few bruises to show for it."

"He was a bad influence on you. Which is why you were causing any trouble at all. Up to no good. He was the help, for pete sake! If Kaleb didn't need him around and hadn't pled with me to keep the boy on, I would have banished the little imp to never come back to Carter House, ever again.

"And now... we are."

"We are, what?"

"Banished from Carter House."

Constance unexpectedly whimpered and then a sob broke from her lips. Pulling a handkerchief from the cuff of her dress sleeve, she began to mop her eyes. Janey thought to leave her alone and getting up from her chair, she moved to the door. Before she left the parlor, she turned and said, "Tom isn't an imp anymore, mother. He's a grown man, and... I like him." Hurrying out before Constance could formulate a reply, Janey retreated up the stairs to her room, slamming the door for effect.

Later, she found herself sitting alone at the large dining room table, her meal complete. Constance had also withdrawn to her bedroom and chose to eat her lunch there. Tabby hovered around the table, occasionally patting Janey on the shoulder when she passed. Janey finished her tea and said, "How's mother, Tabby? Is she terribly angry?"

"Uh, no, Miss Janey. She just be sad. Sad about losing her house, sad about losing her husband of so many years..."

"Is she angry with me?"

"Now, Miss Janey, don't go talking like that. Your mama love you."

"I'm sorry you had to hear what she said about working folk. I've never heard her talk like that before. She made it sound like you were less than..."

"It's okay, Miss Janey. Percy and I know who we are. We're proud of what we do and that makes us good at it. Besides, I don't think Missus Constance was even thinking about us when she said that."

"So, why isn't she down here having her lunch with me? Is she trying to make me feel bad?"

"Now, Miss Janey, like I said, she just sad. She git that way a lot nowadays."

"I'm going up there."

"Might be best you stay right here, sugar. Mayhaps you have some more tea?"

"No," Janey said, and pushing out her chair, she went upstairs to stand outside her mother's door.

"Mother, it's Janey, I want to talk to you."

"Not now," Constance rasped out.

Janey tried the knob and found the door locked. "Mother, please."

"Leave me, Janey. I'm not in the mood."

"I was so looking forward to coming home and spending time with you. Now this, and it's not even been two days."

"Maybe tomorrow, Janey. Right now, I don't wish to see you, or hear what you have to say. Go on now."

Janey's temper flared in a way it hadn't for a long time. She was feeling fourteen again and memories flooded in of past times when she had heard those very same words. She wasn't going to get down on her knees. No, not any more. Turning away, she stomped down the stairs and out the front door. Tabby came to stand at the screen, drying a dish with a towel as she watched Janey depart. Shaking her head, she muttered, "Such a shame."

6

Janey made her way down to Main Street, not sure where she was going. Maybe to the café, perhaps over to the newspaper to talk with Cap McKendry, or better yet—the school house. It was her second residence now and she had rooms there; small rooms, but rooms just the same. She could begin the impending task of getting the place ready for August. But not knowing if there were any lamps or candles, just in case she had to carry on into the night, soured her on the idea. There was always tomorrow.

Because it was still lunchtime, n A Walk Inn was hopping, Biddy, and the teenaged Ellie Fleming, moving frantically among the tables carrying pots of coffee and pitchers of water. Boots McCann stood behind the counter directing the short-lived chaos of meal time, his sharp eyes never missing a thing.

Brenner's was quiet and Janey figured there would be a few folks in there for their afternoon meal; Boots didn't serve beer. Looking up, she half expected to see Tom leaning on the balcony railing. Instead, he sat tipped back on a chair taken from his room, his shoes resting on the balustrade.

"Didn't expect to see you again today."

"It's my town, mister, I can come down here as many times as I like. I'm a grown-up woman now as you can see. What are you up to on this hot afternoon? You're not spitting on the good citizens of Gowan as they pass, are you?"

"No... not the good ones," he said and laughed. "Just enjoying the afternoon. I have a few more days until I'm off to Carter House. Then, I'll have to give in to a life of quiet isolation, unless I come to town on occasion, or should I say, if I'm not too exhausted. I suspect my uncle is going to put me to work. Want to come up here with me?"

"Certainly, not much on tavern life, but I'll make my way through."

"It's an inn, Janey. Compared to some I know in Salem, like... The Stake, Brenner's is mild. I'll meet you on the inside balcony." Tipping forward, Tom got to his feet and climbed back in through the window. Janey went up the steps to the boardwalk and pushed her way through the batwing doors.

Colin Brenner was bartending. He stood watching her intently as he wiped glasses, stacking them on a back shelf as he went. The LeBarge boy was quietly sweeping the floor in a back storeroom with the door open. He only glanced up at her for a second. Beth Brenner sat at a desk on a raised platform back in a corner. Her little rostrum was surrounded by a fancy balustrade. A short, narrow set of steps, at the side, granted her access. Beth's setup reminded Janey of a judge's bench. She was holding court.

Brenner's was all dark, varnished wood, and brass. It smelled of spilt beer and tobacco. The open staircase had a slight curve to it as it rose to a gallery running around all the walls except the south side. The wall on that side was covered from floor to ceiling with giant pieces of framed art work, deer, moose, and elk's heads along with ancient muskets and fowling pieces strapped to long plaques.

The balcony like gallery offered access to the sleeping rooms. Numbered doors, one through twelve, lined those walls. Door number ten opened above her head as she passed beneath the balcony.

Before she could look up, Colin said, "Well, if it isn't Janey Carter. Don't think I've ever seen you in here. Well, least not since you were a little, bucktoothed tomboy."

Beth hollered, "Now, Colin, you leave that woman alone. It's been years since Janey's had buckteeth. Can't you see? She's a woman now." Rising from her desk, the fifty-something year old woman painstakingly made her way down the short set of steps. Janey wasn't sure if the creaking she heard was the treads or Beth's joints.

Sandy Brewster and Sully Albright, from the slaughter house, were sitting at the bar drinking their lunch, accompanied by Otis Loeffler from the butcher shop. They all turned together to ogle Janey.

Sully was the youngest. Sandy and Otis were grey haired business men in their late fifties, both having inherited their businesses from their fathers back in the days of Uriah.

Beth walked up to her and taking her hand said, "Care for a drink, Janey? Got some good gin behind the counter."

"Hello, Beth, how are you? Been a long time."

"Yes, but you were off to college. Thought I'd never see you again. Figured maybe you'd hightail it for Boston. You want something to eat? I can send Colin into the kitchen to bring out some roast chicken, or maybe some meat loaf and potatoes? It's a good meat loaf."

"No thanks, Beth, I've had my lunch."

"So, you just come to say hello, or..." Beth's eyes strayed to the balcony above the front door. "Oh, I'll betcha you came to see your pal, Tom. You two were thick as thieves back in the day." Janey turned and looked at Tom, standing at the railing upstairs. He gave them a shy wave.

"Yep, that's why."

"Well, you go on up, then. Looks like he's itching to get you upstairs into his room." Patting Janey on the arm, Beth chuckled and turned away. Janey moved toward the foot of the stairs at the other end of the bar, greeting Otis and Sandy, but ignoring Sully. They nodded and smiled, but it was Sully who broke the silence.

"Well, Janey Carter, long time, no see. Want a beer? You can sit down here with me and we can talk about the good times." Sully's white tee shirt was covered in blood and his grin was frightening.

30

"Well now, Sully Albright, you know… I don't remember any good times with you."

"We could make some new ones?"

Janey took in the pale blue eyes, and the crows' feet already forming at the corner of them. His longer, greasy, dark hair was already receding; just like his father's. Janey had to admit to herself that she was never really attracted to him all that much as a teenager. There just wasn't any chemistry to speak of. They had spent nearly as much time together as her and Tom. Sully worked the killing floor over at the slaughter house and had grown quite good at using his sledgehammer on unsuspecting cows and pigs.

"Another time, Sully."

"Okay, another time. But… don't forget."

Janey smirked and turned away. Moving up the stairs, all eyes followed her. Seeing that the three men at the bar watched intently as if waiting for a view up her dress, she moved back against the wall out of their sight until she got to where Tom stood.

"Come in," Tom said and grabbing one of two chairs flanking a small lantern table along the wall, he stepped inside.

"You put that back when you're done, Tom Lynn. I don't want no shenanigans, you hear me? You're a grown man, now," Beth hollered as Janey stepped into his room.

"Yes, ma'am," Tom said and shut the door.

Janey had never been in the tavern's sleeping rooms. They were small but elaborately furnished.

Tom dragged the chair through the window and Janey followed him out. "Let's sit here and spy on the town," Tom said.

"Could be fun, but let's not get too vulgar. I am just now home and I vowed to myself I would be a more diplomatic person upon my return. Besides, I am the school teacher… now."

"Very well, no vulgarity."

Tom set Janey's chair next to his. "Good enough?" he asked.

"Good enough," Janey said sitting down.

Tom returned to his chair, keeping his shoes off the rail.

"Sorry, would you'd like a drink? Beer? Gin?"

"No, but thanks, I don't partake much. Maybe wine once in a while.

31

Yes, I know, one can never trust a teetotaler, but…"

"I'm sure you have your reasons. Never been much on idioms or old wives' tales. So… to each their own. Can't say I have much use for alcohol, either."

"So, how do you feel about… new wives' tales?" Janey said and chuckled.

Tom laughed. "Still got that sense of humor, I see."

"For as long as I can."

"So, Janey, what brings you down from the mountain?"

"Well, if you must know, my mother and I had a row."

"And not even two days have passed. I'm sorry to hear. May I ask you, about what?"

"You can ask… but I won't tell."

"Very well," Tom said and growing quiet, he looked away up the street toward Headmost. Janey stole a look. Tom's hair was now parted in the middle and was free of pomade. His once chubby face had become somewhat strong featured and he reminded her of Douglas Fairbanks. He smelled of bay rum and his suit was of a decent cut. He turned to catch her looking. Grinning sheepishly, she cast her eyes to the railing and picked at a splinter.

"Now there's a look one doesn't see too often," he remarked. Ignoring the comment, she asked, "So, what is it you will be doing up at my house? Do you know?"

"Oh, probably the usual. You know? What I used to do back in the grander days. Managing the stable, taking care of the horses while my uncle tends to everything else, like the house, the orchard, the lawns, and the gardens."

"So, you said Kaleb wrote you a letter asking for your help?"

"Yes, I did. My uncle's on his own and still trying to make it work. Mentioned he was thinking about disappearing and leaving Benjamin and his new wife to fend for themselves. He had no money, though, and had not been paid for quite some time. I guess every time he approached your father, Benjamin was either coming or going. So, until he can get a little bit of the money he's owed, he'll have to stay."

"You know, Tom, I can go up there and demand that my father pay Kaleb. He had always been a loyal employee and well worth his salt."

"Well, we will see. I have yet to lay my eyes on Carter House. It's been a while for me, as well. Hey, would you like to go over to Boots for some ice cream? It appears to have slowed considerably. We could probably get a table… now. My treat, what do you say?"

"Are you sure? You haven't even started your first day of work. You probably don't have much money, either. If your uncle's not getting paid, there's a good chance that you won't."

"I'm good, don't worry about me, Janey Carter. What do you say, Boots?"

"Very well, better than hanging around this ol' tavern."

"Inn," Tom said, "It's an inn."

"As you wish," Janey said snidely with a hint of mirth.

Getting to their feet they moved to the open window, Tom allowing Janey to go through first. Remembering Beth's stern command, he spun around and grabbed the chair. "I was commanded to return this once I was finished."

"Well, that's Beth for you. Colin may run the bar, but Beth runs his world."

"I have no doubt," Tom said. "A more tasteful and orderly room, I have never slept in."

They laughed together and exited the door. Tom meticulously replaced the chair, moving it one inch left, then right, then back again, as if he couldn't find just the right place. When he finished, he turned and grinned at Beth who glared from her perch. "How's that, Beth? Good?"

"Thank you, Tom," she said, obviously annoyed.

Janey and Tom bounced down the stairs together. Tom threw Beth an impish grin and crossed his eyes.

"Scalawag," she said, teasingly.

"Goodbye, Beth," Janey said.

"Good day, young lady. Say hello to your mother for me."

"I will."

Janey saw Sully now sat alone. Sandy and Otis must have snuck out the back door to avoid the eyes of gossips. The Cow Killer had graduated from beer to what looked like whiskey. She wondered if he remained to see if she would come down alone, probably hoping he could talk her into that beer.

"Goodbye, Colin, good bye, Sully," Janey said. Collin nodded and grinned, adjusting the fancy garters on the sleeves of his white silk shirt. Sully said nothing, a scowl on his face.

The two walked toward the front door and Janey could feel Sully's eyes boring into her back, or maybe, it was her backside. She resisted tossing a glance over her shoulder. Taking Tom's hand, she smiled to herself. Tom didn't reject the move and gave it a little squeeze.

Crossing the street, they went to the café. Janey pulled her hand from Tom's when she saw Ellie glance out a window. Tom looked at Janey and meeting his eyes, she, for the second time that day, smiled sheepishly.

"What was that all about, anyway? Somebody just might think you like me if you keep doing that."

"Oh, Tom, it's just… Sully was giving me the eye. I wanted to send a message."

"So, you were using me?" he said humorously.

"Oh, I don't know if I'd say that. Did you disapprove?"

"Well… no. I suppose not."

"Then you benefited, yes? There might be a few more times in the future that I might have to latch on to you."

Tom grinned at her and said, "Very well, latch away. Now, shall we have some ice cream?"

"Let's hope Boots' has chocolate."

Tom opened the door and decided it might be better if he let Janey go in first. All heads turned. The place had emptied out considerably. Biddy and Ellie were still cleaning up after the rush. Ellie moved to get menus, but Boots grabbed them instead. "I'll take this, Ellie," he said, his deep voice booming. Moving to where they had taken a clean table at one of the windows, he placed the menus on the varnished pine of the table top. Janey smiled up at him.

"Janey Carter, home from college, huh? And I see Tom Lynn's back in town. Left Gowan as rascals and came back grown folk."

"How are you, Boots?" Tom said.

"Yes, how are you?"

"Doing well, as you can see. Just might have to hire some more help.

Three rushes every day for the last year. I guess it's good for me that the people of Gowan don't much like cooking for themselves. Either of you looking for a job?"

"Not me, I'm the new school teacher."

"Oh, yeah, heard ol' Durnell has abandoned us for distant lands. You know, she taught me when I was a kid. 'Bout time she flew the coop, probably used that ruler on me as much as she did you, hey, Janey? Never thought I'd see you taking on her mantle. Figured once you left Gowan, you'd never come back. Now... here you are."

"Yep, here I am."

Boots looked at Tom, they locked eyes and Janey wondered if they were going to have words over something that happened years ago. Then Boots face softened and he said flatly, "How about you, Tom? Need a job? I need someone to clear tables, wash dishes, and maybe help Clyde in the back with cooking. Of course, you'll have to take orders from me... what do you say?"

"Sorry, Boots. I'm working up at Carter House with uncle Kaleb. Start in a couple days. You remember Kaleb, right?"

"Oh, of course. Haven't seen him for some time, though. Well, except for maybe once last week when he drove that big Pierce Arrow down here for groceries. Parked right in front of McCarthy's, had what looked like three teenaged girls hiding in the back seat, mocking people walking by. You know? Sticking out their tongues, laughing, stuff like that. One time they got out and played what looked like a game of tag or something, then jumped right back in and stayed out of sight for the rest of their time down here. Every one of them had dark hair down to their butts and dressed like they was in the hootchy-kootchy show, or something. Not a shoe among them. That's another thing too, never saw their faces. They was wearing veils. Darndest thing. Didn't get over to talk with Silas or Mary about 'em. Figured I could do it tomorrow when I go for supplies."

"You sure it was my father's car?"

"Well, sure! Kaleb was driving and was the one to go in for the groceries. Not many people around here can afford a car like that... oh, sorry, Janey, I didn't mean..."

"It's okay, Boots. I am thinking, if your business keeps going like it is, you just might be able to afford one of those, yourself." She threw Boots a snide grin and watched him blush. He looked at Tom who gave him a confirming expression.

"Sorry to hear about your folks splitting, Janey. Feeling kind of bad for Constance, such a lovely woman, your ma. Heard your pa remarried? Some woman from Scotland? Biddy tells me those girls I saw were her ladies-in-waiting. You hear that, Janey?"

"Nope, but I haven't been back long enough to start loading up on the gossip, yet."

"Well, okay, guess I'll leave you two to your meal."

Janey picked up the menus and handed them back to Boots. "We're just having ice cream. A bowl of chocolate for me."

"Same for me," Tom said, his consistent smile now more like a sneer.

"Very good, I'll get that for you."

Boots turned away and Janey watched him go, the cuff of his right pant leg caught in the top of one of his cowboy boots.

"That's why they call him Boots McCann. Don't think you'll ever find another soul in Gowan who wears cowboy boots. Tom looked, snickered, and turned his face back to Janey to speak, but she beat him to it, "So, you said you're going to write a book? About what, if I may ask?"

"Well, you may ask. So, like I said, I studied folklore. It was offered in the School of Sociology. You know, the study of society? I wanted to write about the folklore of Massachusetts."

"Terribly odd, Tom. A stable boy wanting to write about folklore."

"College will do that to you. Honestly? I've always had an interest."

"Since when? I always thought the only thing you were interested in was horses and causing trouble. Well, I guess there was Violet Dent, the banker's niece. You remember? She used to summer in Gowan—much like you. Helped out as a teller before they hired on Vivian Bishop."

"Yes, but I'm trying to forget. She still haunts my dreams—and not in a good way."

"You had a thing for her, if I remember. I think your first true girlfriend." Janey giggled and reaching across the table, she lightly punched Tom in the shoulder.

"Janey, could we get back on the subject and not talk about the failed loves of my life? Unless, you want to start talking about Sully Albright?"

"Okay, fine. So, what was your motivation? For the book, I mean."

"So, you know why the ground under Carter House is called Nixie's Bluff, right?"

"Oh, of course. I've heard stories from the old days when there was nothing but a cabin up there. They converted it to that stable you used to sleep in. That was the year I was born."

"Well, anyway... my uncle used to always tell me about the wee folk in the woods behind the house. So... I went looking. Not expecting to find hide nor hair. Figured I could at least tell uncle Kaleb that it was all talk. So, uh... this stays between you and me, huh, Janey? I don't need folks thinking I'm off my rocker?"

"Agreed."

"So, I'd wandered off quite a distance to the north on Parson's Ridge, just sky larking, poking things with a stick. You know, kid stuff?"

"Yeah, I had a stick, once," Janey said and giggled.

"Come on, Janey, this is serious. I'm baring my soul to you and you want to poke fun at me."

"Yeah, well, that's better than a stick, right? Okay, sorry... go on."

"Anyway, there's a rather large pool back up in there. I stopped to rest and was just looking at it. The sky was clear and the sun was hot, but the leaves kept it off me. It was rather shadowy in there, and... well, there was a group of boulders sticking up on my right, next to that pool of water."

"Yes, I remember that place, so..."

"So... I'm standing, watching the water striders skating around on the surface and out of the corner of my eye, I caught something moving. Like someone lifted their hand to scratch their head or something like that. I look that way and in the shadows of those rocks, I could just make out someone sitting there. An ugly little man with big ears, short brown fur all over his body and a black tuft of hair sticking up from top of his head. He was grinning at me, not making a sound. I screamed and ran. Didn't take long for me to get back to the stable. Kaleb was mad as hell because I'd wandered off. I was supposed to be mucking stalls. So, believe me, I had nightmares for a year after."

"What was it? Some kind of a monkey escaped from a circus, or…"

"I don't think so, but…"

Before Tom could finish, Boots appeared at the serving window with two dishes of chocolate ice cream. Clyde came up beside him, his white cook's hat matching his hair, but contrasting his dark skin. He had been the cook there for as far back as Janey could remember. He said something to Boots who nodded and walked away. Picking up the bowls, Clyde carried them out to their table.

When he arrived, he said, "Hello, Miss Janey, how you? Long time since you come around. And Tom Lynn, here you are. Seems I don't ever see one of you without the other. You like two peas in a pod."

"Well, if it isn't Clyde Meeks, good to see a friendly face," Tom said.

"Hello, Clyde, still cooking for Boots, I see."

"Well, yes'um. Boots say someday he going to retire and because I been here so long, he just gonna give me this ol' cafe."

He laughed and set the bowls on the table. "Got to get back to it, good to see you." They both smiled at him as he turned away, but then he stopped and turned back. "Oh, by the way, Miss Janey," he said, and reaching into his pocket he pulled something out and handed it to her. Dropping a button sized object into her palm, he said, "Found that over where your daddy's car was parked in front of the store. Thought maybe it fell out when those strange girls was running around. I figured you can see that it gets back to whoever it belong to, up Carter House."

Janey studied it for a few seconds and turned to question Clyde further, but he was already walking away. Tom reached across and rolled it around in her open palm with his fingertip. "Odd looking thing, if you ask me."

"Yes, looks like solid gold, and it's warm to the touch. What's that on it?" They looked closer and lightly bumped heads.

"Ah!" Janey said.

"Oops! Sorry," Tom said, now his turn for that sheepish look.

Janey laid it on the table to avoid another accident. There was some kind of a symbol carved into it and a small hole at the rim where a single link of a tiny gold chain still remained. The expensive mineral was unpolished and left Janey with the impression that it was ancient.

"Looks like a charm from a woman's bracelet or necklace."

"Allow me," Tom said and picked it up.

"Hmmm… haven't a clue what this engraving is. Why it would be lying on a street in Gowan is beyond me."

"Like Clyde said, one of those barefooted girls probably dropped it when they got out of the car. Makes sense, huh?"

"Yeah, I suppose. Leave it with me and I'll return it when I go up to Carter House."

"Okay," Janey said, "But if you don't get it there, I'll wrestle it away from you and take it myself. Have some chewing out to do. Just not sure when that's going to happen."

Tom stuck the bauble in his pocket and they dug into their ice cream. There came a lull in their conversation as they enjoyed their treat. An occasional eye was cast their way, mostly café customers who knew who Janey was, poor folks from the cottage district. Citizens who took advantage of Boots' 'free lunch time coffee' and the cooling fans hanging from the ceiling. Those able to afford a piece of pie, shared it with family members, just good folk looking for camaraderie.

The not so good folk would be gathering at Zelda's in a few hours for a late night of drinking, fighting, and fornicating. Some would walk home in the early hours of the morning, making the staggering trek from one end of town to the other. It was always suspected that the holding cell over at the police office would be filled to capacity, nightly. Nealy needed to feel he was doing his job.

Before Nealy, Merlyn had to do it, but he was known for borrowing a horse drawn wagon from Sandy Brewster on occasion, and hauling the lush's home, instead of locking them up. Knowing them all personally, he would drop each one off at their perspective cottage. "Nothing else to do at that time of the morning, anyways!" Janey had heard him say to Cap McKendry once. But Merlyn was getting old and fat. Nealy was zealous and seemed to never tire. Merlyn got to stay home at night, now, and rarely got called out unless things were going badly for Nealy.

Janey and Tom finished up and sat talking and drinking coffee until the gloaming. When they'd had their fill, they got up and moved to the cash register where Tom paid their bill. Boots worked his way over and grinning at Janey, he said, "Good to see you again, Janey. Tell your ma hello for me, and your pa if you see him. You know, Janey, Tabby, she comes in sometimes to get her and Percy something to eat. Hell, tell them hello for me, as well."

"I will, Boots," Janey said and looking around she saw all eyes were on them. Getting an idea, she leaned forward and whispered something in Boots' ear. His eyes widened and he practically shouted, "Are you sure about that, young lady? That's a basket full of dollars!"

"Yes, I know. Just start me a tab, and make sure you add a little something for Biddy and Ellie. I'll be in tomorrow to pay up. You know you can trust me."

"Certainly do! Okay... Biddy?" he shouted to the older waitress.

She turned and gave him a questioning look. "You and Ellie start cutting pie, our new school teacher is buying. Pie on the house!" he sang out, making sure everyone could hear. Janey and Tom left the café to a chorus of cheers. Not so much for the local, rich girl, but the idea of a free slice of pie. Boots would bask in the glory of it. Janey didn't mind.

"Walk me home, Tom?"

"Sure thing."

Outside, they stood quiet for a minute and then Tom said, "That was rather bold of you."

"You know, Tom, I never have been wanting for anything. Thayer was the hardest thing I ever had to do, but we had three squares, a roof over our heads, and we kept warm in the winter. Those people back there have known nothing but hardship. I can only imagine what they thought of us Carters sitting up on that bluff. Probably thinking that we weren't only looking down the bluff at them, but probably our noses, as well. You ever just want to be generous, Tom? Ever want to just be helpful?"

"Well, Janey, keep in mind... I am one of those people."

"Yes, but not to me, Tom, or maybe as a child I always thought I was one of those people... one of thee people."

"I've never held your wealth against you, Janey. It really wasn't yours, was it? It was your father's, and his father's. What I saw back there, just five minutes ago, tells me I'm right. The real test will come when it all becomes yours as the sole heir."

"Thank you, Tom," she said.

"You're welcome."

40

They walked in silence, both deep in thought. It would be hours before the throng of drunks from Zelda's would make their northward trek and some wouldn't make it by Nealy, who would park his car in front of McCarthy's and await their arrival. Since Nealy was a talker and working overnight always brought a certain degree of loneliness, having a few drunks in the holding cell meant there would be someone to talk to.

Nealy Garret was known to only pick up drunks who had no family. It was an act of kindness for those who had a wife and children waiting for the man of the house to return home. Everybody knew this and some of Zelda's regulars actually looked forward to being arrested so they didn't have to return to an empty house. A few would leave the roadhouse early because that early morning walk north to Grunewyck for work, with only a little sleep and the remnants of a hangover, was trying. Some would probably stop in at Brenner's on the way past to tip back a few more. A change of scenery.

Reaching Headmost's open gate, Janey wondered if Tom would walk her all the way up to the house. He never paused and she smiled to herself. They soon found themselves enveloped by the dark of the trees as they moved up the pea graveled lane even though it was early evening.

When the two reached the fountain, Tom stopped and turned to face her. The two stood shielded by the great granite statue of a scantily clad woman dumping water from a pitcher. They sat on the basin wall and talked some more well past sunset. Janey, on impulse, asked, "Would you like to come to dinner some night?"

"Well, it better be soon, I still have to make an appearance at Nixie's Bluff or uncle Kaleb is going to think I stiffed him."

"You still have a few days, so... how about tomorrow night? It would be a good sendoff dinner before you have to get to work and stop being so lazy."

Janey laughed and Tom looked at her in a way that said she had captured his heart. Owls called, crickets chirped, and frogs could be heard from the nearby lilypond. Her uncle liked ponds and had planned to build several more, but then he died and ponds didn't matter.

Then there was the moon rising over Prosper's peak, the cool breeze washing over them, and the warm lights from the front windows. He moved in close and kissed her softly on the lips. Janey expected it and didn't resist. She had longed for that moment. If she only knew how long Tom had dreamt of that moment, himself.

He sighed, smiled, and said, "Wow." Janey smiled back in that sheepish manner for the third time that day. Tom got to his feet and without another word, he started down the lane toward the gate.

"Tomorrow night? Six o'clock?" he said, looking back over his shoulder.

"Yes," was all Janey said as she watched him melt away into the shadows, remaining until the squeak of the gate's hinges and the clang of the latch.

7

Gowan had no pole-type street lamps, but every shop on the boardwalk had a light fixture, or two, at the front of their establishments. Lamps that would remain lit until dawn. The cost of the electricity to power those lamps was included in the townsfolk's taxes, but came free to the shop owners. Everybody recognized the importance of a well-lit street.

All the shops were dark inside and only Brenner's and the café showed any life. Tom soon found himself walking north in the middle of Main Street. He felt a spot of heat in his pocket and reaching in he touched the bauble. It was warm to the touch. Taking it out, he looked at it. His pocket cooled, but the tiny piece of gold did not. Unless it got hot enough to burn him, there really wasn't a problem, but he was still perplexed. He would leave the bauble in his room and wait to see if it cooled down. Dropping it back in his pocket, he continued toward Brenner's.

Two men had been walking ahead of him and he soon caught up. One of them must have heard his footsteps and turned to look.

"Hey, who's that?" Cal Loeffler said.

"Tom… Tom Lynn."

The two stopped and turned to face him. The other man was Charley Bates Jr., the slaughter house drudge.

"Hey, I know you, Tom Lynn?" Charley Bates Jr. said.

"So do I," Cal added. "You used to work up at Carter House. That was a long time ago. What you doing here, now? You living here?"

"No, I'm back to help my uncle Kaleb, seems he's got his hands full up there on the bluff."

"Hey! You think ol' Ben Carter would hire me? Getting so sick of that slaughter house. You know? Cleaning up cow guts and all, Ol' Sandy Brewster yelling at me all the time. Charley, do this, Charley, do that. Get off your ass, Charley, there's shit to be done! Getting so sick of it."

"So, where you headed, Tom?" Cal asked as the lesser of the intoxicateds.

"Brenner's"

"Going for a beer?"

"No, that's where I'm staying til I get up to Carter House."

"Hell, I'll buy you a beer? Hey, Cal, I'll buy you a beer too. Let's go have some beers!"

"Alright, Charley Bates Jr., you ol' gut sweeper. Just one, though, then I have to git to my bed," Cal said.

Both men lived above their places of work down at the end of Main Street. Cal lived above the butcher shop with his father; his mother, several years deceased. Charley Bates Jr., originally from Grunewyck, had a small closet at the back on the second floor of the slaughter house. He often complained of having to put up with that never ending stench of cows and pigs; alive or dead, and the flies; oh, the flies! They made him long for the winter months.

Nealy Garret was in his usual spot, the glow of his cigarette marking his presence behind the wheel.

"Uh-oh, Nealy Garret! Fly right, you two," Charley Bates Jr. whispered.

"Ah, damn. Don't want to spend the night in the hoosegow. Goddamn Nealy will talk your ear off. You never get no sleep. Darn bunks aren't too comfortable, neither."

Tom said nothing.

Nealy greeted them from the dark interior, "Hey, boys."

They all knew that being single meant you were suspect, but Tom knew Nealy would have a tough time proving him drunk—since he wasn't. Cal and Charley Bates Jr., on the other hand, were prime targets.

Nealy never made a move, though. He'd already been there. He knew that if he took either one, somebody wasn't going to get their meat in the morning and he liked to have a steak with his eggs for breakfast. Both Sandy Brewster and Otis Loffler would come down hard on Merlyn for taking away their good help, slowing them down on a business day. Then Merlyn would come down on Nealy—with both feet. He knew to wait for the rowdier, factory crowd; less repercussions that way.

"Hey, Nealy," they sang out in unison and continued on to Brenner's without incident. Tom followed, grinning at their drunken antics.

8

Janey greeted Percy in the midst of the evening lamp lighting and moving into the kitchen she hailed Tabby and asked, "Mother ever come out of her room?"

"Ah, yessum, sugar. She came down for a while to chat with ol' Beulah on that talking gizmo in the entry hall. Wasn't for that contraption, she have nothing to do in the evenings except sit out on that porch and watch the sun go down. I so wished you hadn't fought, would have been so much nicer to hear you talking in the front parlor, maybe sharing a little bit o' that claret she keep hidden in the side board. Oh well, maybe tomorrow evenin' will be better."

Janey sat down at the small breakfast table and they chatted while the old woman moved about preparing for the next day. When her eyelids got heavy, Janey kissed the old woman's cheek and embraced her. "Good night, Tabby. I told Percy not to worry about the lights upstairs."

"Okay, sugar. You take this, then," Tabby said, handing Janey one of the fancy glass hurricane lamps that she had burning in the kitchen. Janey left by the door at the back of the room. Stepping out into the narrow corridor that led to the entry hall, or the other direction, to the back staircase, she heard Tabby say, "Night, sugar. Sleep well."

"Night," Janey said and took a left to move up the creaky treads. The door to her mother's room was closed and putting her ear to the wooden panel, she could hear her mother snoring. "Good,' she said under her breath and continued down the hall. Moving past an open doorway on her left, she glanced up the stairs that led to the attic rooms and the cupola. She wondered if it might be cooler to sleep up there. Something to consider while dressing for bed.

The next door, adjacent to the landing of the main stairwell, was her room. The one that she used when she came to visit as a little girl. The door was open along with one of the windows. A vase of fresh flowers graced her vanity. She smiled and murmured, "I love you, Tabby. You're so good to me."

After placing her lamp on the nightstand, she shut the door and turned on the light at the ceiling. Shucking her clothes, she stood naked before the tall floor mirror. Cupping her breasts with both hands, she raised them slightly before letting them drop, then turning her backside to the mirror for a few seconds, she said, "Good enough." Pulling her gauzy, sleeveless gown over her head, she thought of Tom.

The heat in the room was close to unbearable with the door shut. Sliding open the sash of the second window, the evening breeze washed over her body as she gazed at the fireflies flitting among the trees.

The house had acquired steel mesh window screens only five years prior. She could now sleep with the windows wide open and not worry about bugs. In her younger days, cheesecloth sheers draped all the bedroom windows and if any kind of a breeze blew, mosquitos were sure to find their way inside to make for a miserable night.

Tabby and Percy slept up under the roof. She remembered it to be stifling up there in the summer and freezing in the winter. The small windows under the eaves and in the cupola could help bring the temperature down to a reasonable level, but only if every single one of them was open.

Janey's thoughts returned to sleeping in the cupola. She wanted one more look at the town before bed. Taking the lamp, she stepped quietly into the hall. Percy was now in the kitchen with Tabby and they were talking in low tones.

The narrow stairs had several turns, each one punctuated by a small landing. Janey passed the door to the Snoaks's attic rooms, and after two more turns she found herself at the top. The large chandelier hanging from the ceiling of the cupola remained unlit. A three-foot-wide wooden walkway, built to allow viewing from all sides, came with a balustrade to keep one from plunging to their death in the entry hall below. Janey moved around to the front to look out over the town.

Main Street was empty of souls; except for the police car. "Still ambushing drunks, hey, Nealy?" she whispered to herself.

Her eyes traveled the length of the street out toward the school house, but all she could see was the lantern lit windows that glowed among the trees. The chandelier in the cupola of Sweeny's Funeral Home burned, and from there, her eyes moved up to Carter House.

The belvedere atop the tower glowed along with every window in the place. "What are you doing up there, Benjamin Carter? Having an orgy with your new wife and her ladies?"

Janey often wondered if her father might be some kind of a deviant. His behavior in the past said, yes. But there was never any solid proof. Benjamin would often return after weeks in Kingsport, grumpy and bleary eyed. Locking himself in the guest bedroom on the third floor, upon his return, he'd be in there for days with only the maids (always the younger ones) tending to his needs. He always seemed overly cautious in the days that followed any excursion. 'Guarded' was the word some people would use.

Pressing her mother for what she might know, Janey would learn nothing. Constance was loyal and would only say, "Leave your father alone, he is a good provider." Janey began to imagine that he held multiday parties, entertaining business men at their shantyboat anchored in the Kingsport marina. She was sure that other women were involved, but Constance wasn't at all concerned; as long as the money kept flowing and that she had free access to it.

The chandelier in the belvedere of Carter House blinked as if a body had passed in front of it. Then it went dark. The dormer windows followed suit, and then the second and first floor. The house became indistinguishable in the night. Then, what could only have been a candle, appeared on the veranda, an almost indiscernible pinpoint of light. It moved out onto the lawn trailed by three more. Soon, other flecks of light moved out from the trees at the west side of the lawn and joined them.

They formed a circle and started to move as if the bearers of each light were dancing. A spiral formed and spun in a mesmerizing fashion.

46

One speck of light broke away and moved in the direction of the natural stone bridge that stretched from the front yard, over the lane, and into the woods on the east side of the house. The others followed and entering the trees, the specks of light disappeared.

It left her with a strange feeling. What was going on up there? Was her father involved in that? How unlike him. Maybe party games? But why go into the woods in the dark? And where was Kaleb? Taking her lamp, Janey returned to her room, her mind abuzz.

CHAPTER THREE

GOWAN

1

~

1

4:30am, Saturday, July, 1935

The village was waking up. The cockcrow was just minutes away, and although not as mysterious as the gloaming, the rising sun brought a certain type of joy to many of the town's citizens. The light came up in the world, confirming that the planet still turned, that summer was still present, and the living could go about their day as they had for centuries. The wicked would seek their beds, wherever they be, relinquishing Gowan to the sun worshippers. It was the way of the world. So, not only would the sunrise disclose the smiles on good folk's faces; it would also retract the shadows to reveal the debris left behind by acts committed while darkness lay upon the valley. In nature, everything has to balance.

2

5:00am

Sully Albright stood at the center of the killing floor. The day was already heating up and even though he remained free of the sun, he was still sweating, and as he put it, 'like a pig.' He clutched his sledgehammer with both hands, its head stained with the blood of many kills. Sully believed it was bad luck to wash it off.

He watched Charley Bates Jr. moving about the corral outside of the large, overhead door. Three fat steers were being herded to the chute that came through a corner of the east wall. The steers would gather in a small pen there and when Sully gave him the signal, Charley Bates Jr. would open the gate to let them come out onto the floor; one at a time.

Sully, sporting a black eye, was seriously hungover and seething about Tom being with Janey, telling an indifferent Charley Bates Jr. how he would like to beat Tom to a pulp. By the time he got to Zelda's and the chaotic party within, he was a bomb set to explode. Going from beer to whiskey didn't help matters.

By one thirty in the morning, he'd already had his first fight. He had taken his anger out on some loudmouth who came up from the tiny burg of Lilting. When the bouncers pulled Sully off, he didn't fight them. Tip Thomas had shouted in his ear, while they held him, "You don't calm yourself, Sully boy, I'm going to let these fellas beat you raw and toss you outside." Sully knew better than to take on the burly, scar faced men that kept the peace within those walls. That included Tip, who had a few scars of his own.

Sully watched Charley Bates Jr. with an evil eye. "Sissy," he muttered. Sully had invited the kid out to Zelda's one night and Charley Bates Jr. had declined. It's not that he didn't like Zelda's; he just didn't like Sully. The cow killer would never let him forget it.

Charley Bates Jr. always locked the door to his little room when he was inside. He rued the day he came to work for Sandy Brewster and was always looking for other employment. The 'Help Wanted' sign at Boots' hadn't escaped his eye. He joked once to Cecil Walker, when he went for a haircut, that maybe Sully would get trampled to death one day and he could take over his job. After a laugh, he added in a more serious tone that he liked animals, even cows, and wasn't sure he could kill them. Cecil had said, "Then what the hell are you doing working for Sandy Brewster?" That's when Charley Bates Jr. decided he was going to quit come September.

Charley Bates Jr. got the steers into the waiting pen and followed them in, closing the gate behind him. Climbing up to sit on the top rail of the pen's fence, he waited. The sun was now up and nearly blinding Sully, who stood impatiently waiting.

"Close the damned overhead, Charley! Don't want that damn sun beating down on me while I'm working… you dumb shit!"

He did as Sully asked, mumbling, "Yeah, but I really like the thought of something beating on you."

Sully was going to work all day under electric lights, making the killing floor even eerier. When the sun moved around to the south side of the building, Charley Bates Jr. would open the overhead back up. After fulfilling Sully's request, he returned to the holding pen.

"Hey, panty waist! Open the gate and send me my first victim!"

Charley Bates Jr. did as asked, sending the first unsuspecting creature out onto the floor. He watched the steer walk right over to Sully as if expecting a hand full of oats; it got the killing end of that hammer instead. When Sully's tool of choice started its downward arc, Charley Bates Jr. turned away and covered his ears.

3

5:30am

The morning sun found the usual throng of laborers who didn't work in Gowan, trudging their way to Grunewyck. With brown paper sacks, metal lunchboxes, and coffee filled thermoses in hand, they made their way through Whip-poor-will Hollow. The ones who could afford newer work boots, carried them, walking barefoot until they passed through the ford at the ravine. If anyone of the cars that came through, heading in the same direction, had open seats or running boards, rides would be offered, but always on a first come, first served basis. Sometimes an empty pickup truck would come through and stop long enough to load up and transport the perpetually weary.

It was a thirty-minute walk but seemed longer for those who had been out late at Zelda's. The lot of them would have to circumvent the multiple hairpin curves before stepping out of the hollow altogether for a straight shot into the town. Even though the sun shone, that didn't matter in the Hollow. They wouldn't feel its warmth again until they topped the rise just south of the Davidson's farm. It was an unusual, but normalized phenomena. For some strange reason, the light of that great orange orb could barely penetrate the shadows of Whip-poor-will Hollow.

The return trip in the dark was worse, and the men moved in a tight bunch like a flock of sheep that perceived danger at every turn. Fear overpowered exhaustion during their trek, for evenfall wasn't a good time to be lingering in Whip-poor-will Hollow. They were always grateful for the summer months when the sun didn't seek its bed until well into the evening after they had safely passed through.

The winter months were hell and those who didn't own property in Gowan, who weren't still living in a cottage that had been passed down through generations, often moved their residences to Grunewyck to save them from ever having to pass through that place. Grunewyck had their own taverns, none as dangerous or exciting as Zelda's, but good beer was good beer; no matter where you drank it.

Ϥ

6:00am

Sandy Brewster, using a heavy cart, was hauling steer carcasses across the street to Otis Loeffler's butcher shop. His white T shirt and dungarees were striped with blood. Unlike Sully, he could afford to change them daily, keeping his wife, Addy, busy with laundry.

He struggled to get the usual number of carcasses over to the butcher shop before the breakfast rush at Boots'. Nobody wanted to see dead cows and pigs in the street being pushed by a big man in bloody clothing while they were in the midst of breakfast.

Otis Loffler was having an argument with his son, Cal, while standing in the open overhead door at the far end of the cutting room. The butchers, Billy Bond, John Sibley, and Thomas Scruggs, created select cuts of beef and pork to be trundled up the ramp and into the back corridor by Cal.

Otis would be waiting there to arrange them in the glass fronted display coolers on fresh paper. After that was done, he filled the orders for McCarthys, Boots' A Walk Inn, Brenner's, and Zelda's. That's what the two men were arguing about—Cal complaining about having to make deliveries.

"Morning, boys," Sandy Brewster said as he approached, the cart wheels squeaking, the eyes of the dead steer, staring.

"Look, Billy, your first customer for the day," Otis called out, "Might want to be sure to ask him if he wants a shave with his haircut!" Billy grinned and continued to run his best knife up and down the well-worn strop hooked to his table.

They all laughed, and cinching up their bloody aprons, they helped Sandy pull the carcass from the cart. Billy grabbed the meat hook attached to a chain hanging from a pulley at the ceiling, then walking it over to the cart, he pushed it through the soft tissue under the beast's jaw. Cal cringed at the sound.

Billy began to turn the crank that would lift the carcass to hang in the middle of the large open room with its sawdust covered floor. There were other hooks and chains hanging there, lightly clanging, waiting their turn. Soon the room would be filled with dangling bodies, slowly swinging, the butchers methodically working their way through the lot.

Slicing and cleaving, Billy's blades moved effortlessly in his scar covered hands. Stopping for a minute, he watched Sandy push his cart back to the slaughter house. The sun breaking over the trees behind the cattle yard would be on him for all of fifteen minutes, bathing him in its light. A grin broke his lips and after throwing a nod at John, who had stopped to give him a curious look, the master carver went back to work, still grinning.

5

8:00am

Tabby and Percy had been up for hours prepping the house for the day. They both liked their jobs immensely and they were good at it. Their parents had made their way north during The War Between The States to avoid being captured and sold into slavery. Tabby had been born in Gowan. Percy was up from Springfield. They had met one day when Percy was charged with a delivery of horses to Carter House. He met Tabby, and the rest was history. Percy cajoled Kaleb into asking Benjamin Carter to hire him on to help with the grounds and horses. It didn't take much convincing; Percy was qualified, and wealthy men rarely turn down an offer of help—especially when no terms of payment were discussed and nothing went down on paper. Benjamin would pay what he thought his employees were worth.

Percy was opening curtains and windows at Headmost to let in the sun and morning breeze. Tabby was hard at work in the kitchen making breakfast and preparing to do some baking. Headmost House was the last on Cal Loffler's delivery list of beef, pork, smoked bacon, chicken, and goose. At one time, Carter House had been the top of the list, but all delivery requests to the bluff had been placed on hold the day Constance was forced to depart the mansion. Nobody had called to start them again after Ben's return. Otis worried. Benjamin Carter had been a big account; the man loved his meat.

Tabby slipped two apple pies into the oven and checked the clock. She would have to wake Constance and Janey as soon as the tea was on the table. Percy, finished with his task, waited in the kitchen before heading out back to chop firewood. A chore that had to wait until the house was awake. He grabbed Tabby, spun her around and embraced her. She giggled like she was fifteen again.

"Now, Percy, I gots work to do."

"I know and so do I and I is doing it," he said raising his eyebrows several times and smiling like a Cheshire Cat. They exchanged a kiss, and pulling back, Percy held Tabby at arm's length, just staring into her face.

"You know I love you, Mrs. Tabitha Snoaks, you know I do."

"I know, you silly old man."

"Tell me, Tabby."

"Oh, you know I do."

"No, I wants to hear you say it. If anything happen to you, I'd just go and jump in that ol' Spry River just like your daddy do."

"Okay, I love you, Mr. Percy Snoaks. Now, get a drink of water and head out back. The tea is steeping on the table and I'm going to wake the ladies."

6

9:00am

Eighteen-year-old Paul LeBarge was finishing up with sweeping the floors at Brenner's. Next on his list was to check the outhouse and make sure there was a roll of fresh paper as well as to clean the toilet seat. The waxing and polishing of the tavern's woodwork would follow. It would take most of the day.

Paul liked his job, though. The Brenner's trusted him and didn't rush him through his tasks. He repaid them by maintaining a good work ethic. There was also the free room and board, and above all else, they treated him like he was their own. The tavern was a place he could call home.

Paul was an orphan. Wandering in one day on his trek north to Aylesbury, he stopped to beg a bite of food and the Brenner's put him to work. Colin was teaching him to bartend. On typically slow evenings, like Wednesdays, Colin would let Paul take over so he and Beth could have a night out to motor over to Luigi's in Grunewyck for some Italian food.

Colin and Beth were taking their lunch in their big house across Ovis Street at the back, and Paul was to call them over, using the Triangle Dinner Bell hanging from a back porch beam. He rather enjoyed using it, running the short but heavy metal rod as fast as he could around inside its frame a multitude of times to summon the Brenner's; he wasn't sure why it filled him with such a childish glee other than that it felt mischievous.

Paul had swept his way to the front door and standing just under the gallery, he heard a noise. There wasn't supposed to be anyone in the place but him. He was pretty sure the noise came from number ten, Tom Lynn's room. Tom was across the street at Boots'. There came the sound of a chair being knocked over, followed by the squeak of bedsprings.

Leaving his broom, Paul climbed the stairs. Number ten was a corner room and a tad bit larger than the others. Stopping outside the door, he listened. It was when he put his ear to the mahogany panel that he heard a slight scratching sound like little claws on wood—and there was panting. Paul knocked and said, "Tom?" Silence.

Knocking again, he heard a low, indiscernible squeaking of words that wasn't English. Finding his ring of keys and sorting out #10, he unlocked and opened the door. There was a loud, *plop!* on the floor just out of sight between the bed and the highboy dresser. It was like the time an opossum had gotten into his bedroom at his foster parent's cottage down in Rhode Island. He had to sling it out of the window by its tail when it stopped to play dead in the middle of the floor.

The window on the north side, overlooking the roof of Philip Shannon's office, was open all the way. Paul could still hear what sounded like a small dog panting.

Getting down on the floor to look under the bed, a brown streak shot out the other side and rocketed through the open window. There was a pintsized laugh and the curtains whipped. Paul dashed over and poked his head out. Nothing.

Turning back, he scanned the room. Everything seemed to be in its place. Moving to the street side window, he checked the outside balcony for good measure. Satisfied that it was out of his hands, he started to turn away when the door to the café across the street opened.

Little Ellie Fleming came out and began to erase items on the 'Specials' sandwich board where it roosted on the boardwalk. Paul liked Ellie. They were now having regular conversations. She always seemed excited about everything he said and was probably one of those optimists he had heard about. It was something that appealed to a boy who'd known nothing but hardship, least up until the Brenner's had taken him in. When he had finally gotten up the nerve to talk to her and she had not rejected him, he felt like he could fly. He wasn't used to feeling such exhilaration and the moment would become a milestone in his life. He and her were about the same age, her being a little older by a few months. She still wore her light brown hair in the Marcel wave craze of the twenties. It made her head appear bigger than it was. She could have been bald for all he cared. Her face, and bright, active brown eyes, had captured him. It was all he could do to keep from staring when they were together.

Ellie, fussing with the board and trying to keep it on its feet, had her back to him as she erased. A gust of wind came and lifted the hem of her cranberry-colored waitress uniform. It had been all of maybe five seconds but enough to expose her thighs and a pair of pink tap panties. Paul quickly turned away. Catching his face in the mirror, he saw it was redder than the tomatoes he often cut for the patron's stew. He squinted at himself and said with disgust, "Pervert! How you ever going to talk to her again?"

He hurried from the room, locked the door, and did a fast walk down the stairs. Picking up his broom, he went back to work. Had anyone entered the tavern at that time, they would have heard him mumbling to himself, "Not your fault, not your fault..."

7

10:00am

Thirteen-year-old Melissa 'Lissy' Potter was making her way to Gowan from Grunewyck. She had gotten wind of a new school teacher in town—a Miss Janette Carter.

Lissy was dead set on meeting this woman before school started. If her new teacher wasn't in her rooms at the schoolhouse, Lissy would find out where she lived and go there. She could politely introduce herself, look the woman over, and if she wasn't invited in for tea, she could leave; simple as that.

It was the girl's great dislike for the previous, Miss Durnell, that put her on the road this Saturday. Lissy was pretty excited about the prospect of not having to spend another year under the rule of the 'old biddy'. She had received her information about Miss Carter through the grapevine. Her mother and her gossip mates hadn't much of anything nice to say about her. This led Lissy to believe that she and her new teacher must have a lot in common. Kindred spirits, she thought, like Anne from Green Gables would have said.

It was noted within the records of the ramshackle school system of the Spry River Valley that Lissy Potter was smarter than the average student. To supplement that, her curiosity was said to be prodigious and those who admired her, never failed to mention that, "The girl was fearless."

Her grandmother had said the same thing back when Lissy was younger. She liked that some people thought of her that way, but she knew in her heart that no one was entirely without fear. Lissy Potter consciously sought to get a handle on it early in her life and had developed a theory that her fear could be controlled and used to her advantage.

Lissy felt it smart to act quick when she sensed people were trying to get the upper hand. Some said she acted inappropriately, but she did what she felt was necessary. Her own mother was known to just smile and say with resignation, "Yep, that's my Lissy. She's a handful."

The precocious teen decided that this would be the year she would, for the first time, benefit from going to school in Gowan. She was one of the few children that had shed tears when they discovered the smoldering ruins of her old school in Grunewyck. A badly installed boiler system had exploded and the building had burned in the night. Gowan's little school house, as she feared, proved to be a couple of steps down—Miss Durnell being a big part of that. Lissy harbored high hopes, though. She, too, wanted to go to Thayer like Miss Carter. Lissy was on a quest.

Passing the Davidson's place out on the road that led to the Hollow, Lissy smiled and waved at the children playing on the porch of the large farmhouse. The oldest Davidson boy, Martin, swung on a tire swing. He was a quiet lad that Lissy thought was handsome. He had shied away on her approach, though. She figured it would take a little more time. So, since she thought he would be a friend worth having, she was going to work on getting closer.

It was the Davidsons who supplied a good portion of Grunewyck with farm fresh eggs. Lissy wondered if the constant cackle of a thousand chickens could drive someone crazy. That was how she was going to do it. The store needed fresh eggs daily. Lissy was going to volunteer to personally go to the Davidson's farm early every morning and pick them up. She could take the Potter's pony cart. Samson, their little black pony, was friendly and quite cooperative. Samson liked her; she could just feel it. But the compensatory apple, offered on occasion, helped matters.

The Hollow soon lay before her, widening out as it stretched from the base of Parson's Ridge, east to the Spry River. Lissy wouldn't stick to the road; too many turns. She would cut through the trees until she reached the swampy portion and then turn west to the road when she was beyond all the annoying hillocks.

Making her way through the trees, she kept her eyes open for fairy circles. If they were to be found anywhere near Grunewyck, it would be in the peculiar confines of the Hollow. She entered a little glade, searching intently, trying to keep in mind that they were not her main goal for the day; Miss Carter was.

Lissy so badly wanted to find a fairy circle, though, much like the one she had come across at the Gyles' farm north of Grunewyck. Yet, today, her search was proving unproductive. Lissy sighed in dismay and moved on.

An opening in the tree line admitted her into a second glade. It was much larger than the first, but just as well shaded. Three quarters of the way across, Lissy flopped down to rest and peel sticky pea vine from her butterscotch-colored dress; disappointment playing across her freckle covered face. Continuing on, she wound her way through a grove of old oaks. After several hundred feet of trudging through dead leaves and decaying acorns, she walked out of the trees and nearly stumbled into the very thing she sought.

Stopping abruptly, she stared with excitement at the ring of bright red toadstools with their small crème-colored warts. Manitas or Anitas? She couldn't remember what Durnell had called them. Her school mate, Abe Spooner, had taken a small bite out of one on a dare. Then he really did start seeing fairies. He got terribly sick afterwards and didn't come back to school for almost a week.

Walking around the wagon wheel sized ring, she avoided stepping inside. That was against the rules. It was either the fairies would take you prisoner or harass you for the rest of your life, Lissy couldn't remember which.

The thought to hide and wait to see if the fairies would come, entered her mind, but that wouldn't be until the gloaming. She didn't have the time, and besides, it would have been just plain stupid to be in the Hollow after dark. Turning away, she continued toward the Grunewyck Road, now visible in the distance.

After nearly a mile, Lissy had to skirt a large pond nestled in the trees. She couldn't remember it being there the last time she came through. But things were always changing in the Hollow. The water in that place did funny things and went wherever it wished. Looking into the pond, she thought it a lot clearer than it should be. She could actually see the bottom, and oddly, there was a current down there causing the pondweed to bend, wiggle, and wave.

She planted her backside on a fallen tree trunk and began to munch on an apple from her bag. The woods were filled with the eerie calls of woodpeckers, jays, and other birds. Frogs were putting forth their undulating trill, and the gurgling of water from an unseen source, filled the air. The fluttering leaves filtered the sunlight and its rays danced over the ground, making it appear as if the soil itself was alive. Lissy felt it would have been a rather pleasant moment had it not been for the perpetual chill that accompanied her every visit to the Hollow.

Lissy soon became lost in thought trying to formulate a story to tell her folks as to why she had skipped out on her chores. It was Saturday, after all. She could tell them that gypsies had kidnapped her and it had taken all day to escape, or, perhaps, she had fallen while crossing the ford and the current had swept her into the ravine. She would add that it had floated her so far away that it took a good part of the day to walk back. There were all kinds of dangerous things that could happen to a young girl out in the woods. Who could question that?

It was on finalizing the crafting of her excuse that she realized they would want to know why she was in the Hollow to begin with. Her brain hurt from creating a story and she decided she would hold off trying to figure it out until later. Right now, she was going to decide whether she wanted to soak her feet in the cool, clear water of the pond, or go as far as shucking her clothes completely to go skinny dipping. No one would see her there because there weren't that many people with the nerve to venture this far into the Hollow. She chose the former.

Removing her 'clodhoppers' and her wooly grey stockings, she set them aside and stepped into the pond up to her ankles. The cool mud squished between her toes. She studied her reflection, her squarish face and button nose. Then there were the dimples that showed even when she wasn't smiling, making her cheeks look chubby. On top of all that, even though she was brown of hair, freckles covered everything. Her dark eyes turned down at the corners and often people commented that they were a little too fierce for a girl her age.

Those dark eyes caught movement way down deep and she figured it was just a fish. Yet she couldn't dismiss the distinct shape gliding through the pond weed. Maybe a trick of the light. Watching closely, without blinking, she kept her focus on the long waving strands of vegetation. Lily pads and luxurious green Watermeal floated on the surface. Cattails and Arrowhead hung over from the shoreline, and even though pretty, they were all blocking her view.

Suddenly, a slender shape swam out into the open and then disappeared again. It looked to Lissy like a tall, slender woman, snaking around among the plants, her long, thin hair trailing back in a kind of fringe from a nearly bald pate. Lissy lost sight of the creature and strained her eyes to make sure she didn't miss its return.

The woman-like thing suddenly shot out from a wall of weaving grass blades. Lissy gasped and stepped back out of the water. The thing streaked left across her field of vision; just three feet below the surface. Long, skeleton thin legs undulated, it's slender arms flat against its sides. An algae green, chemise-like garment incased its body and tattered strips of the fabric fluttered as it moved. The thing soon whirled down toward the bottom and disappeared again.

Lissy felt the fear of the unknown, but that didn't overrule her excitement. Her curiosity drove her to lean forward for a better look. Then, it was right there in front of her, having slid out from under a patch of lily pad on her left. It crouched on the silty slope just under the surface, staring up at her with large, bulging, lidless eyes. It gave Lissy a wicked grin, exposing a set of horse-like teeth, stained green. Then a twisted hand with long pencil-like fingers moved stealthily in the girl's direction. Breaking the surface, the hand seemed to float toward one of Lissy's ankles. A soft paralysis, starting at her toes began to move up her body.

"I'm being hypnotized," slipped from her lips, her words barely a murmur. This was followed by a voice in her head suddenly shouting, "Lissy!"

She shrieked and back pedaled, tripping over the log. Frantically crab walking backwards, a tree trunk soon blocked her path. Lissy stopped and sat down hard. The slight paralysis left her body and when she felt normal again, she searched out a hefty stick to use as a club and returned to the pond.

Whatever it was, it had gone. The only other witnesses to the event were a couple of damselflies, their greenish-blue bodies gleaming as they flew in their bouncing manner, and a curious bluejay darting from branch to branch above Lissy's head.

Coming to a halt behind the log, she wondered if it had all been in her head. Maybe her overwhelming desire to see a fairy had caused her to conjure it. Dropping her stick, she gathered up her sack, shoes, and socks. Then hurrying away, she abandoned her half-eaten apple to the mud.

Lissy continued barefoot to where the trees opened into yet another large glade. Stopping long enough to put on her socks and shoes, she cast the occasional cautious glance back toward the pond.

It was a good thirty minutes before she stepped out onto the hard packed mud of the Grunewyck Road. She hadn't gone more than a few steps toward Gowan when she detected a brief, tinkling laughter coming from far up the ravine. Crouching for a better view through the trees, she watched for movement.

The ravine was unchartered territory. Lissy had never ventured there. It was also private property. It belonged to the Carters, as did the cave up the slope, its large gaping maw, partially hidden from sight by trees and thickets. Ghillie's Gate, they called it, but she didn't care, she wasn't going up there.

The laughter came again. Leaning a little to her left, she gazed through the tree trunks in the direction of the covered bridge at the far end of the ravine, and the lane that snaked its way up to Nixie's Bluff. She could just make out assorted colored clothing moving through the green leaves of the low hanging branches.

Three girls with long, dark hair came into view. They were playing tag among the trees just this side of the bridge. There was something odd about the way they moved. It took Lissy only a few seconds to realize their movements were more animal-like than human. That set her back a bit, but also sparked a more tenacious curiosity. She wanted a closer look.

Holding her bag tightly in her arms to keep it silent, she found a path covered in wet leaves and moved down it, her shoes barely making a sound. Arriving at the bottom of the slope, she quietly worked her way west.

It was a whole different world down there. Centuries old trees, shielded her from the sky, their late summer leaves fluttering in the breeze. She could see that the path went on for a good mile or so, hugging the edge of the short, vertical bank that contained the road-width body of murky water that stretched from one end to the other. Clusters of exposed, twisted tree roots protruded weirdly from both sides looking like they could come alive at any second to wrap her in their gray, muddy arms and drag her into the water to drown.

Birdsong had been replaced with a mixture of frogs, crickets, and katydids. Lissy thought that odd. In fact, the only bird she saw was the occasional owl that sat fearlessly scrutinizing her as she passed, large dark eyes causing her to shudder.

When Lissy was close to where the girls were playing, she saw they were dressed like the women she had seen in a hootchy-kootchy show at a circus down in Springfield. She had joined a group of young boys spying under the bottom of the tent at the back. Inside, a dozen or so men, seated in chairs, cheered on some scantily clad women dancing on a stage, shaking their bellies to music, and making come-hither gestures with their hands.

The girls among the trees wore low riding gossamer pants with wide decorative waistbands covered in gold baubles. The cuffs of their pant legs were similar and wrapped tightly at the ankles. Their blouses were short of sleeve, outlined with decorative trim, and made of the same material as the pants. Falling many inches short of their hips, their tiny blouses exposed a great deal of midriff, allowing Lissy to see that not one of them sported a belly button.

Each outfit was of a different color and transparent enough to show the girls wore nothing underneath. Their bodies were long and slender. Not one of them had anymore atop than Lissy had in her tenth year of life. They were of varying heights, small, medium, and large, but all taller than Lissy by several inches. There wasn't a pair of shoes among them.

Flowers adorned their long, dark hair along with other woodland debris. The shortest of the three had a white patch in her hair just above her forehead. The bigger of the three bullied the others in their play, one time even putting the smallest one on her back, both admitting short, high-pitched squeaks.

It was their faces that brought Lissy the most concern. They were odd, reminding her of something. The tallest had a wider, flatter nose, the other two, small and button-like. All had dark, beady eyes. They reminded Lissy of polecats, only—without the fur and tail. Creatures that would kill every one of your chickens if you weren't careful in how you cooped them up at night.

One spun away from the others to escape being tagged and her hair flew up to expose small pointed ears. Lissy pressed a hand against her mouth to suppress a gasp and almost dropped her bag. Ducking behind a tree, she frightened a woodcock that burst from a patch of briar and rocketed into the sky. The three girls melted away into the landscape.

Lissy's heart was now in her throat and a dose of adrenaline coursed through her veins. She looked in every direction, but those unusual creatures were nowhere to be seen. She continued slowly up the path toward the covered bridge to see if they might be in the lane leading up to the house. But no, they were hiding. She could feel them watching. Then the sensation waned and she knew they had gone.

Moving up to stand on the driveway leading to the carriage house, she studied the covered bridge behind her. It was the fanciest bridge she had ever seen, even more so than those up around Dunwich and Aylesbury. But the Carters could have any ol' covered bridge they wanted. The weird thing about this one was the faces carved into the wood underneath the eaves.

Some were cherub like, but others were ugly and looked like goblins. Gargoyles! That was it! The faces of the cherubs were distorted in fear like they felt threatened by their menacing companions. From where she stood, Lissy could see the backs of the two statues that had been placed at the other end as if to guard the opening. They sat upon the large wooden railings, and appeared to be snarling at anyone who came forth from the Gowan side. More gargoyles!

The wide body of water ran under the bridge and ended in a large pool just to the west. At the far end, up under the trees, there was a small sandy beach. Upon it, several large flat rocks stretched out into the water, and just on the far side, a short rock wall covered in vegetation with a cascade of water running down it. So, it was a spring that fed that dark pond, after all!

It was shadier on that side of the bridge, and the sun never touched the water. She wanted a closer look at the cascading spring. So, moving to the other side of the driveway, she pranced down a narrow path that led to her destination.

Stopping at the bottom, she scanned the area and then froze. A decrepit looking hag now knelt atop one of those flat rocks. Lissy hadn't heard a thing; it was almost as if the crone had appeared out of thin air. She wondered if it might be one of the three girls, but no, not unless one of them had transformed into an ugly, old hag dressed in rags.

The creature pulled something from the water and held it up. It was a man's shirt, white in color, much like the ones Lissy's father wore. The old woman held the garment up to expose a large red stain and then plunging it back into the stream, she began to scrub it frantically against a stone just under the surface. The woman blubbered and talked to herself, fretting and shaking her head, her long, greasy grey hair hanging down to curtain her face.

Lissy wasn't sure whether to approach or run away. She took a step back and her shoes scuffed the path. The hag jerked her face around and glared at the girl. Dark eyes gleamed from behind thin strands of hair, and the mouth, under a large hooked nose, formed a wicked grimace. Raising the piece of clothing out of the water with both hands, she shook it at the girl, showing her the large crimson stain. It was as if the washer woman expected Lissy to know who the shirt belonged to and the reason why it was stained with blood.

A keening wail rose on the breeze and Lissy realized it came from the mouth of the old crone. She shuddered and the hair rose on her arms and back of her neck. Her bladder gave up its water, and spinning around, she ran.

The wailing noise in her ears now crescendoed and became loud and unbearable. Dropping her lunch bag, she pressed the palms of her hands to her ears and ran faster than she ever had before. The woman's cry turned into a long-drawn-out scream that suddenly broke; only to begin again.

Lissy wanted so badly to outrun that noise, but the ravine had captured it and encapsulated her within its resonance. She began to sing *Ring Around the Rosie* as loudly as she could, trying to drown out that terrifying wail.

Upon reaching the Grunewyck road, the terrifying cry faded away. When it registered that the sound had ceased, Lissy rested just long enough to take several big gulps of air and attempt to ease her splitting sides. Her underwear was soaked. Making sure the road was clear of human traffic, she pulled up her dress and removed her sodden knickers. They would only slow her down and chaff her thighs. Tossing them out of sight into the long grass, Lissy broke into a fast jog toward home.

She cut across the hillocks instead of going around them, and she didn't stop to rest until she reached the Davidsons. Without warning, the tears came as she stood in the middle of the road. She had never been this scared before.

When Lissy realized that Martin watched her through the chicken wire at the coop, she took off again; running with her face pressed into her hands. Tears streamed and sobs broke from her lips. Somebody was calling out to her; a woman's voice. She didn't look back. For the first time since she was a small child, Lissy seriously wanted for her mother.

8

11:30am

Danny Billings stood on the Gowan station platform, checking the pocket watch his father had given him on his last birthday. "You got to have a good watch if you're going to be a station agent, one that's worth their salt, anyway," the old man had said before handing the ancient Rosedale to his son. Danny had been so overcome with emotion that he had hugged his father. It was not something he did regularly.

The noon train would soon arrive and Danny had his hands full. Gil was at home, sick. Danny would have to do it all by himself. He had two young passengers bound for Ipswich who couldn't control their glee at visiting their grandmother. Then there was Bessie LaVern's mother, Audrey, who had a sick relative up Aylesbury way. They occupied the two benches set against the station wall, sheltered by the porch like platform. It was a comfortable, shady spot that the sun only touched for a short time before dropping behind the trees atop Mount Ovis.

All the necessary tickets had been sold and all Danny had to do was get his passengers and their luggage on board. The rest of his day would be filled with menial tasks such as sorting the mail for Anson Teal, the postman, and a few other things which included a little housekeeping. If there was time, he might even pull the weeds sprouting around the ties that supported the two shiny rails. He listened for the air horn of the locomotive and then checked his watch again. The Coast Bound Flyer would whistle upon leaving Brimfield, the sound floating all the way up to Gowan. It would give Danny ample time to have things set up for its arrival.

The young agent scanned the sky, hoping for some sign of rain to cool things off. His eyes passed over the cupola of Carter House rising up above the trees in the distance. Something blinked, like a window had been opened, reducing the amount of glare on glass.

There had been talk of odd things going on up there. Danny knew Janette, but she was three years older and they didn't travel in the same circles. She was always polite to him, though. He often told his pals that he thought Janette Carter was quite the looker. It wasn't news that Janette and her mother had taken Headmost House, as old Ben Carter had divorced the both of them, having met and married another woman in England, or Scotland, or… some place over the pond.

Danny had been present on Carter's return with his new wife. Gil told him that Carter had purchased every seat on the train for the return trip. Privacy reasons. Danny had seen the new bride dressed in all her finery, caped and veiled, leading Carter by his hand as if the old man didn't know the way to the car. Kaleb Knight had pulled the Pierce around to the south end of the platform; out of sight of the nearby houses. That was against the rules, but Gil said nothing, and if Gil didn't—Danny didn't. The whole event was the first sign that something was amiss, leaving Danny with a bad feeling.

Then there were what Gil referred to as, "Those ladies in waiting." There were three of them, caped and veiled like their matron. They wore clothing so thin; Danny could see they weren't wearing a stitch underneath. Their bodies were no more developed than his sister had been at eleven years old, just taller, their torsos, slender and long. It wasn't normal. This caused his mind to go into a quandary, bringing a headache. He had to deliver the luggage to the Carter House kitchen. Kaleb had done most of the work once he was inside. It was like the old groundskeeper didn't want Danny in the house. Those girls had remained just out of sight, whispering and giggling in their squeaky voices.

The following day, he had been waiting for the Coast Bound Flyer returning to Gowan as the MA & RI Rambler. It was right at the gloaming. He stood alone on the platform, readying himself to greet two passengers (Mayor Wilton's boys) returning to the village. Gil was inside preparing to close things down for the night.

There had come a loud whispering, followed by giggling just like those girls up at Carter House. The sound had come from the trees beyond the tracks. He felt like someone was watching him, and then those three girls appeared, dressed in their hootchy-kootchy outfits.

The three of them were just visible in the gathering shadows of the trees as they stood together, their eyes on him. Danny gave them a slow wave and they giggled again. Putting their heads together as if in conversation, they stared back and he saw their eyes pick up a glow like polecats caught in lantern light.

The tallest of the three slender creatures took a step in his direction and began a kind of dance, all three singing a song that was strange to Danny's ears. The dancer's moves were seductive. He started to sway along with her as if spellbound. He became aroused; the bulge in his trousers apparent.

Gil had stepped into the ticket bay that projected out onto the platform and saw his assistant swaying and humming a tune. "Everything okay, out there, boy?"

Danny snapped out of his trance and the source of his mesmerization melted back into the trees.

"Just fine, Gil. Still waiting on that train," he said, not wishing to divulge the odd thing that had just occurred. Later, in relaying his tale to Paul LeBarge, his confidant and partner in tomfoolery, Danny shared that it had felt a lot like being drunk on whiskey with one serious hard-on.

There came the short, 'Toot, toot, toot', that the engineer of the noon arrival was so fond of whenever he came in sight of the station. Danny shouted in his best station agent voice, "Coastbound Flyer to Grunewyck, Aylesbury, Arkham, and points beyond, now arriving. Prepare to board in five minutes. Five minutes, folks." Danny smiled to himself; he was getting pretty good at his job.

The three passengers got to their feet and moved toward the edge of the platform. Danny began pushing the luggage cart to the spot where he knew the baggage car would stop. Glancing over at the trees, his thoughts turned to those three strange girls, hoping they would return. He liked the way they made him feel.

9

12:00pm

The bell tower at the village green began its peal shortly after the sound of the train whistle. Shop owners, and their helpers, closed up for an hour or so with 'Out To Lunch' signs appearing on doors and in windows. Some went home for their noonday meal, but most went to the café.

Boots was ready for them. Ellie, Biddy, and Clyde, were poised and ready to go. Paul LeBarge was in the kitchen at Brenner's with every stove burner occupied, sweat pouring from his brow. Plates of meatloaf, fried chicken, bratwurst, potatoes and other assorted vegetables covered the prep tables, ready for the rowdier crowd that wanted beer with their meal.

Grunewyck's noon bell could be heard peeling from beyond the Hollow, a town seriously anticipating a much-needed break from their daily labors. The doors and gate to McGowan's Basket Factory and Anderson's Box & Crate Works opened and the workers piled out to find seats in the shade to eat their lunch and drink their beers.

Men and women perched themselves on loading docks, short walls, and nearby rail fences. Some sat on overturned buckets, in the seats of company trucks, and on the grass itself. Home rolled cigarettes and cheap cigars were lit after their meager meal was consumed and the air filled with chatter. Conversations centered on local gossip: the Carters and their separation, the strange lights seen bobbing around late at night in Whip-poor-will Hollow, and the fearful rumor that the factories may close next year due to acquisition by the state government. Boston needed water, and a reservoir had to be built, but nobody seemed to know where exactly. The powers that be, wanted to stave off resistance. So, transparency was pushed to the back.

Nobody, in any one of maybe a hundred villages, wanted to accept the reality that it just might be theirs that was to swirl down the drain of extinction. The thought of such a loss was hard to accept. So, the news was shrugged off as if it were a troublesome fly. There had been no official word and very few, if any, were going to go off half-cocked. They had enough to deal with and were doing their best to not fret about something that might be purely a product of the grapevine.

Their view narrowed toward the end of the workday, a time when the focus was just on getting home, greeting their wives, playing with their children, eating their supper, poker, drinking, and chasing after dubious women. Tomorrow would be another day.

10

12:40pm

Cora MacLean swept the gallery porch of the Lost Collie tavern on the south edge of Grunewyck. The place was never as busy as it used to be back in the day. Prohibition had made her, and her husband, Al, wealthy. They had been the only establishment in the town willing to thumb their nose at the law and offer alcohol on the sly. The Lost Collie tavern, handed down to her by her father, had evolved into a speakeasy in the roaring twenties, and boy, did that place roar.

Now, it was just an out of the way stop serving Grunewyck regulars, farmers, Gowanites stopping in for supper on their return home, and the occasional weary traveler.

Cora had immigrated with her parents, older brother Dugan, and younger sister Chastity, from Scotland in the nineteenth century when a feuding clan had burned her father's pub to the ground. They had barely escaped with their lives. Dugan had died the first winter in Massachusetts, not understanding that in the new world, one could freeze to death. They had buried him in the cemetery there in Grunewyck and didn't have the heart to leave him. So, the Grahams built their tavern and there they stayed. Now, the state conveyed that they just might take the town, and if so, all the souls buried in the graveyard would be relocated to municipalities that stood on higher ground.

The Macleans didn't want to think about that hardship. Cora told people that at her age she just wanted to take care of her tavern and enjoy what remained of her life. It wasn't that her and Al couldn't afford to shuck it all. They had been frugal and could afford to move. They just didn't want to.

Lost in thought, she pushed her broom around, her arm pits damp with the heat. She stopped and gazed down the road toward Whip-poor-will Hollow. The sound of running feet had caught her attention, and soon a young girl appeared moving toward the tavern in a lurching stride. Something told Cora that the youngster had been at it for some time. Leaning her broom against the wall, she stepped out onto the line of large flagstones that ran to the road.

It was Lissy Potter.

Cora was good friends with her mother, Colleen, and her husband, James. She had often engaged the girl in conversation when going for supplies at Potter's General Store. Lissy, more than likely, could be found seated on sacks of potatoes or a crate of goods, where she had been ordered to remain and think about some misdeed she had committed. Cora told Colleen that she believed Lissy was just overly curious about the world. She knew that the girl was smarter than most of the kids in the village, except for Serenity Trask, an infirm, wheelchair bound wealthy girl who received her scholarly instruction from Gregory Bly.

Lissy could be seen spending a lot of time at the tiny library in Grunewyck. Ethel Lancaster, the librarian, once shared that Lissy was an avid reader and had the potential to make something of herself. Cora told Al that she believed Lissy's title of troublemaker was underserved. Al told her to mind her own business.

Cora called out to her as she passed in her limping run. Lissy was shielding her face as if she didn't want to be recognized. The girl ignored the old woman and continued on as if Cora wasn't even there.

"Melissa Potter, is something wrong?" she called again. Still no response. Lissy was covered in dirt and her hair was a mess. Something bad had happened.

Cora walked out to the edge of the road and shouted, "Lissy, wait!" She took in the condition of Lissy's knee length, butterscotch colored dress with what had once been white trim. It was tattered now as if Lissy had been busting thickets. An upside-down, V shaped shadow at the back, below Lissy's waist, was all too familiar to Cora. It brought her father's voice forth from the grave to echo in her head, "Lass... you've pissed yerself."

She watched until Lissy was out of sight and then turned to look down the road in the direction from which the girl had come. Cora half expected to see someone, or something, emerge from the distant woods in pursuit. But there was only Martin Davidson swinging on the tire swing in front of his house. She waved, but he didn't acknowledge and left the swing to go inside. She raised her eyes to the belvedere of Carter House showing just above the tree tops far in the distance. She wouldn't be surprised if there was a connection. The grapevine had flourished with all the talk of Benjamin Carter and his new wife. The sight of the place gave her the willies.

Cora believed that Janey was the only decent one of the bunch. She rejoiced at the news that, "Janette Carter will be taking the position as schoolteacher over in Gowan." Maddie had told Merlyn Cobb, and he had accidently let it slip to Beulah McKay. Constance confirmed it, and the word spread like the 1918 pandemic. Janey was soon the talk of the two villages.

Walking back to the tavern porch, Cora was going to give Colleen Potter a call and give her a heads up about Lissy.

11

1:00pm

Tom Lynn prepared for his visit to Headmost House. Paul LeBarge had drawn him a bath and laid out towels. Tom sat on an old, cane bottomed chair next to the tub, his bare body covered in a slight sheen of sweat. The water was too hot and he wasn't ready to climb in yet. He would let it cool. The two windows were open in room number nine, also known as, 'The Bath Room'. Cream-colored cotton, serving as curtains, undulated in the afternoon breeze.

Tom, at first, worried someone outside might get an eye full, but the two windows looked out on the roofs of the attorney's office and the butcher's shop. So, unless someone had binocular's or a telescope down in that first cottage across Cemetery Lane, he was safe from being accused of parading his nakedness.

He checked again to make sure he had locked the door as Beth didn't seem to respect her boarder's privacy all that much. She had walked in on Tom just the day before. She brought him his clean laundry and tossed it on the bed saying, 'Ain't nothing I've never seen before. Hell, I raised two boys of my own," then laughing, she left the room. So, he took to locking the door, the key tied on a cotton string around his neck.

71

The gold bauble that Clyde had given him and Janey, was missing from his dresser top where he had placed it before bedtime. He hadn't given it the attention it needed. It should have been locked away. Perhaps someone had come out of one of the rooms adjoined by the outside balcony, entered his, and helped themselves. He made a mental note to ask Beth or Paul.

The foremost thing on Tom's mind was making the best of his dinner at Headmost House. Janey was dead set on accompanying him up to Nixie's Bluff and he needed to talk her out of it. Tom knew once Janey had accomplished her little affray with Benjamin, the old man would tell her right to her face to get out and never set foot in Carter House again. He might even disown her. So, Tom's only chance to see her, once he started work, would be a visit to Gowan every once in a while, and hope Benjamin didn't find out. There was a good chance he too could get kicked out and that might extend to Kaleb. Benjamin Carter was that way.

The water had cooled considerably and climbing in, he took the soap and began scrubbing, all the while suspecting even after toweling dry, he would still be just as wet minutes later. The day was heating up.

3:20pm

Sally Combs stood behind her counter, checking out the latest in daywear for women, a supply catalog spread out before her. The shop sold an equal amount of clothing for men and women. Workboots and high heels shared the same rack of shelves on the south wall. She had thought to add on to the building, but that plan had been put on hold. The reservoir spelled the end for Gowan. There was no official word yet, but Sally knew better, and besides that, she now had other plans. Her eyes traveled up to Bessie LaVern, her assistant and sales person. The eighteen-year-old Bessie, had her back to her and was bent over, pulling men's flannel shirts from a box to hang on a rack.

Even though it was already the mid 30's, Bessie still sported a rather risqué blue flapper dress. They were her favorites and when Sally began replacing the few she had in stock with the form fitting day dresses that were the style at the present, she offered the outdated flapper wear to

Bessie at a great discount.

Sally never thought Bessie would wear them in the daytime while she worked. She thought to ask her to curb her desire and wear something closer in design to what hung on the racks. That frame of mind didn't last long when she saw how good Bessie looked in them; especially when positioned as she was.

No one ever questioned Sally as to why she never married, never had a date, or never joined in the chatter of friends when the topic of conversation turned to men. She was known in the gossip circles as a spinster.

Bessie was good at keeping secrets, especially since the feeling was mutual. They both stood to suffer the slings and arrows of the people's malice should the truth ever be disclosed. Sally imagined she would be forced to close up shop and leave the county. At the moment, if there was any question, it remained with the gossips like ol' Widow McKay. Sally was sure some people just didn't want to know. So, if there was no evidence, then... ignorance was bliss.

Bessie was just a girl that worked at the clothing store and was a friend to her boss. She was good at keeping up appearances and did everything expected of an eighteen-year-old girl in small town Massachusetts.

Since Sally couldn't afford a big house out back across Ovis Street, she still made her home above the shop. She could access her rooms without leaving the building. Some days she would hang the 'Gone To Lunch' sign on the door, lock it, and the two of them would retreat upstairs, taking an hour for tea and other assorted pleasures.

Sally's plan was to close up shop and move to Boston. Her and Bessie could travel separately and meet up later in the big city. She could open a new shop on some busy street there, selling only women's popular styles. If Gowan was in peril of disappearing from the map, then the opportunity may be just around the bend. She might be able to finagle a hefty price from the state for her property, and then her dream could come true. Sally felt that Boston would be more conducive to her way of life and there would be a whole lot less sneaking around. It was time to leave her home of thirty years and say goodbye to village life.

Coming out of her trance-like state at the sound of a wooden hanger hitting the floor, Sally saw Bessie had dropped a shirt. Turning back toward the counter, Bessie bent to pick it up, her sizable breasts straining to break free of their bonds. Flapper dresses weren't designed with the big chested in mind. Sally took a step to her left for a better view. When Bessie came upright, their eyes met, grins were exchanged, and Sally gave her a wink before returning to her supply catalogue.

4:35pm

Janey sat at her vanity wearing only a slight sheen of perspiration. Studying her face in the mirror, she said with a haughty British accent, "To wear make-up or not to wear makeup, that is the question." Chuckling, she applied only a little. There was really no need for it. Her skin was smooth and unblemished except for a tiny mole by her right ear. Brushing out her short, straight, blonde locks, she marveled at how they formed an almost perfect bowl shape around her head. The hairdresser over in Bournemouth was good at her job and had even bragged that Janey had been her thousandth customer for the outdated bob cut. It would be the first, as well as the last, for Janey. She was going to just let it grow back to shoulder length.

Standing, Janey looked her body up and down in the mirror. Other than her somewhat knobby knees, she thought she looked pretty good. Turning sideways, she studied her perky breasts before taking in her belly and backside. Turning her buttocks toward the mirror she found herself somewhat relieved that they remained round and firm. She figured at some point in the future, she would just have to stop fearing that her butt was going to drop, and then flatten out like Percy's favorite snow shovel. No sense in worrying about something she had no control over. For the moment, though, everything looked good, and with Tom coming over, that's all that mattered.

The heat had come up quick. So, before she dressed, she powdered her entire body. She had stopped by Sally's, and Bessie had talked her into a bandeau style bra and tap panty set of a new material called Rayon. It looked and felt just like silk but was a lot cheaper. Janey had chosen 'Light Rose' along with garters and garter belt. Then, a pair of black chiffon seamer stockings to help hide her knees and a blue

Parisian tea dress with little white flowers. Sally said she was afraid the dresses would never sell in Gowan and was thrilled that Janey had chosen one of the four she had in stock. Janey didn't want to go all out and wear something too formal, especially something high fashion like those evening dresses that had no sleeves and hung to one's ankles. Nope, not in rustic Gowan. A day dress would be just fine.

She finished dressing and slipping on a pair of black flats, she checked herself out one more time in the mirror. The dress was just tight enough to compliment her figure, but not so much to show her panty line. Leaving the room, she stopped to stand at the top of the stairs, just listening to the house.

It had been difficult to convince her mother to allow Tom up for dinner. Janey wasn't confident her mother wouldn't fly off the handle and start berating Tom to his face. She was going to go downstairs and confirm that Constance's promise to remain civil would be kept.

Below in the entry hall, the grandfather clock chimed five. Janey had an hour to check and make sure everything was in order; starting with her mother. That, in itself, may take up a good portion of that time. "Your best behavior, Janey Carter, your best behavior," she told herself, and bouncing down the stairs, she announced at the bottom, "Well, I am ready," to no one in particular. Moving into the parlor, she greeted her mother and kissed her for good measure.

҉

5:55pm

Tom stood hesitant on the portico of Headmost House. He was prepared for a cold response from Constance and was feeling a little nervous. In his hand was a basket full of things like fruit, the locally made cheese from Prospect Dairy, a jar of apple butter, and other assorted items that could be passed off as gifts. Mary McCarthy had taken care of it for him. She became quite excited when he had asked her. Following her around the store as she picked out items to place in a decorative basket crafted locally in Grunewyck, had him chomping the bit.

Tom tapped lightly on the door and Percy appeared as if out of nowhere. "Mr. Tom Lynn, my... how you grown. I can still see that little scamp in your face, though. So, how you?"

"Good to see you again, Percy. I am just fine," Tom said, ignoring the scamp remark. He just smiled big and followed Percy into the entry hall.

"You wait right here, now, Mr. Tom. Let me announce you to Missus Constance and Miss Janey." He walked to the door of the parlor and said, "Mister Tom Lynn has arrived."

Janey jumped to her feet from the loveseat that sat just across from her mother's chair and stood facing Percy. Constance remained where she was, looking like the previous queen of England. "Well, Percy, show him in. Don't leave him standing out there," she said.

Percy motioned for Tom to come in and then remained beside the doorway waiting to be dismissed. Tom walked in, grinned at Janey, and then turning to Constance, he offered the basket. "Misses Carter, I brought you a little something. Mary, down at McCarthy's, was good enough to make some excellent choices for me. I hope you like them."

He smiled politely and waited. She dropped her hands to her lap from the arms of the chair and gazed up at him. For some reason, the hardness left her face and she gave him some semblance of a smile. Then offering up her hand, he gave it a gentle shake. "Welcome to my home, Tom."

"Thank you. It's been a long time. Hope you are well."

"Percy, you take this out to Tabby and see if she needs any help setting the table."

"Yes, Missus Constance," he said and grinning from ear to ear, most likely because the introductions had gone well. He took the basket and exited the room at a swift walk. Tom took a couple steps to his left so as not to block Constance's view to Janey and then turned and said, "How are you, Janey?"

"Fine as frog's hair," she said and giggled. "Ummm, now..." she added and winked.

"You two can sit over there," Constance said, pointing to the loveseat that Janey had just vacated. "Yes, sit here with me, Tom," Janey said and cozying up together, they met Constance's gaze with submissive expressions. They would allow her to be the one to start the discussion. Both Janey and Tom already knew what to expect in the way of conversation.

It started out light and moved to more serious matters and finally the abandonment and separation. Percy announced dinner. Tom and Janey helped her mother from her chair and they gathered at one end of the long mahogany table with Constance at the head. Janey and Tom sat across from each other, smirking playfully.

Tabby served the soup and they began their meal. Tom was first to speak and picked up where they had left off in the parlor. "I am terribly sorry about your situation. It must be most difficult for you and Janey."

It was a turning point in their evening. Constance's eyes welled with tears and she looked away as if to study a large portrait of Uncle Bart's wife, Trudy, who still graced the wall of the dining room. Looking back at Tom, Constance gazed at him for an awkward moment and then said, "Thank you, Tom, that is most gracious of you."

Even Janey was somewhat surprised at the elegant manner in which Tom had expressed his words, and a slight smile braced her lips. The statement opened a flood gate and Constance began to talk as if Tom were an old friend rather than that annoying boy of twelve. The rascal, who stole cookies and apples from the kitchen at Carter House and whipped up Benjamin's foxhounds into a barking frenzy just to irritate her.

Constance conveyed all she knew of her selfish husband and his trip abroad that had turned the tide on what she considered to be a wonderful life. And even though she had not spoken with Benjamin since his return, she had gleaned from Beulah McKay all she figured she needed to know. The local gossipers were a tight knit bunch and like a pack of spies, they intentionally endeavored to know everybody's business. Philip Shannon, even though an attorney bound by attorney-client privilege, was also part of that network. His loyalty was equally split between the husband and wife of a family that was largely responsible for his wealth.

"The gold digger's name is Mabel. She used the last name of Morgan, or... Morrigan, something like that, anyway. That's what the papers, filed by Benjamin, say. I doubt it, though. I suspect it's a fake, and more than likely, one of many alias's. He met her while traveling in the borderlands of Scotland. That platinum blonde tramp got her hooks into my Ben, and somehow, oh... what's a good word? Help me out, Janey? Charmed him? Enchanted! Yes, that's the best word, I think! There is no other way. She cast a spell over my Ben. The little leech."

Janey and Tom sat unspeaking, glancing at each other on occasion as if in disbelief. "Now, she's sitting up there in my house. The house my husband built for me!" she said, pounding on the table once, causing the settings to jump.

Her lamenting continued on until Tabby moved to serve dessert. Constance's pie remained untouched, though, as she rose and left the table, having worked herself into a tizzy. Before she took up her cane and ascended the stairs to her room, she turned to Tom, who had risen to his feet as a gesture of proper etiquette, and said, "Nice to see you again, Tom. Thank you for listening to an old woman blather on about her woes. Good night, everyone."

Before Tom could respond, or Janey could move to embrace her, Constance turned and left the room. Tabby stood in the kitchen doorway with a crock of vanilla ice cream that she had hoped to slaver on the apple pie. Janey looked at Tabby and shrugged, "More for us, I guess."

Tabby smiled and going to the table, she put a satisfyingly sized scoop on each piece of pie. Picking up the plate with Constance's piece, she returned to the kitchen and closed the door to offer the two some privacy. Taking his plate, Tom moved around to pull out a chair next to Janey.

They ate their dessert in silence, both mulling over Constance's words. Janey finished her dessert and said as if to her pie plate, "I wonder if she blames me."

"I don't see how it could be your fault," Tom said with a look of concern.

"Well, it doesn't have to actually be my fault. I mean, maybe because I wasn't here when she was forced to move out. To, uh... buttress her against the hardship, so to speak."

"Confront her, Janey. Do it when she can't get away. Pull up a chair and set it right in front of hers in the parlor when she's in there. And even though it's not a concern of mine, you have some unfinished business that needs finishing."

Janey gazed at Tom in a new light. Once again, words she never expected to hear come out of his mouth. She wondered if she had been underestimating him.

"Now, shall we go outside? I'm stuffed, and I need some air."

"Why certainly, let's do that. Tabby! We're outside."

Tabby opened the door from the kitchen, a mixing bowl under her arm. Janey and Tom could see Percy inside at the small breakfast table quietly devouring what must have been Constance's Pie Ala Mode.

"Okay, sugar. I'll have Percy hang a light for you on the porch."

"Very well, we won't be going far, though. Lovely meal by the way."

"Yes, good meal, Tabby. Thanks so much for your trouble."

"Twas nothing, Mister Tom. Good to see you again. So many years, so many years," she said and smiled.

"Good night," he said and taking Janey's hand he towed her to the front door and outside, leaving her to wonder why the urgency.

Tom kept her hand in his until they reached the other side of the fountain and then sitting on the edge of the huge basin, he released it.

"Sorry, I just needed to get out of there. Too many ears for what I want to say."

"Too much for you, was it?"

"All that your mother said got my mind buzzing. All that talk about Ben's new wife. I want to know more, Janey. I want to go to Carter House. I could show up early. I am sure my uncle won't mind. I can't help but feel something else is going on here. Maybe none of my business, but…"

"No, I feel the same. In my mind something doesn't jibe. Is this woman so provocative she could influence my father the way she did? And platinum blonde hair?"

"Well, that's coming from Beulah, or, whomever. But… on a different note, I think people are looking the other way because of… well, like I said, it's none of their business. But it is yours and your mother's business. Is your attorney, Phil Shannon, looking into this? I'm sorry, maybe I'm out of line?"

"Ummm… no, I think my spite for my father has been overpowering my need to be concerned about related things. Maybe I'm using it as an excuse to not have to act. You know? Just to get on with my own life and let the forces that be, take him down for what he did to my mother."

"And… you?"

"What? Oh! Okay, yes, and me. But now you've lit a spark, Tom.

So, what happens after we've knocked him down a peg or two? What about that woman and her hand maidens? It will have a domino effect, so to speak. Perhaps… Merlyn Cobb should get involved?"

"Maybe. That woman is in his territory now. But of course, somebody needs to meet her… evaluate her, and determine if she's some kind of a criminal."

"I can do that," Janey said matter of factly.

"I was thinking more like… Cobb."

"No, I am going with you when you go up. I am going to talk to father and get a look at that woman."

"Could prove to be a little perilous, if you know what I mean?"

"Are you afraid? I think you can do the same, and together, maybe we can convince somebody to look into this matter. Perhaps… a Pinkerton?"

"No, I don't think we want that kind of attention. But you should know, I'm concerned about my uncle Kaleb losing his position because of our association."

"Unless my father has completely lost his mind, I don't see that happening."

"Why would he dismiss everybody else and not Kaleb?"

"That's what I'm saying, Tom. He couldn't part with Kaleb, considering how long they've been together. So, unless this woman has influenced my father to the point where he isn't in command anymore, or… he's been put out of commission..."

"Exactly. What if something has happened?"

"Don't say that, Tom. We may not be close, but he is still my father. I got a bad feeling about this."

"That makes two of us."

They talked until late and then walking Janey to the front door, Tom left her to return to Brenner's. With his back to the house, he didn't see the curtain in an upstairs window fall back into place.

8:30pm
An antsy Nealy Garret pulled into Zelda's parking lot, sat for a minute to scrutinize things and then got out of the patrol car and went inside. It

was early yet, and there were only a few drinkers in there. Tip was behind the bar reading a magazine. Nealy's plan was to have a beer, scope things out, and leave before the action started at nine. Tip was trying something new by bringing a little burlesque and vaudeville to small town Gowan. The actors and dancers had gathered back in the corner of the cavernous room near the stage. Nealy had already expressed to Merlyn that he was convinced that those dancers were actually prostitutes. Merlyn told him in stern fashion to let sleeping dogs lie.

If it was true, what he had heard about the state water commission's plans to take the valley, he would be out of a job soon anyway. So, at this point in his law enforcement career, it didn't matter.

The patrons sitting near the bar got up and took their drinks to distant tables where they could keep a close eye on the lawman and make a quick escape if necessary.

Nealy didn't recognize any of them. He suspected they were up from Lilting or Brimfield; maybe some of the outlying farms.

"Give me a beer, Tip."

Tip poured the best stuff he had on tap into a mason jar and set it on the counter. "On the house, Nealy."

"Thanks, Tip. So… how's the burlesque business? Those are some right pretty women you got back there."

"Well… Nealy, revenues up, and I'm thinking about adding a few more dancers for even bigger shows."

Nealy rotated on his chair, putting his back to Tip. He took a swig of his beer and said, "So… is that all they are, Tip? Dancers?"

Tip gulped and prepared for some kind of harassment. Nealy was known for that. Not that Tip didn't have the upper hand, as all it would take was one phone call to Merlyn Cobb and Nealy would be banned from his establishment. If Nealy persisted, Judge Benson would be consulted and Nealy Garret might have to take a job outside the county; one limited to farm work. Nealy knew this and thought it better to back off rather than strike too much alarm in the hearts of those who dwelt in Zelda's world.

Nealy was known for shooting first and asking questions later. Gowan, at the present, didn't have more than a couple of troublemakers left. That's because the majority were in the ground. Fifty-two-year-old Brad Conklin, caught in the midst of raping thirteen-year-old Lyla McKenzie out behind the slaughter house became the first. Refusing to follow Nealy's orders to turn Lyla loose, Conklin pulled his infamous pig sticker and got a forty-four-caliber hole through his chest for it. Two months later, a drunken Wayne Spade, who had been gunning for his cheating ex-wife with a double barreled twelve gauge, made the mistake of pointing it at Nealy. A month and a half after that, Lucious Weber tried to escape when Nealy was locking him up for the night. He punched the officer and ran. Lucius took a round in the back of his head for his trouble while fleeing across the village green. So, Tip didn't want to be number four. The thought of that bullet plowing through his skull was almost unbearable and, even worse, how easily it could happen.

Turning back to face Tip, Nealy swigged some more beer, put the jar with what remained on the bar, got up, and walked away. "Thanks for the beer, Tip, gotta get back to work."

Nealy departed and everybody relaxed. Pete Agar, Gowan's only beggar, came up and swigged down what remained of Nealy's beer. Tip gave him a smirk, took the empty jar, washed it out, and went to wiping the bar. About halfway toward the opposite end, he muttered to himself, "Work, yeah, right! Like you know what work is, Nealy Garret." Chuckling to himself, Tip finished his task and then poured himself a shot of whiskey to calm his nerves.

16

10:15pm

Sixty-eight-year-old Sam Shoats surfaced from a nightmare he was having about his older brother getting caught in the corn auger back in 1879. There had been a noise outside the farmhouse. Something wasn't right. A four o' clock milking was coming up and he had only been in his bed for a little over an hour. His wife, Aileen, snored beside him, oblivious to all. They slept with all the second-floor windows open because the night was hot and humid. The sweat made his nightshirt stick to his body and looking at his wife, he shook his head, and muttered, "How the hell can you sleep under a damn blanket?"

Prospect Dairy was usually quiet at night, but Sam was a light sleeper. World War One had made him that way. Rubbing his eyes, he realized the cows were raising a ruckus. Normally, they would have been outside in their pen on a hot night like this one, but there had been things going on—strange things. The most obvious were gates, doors, and windows he'd found open that he was sure he had closed and latched. Two nights before, Sam discovered one of his best Guernsey milkers down in the meadow, a rope looped around its neck and tied to a fence. It's utter had been completely dry. That was one full can of milk he wouldn't be selling.

Leaving the bed, he moved to the window and looked out into the yard that stretched between the house and the barn. The moon shone like daylight. Nothing was moving out there that he could see, however, the lowing from the barn and the occasional bellow said something was going on just out of sight. Pulling on his trousers and grabbing his twelve-gauge double barrel, Sam tiptoed down the stairs. Slipping on his boots, he grabbed the lantern sitting on the kitchen table. He kept it lit all night just for this very thing, the wick set at its lowest point. Turning it up, Sam left the house, checking to be sure the door hadn't locked behind him.

Stopping outside the barn door, he wondered if it might have been better to bring his Smith & Wesson revolver instead. It had six shots and was less awkward to weld. But the long gun was good if there were a bunch of trespassers. He was more likely to hit something with a load of buckshot than randomly tossing bullets into the dark.

With the shotgun in his right hand, he set the lantern down and quietly opened the door. Holding it open with a foot, he picked up the lantern and raised it high. The light showed the cows eyes wild with fear. The barn grew quiet, but someone, or something, was in there with them, Sam could just feel it. Stepping over the threshold, he hollered, "Who's in here?"

All hell broke loose.

A loud scrambling and scratching of claws on wood, coupled with squeaking and cackling, filled the barn. The cows began to panic, reeling, and jumping, slamming into walls and roof supports. Sam moved right, creeping down the aisle between the outside wall and the railing that kept the cows from running out into the dooryard. The aisle opened into a larger room at the north end. There was a large group of knee-high shadows moving fast along the back wall. They began leaping out an open window as he brought the shotgun to bear. Whatever they were, they had all escaped before he could draw a bead.

He lit several more of the lanterns hanging from overhead beams, then taking the one he'd brought, he entered the holding pen. Moving through the herd, Sam checked the animals as he went. They calmed with his presence; their source of agitation gone. Making his way over to the stanchions, he pushed cows out of his way as he went. When he arrived, he found four of the bovines with their heads locked in for milking.

"What the hell?"

Upon closer examination, he noticed the floor beneath their utters was puddled with milk.

"Well, definitely got myself some milk thieves."

The four udders were in varying stages of fullness, one being completely dry. After releasing the four cows, he exited the west door into the corral. The brightness of the moon made the lantern almost useless. Walking along the barn wall, he came to the open window and checked the ground for tracks. Bewilderment crossed his face, and reaching down, he touched one of the spoor. It looked like the imprint of an infant's bare foot, except—there were claws.

There were other kinds there as well, tracks similar to racoons, opossums, or the polecats he trapped in the winter months, except— much bigger. A chill, triggered by the unexplainable, crawled up Sam's spine.

He moved across the cattle yard to the shoulder high four rail fence, being careful where he put his feet. Aileen would get angry if he tracked cow flop into the house. Setting the lantern on the ground, he climbed up onto the bottom rail and gazed out across the meadow to the trees beyond.

The moon's light vacillated across that open green, the night breeze caressing the ankle high grass. He thought he saw movement at the tree line. The thieves were out there and for what he could make of them, they seemed to be playing. He hollered, "You're trespassing! Get off my property!" They stopped their activity and peered in his direction, dozens of eyes reflecting the moon's brilliance, showing green, red, and somewhere in between. This gave Sam a bit of a shock and in his fear, he stuttered out, "I have a gun… and I will use it."

The creatures didn't move other than to blink. He pointed the shotgun at them and let go with the left barrel. He knew the distance was too great for the shot to be affective, however, it made him feel better. A display of authority.

The blast broke the stillness, reverberating throughout the valley. There was no way Aileen could have slept through that, but it was him out there defending their property, not her. If she had a complaint, she could damn well come out here and take care of it herself.

Even before the muzzle flash had receded, the eyes vanished into the gloom. "There! Take that, you… you milk thieves!" The response was a shrill laugh that wafted back to him on the breeze, followed by a chorus of mirth filled cackling.

The power he often felt whenever he brandished his gun, drained away. A helplessness in the form of a lethargy overcame him, and his hands began to shake. Grabbing up his lantern, he secured the barn before hurrying back to the house. Sam Shoats no longer felt he was lord of the manor.

¶

11:45pm

Benjamin Carter slowly regained consciousness only to find himself lying on the roof of Carter House. He was in pain, like someone had tossed him out a window of the belvedere rising up behind him. The mist swirled and made him think he was dreaming, but the pain, and the blood soaking his nightshirt where it covered his scraped knees, told him otherwise.

The last thing he remembered was waiting in his bed for Mabel. She showed up to stand in the doorway, accompanied by her ermine faced temptresses. The three so called ladies-in-waiting followed her everywhere and always referred to her as Mab in their squeaky, little voices. When he had asked why Mab, she never answered other than to tell him he could call her that as well, if he wished. He refused.

She had appeared dressed in a gossamer sheath that left nothing to the imagination. Her hourglass figure and full breasts always cast a spell over him, leaving him to think of nothing else other than making her his own. Benjamin thought back to when they'd met, leading him to now wish that they never had.

He had been out late, sharing whisky's with business partners at a local pub just north of Jedburgh, Scotland. The meeting had been about a property he hoped to acquire, an old castle in Roxburghshire that he was sure he could have for a song. Benjamin knew if he could pull it off, it would be an act of thievery. The owners knew it too and had resisted the sale. Out of anger and drunkenness, he left and went back to the castle to make a list of all the things that would diminish its value.

Benjamin met her there in the twilight. "Just strolling the grounds," she said, for she too had an interest in the property. He was instantly smitten. He made advances toward her and she accepted them.

They made impulsive love in a grass covered courtyard. The next thing he knew, they stood at some pagan alter in front of a man who he suspected wasn't a priest, or maybe, wasn't real—period.

Everything after that was a blur. The arrival of her three ladies at the inn the day of their departure, the awkward boat trip home, and the train trip from Kingsport. He didn't even remember having Shannon draw up paperwork, but it was there. Mabel's ladies soon got involved in the love making, all four of them in bed with him at the same time. It was all so surreal, one session flowing into the next. It got so he didn't know which one he was having sex with. Benjamin felt as if he never recovered from the state of intoxication that the whisky had brought the night he met Mabel.

Kaleb seemed distant when they met at the station. The two hadn't spoken much. Every time he attempted to communicate with the groundskeeper, the man seemed to be in just as much of a stupor as himself.

As hard as Ben tried to break free of his own catatonia, he found he made no progress. Mabel and her handmaidens had taken control. She did all the dictating and he complied. The same for Kaleb.

This night, her three mischievous brats stood behind her, staring with those small, beady eyes. Giggling in their squeaky voices, they cast glances at each other as if communicating without words.

He had grown tired of them, and in a moment of clarity, he told them to get out. Leaving the marital bed, he picked up a long-handled clothing brush and held it in a threating manner. Moving toward them, his mind suddenly filled with fog and a feeling of great fatigue took control of his body. Benjamin recalled falling, but never hitting the floor.

Now, the evening breeze rippled his nightshirt and swirled the mist about him. He could hear the wildlife and insects in the woods. An insane orchestra. A wicked giggling resonated from the open windows of the belvedere. Rolling onto his back, he propped himself up on one arm. He could see the woman he thought he knew, standing with her minions. They began a low chanting that escalated in volume, filling the air and initiating a strange buzzing sound inside his head. The noise echoing in his mind was soon accompanied by a cacophony of sound emanating from the dark clouds directly overhead. Getting to his feet, he thought to force his way back inside and deal out some punishment.

The racket above his head became deafening, and his eyesight diminished. He felt as if he was going to pass out and stumbling forward, he sought the side of the belvedere for support. Before he could even put a hand on anyone of the pilasters supporting the roof, something seized him under his arms and lifted him into the sky. For the first time in his adult life, Benjamin Carter screamed.

Kaleb Knight dreamed of a man screaming and when he woke up, he realized that it was no dream. Getting up onto his knees, the groundskeeper's hands sought the window sill. Peeking over, he saw some great flying beast lifting a man from the roof of Carter House into the clouds above. Benjamin! He covered his mouth with a hand to stifle his own scream.

He soon returned his hand to the sill, his fingers resting on an iron horseshoe tacked there. The mind fog that formed daily upon awakening, dissipated. Removing his hand from the horseshoe, he found the fog started to roll back in. When he returned it, he got the same results as the first time. It was doing exactly as his grandfather had told him it would; ward off evil. There was one nailed at every window upstairs where he lived, but not the trapdoor that led to the ladder that would take him down into the stable's tool room.

Returning his eyes to the house, he muttered, "They finally got him."

Seconds later the backdoor to the house flew open. Mabel stepped out onto the gallery porch in her gossamer gown, her three minions following.

"Shit! Looks like I'm next."

Kaleb watched Mabel point toward the stable and the three nearly naked imps gleefully skipped in his direction. "Shit!" rolled out of his lips again as he scrambled off of the bed and ran for the trapdoor.

Quietly closing the hatch, he slid down the ladder to land in a pile of straw. The mind fog was returning. It was going to keep him from getting away. He felt faint and falling against the heavy iron grill that served as a door, the fog dissipated again and his mind cleared. So, perhaps it wasn't the horseshoe itself, but what it was made of that dispelled the evil.

"Iron," he muttered to himself.

Letting go of the grill, he quickly moved to a storage box and pulled out a small iron prybar. Taking it in hand, Kaleb opened the grill and stumbled into the aisle that ran between the stalls. There was a large double door at each end that he kept barred at night. Pointing himself toward the one on the east side of the stable, he ran.

His bare feet slapped on the floor, and above that, the sound of Mabel's lot trying to force open the big doors behind him. The horses reared back in their stalls, snorting, their eyes wild with fear. Unbarring the east door, he slipped out and closed it. Not thirty seconds later the familiar sound of the trapdoor to his rooms slamming open. "Upstairs now…" he panted to himself. Turning, he dashed into the woods, prybar in hand, doing his best to disappear into the trees.

CHAPTER FOUR

BENJAMIN CARTER AND THOSE TO FOLLOW

~

1

Philip Shannon, the local attorney for all of Gowan, stepped out onto the boardwalk to look around. The sun was breaking the horizon and the street was quiet. Typical for a Sunday morning. Going back inside, he failed to relock the door. Five minutes later, he wished he had stayed in bed. He was pretty sure it was Kaleb Knight that stumbled in wearing just a dressing gown. Dropping a short prybar onto the floor, the old man followed it down and lay as if unconscious, his breathing ragged.

It startled Philip and he dropped the file he had been carrying, sending papers in all directions. He knelt next to the inert Kaleb, the tell-tale odor of human excrement, among other things, rising up to his nose. The groundskeeper, besides being covered in mud, had also shit himself. Burs and broken pieces of pea vine were stuck to his muslin nightshirt. Kaleb wheezed, sometimes his breathing stopping altogether before resuming. Getting to his feet, Shannon went to the desk and picking up the candle stick phone, he called Chief Cobb at home. Merlyn answered on the first ring, his early morning, 'haven't had my coffee yet' voice grunted out, "Cobb."

"Merlyn? Philip Shannon here. You better get over here, fast."

"What's going on, Phil? Damn, man, you better have a pot of coffee brewing."

"Just come, please!"

Hanging up the phone in a frantic manner, Philip turned to find

Kaleb's eyes open, his mouth moving, but not a sound coming out. He knelt beside the man who made eye contact, his eyes wide with fear. Philip began to think kneeling so close might be a bad idea. If Kaleb vomited, his nightwear would take the brunt of it. The lawyer made an attempt to slide back, but Kaleb grabbed his arm, soiling the burgundy velvet cuff of his robe. Philip screwed up his face in disgust and pulled away, bringing Kaleb up off the floor. Kaleb promptly grabbed him with his other filthy hand and looked him square in the face. Philip saw the insanity in the man's eyes.

Kaleb rasped out, "Benjamin... taken." Then gulping like he couldn't catch his breath, he added, "Tom... tell Tom... don't come." The afflicted man emitted a loud groan and releasing his hold on Philip, he collapsed back onto the waxed boards of the floor. He began to seizure, and exhaling one long breath in what Philip knew all too well as the proverbial death rattle, Kaleb lay still.

Merlyn soon burst through the door, his face red from exertion, his breathing not much better than Kaleb's had been. Philip got to his feet and stepping out of Merlyn's way, he rubbed his hands together in a nervous fashion and said flatly, "I think he's dead."

2

Merlyn stood at the back of the preparation room at Sweeny's, a toothpick in his lips. He leaned back against a cupboard, arms crossed, his wide brimmed fedora pulled low over his eyes. A toothpick rolled from one side of his mouth to the other and back. He didn't like having to go to these damn autopsies. Doc Bolen had made an appearance at Philip's office and officially declared Kaleb Knight deceased. He put in a call to Sweeny's, and Bruce Nelson, the county coroner, was summoned. Vern and Duncan Sweeny, the twins, showed up and loaded the body into the truck that served as their hearse. That attracted attention, of course. Widow McKay had been leaning on her cane outside of Boots', and upon returning home, she called Helen Blake, the telephone exchange operator. "Oh my, Helen! Yes, right inside his front door! Dead as a doornail!" By lunch time, the whole town knew that Kaleb Knight of Carter House had died of mysterious causes in Philip Shannon's office.

Readjusting his massive bulk, Merlyn thought about all he was going to have to do and how much of that, he could trust Nealy to take care of. That was going to be practically none of it. The first thing on his list was to notify next of kin. Tom Lynn would do. It was convenient that Tom was still at Brenner's. Number two on Cobb's list: go up to Carter House and inform Benjamin Carter that his man was dead.

Bruce was just finishing up and Louis Sweeny was ready to go to town on the body in preparation for the funeral. "Massive stroke, plain and simple. No foul play here," he said. "I'll send the sheriff—and you—a report in the mail. You should have it by Tuesday. But I'll tell you right now, it was just a simple ol' stroke. Of course, you'll want to determine why he was covered in mud, plant matter, excreta, and why he was out in only a nightshirt. If I were a policeman, I'd be wondering if, perhaps, he had been frightened to death. Maybe trying to get away from somebody who meant to do him harm." Bruce moved to the wash basin, grinning over his shoulder as he washed his hands.

"Well, doc, I'll give it some thought."

Merlyn didn't like Bruce; never had. He was arrogant, pretentious, and about a dozen other things that the lawman could think of.

"And since you're not a policeman, I'll take it from here," Merlyn said and nodding good bye to Louis Sweeny, he moved to exit the room. "I'll be up at my office if you need me," he said, and opening the door, he heard Bruce say, "Good day, Chief Cobb, I'll send you that report."

Instead of his usual smartass remark, Merlyn just tapped the brim of his hat and then headed up the stairs. Returning to his mare, who stood tied to the porch railing at the front of the old mansion, he boosted his nearly three hundred pounds up onto Little Massy. The horse grunted and turned away from the house, making for the road without Merlyn's prompting. She knew where to go.

Sandy Brewster stabled most of the horses in Gowan. He had built a corral along the north side of the slaughter house many years prior. He was making good money from his little side venture, and he had Charley Bates Jr., who was good at taking care of horses, to help. Then there was Sully, who he had to continually warn not to joke with people about their horses being accidently led onto the killing floor. It just wasn't good for business.

91

3

Merlyn stood outside room number ten at Brenner's. Colin had told him to go on up, and that he was pretty sure Tom Lynn was still up there. He knocked with three loud raps and Tom opened the door almost immediately, his face clouded with concern. "Chief Cobb... what did I do, now?"

"Can I come in? Got something to tell you and might be best if it was in private."

"Certainly," Tom said, and stepping aside he closed the door after the chief came through. Merlyn tipped his hat back and rubbed at his forehead, hemming and hawing. "Got bad news for you, Tom. So... I suppose I'll just come out and say it since we're both men here. Your uncle Kaleb... is dead. Died in Philip Shannon's office early this morning."

"Wha... what happened? Do you know why?"

"Coroner said stroke. That's all we know, right now."

"Well... he was old. My mother's oldest brother, you know? Probably a good thing she's already gone, and that he never had kids. He was pretty devoted to the Carter Family. I suppose Constance and Janey might take it kind of hard."

"I suppose. You mind telling them, for me? I'm only supposed to notify the next of kin. That be you. I can tell them if you want, but..."

"No, you've done your job, Chief. I'll take care of it. Now, I suppose I'd better head up to Carter House and check in with Ben. I'm figuring there will be a lot of work that needs doing. Does he know about my uncle?"

"Not that I can say. But you ought to know... one of the things Kaleb told Shannon before he died was to tell you... not to go up there."

"What?"

"You heard me, Tom. Don't go up there."

"But I have..."

"You have nothing. Heed your uncle's words, stay away from Carter House. There's something going on up there and until I can get to the bottom of it, it'd be best you and Janey kept your distance. Kaleb was still dressed in his nightshirt and covered in dirt; among other things. Phil said the man looked scared out of his wits. Whatever made him run

92

all the way to town, probably scared him bad enough to give him that stroke. So, I'm going to tell you one more time, stay away. Least until I get back to you. Hear me?"

"Well… okay, but how soon do you think?"

"No clue, but like I said, I'll be in touch."

"Okay," Tom said, his squinting expression saying he just might not wait.

Cobb opened the door and walking out, said, "See you." Beth was at her desk, and Colin was still behind the bar counting bottles. Paul watched through the crack of the kitchen door while drying a plate with a dish towel.

"What's up, Chief?" Colin hollered.

Merlyn shouted back as he moved toward the batwing doors, "Kaleb Knight died this morning, right next door on the floor of Phil Shannon's place. Hell of a thing." The big man stepped out and crossed the street toward the café. His free morning coffee was late in coming and he wasn't too happy about it.

H

Tom had not been that close to his uncle. Kaleb had always been something of a grouch, but he had always treated Tom fairly. The old guy had often defended him when the Carters were looking to punish him for some minor infraction and always made sure Tom got paid for the work he did. Tom wasn't really feeling anything other than shock and remorse. Taking the open suitcase from atop his bed, he closed it and put it back in the corner before leaving the room. Locking the door, he went down the stairs.

"Looks like I might be staying a little longer. Does that work for you?" he said to Beth.

"Why certainly, Tom. As long as you need. No change in rate."

"Thanks," Tom said and walked out to stand on the boardwalk.

"Sorry to hear about your uncle," Colin hollered out.

"Yes, such a shame," Beth said from her desk.

"Thanks again," Tom said without looking back.

Paul came up behind him to sweep the boardwalk in front of the tavern. "Sorry to hear about Kaleb, Tom."

"Thanks," Tom said and smiled. Word travels fast in a small town. Your business was everybody else's in a village like Gowan. He was going to be the recipient of a great many condolences before the week was out. Tom turned and headed south just as Tabby and Janey stepped out of Boots', both carrying picnic baskets.

"Janey!" Tom called.

She smiled big, and waved, appearing somewhat relieved to see him.

"Tom," she called, "Come here."

He hurried across and when he got close, Tabby said, "Hello, Mister Tom. Glad to see you. Some kind of a stir going on around town, haven't heard yet what it is. Boots wouldn't say."

"Yeah," Janey said, "Boots wasn't his usual loose lipped self. We're down bringing a few dozen of Tabby's oatmeal cookies in trade for Clyde's famous fried green tomatoes and a pan of corn bread. Wanted to give Tabby a break on a Sunday afternoon. We saw Biddy was on the phone with Helen. Boots had to warn her about spreading any gossip when working. Want to come up to the house for lunch?"

"Well, I suppose, haven't got much else to do."

Janey frowned and started to say something and then changed her mind. There came an awkward silence but Tom broke it, saying, "Janey, I have something to talk to you about. Can I have a minute."

"Certainly. Tabby, you go on, I'll be right behind you."

Tabby reached for Janey's basket. "No, no Tabby, I'll bring it, you don't need to feel you should be carrying both. I won't be long."

"Okay, Miss Janey, but be quick, please, we need to get that cornbread to the house or Missus Constance is going to get angry. You don't want Mister Tom seeing that."

"Oh, I've seen that. Most of the time it was directed at me," Tom said, grinning.

"Well, okay, Miss Janey, I got to get the table set, so... I'll see you at the house."

"I've got bad news for you," Tom said even before Tabby got to the newspaper office. "So... prepare yourself."

"What is it, Tom?"

"Well, you know that thing that seems to be stirring up the town? I know what it is."

Janey faced him and their eyes locked.

"Out with it, Tom."

"Uncle Kaleb is dead."

Tom watched the shock come into her face and her mouth drop open. The tears welled in her eyes, but she kept them in check and said, "Kaleb... Kaleb is dead? How do you know this?

"Chief Cobb came up to my room and told me. He didn't mince words."

"But... how..."

"He died in Philip Shannon's office this morning. Said it was a stroke. Well, Doc Bolen and the coroner, said so, anyway."

"So, you'll have to take over for him?"

"Well, depends on what your father says. Cobb told me to stay away from Carter House for a couple days. I guess Kaleb was in a bad state and Cobb needs to go up there and talk to your father to find out what might have sent Kaleb running away in the dark in just his nightshirt."

"Nightshirt? Oh, my, Tom, you suppose something happened to father?"

"I don't know, but Cobb is not going to tell us. We need to get it straight from the horse's mouth. We need to talk to Philip Shannon."

"When, though? I need to get this bread home. We could always come back down later, maybe call, just to make sure he's in. Hopefully he'll answer."

"Yes, certainly, but we need to break the news to Constance, first. She's going to want to know and she'll be put out if she should find out that we knew and didn't tell her."

"Okay, let's get going so we can get through it, have our lunch, and get back down here."

"Well, we do know where the shyster lives, shouldn't be too hard to find him. But like you said, the coward may not answer his phone or his door if he knows it's us."

"We might have to bully him, maybe you can kick in his back door if he doesn't answer?"

"Perhaps," Tom said, grinning like the idea appealed to him.

"Let's hurry it up," Janey said, and picking up their pace, they tried not to look like they were on a mission

5

Constance cried when they broke the news. Not a wailing kind of crying, just a slow, quiet weeping as she sat in her chair, wiping at her nose with a frilly handkerchief. Tabby did too, holding a dish towel to her face while Percy stood behind her, his hands on her shoulders, repeating in is low voice, "Gonna be okay, sugar. Gonna be okay." Occasionally he'd look at Janey and Tom and then shake his head slowly in disbelief. The news ruined the meal and they all ate in silence. Afterwards, Constance dismissed herself from the table and standing in the door of the dining room, she said, "I'm terribly sorry, Tom. I know he was your closest living relative. I'm so sorry."

"Thank you, Constance."

She turned away to retire to her room. Janey got up, and hugging Tabby, told her, "We have to go see Philip Shannon. I'll be back before supper and maybe you could set a plate for Tom as well."

"I can do that, Miss Janey. Maybe you can share some more news with us. Percy and I would like to know."

"Okay, very good," she said, and taking Tom's hand, they moved to leave with Tom thanking Tabby for the meal.

Walking fast down the drive, Tom said, "Constance was pretty upset about Kaleb. I didn't expect that."

"Well, he was part of our history. We went back a long ways and we got a little closer to him when Josephine died. I also think that he was one more thing that she lost. I mean, first her marriage, then her house. My father, built Carter House for her, and then divorced her and kicked her out of it. Now me… yes, I'm sad about Kaleb, but I am more upset that it hurts my mother as much as it does. I desperately need to give my father a piece of my mind."

"Can that wait until after I see if I'm going to replace my uncle? If I'm out of a job, I either have to prepare to go back to Salem or find work here. Have to pay my room and board, you know."

"Okay, I can wait, but it's got to happen soon. I also want to get a look at that woman. And if there are three other women living in that house, besides that gold digger, I suspect my father may think he has himself a harem. I need to shame him, or at least, try. I think he needs to know how I feel. Also, have you ever given any thought to, perhaps,

96

working for my mother? There is a lot for one man to do up at Headmost. Percy is struggling. Besides that, we have the rooms. We could put you up?"

"If it will make you feel better?"

"It will," Janey said in mock defiance and then chuckled.

They continued on, hand in hand for all to see. When they arrived at Shannon's office, they found the door locked.

"Oh, well, maybe tomorrow?" Tom said with dismay. Janey huffed and pushing Tom aside, pounded on the door, and called, "Philip Shannon, it's Janey Carter. Are you in there?" Still no response.

"Not home," Tom said.

"Or hiding." Stepping back, she peered at the windows above their heads.

"We can come back later."

"I suppose, but… I'm not ready to leave you. You are still going to stay at Brenner's, right?"

"For another day, at least."

"I'm going to talk to my mother about hiring you on."

"Well… I don't know. You can try, I guess, but I'm not going to expect much. How about a beer? I feel like I need a drink."

"Maybe a small glass of wine. It's not even five o'clock yet."

"I don't want to wait, but I'd be suspicious of whatever Colin has for wine. It may be a bit second rate."

"It will do for Gowan," Janey said, and squeezing Tom's hand, she towed him toward the tavern.

6

Merlyn Cobb relieved Nealy of the Model A, saying he would have to either do his patrols on foot or saddle up the horse. "Okay, Chief," was all he said, but when Cobb left the office on his way to the car, Nealy shook his head and said, "I'll be damned if I'm riding a horse. Hate that damn horse."

There was no one for Nealy to harass since Maddie had the day off. He decided he would just stay at the office and read his latest copy of *Saucy Detective Stories*. Someone had picked him up a copy over at the Grunewyck drugstore and he had been holding off on reading it. He would just sit and wait until Merlyn brought the car back. His excuse would be that he stayed in the office to answer the phone. Nealy figured there wasn't going to be too much going on around town, anyway, and besides, he was mad at Merlyn for disrupting his routine.

7

The patrol car stopped in front of Philip Shannon's office and Merlyn honked the horn. The 'Closed' sign was hanging in the window, but he knew Phil was hiding in the tiny back office, or upstairs in his posh apartment. Philip poked his head out and looked up and down the street, locked the door, and jumped into the car. Merlyn started rolling even before Philip got his feet inside. He glared as Merlyn pulled a tight U turn right there on Main Street.

They soon arrived at the sign declaring: 'Carter House-Private Lane-No Trespassing'. Merlyn whipped the Ford in, jostling Philip. The car bounced and swayed over the rough surface. Philip sat quiet, clinging to hand holds, his teeth clenched.

"You think ol' Ben could have paved this road after all these years. He has the money, right?" Merlyn said.

Philip was a tall man, but slight of build and walked with a stoop. Having lived in Gowan all of his forty-two years, the only time he had ever been away was to go to law school. When he returned, Benjamin Carter had snapped him up on the spot to become the family's attorney. He now handled all of Benjamin's affairs—good and bad.

He was the kind of guy who liked nice clothes and expensive shoes. His egg-shaped head was balding, so he kept his hair cropped close. He detested physical labor and the dust now leaking in his closed window had him swiping at the fabric of his suit and muttering with displeasure. His biggest worry at the moment was that he knew the Carter Estate was going under. Eventually there would be no more money. Without Carter capital, The Bank of Gowan would fold. So, Philip had been taking some of it, little bit by little bit; skimming, as they say. No one would notice.

Philip also knew that all the rumors about the state wanting the Spry River Valley, for its new reservoir, were true. He had been charged with sharing the news with all who needed to know; however, it had been suggested that he hold off issuing notice until the last minute. Mayor Wilton should have known months before. If Philip told him too soon, there might be more obstacles thrown into the path of progress, especially if some of the more powerful folks joined other powerful folks from the multitude of towns and law suits were filed. The money he was paid to hold off until they sent him word was a sizable amount. There would be no time for the community to take action before the demolition companies began their destruction.

He never listened to his pappy much as a younger man, but the one thing that did stick was, the old man's favorite phrase: "Gotta git while the gittin' is good." Philip was going to do just that. As soon as he had collected the deeds and wrote the checks for the meager amount the property owners would be receiving, he would slip away before the town could gather a mob to tar and feather him and run him out of town on a rail. The village of Gowan was dead any way you looked at it.

There had been no paperwork drawn up to bequeath all of Carter's properties to the new wife. Mabel wouldn't receive a thing, and from what Philip knew, she hadn't asked. It would all go to Janey, unless Constance was still living at the time of Benjamin's death. But eventually—all to Janey. Unless of course, Mabel had plans to murder the entire Carter Family. Having met her just one time, Philip wouldn't put that past her. He suspected she was capable of such an act—and would, in all probability, get away with it.

Philip had shared with T.H. Enborne, an attorney over in Grunewyck, that "That woman is pure evil, I don't understand why Ben can't see it. I suspect, though, it's because he had been in a state of stupefaction ever since he met her. That witch has neutered the most powerful man in Gowan... and the surrounding counties, for that matter."

Philip had told Kaleb at the station, that day, that he best not get on Mabel's bad side. The look in her eyes told him that they all best stay out of her way. He knew that a smart person should pick and choose their battles carefully. Nobody but Mabel was going to win the fight that loomed on the horizon.

The lane wound through the trees. Sunlight barely made its way through the dense canopy of leaves. It was a land of shadows and remained that way clear up to the bluff where the lane passed under the natural stone bridge. There was a very narrow dirt path that led from the east end of that bridge, through the trees, and down to Ghillie's Gate. Who had been using that path so often that it had been worn to a shallow trench? Philip didn't know; but it wasn't the Carters. He supposed, and told people so, that the path must have been there long before Angus McGowan and, possibly, before the United States was even a country.

Merlyn drove slow and Shannon grew more impatient. He never liked Merlyn all that much and referred to the bigger man as, "That slob," when in the company of folks who he knew didn't like the old cop. Merlyn's uniform shirt and bib overalls were always soiled with dirt and food stains. He obviously was not one to bathe much and his work boots were often covered with horse crap. He wore his long-barreled Colt Peacemaker in a scuffed western style holster at his hip. Philip let it slip to Mayor Wilton, "I wonder if that revolver ever saw a cleaning brush, beings it's probably never left his holster in all the time he'd been Chief of Police." All Wilton had to say about it was, "Merlyn's a good man."

The car finally rounded the bend and the covered bridge came into sight. The creepy gargoyles were still there. No one had stolen them—yet. There was something odd about them, now.

"Something life-like about those damn things, you know?" Philip said.

"What's that?"

"The gargoyles."

Merlynn didn't even look their way, an indifferent, "Uh-huh," slipping from his lips.

The model A moved through the old wooden structure, and coming out the other side, Merlyn shifted down a gear so they could make it up the hill. Passing under the natural stone bridge, the car burst into the sunlight, blinding the men to a squint.

The drive ended at the large carriage house attached to Carter's stable. Merlyn didn't go that far. Braking, he slid the car to a halt in the drive just adjacent to the mansion's back porch. The dust whirled and Merlyn sat, just looking around. Philip leaned forward as if to see what it was that Merlyn was looking at. Not seeing anything, he got out and stood beside the car, waiting. Merlyn left the engine running, set the brake, and got out. They both stood studying the house as if they couldn't decide who should lead.

The grass had gone uncut and the shrubbery untrimmed. Weeds had sprouted up everywhere and a good many vines were climbing the walls. The paint was starting to peel in some places and several of the fish scale shingles on the slope of the mansard roof had blown off. The carriage house and other out buildings were in no better shape.

Curtains had been drawn all around the house and not one of them was open except up in the belvedere where the once elegant drapes now flapped, ragged and water stained. It hadn't been that long since Constance and Janey had been banished, but the condition of the place gave the impression it had been a decade.

Merlyn walked to the carriage house, swung one of the double doors open and went inside. Philip, not wishing to be left alone, followed him in. They saw that both of the Carter's horse drawn carriages and the Peirce Arrow were still there. The fourth stall stood empty, but they knew Constance had taken possession of the Cadillac the day of her departure.

Merlyn walked through and opened the door in the back wall that led to the stable. Moving into the center aisle he could see all of the stalls stood open and not one of Benjamin Carter's horses remained. Philip joined him there and said, "Where are all the horses?"

"Not a clue," Merlyn monotoned.

The double door, behind them, at the west end of the aisle, stood open and swung lazily, its wooden locking bar broken in two and lying on the ground. Phil moved through it to stand in the dooryard just outside the gate that led to the back garden and the orchard beyond. Merlyn soon joined him. They both stood gazing at the back of the house. A curtain falling back into place up on the second floor, caught Merlyn's eye. He stared long and hard as if waiting for it to be opened again.

"Look," Philip said, "The horses."

Merlyn turned and saw him pointing out toward the orchard. Two chestnut colored Quarter horses and a white Arabian moved slowly through the back part of the orchard eating fallen apples.

"Damn, that's not good," Merlyn said.

"Ben wouldn't allow that, you know? So, where is he? He needs to know. We need to tell him," Philip whined as if it was his property that was going to hell, and those were his horses. "And where's the other two? And... why aren't the dogs barking? The dogs always bark when someone comes up."

"No idea," Merlyn said indifferently, tipping his fedora back and rubbing his forehead.

"We need to tell Ben."

"Phil, I believe if Mr. Benjamin Carter were here, he would have been on top of it. When was the last time you saw him or heard from him?"

"Well, I met him at the station, along with his wife, uh... new wife and her servants."

"So, you met her?"

"Well, yeah... for a minute."

"And... she has servants?"

"Uh... yeah. I guess she's kind of royalty or something."

"You guess?"

"That's what I said."

"What did ol' Benjamin have to say?"

"There was paper work for me to take care of."

"What kind of paperwork?"

"Sorry, Merlyn, attorney-client privilege."

Merlyn squinted at him and scowled but left it at that. Looking one more time at that upstairs window, he turned and walked through the garden gate and around behind the stable. The doors to all of the kennels stood open. Only one of the six prized foxhounds was still present, but it was dead, its carcass lying on the dirty straw of its enclosure. Merlyn walked over and nudged it with his foot. A cloud of flies rose and he swatted at them before backing away.

"What happened to it?" Philip said loudly, startling Merlyn.

"How in the hell am I supposed to know? What do I look like, a dog specialist? Maybe you could call that lame ass coroner and get him up here to do an autopsy?"

Philip ignored the comment and walked closer to the dead dog. "Kind of looks like it was scared to death. Just look at it. Kind of like it just keeled over from fright."

"Know-it-all," Merlyn growled and walked over to where the woods butted up against the narrow strip of grass that ran along the east side of the building. He started to say something to belittle Philip, but there was movement in the underbrush just inside the tree line. Something big was pushing through and Merlyn's hand strayed to his holster.

Unsnapping the strap that kept the big pistol in place, he waited. Eventually horse number four and horse number five, both Cleveland Bays burst through. Merlyn jumped back in fear and drew his revolver in panic. The horses stopped to stare.

"No! Don't shoot them, damn it! Just horses, Merlyn, just horses!"

The animals were covered in burs. They appeared lathered up as if rode hard and then left without being wiped down and brushed. They stood chewing, their big eyes blinking at the two men. Merlyn holstered his weapon and moved to them. Grabbing one's mane to keep it still, he took a closer look. The beast had long, partially healed scars on its back. Scratches, like from a large predator.

"Probably going to have to get somebody up here from the slaughter house… or better yet, you get a hold of Tom Lynn and have him come up. He's a horseman, right? He could herd them all into town. Can't have them running loose up here, now, can we?"

"Well, we should at least talk to Ben and let him decide. He can deal with them," Philip said snidely.

Merlyn turned and stomped over to face off with his companion. Staring the attorney down, just inches apart, he said, "Listen to me, Mr. Philip Shannon, something ain't right. You hear me?" Merlyn cocked his head and kind of bent down so he could look into the face of the attorney, who was trying to keep his eyes averted.

"There is something god-awful wrong about this place. If Benjamin Carter were around, this wouldn't be like this. I suspect foul play and I'm thinking we won't be finding Benjamin Carter anytime soon to ask him any damn questions."

Without changing his position, Philip muttered, "We could at least go to the house and knock."

"What's that? I didn't hear you," Merlyn said flatly.

Phil raised his voice in an almost defiant tone and repeated it, "We could go to the house and knock on the door. Please, Merlyn, I… I just need to be sure."

"Alright, fine, let's go do that."

They left the horses, Philip following Merlyn. They moved out of the shade of the buildings and felt the hot sun stab them as they walked to the porch. The door having been open about an inch, slammed shut. Upon coming up the back steps, the sound of a bolt being thrown could be heard, followed by giggling.

Phil remained at the bottom of the steps, watching wide eyed as Merlyn pounded on the door. "Hello the house! I want to talk to you. I know you're in there. Benjamin Carter, is that you? This is Chief Merlyn Cobb of the Gowan police department. Open this door."

There came more giggling from the other side, sounding almost like a tinkling of tiny bells. "Benjamin Carter, come out here. If I have to go get a warrant from Judge Benson, I will. So, you just open this door and we'll have us a nice little talk. Now, it's my job to make sure everyone is alright. So, you just do as I'm asking and everything will be okay."

Philip remained quiet. It was Merlyn's game now.

Merlyn pounded again and said, "I know you're in there! Come out!"

Movement could be heard on the other side of the door. There was whispering and more of that strange giggling. Then someone spoke, a woman's voice sounding like she was speaking in a large empty room, a haunting echo following every word.

"What is it you wish, constable? You are to bring the peace, not disturb it."

There was something far away about that voice; almost mesmerizing.

"I'd like to speak to Benjamin Carter. May I come in, please?"

"My husband isn't present at the moment, constable Cobb. Please go away and leave us in our solitude. You have no call to be here. Depart my property and don't ever come back. If we need your help, we will call you."

"I want to speak to Benjamin Carter, this instant!"

"My husband is away. We don't expect him back anytime soon."

There was more strange giggling as if the statement had a double meaning. "His car is here!" hollered Philip. "How did he go, if his car is still here?"

"Who is that that shouts as if I am deaf?"

"Philip Shannon, Mr. Carter's attorney. I met you at the station."

"Oh! The lowly barrister. I had Benjamin picked up and taken where he needed to go." The giggling was louder and longer this time. Merlyn became enraged at the insolence and pounded again, the door banging in its jamb.

"Who are you," Merlyn asked, trying the door knob. "Mrs. Carter... Mabel, is it? Are you Benjamin's wife?"

"I thought I made it known. You can call me, Mab, and yes, I was married to Benjamin Carter. It was a proper ceremony in a vale in Alba. I am sorry you weren't invited."

"I'll call you whatever I want, Mrs. Benjamin Carter. Now, I am the law in these here parts and if you don't open this door, I'm going to break it down."

"Oh, constable, no need to threaten. You have no cause to be troubling me, please return to your automobile and leave my property."

Merlyn stepped back from the door. "Okay, I guess I'll just have to go get that warrant."

"Please do, constable. Go to your judge and convince him that you need to enter my home without just cause."

Merlyn kicked the bottom of the door out of anger and turned away to a chorus of giggles punctuated by the occasional squeak. He stomped down the steps, past Philip, and made his way to the car. Philip chased after him, saying "Is that it? Is that all you're going to do?"

"Shut up and get in the car, Phil. This ain't over yet. I am going to get that warrant and I will come back and I will knock that damn door down if I need too."

Back in the car, Merlyn glared back at the house and said, "Laugh at me, will you." A curtain in what Philip knew was Benjamin's library was pulled aside and three small faces, with black hair, appeared as if stacked on top of one another. The top one screwed up her face, the second stuck out her tongue, and the bottom one just grinned wickedly and crossed her eyes.

The chief whipped a tight U-turn in a cloud of dust and they sped back down the hill toward the covered bridge with Philip Shannon holding on for dear life.

8

Chubs Stewart had been baking all day, his wife, Page, lending a hand. Blossom Lane, their teenaged helper, had taken their last batch of bread loaves out back into the cooling room and then departed the shop to be with friends for some Sunday fun. The Stewarts were preparing for the next morning. Page had been cleaning out the inside of their glass fronted display cabinets while Chubs baked. He left his ovens and entered the cooling room through the back door to pull the racks inside.

The cooling room was slatted to allow in the breeze. It did have an opening, just not a door. A high, board fence surrounded the entire property at the back, so there was little chance anyone could just wander up and help themselves. Well, that didn't include, insects, birds, or small animals. Blossom's job was to drape cheese cloth over the racks and check periodically that nothing was trying to make off with the baked goods.

Chubs had been thinking a lot lately about screening it in and putting a door on, but baking was laborious work and old ways died hard. Besides that, to hire a carpenter would be costly, plus the price of the metal screen. If he and Page were to believe the rumors floating around, their lifelong dream of owning a bakery was at an end. They were too old to start elsewhere. The two were actually looking forward to retirement.

Chubs moved to the opening and gazed out across the top of the fence and through the space between his and Cap McKendry's house. The trees stretched to the top of Mount Lilie, mostly pine and fir. A lone Whip-poor-will piped, and the night insects could be heard, along with a few frogs. Stretching, he yawned and thought to have a smoke before trundling the racks inside. If Page caught him, though, she'd raise holy hell.

"Chubs! You out there?" she called.

Too late.

"Yeah, I'm getting the racks."

"Well, pick up the pace, will you, I want to get home. My feet are killing me."

"Oh, alright, just hold your horses, will you?"

"Don't you be telling me, Chauncey Lee Stewart!"

Chubs groaned, and turning away from the opening, he moved to the still warm loaves of bread. They sat on two, tall, rolling racks with multiple tray slots. There were only ten trays on each, five loaves per tray for a total of one hundred. They would sell nearly ninety-five of those in a day on a regular basis, supplying the entire village. What was leftover, they took home, often giving a loaf or two to Liam McClary, the local teamster, for delivering their supplies. If ever there were ten or more left over, they would send them to Reverend Hale, in Grunewyck. He would hand them out to the poorest members of his congregation. Like milk, bread was popular with the citizens of the village. Page's daily job was to decorate all items requiring frosting. She especially liked the cakes. Baking had been good to the Stewarts; they could live comfortably for the rest of their lives on the profits they had accumulated.

Chubs stopped and looked perplexed. An empty pan stuck out of the bottom slot of one of the racks. Five loaves were missing. Scratching his head, Chubs looked around like he expected to find them elsewhere. Nope, sure enough, five loaves were gone. Somebody must have come in and helped themselves. They must have jumped the fence because he could see that the gate remained locked. It was a first.

"Page, you better come out here."

"Ah, what now? I want to get home."

"Well, it ain't that far a walk, but…you gotta see this."

Page sighed and taking off her little white paper hat and pulling off her hairnet, she tossed them onto a display table and went out back.

"What in tarnation's wrong, Chubs? You can't do this one simple thing?"

"Lookee here, bread's missing."

"Are you sure?"

"Yeah, I'm sure. Counted the loaves a thousand times myself."

Page counted them and counted again. "We're missing five."

"Uh… yeah, didn't I just say that? Well, anywho, there should have been noise. I didn't hear nothing. Maybe Blossom helped herself?"

"Oh, hell, Chubs, don't go blaming Blossom. She's a good girl. She wouldn't take nothing and would always ask first. You know that."

"Then... who?"

"Well, we got a thief. How many times have I told you to get Ross Baily over here to put a door on?"

Chubs groaned and walked over to look outside. Page came over and stood beside him. They scanned the nearly empty space. "You know, Chubs, we can't no longer keep thinking that the folks around here are good. Too many people we don't know. Aileen, over at the dairy? She told me, when she came in for their biscuits, somebody been stealing milk. Milking their cows right there in the barn whilst they were sleeping. I 'spect maybe the same bunch come down here and helped themselves to our bread. Probably hobos, the sneaky so and so's."

Chubs turned and walked back to the light switch and flipped it up. The single bulb, hanging from a wire above their heads, projected its dim light, and he began a more in-depth search of the porch. Page, taking her cue, began to do the same. "You'd think they would've left tracks."

"Maybe so, but right now I'm just checking behind stuff to be sure."

Page stopped her search and moved to study the white painted wooden ramp that ran down to the well-worn patch of mud at the bottom. There were many prints there, mostly from their own shoes, but there were also a couple of small foot prints that looked like a toddler had walked barefoot through wet grass and then picking up dust with their wet feet, left two muddy prints just at the edge of the ramp. "Lookee here, Chubs, see that?"

"Looks like baby feet. You think maybe one of the poor kids came up here?"

Page remained quiet for a minute, squinting hard in the dim light at the two prints. "Well, I'd like to think it was some poor kid, but there's something very wrong about those prints, Chubs. There're scratch marks where the toes ought to be. You, see? You, see?" she said, and bending over with a groan, she ran a finger over the wood. "Yep, they's claws. Your poor kids have claws... mister know-it-all."

Page stood up and met Chubs' eyes. Something passed between them and they both gazed out at Mount Lillie where fireflies danced and katydids buzzed. A minute passed in silence, then Page said, "You better get that bread inside—right now."

Chubs didn't have to be told twice. Pushing the empty tray to the back of the rack, he rolled them inside. Page kept an eye on the mountain side and when her husband finished his task and the bread was safely in the back room, Page followed him in. "I want you to give Ross a call, first thing, about getting a door put on back there, and while you're at it, call Merlyn Cobb, I want him to know about this." Locking the backdoor, she threw the bolt at the bottom for good measure.

9

Telephone service came to Massachusetts in the late eighteen hundreds. Bartholomew and Benjamin Carter made sure Gowan wasn't left out of the loop and by the turn of the century, the village had their own switch board installed inside the old telegraph office with the back portion fashioned into rooms for the operator. Helen Blake, now in her sixties, held that position for as long as Janey Carter had been alive. Helen spent her days (and nights) operating the switchboard. She didn't get out much. Iris Hazelton, a reclusive woman and the village seamstress, was her second. If Helen needed a day off, Iris was always happy to sit in. Even a few hours would net her an entire day's pay. Helen was content with her job, though and, being somewhat of a recluse as well, the job suited her.

Helen knew just about everything that went on in the village, and anybody's business who had a telephone and that included any farmhouse outside the city limits. Gossip was a past-time in the town, and if any one person was an initiating source in the community, it was Helen. One of her many constant fears was that she would miss a connection that may reveal some tasty morsel of blather. After so many years of party-line calling, people were prone to forgetting they should keep their personal business off the line.

"...what reason I got for a warrant? None your business, Naomi. Yeah, I know you're the Judges wife, but you just tell him I'm coming over. There's things...

"...plain and simple, Merlyn. That's just what Kaleb said. They took Ben. Who 'they' is, I don't know, but..."

"...yeah, five loaves missing, never happened before. I'm thinking maybe poor kids, but there was footprints with…"

"…he's back in town, seen him walking with Janey Carter, thick as thieves if you ask me. I remember that one time, they…"

"…can you believe it? Died right there on the floor of that lawyer's office. Must have run all the way down from Carter House in his nightshirt. I tell ya, Louise, there's something going on up there. I seen through my binoculars…"

"…you see the way that Sally's been acting with Bessie LaVern over at the café? Kinda brazen if you ask me, you'd think they was sisters or something. Maybe… you know, kinda…"

"…who did I just say? Leo Dane, is he there? Now, Tip, I damn well know he starts drinking early, so…. No, he doesn't go to Brenner's, only your place. Well, when he shows up, tell him I want him down here at my office, I need…"

"…witches, I tell ya, Millie, witches. They was sitting out there in Ben Carter's car, while Kaleb was in getting groceries. They got out once and chased each other around, playing like they was little kids, barely had a stitch of clothes on between 'em…

"…that's what I heard, Reverend, they was witches, plain and simple. You know how Mary gets long winded, but she's no liar. Said they came down from Carter House in that big car of Ben's. No, not the Cadillac, that big Pierce. Sat in the dark of the back seat, sticking out their tongues and making faces at people walking by. Got the long black hair and everything…"

"…of course, it was her, Chastity Matthews, yeah… got that sister who owns that tavern over in Grunewyck, you know? Got a dog in its name? Can't remember… Oh hell, yeah, knew Chastity even before she got soft in the head. Saw her go by the house in just her sleeping gown. Out wandering again. Hopefully someone will find her and bring her home. She got the mania, you know? Don't know why no one's watching her, 'spect she's gonna wander off one day and fall in the river…"

Helen loved her job

CHAPTER FIVE

JANEY

II

~

1

Janey and Tom sat in Brenner's along the south wall across from the bar. There were no sleeping rooms on that side and the dark wainscot stretched all the way up to the ceiling. Colin was serving a few regulars that Janey didn't know and Beth was in her usual spot at the back. The judge at her bench.

Tom drank stout, and Janey, wine. Colin had been good enough to break out a bottle of Bordeaux he'd been hoarding. No one in Gowan had ever ordered it. He hoped to at least get rid of one bottle. It was expensive, but Janey was the perfect customer for such a thing. She hadn't frequented Brenner's more than a few times in her whole life and mostly as a child running in the back door and straight out the front, always Tom, or some other boy, in hot pursuit. She couldn't have cared less if she tracked up the floor or disturbed the customers. Beth would grimace and glare at Colin who would just say, "Kids," and shake his head in dismay.

Now Beth looked at Colin and he grinned back. The look was of mutual agreement. Having Janey Carter in their place was good for business. In fact, anyone of the Carter's gracing their establishment was beneficial. When word gets out that Janey was having a drink at

Brenner's, the town's people would consider the inn as more of a place for food and drink, not just a tavern and a flop house for the intoxicated. Colin could give Boots' a run for his money.

"So, how is the wine?" Tom asked Janey.

"Oh, better than expected. Not much on drinking, but it's not hard for me to tell a good one from a bad. The bad ones always gave me a stomachache. That's mostly what we got over at Thayer."

"Those nights you snuck out of the boarding house?"

"That will be our little secret, Tom. Don't need any more gossip going around about us than there already is."

"You can say that again."

"So, any word on the funeral? I suppose Kaleb will be buried here?"

"Yes, at the cemetery, next to Josephine. Michelle, over at the gazette wrote up a short obituary and gave it to Cap McKendry. So, Monday, uh…tomorrow, late afternoon, she told me."

"Not enough time, how will folks know?"

"Out of our hands. Don't expect a lot of folks will show up, anyway."

Janey sat facing the door and looking past Tom, she squinted. The bat wing doors squeaked open and an older woman stepped in carrying a small cardboard suitcase. She was dressed like it was still 1920. Her short, grey hair was fashioned in the Marcel waves of that time, and she wore a flapper dress that stretched to her calf.

The woman looked around the room starting with Colin, the two drinkers at the bar, back to Beth at her table (who now stared, open mouthed), then to Tom, and Janey. A smile parted her lips and she moved their way.

Colin hollered, "Well, if it isn't Cora Graham, all the way over from Grunewyck."

"That's MacLean to you, Mister Brenner. Been married for a hundred years and you damn well know it."

"Here for a drink? Or maybe you'd like to try the stew?"

"Make that a few drinks… and a room. If you got one."

"Well, I'll be damned. Never thought I'd see you grace our place," Beth said, now smiling.

"Oh, Chastity done wandered off again. Least she remembered to lock the door. It's just… I couldn't get inside. So… hope she took the key with her or we're going to have to break a window. Anyway, I need a room for the night, damned if I'm walking back through the Hollow in the dark."

"You're most welcome to a room, got a few, in fact. You can pick which one. Only got Tom staying here, right now. You know, Tom, right Cora? Tom Lynn?"

"Aye, I remember you as a boy," she said. Tom nodded and grinned. Gazing at Janey with familiarity she said, "And Janey Carter. My, oh my, look at you, all grown up and in a fancy dress, none the less."

Janey grinned, stood, and gave Cora a playful curtsy. They all laughed.

"Hello, Cora, long time, no see."

"Hell, haven't seen you since you gone to... where was it? Oh, that's right, you went to Thayer. You're a woman now! And I hear you're the new school teacher, too? Replacing ol' Durnell? Good riddance. Never seen so many unhappy children passing by my place in the afternoon."

"Join us, Cora. Leave that ol' suitcase right where you stand."

Tom pulled out a chair for her and they all sat down together.

"What will it be, Cora? Beer? Whiskey?"

"Now, Colin Brenner, you know me, so... no teasing. I know you got a bottle of gin stashed away under that bar top."

Lowering her head and looking at Tom and Janey out of the tops of her eyes, she said matter-of-factly and so no one else could hear, "I'm the competition, you know." Smiling, she added, "I'm sure if it wasn't for Whip-poor-will Hollow separating Grunewyck and Gowan, the Brenner's and I, would be literally battling for position. Zelda's has its place in the world, too. Just more for the rougher crowd, if you know what I mean? Now, my place, the Lost Collie? And this place here, are about the same, but the Collie is older. And speaking of Whip-poor-will Hollow..."

Janey glanced at Tom as if to question, 'Were we really speaking of Whip-poor-will Hollow?' Tom gave her a slight shrug and turned his attention back to Cora.

"Have either of you been through the Hollow lately?"

"Well, no, not lately," Janey said.

"Not me," Tom added, "Why do you ask?"

"I remember you, now," Cora said. "You were that little rascal, ummm... Kaleb Knights nephew. You were quite the scamp if I remember correctly. You used to make faces through the window at Chastity's house when you'd come down from the bluff. She said she was always chasing you away with her broom."

"True," Tom said, blushing. He exchanged looks with Janey and she gave him a grin.

"You little rascal," she taunted.

"Not anymore," he pled. They all shared a laugh. Colin brought over Cora's gin and set the glass on the table. "There you go, Cora, best gin in the house. Not that bathtub stuff you were so used to back in the day."

"Thanks, Colin. Next time you come back over for a refill, just bring the damn bottle."

"Certainly," Colin said and they swapped expressions, something more along the lines of adversaries trying to be diplomatic. Colin grinned and returned to the bar.

Tom said, "You were saying about Whip-poor-will Hollow?"

Cora slugged back her gin, emptying her glass, and slamming it on the table, said, "Oh, aye, so... it and Ghillie's Gate. You know Ghillies Gate? That damn cave up there on the side of that slope just before you get to the fording spot?"

"Yeah, I know it," Janey said. "I've been in it; it runs clear back under the well at Carter House. Big cavern back there where we pulled our water from."

"I've been in it, too," Tom said.

"Well... there's been strange things going on over there, and this evening there were peculiar noises coming out of that big, damn hole. Beings it's up there in the trees, you can hardly see it. Gave me the shivers, it did. I walk over to Chastity's every week and ever since... well, ever since your father brought home that new wife of his... oh, I'm sorry, Janey... how is Constance? She must be in a terrible state. Getting kicked out of her own home and exchanged for another woman, why..."

"She's fine," Janey cut in to stop the blather before Cora said something that would set her off. Cora had, obviously, already had a few drinks before she even got to Brenner's, making Janey wonder if she didn't have a bottle in her suitcase. "We're up at Headmost House, now. My mother and I."

"Headmost?"

"Yes, my uncle Bart's place."

"He's dead now, ain't he? Drank himself to death, I heard. I imagine the Basket Factory is in your father's hands, now. Whether he wanted it or not."

"Well, yes, uncle Bart was a drinker, and, yes, the factory has always been Carter's, going clear back to my grandfather. As for uncle Bart drinking himself to death… you can't believe everything you hear," Janey said, even though she knew that it just might have been the case with uncle Bart.

"So… the Hollow?" Tom said impatiently.

"Colin! Bring the bottle," Cora said, raising up a hand and snapping her fingers as if summoning a servant.

"So, why you so interested in the Hollow, Tom? You anxious to hear all the stories I have about that place?"

"Tom was a student of folklore at Amherst. He's going to write a book."

"A book? About what?"

"The folklore of Massachusetts, going to start with Nixie's Bluff," Tom said before Janey could interrupt. He scowled at her in a humorous manner, and she stuck her tongue out at him. Their eyes locked and she picked up where he left off. "Yes, Tom had an experience with the little people up there at Carter House way back when we were just kids."

"Oh, my! Well, that's right up my alley. I was born in Scotland, as you may know."

"No, I didn't," Janey said.

"Honestly?" Tom added. "Never detected an accent."

Cora absentmindedly picked up her glass and put it to her lips. Remembering she had drained it. She shouted at Colin again, "Colin, my bottle!"

Colin cut his conversation short with a patron at the bar and snatching up the bottle he hurried over to the table. He was irritated. Setting the three quarters full bottle on the table, he said, "There you go, Cora, drink up. You know it's gonna cost you? That's the good stuff."

115

"Colin Brenner, the only thing you need to worry about right now is if you have another bottle tucked away somewhere because I'm spending the night."

He glared for a moment and then turned away without a word. A chuckle floated to their ears from the back of the tavern. Janey turned to see Beth, an ever-widening grin breaking her face even though her eyes remained on her paperwork. Janey smiled to herself and turned back.

Cora poured herself a glass, swigged it and then looking directly at Tom, said, "So, tell me your story, Tom. Tell me about the nixie. Then I'll tell you all about mine. Scotland is full of them."

"Nixie stories," Janey said, giggled, and clapped her hands.

"Aye, nixie's! The Sidhe! Fairies as you say. So, let's hear it, Tom. I've got all night."

"Well, can't say it was much. I was out in the orchard up behind Carter House. Supposed to be picking apples for uncle Kaleb. One thing I hated more than anything, was picking apples. I left the basket to sneak off into the woods on Parson's Ridge. I went way back in there, just wandering til sunset. If I'd been smart, I would have turned back long before. I sat down on this log next to a large pool of water to rest, and the longer I sat there, the more I started to feel like there were eyes on me. It's just, I couldn't see anyone... at first. Then I caught a slight movement out of the corner of my eye. There were these boulders sticking up out of the ground on the other side of that pool. At first, I didn't see it sitting there. It blended in so well with the stones. All the browns and greys."

Janey's eyes watched Tom intently. Even though she knew the story, she had never asked Tom to tell her in detail what had happened the day he had come running back to the house, his face white as a sheet. The scratches on his legs, hands, and cheeks, looked like he had ploughed through every thicket on the way.

"So, what did you see, Tom?" Cora said, prodding him.

"Well, it looked like a man, a small man, but he had the face of an ape or something. Like a chimpanzee... maybe. Big ears, kind of pointy. A long chin and not a stitch of clothing—just some kind of brown fur... or down? He never moved, never blinked. But he was smiling this strange kind of smile like I had discovered some kind of a secret. I

116

looked at his legs and they were covered in something like dark sheep's wool. When my eyes got down to his feet, uh… there were hooves. I beat it out of there. Ran all the way back to Carter House. Can't say I ever went out there again—by myself, anyway."

"So, kind of like Pan, or what was it…oh! A Faun! That's it," Janey declared.

"No, I don't think so," Cora said, "No horns? You saw no horns?"

"No, no horns of any kind, just a smooth head. Why do you ask?"

"Urisk, is what I'm thinking."

"What?" Janey said.

"Urisk, it's a solitary fairy. They are all over Scotland, it's just you hardly ever see them, unless they get a hankering for human company. They're too damn ugly to want anyone to put their eyes on 'em."

"You've seen one?" Tom asked.

"No, not me, but I remember my uncle, Wallace, telling my da all about running into one on the moor while on his way to our house. That was when we lived just outside Kelso in the Borders."

"Well… it was pretty long ago. I was just a kid, with a pretty vivid imagination, gallivanting around Parson's Ridge."

"Tom, it's called Nixie's Bluff for a reason. So, you weren't the only one. I think it's just folks around here would like to ignore it. Maybe it's just harder to believe because this is Massachusetts and not Scotland, or Ireland, for that matter."

"So, Cora, I get the impression that you feel Carter House is now playing into this. Like… you've got a feeling something else may be going on up there," Janey said, her eyes questioning.

"I wouldn't want to say for certain, right now. I've seen and heard things that bring back old memories. One of those things I experienced just before my family immigrated. Believe me, I too didn't want to accept it. I want to blame it on my age, or just not remembering correctly. I have an imagination too, you know? Aye, I do. So, I too, have to make sure it it's not just my mind playing tricks on me."

"What kind of thing are you referring to?" Tom asked, his curiosity peaking as he stared intently at a very tipsy Cora.

"I was of age, a rebellious teenager, walking back from the village a little after sunset. Our cottage was in a woods that stretched in all directions. I watched a woman walk out onto the road, dressed in a green flowing robe. My worst nightmare was coming true. We didn't walk the roads at night, my ma didn't allow it. As a wee-un, I had made a rather arrogant decision and I was going to pay for it. I reckon you have heard of, or maybe even read, Bram Stoker's, Dracula?"

"Yes, several times in fact," Tom said.

"I have once," Janey said, "That's how I know about vampires, and that's what we are talking about, right?'

"Aye, tis, well, Scotland has their own. The Baobhan Sith."

"Sorry, the what? Come again?" Tom said,

"Bay-o-von sheeth, I suppose is the best way for you to pronounce it. But don't worry about that right now. You can just say, those... things, we'll know what you're talking about. So, the bloodsucking maiden of the Highlands. Something of a succubus, my grandda said. He was an educated man from up Edinburgh way. The university, you know? Anyway, the problem is, those things are not limited to any one place. How silly is that to think, hey? They could be anywhere... and they were in Roxburghshire."

"So, what happened? Janey asked, "With the woman in green."

"I could hear her little hooves clacking on the road as she walked out into the middle to stand and stare. Her eyes glowed and she began to sing my name, not loudly, just this sweet wee tune that drew me toward her. She opened her arms like she wanted to give me a hug. I was close to falling under her spell and she would have had me, but the door of the cottage opened and my da stepped out with a lantern. That brought me out of it, and I ran by her to him. He kept an iron made potato fork just outside the front door with his other gardening tools. Grabbing it up, he ran toward her, swinging. Iron is a bane to the fae, it grounds their magic and they will either die from contact or become mortal and then... killable. I watched through the window as she moved back into the trees. She just melted away into the dark.

I got a serious beating from my da and a long lecture from my mum, reminding me of the dangers of being outside at the gloaming. But things like that didn't happen too often. As a wee-un you start to believe it's all shite. Something made up to keep the lads and lassies in line. I learned my lesson. It's said that once the Baobhan Sith take you, you become one yourself. You find a good hiding spot in a thicket or a cave and leave your human body behind at night when you go on the prowl for the unsuspecting. You return in the morning and remain for the day until the gloaming descends again. Oh! And men can't turn, so death takes them after their bodies are mangled—sometimes beyond knowing. There are two times I know besides my own. Both men, both sucked dry. If a mortal person finds the body of the changeling where it's been hidden away, just like with the stake and crucifix, an iron rod through the chest or even laid on the body, will do the trick. The peasants of the old days used to burn them afterwards."

"So, is that who this Mabel is? A vampire?

"Naw, I am afraid... or maybe, I just suspect, from what I am hearing, this Mabel may just be the Queen of Air and Darkness. Mab, The Winter Queen."

"What?" Tom said, "You're pulling our legs, right?"

"Who?" Janey asked, "You said... queen?"

"It's a long story and I have a theory, but, like I said, I'd rather not say anymore right now."

Swigging the last of her gin, she poured another. "I can say this, though, I have a friend over in Grunewyck, she and her husband, they own the general store there. I've known Colleen Potter almost all of my life, clear back to when we were girls. A time when she was known as Colleen Baker. She has a daughter, Melissa... Lissy, we call her. The girl had some kind of experience over around the Hollow. You know that tree filled ravine that runs from the Grunewyck Road clear back into the woods to the bottom of Nixie's Bluff?" Janey and Tom threw each other a glance and then a grin.

"Has that long pond at the bottom? Well, can't say I've ever heard Colleen fret so much. She had a tough time telling me what Lissy had told her. Something about a washer woman at the stream with a bloody shirt. A Caoineag."

"A cooney-ack?" Janey said, and looked at Tom, who grinned and shrugged before they both turned questioning eyes back to Cora.

"Close enough. A banshee, if you will. It was a scary talk we had, took me right back to Roxburghshire. Now, James, Lissy's father? He lies dead, his own car running him down right in front of the store, right in front of his family. Not even a day after Lissy lays eyes on that washer woman. Now, Colleen is without a husband, and Lissy… a father. But as I said, I dare not say what it is I know. Just keep this moment in mind for the future. All will disclose itself in time."

Cora smiled at them as if she wished to change the subject. Casting her eyes to the table top, she sipped her gin in silence. Janey sat somewhat stupefied, wondering what else she didn't know. Tom appeared to be doing the same.

A few minutes passed with just the sound of Colin busy at the bar, and Paul, moving around and stacking boxes on the back porch, awaiting the arrival of Liam McClary.

With the back door open, an evening breeze blew through causing the batwing doors to gently swing at the front. Janey finished her wine, waved for a refill, and looked at Tom who appeared to be on the verge of saying something. Cora beat him to it. "So, Janey, have you seen Benjamin since you've returned?"

"Uh… no. I've meant to go up and give him a piece of my mind, but so much has been happening. Merlyn Cobb has basically banned Tom and I from going to Carter House until he gets this Kaleb business sorted out. I thought to stick tight until we got the word."

"Don't wait too long. Ol' Merlyn can't stop you, even if he thinks he can."

"It will be soon," Tom said flatly, "I'll play along for maybe a day or two, but that's all."

"Good, I'd go up there myself and just take a look around, but I don't have the same right as the two of you. I'd sure like to get a look at that woman, myself.

"You and me both. The gold digger…" Janey said. Tom chuckled and took a long drink of stout.

"Naw, no a gold digger. Like I said, she's something else. Something we least expect her to be. That's why I'd like to get a look at her. I hear she has ladies in waiting. Hand maidens to do her bidding. Creatures created by her own hand and probably from wee animals like polecats, racoons, or opossums."

"Uh-huh, we heard over at the cafe that they made a showing next door at McCarthy's. Kaleb had driven them down in the Pierce for groceries, and they were sitting in the backseat with the curtains pulled. They were harassing folks who walked by. Clyde, the cook over at Boots' found a bauble or a charm of some kind in the street where the car had been parked. He gave it to me to return to them when I got up to Carter House to start my work. We thought it might be gold."

"What kind of a bauble?"

"Uh… it's gone. Came up missing from my dresser top."

"What? It was stolen?" Janey said.

"I guess so, or…"

"Or, whoever it belonged to, came back to claim it," Cora said, smirking, and then swigged down the remainder of her gin.

"Excuse me," Tom said, "I'm going to the outhouse." Looking embarrassed, he got up and walked out the backdoor.

2

Cora smiled at Janey, and filling her glass with more gin, she said, "So, you're going to start teaching here, soon?"

"Yes, in August. Have to get out there and get things set up. I imagine I'll have a full room, least until Grunewyck gets its school rebuilt."

"Oh, haven't you heard? That's not going to happen. Al said I'm not supposed to say anything, but, oh what the hell, what are they going to do? Hang me? The state is going to take this valley for a reservoir. I suppose whoever is charged with giving Gowan the official word… hasn't yet."

"Most likely, Philip Shannon. Can't say I trust him entirely, but beings I'm a Carter, it might best behoove me to confront him on it. My mother certainly won't, and my father… well, he seems to have fallen out of the picture."

"Words been going around Grunewyck, for almost a week now. It's a sure thing. A few of my regular customers are talking about packing it in and moving. Tobias Whitman, an attorney over in town, is the one I 'spect is supposed to give Grunewyck folks the official word, but that hasn't happened yet. But… you can't fight city hall, they say. If the government decides they want your property, they'll take it; whether you like it or not. I 'spect some will fight. Suits can't be filed until the official word is given. These shysters hold off long enough and there won't be time. Some deadline won't be met because of ignorance of the law and the suit will get thrown out. These chiselers are probably getting paid under the table to stall as long as possible. Imminent Domain, lass, Imminent Domain. Don't expect to have your job very long."

Janey knew Cora meant Eminent Domain, but didn't correct her. She also knew she had missed out on a lot since she left Gowan for Thayer. If she hadn't gone and had gotten even the slightest wisp of what was to come, she would have fought it; rumor or not. Her first step would have been to form a group to oppose any action by the state of Massachusetts to level villages in the Spry River Valley. She could only speculate where it would go from there. Now, if Philip Shannon was holding off telling Mayor Wilton, the intent would be to make any kind of protest, ineffective. It would be considered, 'Too little, too late.' Then there would be no chance, whatsoever, to stop the demolition companies with the incessant hammering of their 'Woodpeckers' when they descended upon the villages to flatten every structure in the valley. It was out of her hands.

3

Tom returned to the table, a scowl on his lips, obviously still pondering all that had been said. Cora belched, took another drink of gin and said, "So… describe the bauble to me, Tom."

"Small like a button, some kind of symbol carved into it. A hole for a string or a chain."

Cora belched again and looked into her glass as if she couldn't decide if she wanted to refill it. They watched her eyes slowly shut, pop open, and then look them over like she didn't recognize them. Her Pince-Nez glasses fell to the end of their chain and she left them to dangle. Grinning, she said, "We'll talk later," and Tom shot her a look of annoyance.

"Okay, had enough of fae talk, time for beddy by."

Pressing a palm to the seat of the chair between her legs, she tried to get up. It slipped and she sat back down hard, her glass hitting the table top with a bang. "Colin Brenner, you ol' numpty boy, is my room ready?" she shouted across the floor. Colin looked at Paul, who nodded. "Let me walk you up, Cora," Janey said.

"Aye, very well, lass, accompanied… accompany me to my woom," she said and giggled.

Janey walked her up to number eight, but only after a bit of a struggle with the stairs. She got Cora onto the bed, pulled off her shoes, and the old woman promptly passed out. Paul had followed them up with the suitcase and hung a key with a string necklace from the inside knob. Janey opened the two windows and departed with Paul locking the door from the outside with a second key. "Thanks, Paul," Janey said, noticing that he acted with a greater degree of timidity than usual. "Yes'm," he said, not meeting her eyes. For Paul, this type of behavior was usually limited to men. He was more talkative with women and girls.

Janey moved back to the top of the stairs with him following at a distance. At the bottom, she waited until he had stepped off the last tread and turning, she blocked his path and asked, "Everything okay, Paul?" His nervousness increased, and he played with the ring of keys, his eyes on them and not Janey.

"What you mean?"

"Oh, I just got a feeling, is all. Everything alright? You can tell me."

"Mam?"

"Oh, forget it, it was nothing."

Janey returned to Tom who was lost in thought as he drank the last of his stout. He looked up at her approach, smiled, and said, "Get her tucked in?"

"She's out like a light. Shall we go for a walk, Tom? I think I've had enough of this place."

"Certainly," he said, and downing the last of his glass, he stood up and gestured toward the door. "After you."

"Good night, Janey," Colin called out with Beth doing the same.

"Put the drinks on my tab, Colin," Tom said. Colin smiled and then leaning in to the one man sitting at the bar, they shared a quiet conversation, both pairs of eyes following the couple out the door.

H

"What do you think, Tom? A short stroll around to dispel the spirits and then walk me home?"

"Sounds good to me."

They moved left to the short set of steps and then down onto the lower boardwalk. Passing the open space between Brenner's and Shannon's office they heard someone hiss, "Tom, Janey."

Startled, Tom grasped Janey's upper arms and pushed her behind him as he faced the dark alcove. Paul LeBarge poked his head out, looked around, and then pulled back in.

"Sorry to scare you… can we talk?"

Tom walked over, stopped as if to study the dark interior, then stepped in with Janey following. "What's up, Paul?" Tom asked.

"I wanted to talk to you about the gold button, or… whatever it was. I heard you talking with Cora."

"Did you take it?" Tom asked taking a step toward the boy. Janey wrapped an arm around Tom's waist to hold him back and said, "What is it, Paul. What do you have to tell us?"

"I didn't take it. I would never do that, but… I think someone was in your room that wasn't supposed to be."

"Who?" Tom said.

"Well… I wouldn't say it was a who. I have to say it was more like a… what."

Tom glared at the boy. "What do you mean… a what? Like an animal?"

"Couldn't be too sure, Tom. It moved so fast, just a brown streak and it was gone with the curtains flapping. I didn't see the button, or the charm, but whatever that thing was, ummm… it laughed at me when I went after it."

"It laughed at you?

"Yeah, kind of like a baby laugh. Like it was having fun with me, or… making fun of me. Like… mocking?"

Tom turned to find Janey's eyes in the dark. She shuddered and taking his hand, she said, "Thank you, Paul. Thanks for sharing that with us. Least we know what happened now."

"I just had to tell you. There's been so many strange things going on around here ever since your daddy brought that woman home. And those girls everybody's talking about? I've seen 'em. Not together, just by themselves, standing in the dark, in different places around… just watching folk. Watching me. Like when I'm going to the outhouse when everybody else is asleep. They's even watching that ol' Nealy Garret when he's up there in his office. One time I couldn't sleep and I went for a walk up Main Street about three or so in the morning... I'm having girlfriend problems, you see? But anyways... there was one standing up on the corner by the smithy's. She was looking up at your place, Janey. You know, Headmost? I was still a good distance away when she saw me and she talked to me.

"What did she say?" Janey asked.

"She had this squeaky voice, it was hard to understand her, but I think she said, "Come to me, come to, uh... Nick Doevron, I think she said.""

"Nick Doevron? Sounds like a boy's name... anyway, what did you do then?"

"I ran like a striped tail cat! She might have been trying to be sexy and all, in that skimpy outfit, but she made me scared. So, anyway, I just wanted to tell you, is all. Please don't tell Colin or Beth. I am not supposed to go in people's rooms, less I have good reason, or go and leave the tavern after Colin and Beth go to bed, 'specially if there are guests."

"Mum's the word, and thanks," Janey said.

"Yeah, thanks," Tom added, still studying the boy.

"Let's go, Tom."

The door at the café opened and an older couple stepped out. Tom and Janey looked to see who it might be. When they turned back, Paul was gone.

They continued down the boardwalk toward the village green, now holding hands.

"Most I ever heard that guy talk," Tom said.

"Yes, exactly. He's afraid of men. You probably had him peeing his pants."

"Do you think he's telling the truth? About the bauble."

"If I know Paul, he is. He made an effort to tell us at his own risk. Besides, I think he's afraid and I don't mean of you."

"Sure, but that thing about an animal taking the bauble has me a little confused. An animal? Sounds like a story some little kid made up."

"Left me thinking, raccoon, but... if it laughed at him... raccoons don't laugh."

"Yes, that's what I mean. But now that we are talking about it, it makes me think of my research and of this, so called, Mab. She controlled the dark fairies and that included all of the different goblins, boggarts, and such."

"I don't want to talk about this anymore."

"Maybe later, then? When we are in a cozy, well lit room? Uh... are you frightened, Janey? I could just walk you home and we could call it a night."

"You know me better than that, Tom Lynn. And what was that thing back there where you tried to protect me from Paul? Chivalry?"

"Ummm... yeah and... sorry about that. Just impulse, been a long time since I've been with you, Janey. I know a lot of other women wouldn't mind and that lets me off the hook. But, if we are going to be together, I guess I am going to have to ask you to cut me some slack."

"Okay, I'll give you a couple more days," Janey said and laughed. Tom chuckled and lightly squeezed her hand.

They stopped opposite the village green and townhall. The bell tower loomed over them, casting a long shadow from the moonglow. The townhall was dark except for a dim light escaping an upstairs window where the police office was.

"Suppose Nealy's up there sleeping?" Tom said.

"Sure do, and if this was ten years ago, we'd probably toss pebbles at the window or knock on the door and run like hell."

"Yeah, and I'm still tempted, but I promised myself I'd be good."

"Party pooper," Janey said and laughed.

Tom took the risk of pulling Janey close as they walked toward the rear of the building. Janey didn't resist and her arm found his waist. A large gazebo sat catty-corner at the back of the building, close to the base of Mount Ovis. Gowan used it as a bandstand. It looked out over several rows of benches, and more lawn.

"Shall we go and sit in the bandstand?"

"Yes, let's do that, it's nice and quiet. A little dark back there, though, but what's to fear in Gowan, hey?"

"Uh... laughing racoons?"

5

They chuckled at Janey's remark as she led Tom across the grass and up the three steps of the gazebo. They sat at the back on the bench that ran around the inside of the balustrade. Crickets and frogs sounded in the trees behind. An occasional automobile passed on Main Street, and once, a work truck with R.J. Wrecking & Lumber written on the door rumbled through. It left the two to wonder if the occupants might be heading out to the roadhouse. There was the occasional drunk staggering past, making their way from Zelda's to the northside cottages. No one intruded in on the lovers as they sat watching the night sky.

It was hot and sticky. Janey wished she had abandoned her hosiery for bare legs. Tom removed his jacket and opened his collar. No words were spoken. Just two people lost in their own thoughts. Out of the blue, Janey said, "I need to make sure you understand something. When Merlyn gives you the okay, I want to go up to Carter House with you; no questions. So, we can either walk or I can get the Cadillac and drive us up."

"You can drive?"

"Why of course, and I can shoot, too. I can even repair things that get broken."

"Easy, now. I'm just asking. If you must know, I can't drive. I can shoot as I am a fair marksman, and many other things, but I never learned how to drive. It's always been horses. But let's walk up, unless you don't want to walk back to town by yourself in the case I have to stay and get things back in order."

"That's not a problem, I've done it a thousand times, walking to Gowan, mostly because I was angry at my father; which I just might be this time, too."

Tom didn't respond, instead he just sat looking at the floor, his elbows on his thighs, his hands clasped under his chin.

Janey had been curious for a very long time what it would be like to kiss Tom. It had been a while since she had kissed anyone romantically, going back to her first year at Thayer when she had snuck out of the boarding house to meet a boy in the ballfield behind the college. Now, ever since their second night together, she found that she was becoming

127

more and more attracted to her old friend. He certainly wasn't the rapscallion he had been. She wondered what had happened in his life to change that.

"Tom, can I get personal?"

"Oh no! What now?" he blurted and then chuckled.

"No, no, I was just wondering, is there someone? I mean, do you have someone?"

"You mean like a lover, or, someone like that?"

"Well, yes. Are you missing somebody right now? Is there somebody waiting for you when you return home to Salem?"

"Uh, no. I have had nights out with a few women, some that I thought might get serious. Mostly at Amherst. It never happened, though. So, no, Janey Carter. I've been saving myself for you," he said and laughed. He was looking at her now, and in the moonlight, she could see the humor in his face. "Just kidding, Janey, don't worry…"

She interrupted, a hint of pleading in her voice, something not typical for Janey Carter. "But… you don't have to be, right? Kidding, I mean?"

The smile ran away from his face and their eyes met. Janey had turned her whole body to face him. So, he did the same. She reached out a hand and placed it on his knee, saying with solemnity, "I like you, Tom."

He pulled her to him, their lips met, and a passionate kiss followed. They separated to look hard at each other's faces as if to ask without words, 'Is this okay with you?' and then it was Janey's turn to do the pulling. The two figures, locked in passionate fervency, remained for quite some time, as did the pair of animal like eyes that quietly watched from the trees beyond.

6

"Was it good for you?" Tom asked, buttoning his fly and buckling his belt.

"As good as it can be, I think," Janey said, smoothing down the hem of her skirt and patting at her hair, "I kept thinking Nealy was going to come out that door any moment and catch us in the act."

"I'm pretty sure he's fast asleep in his chair, just snoring away."

They were soon walking hand in hand up the boardwalk on the café side of the street, Janey's freehand holding her balled up stockings. Tom and Janey nodded at a couple unfamiliar faces gazing from the café window as Boots prepared to close the place. The two lovers shared a joke and laughed together as they walked past the newspaper office. The backroom was well lit and they watched Casey and Kenny Boyd moving back and forth in front of an open door. Janey supposed they were preparing to print the next day's edition of the Gowan Gazette.

Arriving at Railroad Street, Janey could see Percy had lit a lantern and placed it in the bay window of the parlor at Headmost House. The big chandelier hanging from the cupola ceiling was glowing as well. She suspected her mother was in bed and fast asleep, which was good. Constance wouldn't see Tom walking her home at such a late hour sans stockings.

They gazed at the lighted windows upstairs at Sallys. Someone could be seen walking up to peer through the top sash of one. They wore a filmy negligée, sizable breasts showing large dark nipples as they were pressed to the glass. When they saw Janey and Tom passing, they hurried away.

"Did you see that?" Tom asked, "Who lives up there?"

"It's Sally's apartment, but that was Bessie LaVern at the window, Sally's assistant."

"So, maybe… a little slumber party?"

"I think, perhaps, they are going to be doing a little more than slumbering."

"You mean… Sally's a…"

"That's all you need to say, Tom."

"Okay, so…"

"How do you feel about that?"

"Ah… well, none of my business. Not going to hurt me in any way, shape, or form."

"Glad to hear you are so progressive in your beliefs, Mister Tom Lynn. Been that way for as long as Bessie's been a grownup. I don't know who it might have been before Bessie. Sally's been here for a while. Perhaps, a young woman from another town."

"Anybody else in Gowan know?"

"The towns people suspect, I think. There have been some indiscreet actions on Sally's part and there is always a lot of talk. I figure Sally's been tactful enough on the telephone that she hasn't given Helen, the operator, any ammunition. If word ever does get out, I know I am going to feel bad for them. The attack will be relentless. I just feel it's no one else's business who you love. People can just be shits, can't they?"

"You don't need to tell me, Janey Carter."

They stepped down off the boardwalk onto Railroad Street and crossed. The gate remained open and Janey presumed that Tabby and Percy had gone to bed. Their windows up under the eaves were dark.

"This will be far enough, Tom. Bid me adieu, here. He stopped, but she kept going and once inside, she pushed the gate closed, leaving him to stand, scratching his head. She latched the gate and stood watching him through the bars. He started to speak and she whispered, "Hush, people are sleeping." Tom walked up to the gate and pushed his face against the iron pickets. Janey surprised him with a slow kiss and then said, "See you tomorrow, Tom. Sleep well... despite."

"Despite what? Laughing raccoons?"

Janey giggled, walked backwards a few steps, gave Tom a shy, little wave and then turning away, continued up the drive. Tom sighed and said to himself, "Goodnight, sweet Janey," and watched until she was swallowed up by the shadows of the overhanging trees.

7

Janey entered a quiet house. The front door had been left unlocked, but she was quite sure Percy had seen the others had been secured along with the windows. Janey bolted it behind her and taking the lantern from the parlor window, she climbed the stairs to her room. The windows had been closed all day and her room was stuffy. Throwing up the sashes, she allowed the night air to raise the curtains and deliver a cooling breeze to the room. The house was hot, but her room was worse. Disrobing completely, she used the chamber pot to relieve herself rather than her mother's toilet closet.

Pouring some water from a porcelain pitcher into the basin on her table, she used a washcloth to wipe herself down, cooling her skin and removing any evidence of Tom from between her legs. She dabbed lavender all over, wondering if maybe she should just sleep in her birthday suit.

The room hadn't cooled much by the time she had completed her task. Janey thought how much nicer it would be to sleep up in the cupola. There were plenty of cushions scattered about up there and a gentle breeze would blow through all night long. She thought to just run up naked like she did in her preteen years; when it was still uncle Bart's house. The risk contributed to the excitement. She always made sure there was linen folded neatly and stashed away on a shelf up there; just in case someone came up. Donning her sleeveless, sleeping gown, she left her room and climbed the narrow stairs, avoiding all the creaky spots to avoid waking Tabby or Percy.

At the top, she cranked down the great lamp and blew out all the flaming wicks. The space fell dark, allowing her to see outside. An occasional drunk made their way up Main Street, heading for the cottages. The light to Tom's room at Brenner's remained lit, making her wonder what he was up too.

Gowan had grown quiet and her eyes rose to the distant Carter House. Every light was ablaze and she wondered if there was another party; Benjamin having invited all his new friends and none of his old.

Janey's head filled with thoughts about all Cora had said. The old barkeep was impressive with all the knowledge that she possessed and Janey found it sad that the woman was such an alcoholic. A memory came of a time when her and Tom had traversed Whip-poor-will Hollow to arrive at the Lost Collie where they stopped to beg a drink of water.

Cora had obliged them and offered cookies, but her husband, the usually quiet, Al MacLean, had shooed them away after they had their water, suggesting they never come back without their folks. The tavern was no place for children. They left without a thank you to Cora who began to argue with Al, chastising him for his callousness.

Tom snuck back and somehow stole an unopen bottle of beer. They shared it in the Hollow in a small glade shrouded by trees. They both passed out there on the cool green grass, and when they woke up just before sundown, they vomited together. Then running all the way back to Carter House, they arrived just before complete darkness.

Janey stood, watching intently. Soon the lights went out starting with the belvedere, followed by the dormer windows in the mansard roof, the second floor, and finally, the tall windows on the first. It was a reoccurrence of the last time she had watched Carter House. "Becoming a regular thing with you, huh, papa? What the hell are you doing up there?" she muttered.

A foreboding washed over her just like in the Cadillac on her way home from Bournemouth. Nothing was going as she had expected. She had imagined her father would be driving around Gowan in his Peirce with his new wife, showing her off to everybody, but no. Janey had returned to a strange world. The only good things: she'd gotten her dream job and—Tom. She had satiated years of longing at the gazebo this night. It could easily become love. If it did, and they established any kind of a long-term relationship, they still wouldn't be able to live in Gowan.

The reservoir talk had made her sad. Towns were going to die, and all she had known would die with them. There was always Kingsport or Salem. The Carters owned a big house in Salem, unoccupied at the time, but it could easily become home. But what about Constance? And what did she know about the reservoir? Janey feared that her mother's losing of Headmost after having lost Carter House, may be too much for her.

Janey lay in the dark, propped up by her pillows, a cool breeze caressing her body. The crickets and katydids sang their night song, and occasionally an owl hooted from the woods behind. She lay watching the shadows playing across the ceiling as a Whip-poor-will began to pipe somewhere out there in the dark. It triggered a woefulness that crept in to lick at the edge of her consciousness. The princess of Gowan, Massachusetts didn't fall asleep for the longest time.

CHAPTER SIX

GOWAN

‖

~

1

The morning mist had burgeoned in the night, inundating the village and it's Main Street with the voluptuous vapor until the planets' life-giving star rose above Prosper Mountain in the south to burn it away.

It was Monday, the beginning of a work week. The day would heat up fast and the temperature in McGowan's Basket Factory, the mill, and Anderson's Box & Crate Works, would rise to an almost unbearable degree. It would bring the workers to perspiring, prompting the wish that the hours would fly by in order to get them through to the noon bell peeling from Grunewyck's village square.

Shade would be sought, meager lunches would be consumed, and the coveted bottle of beer, savored. Many would nap and have to be woken at the single tone of the bell that sounded the end of their leisurely moment. Roy LaVern, the manager of the basket factory, would be found at the door, a scowl on his face, his eyes moving from the pocket watch in his hand to the approaching faces and then back again.

On the other side of the mist filled Whip-poor-will Hollow, the villagers of Gowan would be going about their daily tasks, many wishing the dog days would wander off and get lost.

Sully Albright's hammer swung relentlessly and the death cry of cattle and pigs rolled up through the village of Gowan. The quicker he got through with his list of chosen victims, the sooner their bloody carcasses could grace the cutting tables across the street at Loeffler's, and… the sooner he could call it quits for the day. Sandy paid him good money for a half days work, but nobody else in the community showed any interest in a job clobbering animals in the head with a sledgehammer. So, Sully Albright had Sandy Brewster right where he wanted him.

Mayor Willy Wilton sat in his office upstairs in city hall, wishing he was somewhere else. His decision to cancel the Independence Day celebration was causing him grief. Maddie would be fielding calls for the next three days, answering the same question, over and over again. "Maddie, are there going to be fireworks?" Willie told Merlyn, "I hope she doesn't call in sick and leave me to answer that damn phone."

"Best you stay off the street for a few days, Willy," Merlyn said. Willy agreed.

Pots banged, plates clattered, and silverware rang as the café prepared for the lunch crowd. Cap McKendry had the presses whining and thumping at the newspaper office next door. The McCarthy's, across the street, silently filled the boxes under the windows out front of their store with fresh produce that had been carted to the village by Liam McClary on his run north to Aylesbury. The boorish Irishman would load up and return to Brimfield where he lived, stopping and dumping his load wherever he needed. He always attempted to beat his record time passing through the Hollow, going as fast as his horses, Oliver and Cromwell, could pull the wagon, Liam whipping their haunches and cursing them in Irish.

New dresses graced the windows at Sally's where Bessie could be found, a smile on her face as she hung the garments for all to see. She had spent the night upstairs with Sally and had gotten an education. Most likely, not the kind that her folks would approve of.

Fiske's Saddle and Leather across the street was abuzz with business as 'Nails' Dubois, sat at the window, repairing boots and shoes for those who didn't want to purchase the newer, cheaply made footwear sold across the street.

Art Jones's hammer rang with a busy tone at the blacksmiths on the corner, along with the reoccurring, *Hufffff!* of the bellows as the muscle-bound Art happily pounded out iron and steel.

The rumble of the Coastbound Flyer could be heard making its way north to greet the woman who waited with her three children, chattering about their upcoming visit to the beach in Kingsport. Danny Billings stood by with his pocket watch in hand, his ears waiting for the whistle of the incoming train. Gil snoozed away in the ticket booth; arms wrapping his chest, his hat pulled low over his eyes.

A muddy, disheveled Chastity Matthews paced up and down the boardwalk in front of the small public library, wringing her hands. Millie Behnke, the librarian, watched her from the checkout desk. It would not be the first time Millie had to close down the library and walk Chastity back to her cottage. Abigail Cunningham, who lived next door to Chastity, acted as the woman's nursemaid most of the time, but her obligation wasn't set in stone. Strictly a volunteer thing. When Abigail thought that Chastity would be fine and appeared to be in a more lucid state, she returned to her cottage and left the woman to her own devices.

There were no patrons in the library at the time, so Millie hung her 'Gone to Lunch' sign and taking the key that hung around her neck on a sturdy gold chain, she locked the door. Stepping out onto the boardwalk, Chastity focused on Millie and then ran to her with open arms, a silly, lopsided grin on her face. They hugged briefly and then Millie took Chastity's hand and they walked together like classmates heading for a day at the schoolhouse.

2

Vern, and Duncan Sweeny, had been going at it hot and heavy, trying to complete the grave in time for Kaleb Knight's arrival. They worked shirtless, their shovels never ceasing. They had been digging graves since they were thirteen years of age, and once they got their rhythm going in any one job, they didn't want to stop. It was a learned thing, and time passed quickly when they arrived at that place in their heads where their implements sang and the dirt flew. Filling the hole at the end of the service, after the dearly beloved had departed, was easier, and not as time consuming. But the goal then was to beat the sun to the western horizon because the living and breathing never wanted to be caught in the company of the dead after dark.

Vern said, "Why do you suppose pa chose four o clock?"

"No idea, probably the best time for him. Had to get that preacher man to come over from Grunewyck. Mayhaps he couldn't come earlier in the day," Duncan answered, somewhat perturbed that Vern had broken their rule of not talking while they shoveled.

They finished up, tossed out their long-handled implements and Duncan boosted Vern out of the hole. Then grabbing each other's wrists Vern pulled as Duncan climbed. Moving over to a stand of ancient maple trees, they sat in the shade and passed the water jug.

"How do you suppose a fella gets out of the hole if he's a digging by his lonesome?"

"Well, I 'spose... hell, I don't know, brother. Why you asking? Why don't you go over there, jump back in, and we'll find out?"

Duncan playfully punched his brother in the shoulder and they began to tussle. There came the familiar sound of the Model T truck their father used as a hearse and Vern checked his pocket watch.

"Damn, it's almost four twenty, what the hell do you suppose took 'em so long?"

"Don't know, but we best get our shirts on and comb our hair. You know how pa is about us looking our best when the grieving show up. What's he thinking, anyway... we're gravediggers, for gosh sake."

The twins got to their feet, pulled on shirts, tucked them in, and shared a comb. Moving to the head of the grave, they stood beside Josephine's headstone, waiting, no distinguishable difference between them other than their shirts. The twins always found joy in that; most of the time, anyway. People couldn't tell them apart and pranks often ensued.

Tom Lynn, being immediate family, led the procession walking with Percy Snoaks. Janey and Constance followed behind. Tabby walked with Ellie who had often waited on Kaleb when he stopped in at the café. She was to hurry back to the café and get right to work, Boots had said. "Just in case the reverend goes long winded."

The rest of the attendees followed behind her, people who knew of Kaleb, but never really spent time with him. The Reverend, Aldo Hale, walked beside the black pickup, one hand on the casket, the other holding a bible while he read passages. Aldo was serious about his work and was considered to be an angry man by anyone who knew him. He worked hard at striking fear in the hearts of those who attended his service in Grunewyck. He considered Gowan to be a godless town as it had chosen to convert its only church into a school. He was among sinners, but it was an opportunity for him to convert the Gowan non-believers.

Aldo was descendant of those who had persecuted the witches at the Salem Witch Trials of 1692. He believed that there was a genetic predisposition that had traveled over the generations to inundate his blood with the ability to sniff out and then pursue the ungodly pagans that dwelled in the Spry River Valley. That is what brought him to Grunewyck in the first place.

Being forced to use the small chapel at Sweeny's for a shorter than average eulogy, had struck a nerve. His protest to Louis Sweeny had fallen on deaf ears. The upside for the Reverend was that being asked to reside over the burial would put him where he needed to be.

Now there was talk about an unholy presence in the house that sat upon Nixie's Bluff. Three witches had made a showing at the general store to sit in the shadowy interior of Benjamin Carter's car and harass passersby. He had practically shivered with delight that his time to shine had finally come.

Tom stopped at a predesignated spot on the lawn, exactly twenty steps forward of where Louis had stopped the truck. The double column of black suited attendees (all except for Ellie who had to wear her cranberry-colored waitress dress) came to a halt and the funeral director climbed out of the truck to come around and speak with Tom.

Vern and Duncan moved to the back of the truck and pulled the casket out just far enough so the pallbearers could take hold. Tom, Percy, Colin, Cecil Walker, from the barber shop, Philip Shannon, and Merlyn Cobb took their respective handles on the casket and carried it to the gravesite where they placed it on the two ropes laid out on the grass next to the hole. Stepping back to line up facing the deceased, the rest filed in behind them. Duncan rolled a short section of tree stump over and placed it in front of Tom for Constance to sit on. Janey pushed her way through to stand next to Tom and rest her hands on her mother's shoulders. Tabby joined her there, with Ellie occasionally standing on tiptoes to look over their shoulder.

When Reverend Hale thought everyone was ready, he moved to face them, his back to the grave. Raising his right hand up as if to snatch something out of the air, he began to speak. His specially prepared sermon would include references to the sinner in the pine box as well as those who still drew breath; folks pretending they were listening.

Tom looked at Janey, who was making sure the Reverend's focus was on his book and not on her. He saw her roll her eyes and he hid his grin by feigning a cough into his hand. Vern and Duncan removed themselves from the gravesite and climbing over the short cast iron fence that surrounded the cemetery, they moved into the trees on its west side. Sitting on the trunk of a fallen maple, Vern opened his tin lunch box. Duncan declared he had forgotten his and with a promise to return, ran off before Vern could protest.

Duncan ran straight north through the backyards of the cottages nestled among the trees. But instead of returning to the house, he stopped at Penelope Southwick's cottage and knocked on the back door. Vince Skelton (who didn't know Kaleb Knight), was sitting in his kitchen tying flies for his upcoming fishing trip to the Bitterroot River in Montana. He heard, "Penelope?" emanate from the backyard next door, followed by, "Well, hello sweety. You come on in here and make me a happy woman… just like you always do." Vince smiled to himself and mumbled, "Make the best of it, boy. I know I would."

Aldo did go long winded, mostly because he liked to hear himself talk. No tears were shed as there was nothing in his talk to inspire them. The sun sank toward the mountain top, soon casting long shadows of the trees it hid behind. Duncan still hadn't returned and Vern grew nervous. "Damn, him," he muttered.

The Reverend wrapped it up and after a short prayer, he closed his book and smiled at everybody to indicate they could depart. Ellie broke and ran for the café. Tabby came to Hale to say how much she enjoyed his sermon. He thanked her with an air of indifference and she quickly turned away in order to catch up with Percy who had walked out toward the lane. Vern watched them leave, saying loud enough for conversation, "Damn you, brother." He took his lunchbox and placed it in the front seat of the truck. Louis asked, "Where's Duncan?"

"Hell, if I know, pa. Told me he forgot his dinner and was going back to get it, but that was an hour ago."

"Damn that boy."

Percy and Tabby remained in the lane talking with Cecil. Louis walked over and after having a word with them, brought the two men back to help Vern lower the casket into the hole with the ropes. When they had it safely at the bottom, Vern pulled out the ropes and tossed them in the back of the truck. Louis cranked the old Ford to get it started and after muttering a few choice words at the crank's kick-back, he rubbed his wrist while climbing into the driver's seat. Poking his head out, he said, "Jump on in, Cecil, I'll give you a ride. You too, Percy Snoaks."

Cecil jumped in beside Louis. Percy, with Tabby, climbed up to sit in the back, their legs hanging over the tailgate.

"Son, you go ahead and get started tossing in that dirt," Louis said to Vern, who stood, rubbing his forehead, "I'll head home and get your brother and bring him back."

"Okay, pa," Vern said, scowling.

Louis turned the truck around and drove away. Tabby and Percy waved to Vern, who, half-heartedly, returned the same. Kicking at a clump of grass, he retrieved his shovel.

Aldo Hale had stopped in his walk back to the funeral home to chat it up with Phil Shannon on Main Street. Nearly thirty minutes passed before the Reverend said his good byes to the lawyer and headed north toward Sweeny's. Another ten minutes went by before Vern saw his father race by, heading in the same direction. Louis had probably sat bending Cecil's ear the whole time.

This wasn't a first for Duncan shirking his duties and waiting until the task was almost complete before showing up. The sun was gone and the gravestones stood in shadow. A chill ran up Vern's spine as he scanned the trees behind him. It motivated him to work faster. "Duncan Sweeny, I'm going to beat your ass," he said to no one—or so he thought.

The gloaming filled the Spry River Valley like a breathable liquid.

Vern's vigor soon waned and he ceased his shoveling to rest. Somewhere a fox barked. An owl cackled from the trees, and someone's dog, over among the cottages, began to howl. It was a long, low, drawn-out sound that could have put anyone's nerves on edge. Leaning on his shovel, Vern's eyes strayed up to the afterglow haloing the mountain and then down into the trees. There was movement in there. Whatever it was, it became a silhouette that stopped just inside the tree line. It appeared to move within a cloud of mist, making it hard for him to discern who or what it might be.

The mist suddenly dissolved and he could see it was a woman. Her hair gleamed a chestnut brown and she wore a loose, flowing dress of green, whose sheen seemed to vacillate in the dying light. She walked further back into the trees and leaned against the trunk of one of them, unmoving, watching him, her hands behind her back. She looked familiar, even at that distance.

"Molly?" Vern called, "Molly, is that you?"

Molly Sharp, was a millwright's daughter he had courted for a while from over in Grunewyck. She sang his name and he felt a fleeting moment of attraction at the seductiveness of it.

"Why are you here, you got no business being here, and where did you get that stupid dress?"

Molly had been the one to call off the relationship. She had told him that she didn't think she could marry the son of a mortician, who may soon be one himself. She made it clear she didn't want to live in a funeral home for the rest of her life.

Vern didn't get an answer from the woman in the trees and this enraged him. Stomping to the fence, he jumped over and moved among the bark covered trunks. It never occurred to him how odd it was that she seemed enveloped in an unearthly light; something similar to foxfire.

"And what the hell is that smell, you got some kind of shitty new perfume on?"

He was angry now and that clouded his perception of what lay before him. Reaching out a hand to take a hold of her arm, he stopped, confused. It was Molly's face, but her eyes were yellow and snake like. She gave him a wicked grin and he saw a mouth full of long, sharp teeth.

Dropping his hand, he stood frozen in fear, stuttering out, "Why... you're not Molly."

"No... not anymore," it said in a raspy screech, and before Vern could turn to flee, she moved with the speed of light to open up his throat with a single swipe of long, keen edged finger nails.

3

Louis Sweeny drove the pickup back to the funeral home after dropping his passengers at Cecil's Barbershop. He never offered the Snoaks a ride to Headmost House, but they would have been content to walk the rest of the way, regardless. They told him how good it was of him to have taken them as far as the barbershop. Cecil then invited them inside to sit under his fan and drink bottles of Nehi soda before they returned to Headmost. They politely declined. Janey, Tom, and Constance, had walked on ahead. Louis was seething about Duncan by the time he returned to the funeral home.

Reverend Hale sat on the steps out front, his horse no longer hitched to the rail next to the drive. Louis composed himself, left the truck running and climbed out.

Aldo rose to his feet and said, "Horse run off, Louis, 'spect he went back to Grunewyck without me."

No one needed to tell Louis what was coming next.

"Could you give me a ride back over to the church? Shouldn't take you too long. Don't much like the Hollow during the gloaming, or... afterwards, for that matter."

"Why, certainly, Reverend," he said and turning, he rolled his eyes and returned to the front seat, putting on his best face when Aldo got in.

After backing out, Louis headed north. "Another funeral, second one in less than a week. I suppose you heard about poor ol' James Potter getting run down by his own automobile right out in front of his store? Well, maybe you didn't. I'm guessing Ralph Monroe over at Monroe's Funeral Parlor handled that one."

"Yep," was all Louis said, and they rode in silence for the remainder of the trip.

141

⚜

Duncan Sweeny had returned home after his 'quicky' with Penelope. Coming through the back door, he saw the Reverend's horse still tied up out front. He never liked Aldo Hale. His mother, Prudence, was upstairs, nipping brandy, as always. So, he slipped out the front door and after untying the horse, he gave it a good slap on the hindquarters to watch it take off toward the Hollow.

Going back inside, he helped himself to a piece of apple pie and standing just outside the kitchen door, he ate with his hands. He watched the Reverend come up and sit on the front porch, muttering something under his breath. Louis Sweeny would be madder than hell when he got back. Duncan had to be sure he was out the door and on his way back to the cemetery before Louis showed up.

He grabbed a glass of milk before slipping out the back, and chugging the contents, he set his mother's best tumbler on the chopping block by the woodpile before slipping through the hedge into the Brainerd's backyard. From there, he began a slow jog back to the cemetery, formulating an excuse for Vern as to why it had taken so long to get his dinner pail.

The moon was just topping the trees in the east when he arrived. The grave was nearly filled, but the shovels now lay on the ground, and Vern was nowhere to be seen.

"Damn it, Vern, why couldn't you be done."

Duncan finished the job and grabbing the second shovel, he hightailed it back to the house, casting glances over his shoulder as if he feared pursuit by some hobgoblin.

♭

Lissy Potter sat in her small bedroom on the second floor of her parent's store in Grunewyck. The room was at the back of the building and never saw the sun. Her mother, Colleen, sat in the parlor at the front, overlooking the street. She had been weeping and lamenting the loss of her husband to Amelia Lint. They had gathered for tea and Lissy saw the opportunity to leave her mother's side for a little peace and quiet. She needed to think.

Her father's funeral had been the day before and she hadn't cried.

142

The accident had unfolded right before her very eyes as she stood at the display window of the store. Her father had pulled up in the car, got out, and came around to stand in front of it, calling out, "Colleen, I'm heading over too..." The car just popped into gear and ran him down.

It got hung up on his body, and Lissy watched the back wheels slowly turn, sometimes slipping on the cobblestones as it pushed forward, inch by inch, dragging her screaming father with it. She stared in horror at the bloody streak being left behind. It was Bill Henley, from the drugstore across the street, who came out and got the car shut off and the brake set. By the time the doctor got there, several men had managed to drag poor, mutilated James Potter out from underneath. They were too late.

Lissy watched in shock as the doctor looked up at her mother and shook his head. Stumbling to a chair with her mother's wailing in her ears, she sat and stared, dumbfounded. Time passed quickly then. No one ever came to get her and when she finally got up to return to the window in a trance-like state, she saw the men carrying her father up the street toward Monroe's, his once white shirt now a bloody rag.

The rest of the day was a blur. Her mother had cried, screamed and ranted incoherently. There had been plenty of townsfolk around to console her, making it easier on Lissy to not have to. At the funeral they all had pretty much ignored her, except for Cora MacLean, who had wrapped an arm around her shoulders and tried to comfort her as they walked from the cemetery.

Now, Lissy, perched on the edge of her bed, listened to Colleen ramble and Amelia's soothing voice as she consoled her. Lissy's father had told her from day one that life was hard and one needed to stay strong. Whenever she had cried about something minor, he grabbed her by her upper arms and shook her to make her stop, sternly saying, "Enough, girl." Lissy learned how to hide her emotions and remain calm in the worst of situations.

Colleen thought her odd for it; Mrs. Durnell, the same. Time and time again the old school teacher had tried to intimidate her, and when all attempts failed, she'd stick Lissy in the corner on a stool, facing the wall, with a dunce cap on her head. Eventually the cap came up missing and Durnell started having them balance a book on their head, instead. After about a dozen times of the heavy book slamming on the floor scaring the bejeezus out of her, Durnell gave it up and just made them sit there with their heads bare. It was a victory for the scholars, and Lissy became a school house hero. Now, there was vengeance on her mind. Someone had to pay for the death of her father and she had an inkling of who that someone just might be.

Days before, she had overheard Colleen talking with Cora MacLean on the telephone. Cora had called to say she saw Lissy hobbling by the tavern and had asked if everything was alright. Colleen relayed what Lissy had told her about her day over at the Hollow but didn't believe a word of it.

In their walk home from the cemetery, Lissy confirmed everything her mother had told Cora over the telephone and the old woman had a reason for every event that Lissy had experienced as if she too had undergone similar things as a girl.

Their whole conversation funneled down to one person: Mabel Carter. Cora told Lissy that she believed Mabel wasn't who she wanted everybody to think she was. Lissy asked, "If that's the case, then who was she, really?" Cora told her everything, leaving Lissy to believe that it was Benjamin Carter's new bride that had taken her father. Cora left Lissy at the store with an embrace to return to the Lost Collie.

Now, Lissy wanted to go up there and burn down Carter House—with Mabel in it. She figured she might get Benjamin Carter as well. It was his fault, after all, for bringing that woman there. Mabel was supposed to have used some kind of magic, and Cora had been convincing. Lissy didn't want to cry—she wanted to hurt someone.

6

Sally faced off with Bessie in the storeroom at the back of the shop. Heated words were being exchanged. Sally was in one of her moods and was livid over a comment Bessie had made about how attractive she thought Janey Carter was. Even though a mere observation, Sally construed it as a threat to her future plans.

"Then, why'd you say it, Bessie? It was hurtful."

"It was nothing. I was just saying what everybody already knows and probably isn't saying."

"Well, we could have gotten along without it."

"Oh, Sally, it was just a passing thought that slipped out. I didn't mean anything by it."

"So, you're looking at others?"

"Of course, I look at others. What do you mean, others? Sally, I've got eyes, I see other people. Can't help it."

"You understand I'm trying to build something here, right? I'm trying to make a life… for us."

"So… I can't look at other people because you're insecure?" Bessie's voice was rising by octaves, her brow clouded and there was fire in her eyes. Sally looked hard into her face. Reaching out to touch Bessie's hand, the younger woman pulled away and crossed her arms, glaring.

"Don't… not right now. I think I'm going home, maybe I'll see you tomorrow."

"Please, Bessie, don't go, I'm sorry, I just…"

"You just, what? Want to control me? You're acting just like my mother. I don't need that. I don't need someone else telling me what to do."

"I'm sorry, I'm just in my mood… you know?"

"I'm going. I'll be back in the morning. Maybe you can come up with a better way to say what you want to say."

Bessie walked to the backdoor, opened it, and stepped out. She gazed out across the small yard and over the hedge into the windows of the big house across the street. It was a large Queen Anne style owned by Judge Benson. All the windows were lit and she could see his family moving about inside, the children playing in the parlor, the Judge at his desk in his study, and Mrs. Benson moving in and out of the dining room, checking on the children. Bessie could see the maid trudging up the stairs carrying what looked like linen, and the Benson's cook, Amarilla, crossing a hallway into what Bessie knew was the pantry. It was what Bessie had always conveyed to friends as something she wanted— someday. A big, busy house with a family. Then Sally came along, and all that changed.

From behind her, she heard, "Bessie, I'm sorry, please, can't you accept my apology?"

"I'm sorry is not an apology. Saying I apologize, is." With that said,

Bessie shut the door, walked down the steps to the cobblestone apron at the bottom and followed the narrow walkway around to the street. She stopped and looked around as if not sure where to go. Mumbling to herself, she said, "This could be a mistake," her eyes welling with tears.

Sally sobbed at the latching of the door and covering her mouth with her hands, she paced back and forth in the small storeroom. Stopping, she threw up her hands and growled, "Oh no you don't," and gave chase. Instead of following the path around to the street, though, she went straight out through the back gate that was positioned within the hedge at Ovis Street.

Scanning the houses on the opposite side, she caught movement in the dark space between the Benson's house and Blanchett's. Knowing Bessie like she did, Sally figured she would seek some out of the way place where she could cry without being bothered. There was more movement and Sally whispered, "Bessie." She practically flew across the street, and up the short cobblestone driveway that led to the Benson's carriage house. Then, in a fast, stomping walk, she entered the woods, looking hard for whatever she had seen.

April Benson, the Judge's oldest daughter, had just returned from the McCarthy's after taking one of her mother's famous apple pies to Mary's back porch. She no sooner got the door shut at their rear stoop, when she saw Sally Combs enter their backyard, stop a minute, look around, and then run out of sight into the trees behind the carriage house. A look of concern crossed April's face and she hurried from the window to the sewing room to tell her mother of the odd occurrence.

Sally stopped and peered into the trees. Not seeing anything, she started to turn away. Out of the corner of her eye she caught the shape of a face among the tree trunks. Somebody was standing next to a massive oak, watching her.

"Bessie? Is that you?" No answer. Sally went in carefully, picking her way around thickets and fallen trees. Dark blonde hair picked up a gleam and then disappeared. "Bessie, please. Stop messing with me. I'm sorry, I promise I won't get mad again."

The face turned away and a dark silhouette passed through an opening in the trees contrasted by a trace of afterglow. Sally moved faster, trying to catch up, afraid Bessie, in her anger, was trying to get away. Blond hair gleamed again and Sally rushed over to the shadowy figure that now leaned against another large tree trunk, it's hands behind its back. There was some resemblance to Sadie Mills, a past love interest of Sally's from Grunewyck. Sally stopped and looked confused. The woman in the green dress smiled at her and stretched out her arms.

Sally shrieked, barely feeling the slight sting at the side of her neck. She swooned and the creature caught her. Pulling her close, it kissed her lightly on the lips before working its way down to Sally's spurting carotid.

Naomi Benson stood on the back porch with her daughter, April. "Honestly, ma, she was right there, I saw her. I think she went into the woods."

"You sure it was Sally Combs?"

"Damn sure, ma, it …"

"April Leigh Benson! How many times do I have to tell you not to swear, I…"

A shriek resonated from the trees, interrupting the scolding. The two shirked back, gasping and covering their mouths at the same time. Their fear filled eyes found each other, and Naomi instinctively grabbed her daughter and pushed her back inside. She bolted the door and taking April's hand, she rushed down the hallway to do that one thing she was told never to do; interrupt the Judge in his study.

7

Merlyn was about ready to call it quits for the day. Sitting at his desk, he was finishing up some last-minute paperwork. He had put a call into the Boston field office for the FBI to see if they had anything on Benjamin Carter's new bride. They were taking their sweet time about getting back to him.

Nealy was acting his usual hyper self, pacing the room. "You hear about that girl disappearing over in Grunewyck? My cousin, you know? Sam Givens? He was telling me that he got it from some barfly over at the Lost Collie. I think Sam said it was Cyrus Sharp, who said that his niece, Molly, got all bent out of shape at her folks and stomped off into the Hollow. She never came back. Then, Sadie Mills, the seamstress from over there? Walked away from her shop, leaving the doors wide open. Hasn't been seen since."

Merlyn stopped writing and set his gaze on Nealy. "Yeah, I heard. I'm wondering if they ever bothered to get up a search party? Chief Conway was too busy dealing with the proprietor of the general store who got run over by his own car. You hear about that? Conway probably ain't had the time. Got to give it a couple days, I guess, before they consider them missing. Molly used to be with Vern Sweeny, if'n I remember correctly. Hell, I always thought they'd get hitched. She was the one who called it off, I heard."

Nealy stopped pacing and pulling a small notebook and a pencil stub from his pocket, he jotted something down. Moving over to stand in front of Merlyn's desk, he eyed a framed picture of a younger, thinner, Merlyn, in a brand-new uniform. He was standing next to the Model A that the town had acquired new for his use.

"Something troubling you, Nealy?"

"Well, Chief, maybe it's not my place, but…you ever think that maybe Phil Shannon might be part of these going ons? I mean, he's the Carter's lawyer, right? It's just… I've got a gut feeling about that shyster."

Merlyn continued scrutinizing Nealy. He had always stood up for his officer when people questioned him about Nealy Garret being the best choice for a policeman. That started after he had shot those three men to death over the space of a year. Nealy had always been an excellent shot. That scared people.

Merlyn told them, "Nealy is a good man and a pretty decent officer. He might be a little too feisty, right now, but so was I when I first started. He's got an instinct for police work; he trusts his gut. He's hardly ever been wrong."

Now, that instinct was at play again. Merlyn felt the same way Nealy did about Shannon. Their day together up at Carter House had been the straw to break the camel's back.

"So, tell me what you're thinking, Nealy."

"Well, Chief… now I don't want to be out of line, I know Phil Shannon has been here a long time. I know that ol' Ben Carter hired him to be their attorney way back when and had his hands in just about everything Ben did. You know? Business and such? Phil must have been

R.C. Davis

the one to handle all the legal parts, right? So, this woman you're telling me about, who's up there at that house, well, she ain't no American. What's her name? Oh, Mabel... now she's supposed to be Scottish, right? So, ummm... there's a citizenship issue. So... paperwork, right? I'm seriously wondering if it was Shannon who handled that. Maybe even greasing a few palms to make sure Ben got what he wanted."

Merlyn was listening to Nealy but wasn't looking at him. His eyes were on his desk, the unlit stogey in the fingers of his left hand tapping the edge of the ashtray as if he was lost in thought. "I'm just saying, Chief, maybe it's Shannon we should be talking to."

"I hear you, and maybe your right. Maybe you should stay over in the morning and we can just drop over to Phil's office and have a chat. He'll open his door by eight, beings he's a pretty punctual kind of guy."

"Hell, yeah. If I need to, I can just crap out in the holding cell."

"That old cot is pretty hard."

"Ah, it ain't so bad."

"Nealy... how do you know that? You been blowing Z's on the night shift?" Merlyn cracked a smile to let Nealy know it wasn't no big deal because the officer's eyes filled with fear.

"You just joshing me, Chief? I have to make that damn thing every morning after we let... whatever drunk I catch, sleep it off."

Merlyn laughed and Nealy, realizing he was just kidding, gave a nervous chuckle before slapping his leg. "Gol darn you, Chief, you had me there."

Merlyn tipped his dusty fedora back, scratched at his hairline, grinned, and shook his head. "Okay, so... were going to Shannon's first thing after I get in. The FBI said maybe tomorrow, maybe the next day on that Mabel Carter... or, Mab, as she wanted me to call her. Judge Benson won't give me a warrant to go up there and kick down that door. I suspect it may actually be a good thing if Benjamin Carter's still around. But I doubt he is. So, Nealy, my good man, I'm going back up there, regardless."

"You want me with you? I'll go up there. I can take the shotgun. We can haul her ass out and bring her down for questioning, 'specially if ol' Ben is missing."

"Missing, why do you say that? We don't have no proof."

149

"Oh, that's just my gut, again."

Merlyn looked at Nealy standing there, his feet shoulder width apart, his hands on his hips and his head tilted forward, looking at him out of the tops of his eyes. The officers grey, western style Stetson was pushed back on his head, a hat that Merlyn always said was too small for him. Nealy was saying the exact thing he had been thinking.

Pushing his paperwork into a pile and turning off his desk lamp, he stood, reset his hat and said, "Heading home, Nealy, got to cook my dinner."

The phone rang and Merlyn answered it. "Yes, sir. What? You're kidding? Okay... so you don't kid. Okay, okay, I'll send Nealy up. Yes, sir, right away."

Hanging up the phone, his gaze turned to Nealy who was already shaking his head in disbelief. "Head up to the judge's house. I guess Naomi and April heard what sounded like a scream in the woods behind their place. Take a flashlight."

"Ah dammit, I had my mind set on pot roast and taters at Boots'."

"Just do it. You can get supper, after."

"Okay, but what if I find something? What if there's... bad folk?"

"Well, you got a gun, Nealy. If you're sure they're bad folks, shoot 'em, and then stop over and tell me what happened and I'll give you supper. Now, I'm gone, see you." With that, Merlyn left Nealy blank faced and staring as he left the office, the stairs soon creaking under the big man's weight.

8

Leo Dane stood in the woods at the edge of the orchard behind Carter House. He had walked the railroad tracks north and then worked his way up the west slope of Parson's Ridge. He knew about the narrow path that ran south from the Scottsburg Road; he had used it before. Leo often desired to burgle Carter House, but had been thwarted every time.

Dropping his empty loot bag, he got comfortable on a large stump. It had been a strange walk through the woods. There had been an abundance of wildlife, owl, fox, and weasels, along with an excessive number of rabbits. Frogs croaked in the scattered pools accompanied by crickets, katydid, and Whip-poor-will. It had never been like that before.

The burglar knew all about the gloaming but had never experienced it quite the way he did this night. The wildlife had gotten so loud at one point that it became almost unbearable and he thought to leave and return on a different day. It was as if the creatures wanted to warn someone of his unwanted presence. Then the noise dwindled to almost normal when the twilight gave way to full dark.

Philip Shannon had summoned him to make an appearance at the backdoor of his office. Leo used the secret knock and Philip opened the door to allow him in. Standing in the makeshift file room at the back, Philip explained what he expected of the burglar. It was simple, enter Carter House at night, unseen. Make note of everything and see if there was any evidence of Benjamin Carter on the premises. Philip was also sure to let Leo know, in a roundabout way, he could take whatever he wished in the way of booty as partial payment for the operation.

The night before, Leo had watched the house through a narrow break in the trees from a small knoll just south of the bluff. It was late in the evening when the interior illumination of the mansion dwindled to nothing, starting with the belvedere, the darkness working its way down through the floors. It ended with a troupe of four exiting the front door, candles held high. They were soon joined by more specks of light from the woods west of the house.

This was followed by some kind of ritual that involved dancing and chanting. Finally, the line of lights moved from the front lawn, across the natural stone bridge, and into the woods, where every light blinked out.

Leo took in the neglect of the property as he waited on that stump. Tall weeds lined the walls of the outbuildings and the lawn had grown to over ankle height. Doors hung open and swung slowly in the evening breeze. A peculiar thing that caught his attention was the vines that crawled up the outside of the house, some even appeared to have broken window panes to gain access to the interior. Every window in Carter House glowed, but the light was almost ethereal, not electrical. The belvedere was the exception, its ceiling-hung chandelier projected a luminance that would allow the mansion to be found in the dark from a great distance. Leo checked his flashlight by cupping a hand over the lens and clicking the button on and off. All set to go, now he just had to

151

wait for the right moment.

A waxing crescent moon made its way west, and falling behind the trees, Leo soon lost any useful natural light. He was growing impatient, but when he reached the point where it became almost unbearable, a shadow moved in front of the chandelier and it went out. A minute later, the illumination in the windows of the third-floor dormers followed, then the second, and finally, the first. He heard the screen door at the front squeak open and slam shut. Muttered voices could be heard and soon a song floated out on the night air, a siren's lilt that rose and fell. Then ceasing altogether, it was followed by a chant that filled his ears, getting louder and louder by the minute.

The woods around him came alive with wildlife sounds and as the chant began to undulate, the wildlife kept pace with an almost unnatural resonance. The Whip-poor-wills joined in the rhythm and it all became unbearably cacophonic.

It was as if the planet was breathing, the earth beneath Leo's feet vibrating. Then, scattered motes of light descended from the tree tops and filled the woods almost like tiny, living creatures. They joined the lights gathering at the front of the house, filed into a line and were soon lost from sight. Leo shivered.

The candle bearers soon came into sight as they cleared the house and made their way across the stone bridge and into the woods, the unusual little lights trailing behind. The resonance faded, the earth became still again, and the wild things resumed their normal night sounds.

Leo, trying to recover his composure, waited about ten minutes before grabbing up his bag and approaching the house. He crept among the apple trees, stopping occasionally to listen. When he reached the outhouse, he peeked around the corner but saw no one. Moving out across the open yard, he walked up onto the back porch. Quietly testing the door, he found it wasn't locked. He pushed it open and entered the dark kitchen.

Sniffing the air, he said under his breath, "Ooo-wee, what's that smell?" Turning on the flashlight, he kept the beam low and partially covered with his hand. Being a burglar always brought surprises, but what he saw nearly shocked him. He had anticipated the rooms to be of grand representation as everyone believed the Carter's had lived like royalty, however, the disarray was unbelievable. Chairs had been toppled over, a leg on the kitchen prep table was broken and the flat of its surface tilted allowing everything to slide off into a pile. The floor was littered with pot, pans, and plates of different sizes; some having shattered. He found the dining room nearly the same. Portraits that once lined the walls now sat on the floor either leaning against it or lying flat. Some appeared to have been stepped on. Small knick-knacks and such, covered the boards of the floor, and Leo had to be careful where he stepped. Rugs had been pulled up and piled in corners or draped over furniture. The front parlor was no different.

Bookshelves had been pulled over and literary works lay piled up on the floor as if someone was inspecting each book and then tossing it away when nothing of importance had been found.

Moving into the entry hall, he took the corridor that led to the back staircase and the kitchen door beyond. Leo passed the opening to the second parlor on his right and then stopped outside the door to Benjamin's study. It was shut and when he tried to open it, he found it would only move a couple of inches before hitting some piece of furniture. A breeze blew through the gap like a window inside stood open. Giving up the idea of going in, he returned to the entry hall.

Standing quietly at the base of the main staircase, he listened. Hearing nothing other than his own breathing, Leo shined his light upward. He gasped. The vines covering the outside of the house, also covered the walls within.

Leo ascended the open stairs to the second floor and found the upper hall way was fairly clear of obstacles, but the bedrooms were a jumbled mess. Glancing into the master bed chamber at the end of the passageway, his brow furrowed.

The headboard of the large canopied bed was pushed up against the back wall. It was made, but appeared as if someone occupied it on occasion. Three sleeping pallets lay upon the floor, one on each side and one at the foot. All the other furniture had been pushed against the walls. Plants of different types had been bundled, tied with the blades of some kind of long grass, and hung around the room as if to dry. The room had an odor of herbs and spice along with that familiar woodland smell.

There was just a hint of animal odor.

It was obvious that who ever lived in this house, spent most of their time in this room. Moving to the head of the bed, Leo stepped on a pile of tiny, button sized objects. Shining his light on them, they gleamed. Grabbing one, he examined it closely. "I'll be damned, it's gold," he whispered. He bit it and found his observation to be true. Shoving it in a trouser pocket, it was soon followed by the entire pile, the front pockets of his dungarees now bulging.

There came a noise, ever so slight. He turned his light off and stood quietly in the dark for a minute before tiptoeing to the door. Peering out into the hallway, he saw no one.

Something gleamed on top of the dresser to his left. It was a gold pocket watch; one he had seen in Benjamin Carter's possession. Next to it, a sterling silver pen knife, a gold tie tack, gold cuff links, and gold rimmed spectacles. A set of dentures rested at the bottom of a tumbler full of murky water. Leo took everything except for the spectacles and with reluctance, dumped the water from the tumbler onto the floor and shoved the dentures inside the breast pocket of his jacket.

Moving to leave the room, he tripped over something. Shining his light through the cracks in his fingers, he saw clothing piled there. It was a suit complete with white silk shirt and a pair of stockings. Someone had undressed rather quickly and didn't bother to hang it. It was obviously Benjamin Carter's.

Creeping back into the corridor he slowly made his way to a door that led to the third-floor stairs. They would take him up to the belvedere that topped the tower. A view to the grounds was necessary to make sure the coast was clear. He planned to leave by the front door and take the lane down through the bridge to a little used path that ran to the Meadowlands. Hugging the tree line all the way to Doc Bolen's house, he would then use the village's maintenance shop to shield him as he snuck over to Philip's back door.

The treads creaked no matter where he put his foot. He found the rooms on the third floor were as bad as the second. Passing them by, he moved up into the belvedere. The vines were making their way inside through the windows there, as well. Some as thick as his arms. He shook his head as if in disgust and mumbled, "Such a beautiful, old house, too."

Looking out of the windows and not seeing anyone or anything in his path, he turned back to the stairs, made his way down, and upon reaching the hallway, the noise he had heard earlier, came again. It was a kind of pattering, like small dogs running on a wooden floor. He caught motion out of the corner of his eye and turning to peer back toward the master bedroom, he could just make out a shadow within a shadow standing in a corner. A toddler sized figure stood unmoving. Quickly bringing his flashlight to bare, he switched it on.

"Who's there?" he stuttered out, but whatever had been there, moved with amazing speed into a nearby room. There had been just a brown streak, and... gone. Leo moved with amazing speed too, except in the direction of the main stairs and the front door.

Turning off his light, he jumped down the treads, two at a time. Finding the front door unlocked, he ran outside. Turning left, he made for the short embankment that separated the lawn from the lane. Jumping off, he jogged down the hill.

Above him on the bridge of stone, a woman giggled in the dark. It was a tinkling sort of laugh that increased in volume, a noise that caused him to slap his hands over his ears and groan as if in pain.

The laughing stopped and something moved through the trees on his left. He came to a halt and shined his light in that direction. There was nothing, just brush and tree trunks. Leo shoved the flashlight into one of the gold-filled pockets, but using too much force, he pushed it through the bottom and all the gold cascaded down the inside of his trouser leg to spill out his cuff.

"Damn it!" he yowled.

The flashlight went into a jacket pocket instead and he bent to pick up the baubles. Somebody was coming up fast behind him. With just a few pieces in his hand, he sped away, leaving the rest. Profanity issued from his lips as he picked up speed on the downward slope. He raced through the bridge and coming out the other side, he soon arrived at the first bend in the road. Finding the entrance to the hidden trail, he made for the Meadowlands.

Four dark figures now stood in the lane where Leo had lost the gold. One of them squeaked out, "Shall we seize him?" Another said in a raspier squeak, "He's getting away." The third spoke as flatly as one can with a squeaky voice, "Yes, he is."

"No, let him go. He'll bring the others," Mab said, her voice quite regal in tone. "Isn't that what we want?" she added, looking around at the others.

Her companions nearly shrieked with mirth, and after collecting the baubles Leo had spilt, they skipped and danced away, leaving the woman, in her narrow banded, gold crown, to stand alone and contemplate the fleeing burglar.

9

Leo Dane didn't stop running until he reached the cottages on the north side of Gowan. He had to go deeper into the trees when he came upon a group of people standing in the backyard at Sweeny's funeral home. There was a lot of loud talk and people were acting with urgency. Something else was going on.

Where the cemetery butted up against the woods, Leo stopped and vomited. His lungs were burning from exertion, something he wasn't used to. Wiping his mouth, he looked around, trying to determine the best path through the trees. A horrendous stench filled his nose. "What the hell?" he said, studying the puddle of vomit. "That can't be me. What the hell did I eat?" He turned away and began a fast walk only to trip over something and somersault into a patch of blackberry. Rolling away from the thorn laden vines, he sat up and looked back to see what he had tripped over.

It wasn't a something—it was a somebody.

"Hey, what are you doing here." They didn't answer but just sat with their back to a large ball of roots at the base of a fallen tree. Their legs were splayed out in front and Leo had tripped over an ankle. They said nothing and sat unmoving. Finding his flashlight, Leo switched it on and shined it in their face. A shriek broke from his lips and scrambling to his feet, he back peddled a couple yards before falling again. There was no way that guy couldn't be dead.

It had been a young man, maybe seventeen or eighteen years of age. His throat was torn open as was his chest and abdomen. To add to the horror, they looked like they had been drained of all their blood to the

156

point where they had started to pucker, but there wasn't enough blood on the ground to say they had lost all ten pints to gravity. Scrambling to his feet, Leo vomited a second time before fleeing the scene.

A portion of Philip Shannon's back porch was enclosed to protect the firewood that was stored there in the winter. Because it was late summer, it stood empty. Leo crawled inside and sat back in a corner. He would remain there for a good hour before using the secret knock that would bring Philip down the stairs.

10

Reverend Hale stood at the pulpit in his church in Grunewyck, his back to the empty pews. He gazed up at the large wooden cross affixed to the wall, a bottle of whiskey in one hand and his small book of scripture in the other. He had failed to learn all he needed to know about the goings-on over in Gowan. The more he drank, the madder he got. Louis Sweeny had nothing to offer on the ride back to Hale's church.

"Now, Louis, I seriously believe there is a coven of witches occupying Carter House. I want to force them out into the light for all to see, and maybe even expose that Benjamin Carter, as their warlock leader. It's time for me to get to work."

Louis said nothing, just stared straight ahead and drove the truck.

"I know that the state of Massachusetts is going to come in here and take this valley. So, I gots to get my hands on the guilty parties before they scatter to the wind."

Louis remained tight lipped all the way and never spoke until he bid the Reverend good night.

Stepping down from the raised platform, Aldo moved to the front door and out onto the stoop. Setting the bottle at his feet behind the balustrade, so no one could see it, he gazed down the dark and deserted Center Street. It ran from the train station up to his church where it became a 'T' intersection with one branch running north to the village of Danton, the other, curving around the church to the suspension bridge crossing the Spry River and then a few miles east to the small village of Princeton.

The street was often congested on Sundays as more and more people acquired automobiles and wanted to drive to services instead of walking. Many thought it okay to park their monstrosities on the lawn, something Aldo protested at the end of every sermon. It saddened him that the town was going to be put to death, especially at a time when it was so prosperous.

Aldo planned to look to the towns in the north of Massachusetts, perhaps Aylesbury or, Dunwich. Now that was one town in bad need of saving. Hale had heard there had been a church there; now converted to a general store. Rumor had it the steeple had blown off in a great storm. He told Helen Beck that he could purchase the store from some guy named Osborn and if he did, he would have that steeple replaced. Helen lied and told him she would surely move there if he did.

He still needed to pick up his horse down at Larkin's Livery where it had ended up after running away from Sweeny's. Aldo had plans to ride out to the Lost Collie tavern. Cora MacLean might shed some light on the situation. Everybody knew they didn't see eye to eye on much of anything. She was a friend of Colleen Potter, though, who had just lost her husband. The grapevine had disclosed that their daughter, Lissy, had some kind of an unholy experience involving Carter House and Whip-poor-will Hollow.

Aldo confessed to Harold Penny, the man who cleaned the church and was one of his most devout parishioners, that he was going to confront Cora about what she knew. If she didn't cooperate, he was going to spread the word that her and her bootlegging husband, Al, had a connection to that bunch up on Nixie's Bluff. Then, he was going to petition, whomever, to get that name changed. "It's Parson's Ridge, is it not?" he said to Harold, "Well, then... it should be Parson's Bluff, yes?"

Harold had agreed, but told Aldo, "That mountain, and Gowan, are in the bailiwick of the Carters. That means going up against Benjamin Carter. The people around here are afraid of that man... more than they are of you."

Aldo looked up into the star laden sky and mumbled to himself, "Some things are going to change around here."

A sudden baying filled the air and a pack of five scroungy looking foxhounds broke from the brush across Princeton Road, giving him a start. In pursuit of a rabbit, they ignored his calls as they disappeared behind the church, their baying fading away into the distance. "Now whose dogs would those be?" he asked himself. Picking up his bottle, he put his back to the street and took a short swig before going back inside. He needed to get started on his plan and had a few letters to write.

11

Tuesday morning found Philip Shannon pacing the inside of his office in pajamas and his burgundy dressing robe. He stopped occasionally to glare at Leo Dane in the dim light of a desk lamp. The burglar sat in one of the two client chairs, a tumbler of Philip's best whiskey in Leo's pale, quivering hand.

"You say the place was in shambles? Probably a total loss by now…"

"That's right, can't say I'd give you a hundert dollars for it."

"Doesn't matter, when it comes time for compensation from the government, I'll be lucky to get a tenth of what it's worth and that includes the grounds. There will be my kickback for brokering the deal, which will be the same for every property in Gowan. I just have to convince everyone that what the state offers, is final. That's not something you need to let get around, though. So… there was no sign of Benjamin Carter?"

"That's right, nowhere to be seen. Just those strange women. Oh! And this…"

Reaching into the breast pocket of his jacket, he pulled out the dentures and set them on the desk.

What the hell is that? False teeth?"

"Ben Carter's false teeth. Took 'em from his dresser top. Was floating in a glass of stinking water."

Philp walked over, took a closer look, and gave Leo a look of disgust. "You're telling me, those are Benjamin's teeth?"

"I ain't telling you anything, but wouldn't you think so?"

"He'd never leave the house without them."

"Yeah, unless he was forced."

Philip took a handkerchief from his robe pocket, and picking up the dentures, he deposited them in a drawer. Then resting his hands on the desk, he said to no one in particular, "Wonder what they did with him?"

Leo said, "Got me," shrugged, and took a long drink of whiskey.

"I suppose it doesn't matter. As long as he doesn't show up later. So, you're certain he was nowhere to be seen? Because if you're not, and he does, it will signal the end for you."

"You threatening me, Shannon?"

"I am, and if you don't like it... too bad. You been hanging around Zelda's a lot, lately, I hear. You see the Curtis boys there occasionally, I imagine."

"Yeah, so?"

"Well, I suspect you won't want to see them again."

"Whatcha mean by that?"

"Well, it so happens I pay them a lot more than I pay you. You get my meaning?"

Leo just glared and downed the remains of his glass. Shannon opened a drawer and pulled out a small, metal box. Setting it on his desktop, he closed the drawer. Producing a small key, he unlocked the box and taking out a short stack of cash, he counted out fifty dollars, stopped, and let his eyes travel from the money to Leo's face. The burglar's eyes were wide open and locked on the stack.

Shannon appeared to have had a thought, his brow furrowing. He counted out another twenty-five, added it to the fifty, and set the bills on a pile of papers. Putting the stack of money back in the box, he locked it, stuck it back in the drawer, and then made a show of locking that.

Picking up the money on his desk, he held it out in his left hand as his right snaked into the pocket of his robe. Pulling out a Colt Detective Special, he let the pistol dangle next to his thigh.

"I won't be needing your services any longer, Mr. Dane. Come to think of it, I don't want you to show your face in Gowan ever again. I'm giving you an extra twenty-five dollars for your trouble. Keep that pocket full of gold, it's yours per our deal. I can assure you that you don't want to run into the Curtis brothers because, I can guarantee, it won't be a pleasant experience. If you see them first, best you skedaddle on out of there. Hear me?"

"Oh, yeah, I hear you."

"Good."

160

Shannon handed Leo the money and the burglar snatched it from his hand. Setting the whiskey tumbler on the desk, he got to his feet in a brusk manner and headed for the front door.

"Ah, no, use the back, I don't want you being seen going in and out of my office. Remember what I said about leaving Gowan. You're not welcome here anymore, Mister Dane."

"Don't matter none, it's a dead town anyway. I know you ain't telling folks about the reservoir like you're supposed too. In a couple years there won't be no town to come back to. Think I'll head down to Brimfield, or maybe, Burley. There's some nice pickin's down there. Thanks for the whiskey, barrister," Leo said and sneered. "I also had something else you might want to know about, but now... I'm thinking I will just keep that to myself and you good folk can find out on your own." Leo Dane had nothing to gain by sharing information about the body back up in the woods by the cemetery. He was done with Gowan and the people in it.

Shannon scoffed as Leo passed his desk and headed down the narrow hallway to the back door. As soon as the door slammed, Phil made a couple calls. The first to the chief of police down in Brimfield, and the second, to Zelda's, to leave a message for the Curtis brothers.

CHAPTER SEVEN

GREGORY BLY

~

1

Gregory Bly couldn't shake the mounting concern over his forthcoming walk home. At first, he had been quite pleased with himself for his decision to stop by the Lost Collie tavern for supper.

It was well over three miles back to Gowan, and he disliked having to settle for a late meal once he arrived home. Yet the stop would delay his departure and the gloaming would surely catch him out on that lonely road. Wouldn't be the first time, though. Gregory was willing to risk it.

He loved his job tutoring grammar to the invalid children of the wealthy in Grunewyck. It paid the bills and gave him a chance to stash away some cash for the so-called rainy day. However, he now found himself growing weary of the daily trek. His main worry had been, because of the Depression, was how long would the wealthy be able to retain him. Then came all the talk about the reservoir, and Gregory knew, without a doubt, it was done. His life as he knew it, had come to an end. He would have to move, and he had no place to go.

Finishing up his bowl of soup, he downed the rest of his tea, wishing it were something stronger. Something that could calm his nerves, like—whisky. But he was prone to overdoing it and detested walking any great distance under the influence, plus, there were those horrific hangovers.

Gregory gathered his belongings and raised his tall, lanky frame from the booth. Catching his reflection in the mirror behind the bar, he noticed how the paleness of his face contrasted the brown flannel of his ill-fitting suit. His unruly dark hair, large ears, and long red nose didn't help matters. Gregory was just a naturally nervous looking man.

His appearance had brought him the moniker, 'Ichabod'. Yet only the loafers outside Zelda's ever had the gall to abuse it. So, he didn't go there anymore. His only reason for being in attendance at such a place was to seek the comfort that only a woman could bring. Yet little Lisa Bartek had married off, and he didn't like the older hookers. Sighing loudly, he pushed his spectacles back up his nose with a free finger and moved over to the pinewood bar top to pay.

"Finished up, are you?" Cora said as she stood from counting coins.

"I am, Cora. Time to get on the road."

"Wouldn't you rather stay for a glass of Al's finest, Mr. Bly?"

"Ah… no Cora, not tonight. It's almost three miles of rough and crooked road between here and Gowan, some of the roughest country that Massachusetts has to offer. I'd best make that journey with a clear head."

The marcel waves of Cora's grey hair bounced as she shook her head and rolled her eyes; a sure sign she had heard it all before. It's not like she hadn't just made that trip in order to deal with her sister, Chastity.

Gregory felt the embarrassment of the realization that she would be well aware of the distance between the two communities. His statement only served to increase his unease. He expected a cynical retort, but her face changed to a look of concern and she said, "There's a chance to hitch a ride with ol' Liam McClary on his way back to Brimfield, you know? Least you'd have company."

The image of the pungent blowhard rolled into Gregory's mind. "Thanks, but… no. I've experienced that horrific ride before. I think I'd rather crawl back to Gowan on my hands and knees," he said, chuckling as he handed Cora some cash.

"Aye, but it might be easier for you three sheets to the wind than temperate," she declared, cocking her head, and raising a painted eyebrow.

"Well… I know that would put a few more coins in your purse. It'd be just my luck to wake up over in Brimfield with a hangover and penniless to boot."

"You could always take a room upstairs, least for tonight. The road is no place to be after dark. As you may have heard, there have been odd things about, lately."

Her tone had become grave, and it brought forth the very thing that Gregory had worked so hard to push to the back of his mind. His head filled with images from the week before, and he struggled to hide his disquiet. Luckily, for him, she had stepped away to retrieve his change. Little chance she had caught his worried expression.

Gregory watched her drop the bills in a pile next to the coins she had been counting, and then picking up a couple of quarters she offered them to him.

"Thanks a bunch," he said, overdoing his smile. He looked away, making a show of putting the coins in his pocket. Out of the corner of his eye, he watched her watch him. Her Pince-Nez glasses tumbled from her droopy nose and bounced at the end of their chain. She looked like she wanted to say more but was thinking twice about it. When she finally spoke, the suddenness of it startled him.

"You know… things haven't been quite right over Gowan way since Benjamin Carter returned with his new bride. Mabel, I think her name is? The gossip has it, she consorts with the wee folk, and brought their magic with her to Carter House."

"Pshaw! Don't believe everything you hear, Cora," he exclaimed with bravado. "And why pay for a room when I have a fine little cottage over in Gowan. On top of that, it's bought and paid for, thanks to father."

"Just a wee bit concerned, is all. Colleen Potter told me the other day, that her daughter, you know, Lissy? Came upon a fairy circle just this side of Whip-poor-will Hollow. Word has it, the whole inside was trampled down like someone or something had been having a grand ol' time in there. You know what it means when fairy circles show up, don't you, Mr. Bly?"

"Hah! Yeah, I do Cora. It means that your liquor sales are up!"

Cora didn't laugh and a slight scowl braced her lips. "Laugh now while you can, Mr. Bly, but I came from the Borderlands of Scotland. I know all the tales from the old country. Tales of the Pooka, the shape shifting, goat man, and the child drowning Grindylow. Then there's the banshees, the Caoineag, if I may, who forewarned my family of the death of my uncle. So many tales... Something wicked is coming our way, I can just feel it."

"Yes, a reservoir, but I wouldn't call..."

"Oh, please Mr. Bly, I'm dead serious. Ol' Benjamin Carter didn't do us no favors marrying that woman and bringing her to Massachusetts. Who knows what she's doing up there in that old house?"

"Yes, who knows?" Gregory said, as calm as he could. Then laughing nervously, he placed his Homberg at a rakish angle on his head and then tipped it to her. "I'll be careful to keep my shiny shoes out of fairy circles," he said in a cynical manner, an obvious attempt to bolster his bravado. With satchel in hand, he headed out the door.

"Very well, Mr. Bly... see you tomorrow."

Stepping outside, Gregory slung his bag over his shoulder, adjusted his hat, and walked away. It had been a warm day, and the temperature hadn't dropped much since sunset. He maintained his suit jacket even though the heat made it almost insufferable.

Making his way down the empty road, he soon came to the Davidson's farmstead. The woman of the house was walking around lighting lanterns, her children playing in the front parlor. It made him wish he was already home, even more so, that there would be somebody waiting for him when he arrived. His mother had died over a year prior, and he sorely missed her calming presence. She used to greet him on the porch in the evening, the smell of hot stew and fresh bread rolling out the door behind her. Now he was met with dark windows and an unsettling silence.

Gregory wasn't the marrying kind. He preferred his single life, and the thought of bringing a strange woman into his house made him nervous. He had always sought his comfort with Lisa, or in quiet nights nestled in his bed with O'Henry, Dickens, or Cooper, maybe even risking a late-night reading of something as macabre as Poe.

Now, he found his nocturnal perusing of the classics frequently interrupted by a loss of concentration. This brought moments when he caught himself listening to catch the light purring snore of his mother from the other side of the wall. A sound now replaced with the melancholy tick-tock of the grandfather clock in the dark hallway.

He stopped where the road sloped down and bent right into the gloomy woods. The forest widened out for miles from that point, stretching all the way south to Berryman's Crest, west to Parsons Ridge, and miles east to the Spry River. The track within, zigged and zagged, rising and falling, inundated with annoying hillocks. At one point it adopted an almost insane gradient down into a tree-filled vale.

'The Hollow' was a peculiar place. The land to the east of the byway was marshy and had degraded to a swamp at the lowest point. The Great Chicopee River Basin earthquake of 1817 had hit the area hard, causing a narrow tributary of the Spry River to break free from the main channel. Making its way to within a few hundred yards of the Grunewyck Road, it left the area almost impassable. The dark, putrid water overflowed the road and cascaded into the long, narrow, spring fed pond at the bottom of a ravine on the other side.

Even in the daylight, when the sun still filled the sky, Gregory felt he walked in shadow. There was a strange coolness to the air, an ever-present mist, and a disconcerting gurgle of rancid water.

He reset his hat and moved down the incline as a waxing crescent moon rose above the treetops. With its face partially hidden by a thin layer of overcast, it played hide & seek with the nervous traveler.

An owl suddenly cackled from above his head, and dropping from its perch, it glided away. It startled him and he gasped, nearly letting go of his bladder. His presence seemed to prompt the call of a Whip-poor-will from a thicket on his left, and a duet ensued as one answered from deeper within the woods. He hurried his pace as he moved around the first bend. Making his way into the darker part of the forest, he impulsively started whistling *The Can-Can* in order to calm himself.

A few bars later, he remembered its original title: *The Infernal Gallop*. It came from Offenbach's rendition of Dante's Inferno, and the thought unnerved him. He switched to the *Rocky Road to Dublin* but found that too exhausting. He tried singing, but his voice echoing through the dark trees made him feel like he was being mocked. Passing around his first hillock, he heard a loud rustling in a grove of low spruce, followed by the obvious sound of something scuffing over the packed clay of the road behind him.

"Hello?"

166

Not seeing anything unusual, he called out again, "Hello! Is someone there?" Bending forward, he looked hard into the night, straining his eyes. He then experimented by scraping the sole of his shoe over the surface, hoping that it was his own footfalls echoing—but no, it was different. With a quick intake of breath, he hurried away, keeping an ear cocked aft just in case. He reminded himself that he needed to start packing a lantern. He found himself wishing for one of those newfangled flashlights that he saw at McCarthy's store. Sadly, they were a small fortune, and he needed to make good use of every penny.

After a few hairpin turns and the last of those annoying little hillocks, the road straightened for about two hundred feet before sloping down yet again. He stopped and listened as the water babbled in and out of the deep pools and over the partially sunken trunks of fallen trees. In daylight, one could see their dead branches eerily projecting skyward from the water as if seeking to be liberated.

There also seemed to be a constant murmuring in the background, almost as if a large group of people were in a meeting just out of sight in the gloom. The stink of rotten wood and vegetation filled the air, along with some smells he couldn't recognize. A sudden splash startled him. "Just a turtle coming off a log," he said under his breath.

It was a week ago, in this very spot that from the corner of his eye, he caught a dark figure emerge from the forests edge. At first, it had walked on all fours and the best he could tell it was a sheep or a goat. But then it rose up on its back feet in the middle of the road and stood as if staring. He yelled at it, threatening violence, but with no effect. Then stomping toward it a few steps, he shook a fist, hoping to scare it away.

It certainly had the look of a large goat with long curling horns—but goats don't walk on their hind feet. Then there was a noise like the heavy breathing of a horse, or cow, along with a wet dog smell. It had finally moved on, quietly melting away into the woods to leave Gregory trembling and on the verge of hyperventilation. Cora's comment about the Pooka came to mind and shuddering, Gregory picked up his pace.

He knew that Ghillie's Gate sat just five hundred yards, or so, up the slope to his right. As a child he had played in and around it. One time his schoolmates dared him to venture inside. To prove he was no

167

chicken, he took them up on it and soon found himself deep enough inside that the mouth of the cave was only a small pinpoint of light behind him. Figuring he had gone far enough, he turned back only to find his schoolmates had abandoned him.

Rumor had it that the tunnel sloped away to form an underground lake at the bottom of the Carter House well. He never cared enough to try to find out if that was true. A kid could easily drown if he wasn't careful, and down there, he never would be found.

Gregory stood for the longest time as the veiled moon rose higher into the sky. "Just keep moving, Mister Bly, you're not going to get home unless you do," he said aloud. Then forcing himself down the steep grade, he moved into the thin, swirling cloud of vapor.

Frogs and night insects were creating quite a clamor. A Whip-poor-will sounded off to his left, but then stopped abruptly as a banshee-like cry rolled out of the ravine on Gregory's right. It was almost like whatever had emitted it sought to quiet the first; as if the bird had spoken out of turn. His hair stood on end and he began to tremble.

"Perhaps, a wildcat?" he muttered.

He picked up his pace and started whistling *Gary Owen* as loud as he could, the whole time wishing the jovial blades mentioned within the lyrics were with him now. He could use some fearless Irish rovers at the moment and would even condone the brandishing of swords if necessary.

The moon's illumination penetrated the light mist just enough to cast shadows of tree trunks across the roadbed. Moving through those silhouettes, Gregory stayed as far left as he could to avoid the ravine side of the carriageway.

Just short of the fording place, he came to an immediate halt, his right foot poised in midair. Before him, he could just make out a thin, skeleton like arm stretched out along one particular dark length of umbra as it lay on the wet clay of the road. The excessively long fingers of the algae-tinged hand, slowly opened, closed, and opened again. Its lengthy finger nails appeared to be curved like claws.

Gregory's eyes moved back along its length until they came to the thing that the arm was attached to. He gasped. It looked like a scrawny, old woman with long, wet strands of thinning hair clinging to an almost completely bald head. She lay with the side of her face in the muck, a large set of horse-like teeth protruding. They ground against each other, and the almost unbearable noise filled Gregory's ears. Then the creature moaned something unintelligible and chomped at the air.

The thing wasn't looking in his direction, but he could just make out its large, bulging eyes, seemingly focused on a point behind him. Frozen with fear, Gregory watched as the arm started to sweep back and forth over the surface. He quietly put his foot down and sidestepped to the right to avoid the grisly appendage. His movement was detected, and the thing started searching as if blind, its hand undulating through the air and clawing at the surface of the road.

Gregory stifled a shriek as the thing pulled itself slowly back into the burbling murk. He moved disjointedly up the road, fearful of what else may lay before him. A subtle keening suddenly filled the air as if the creature was in despair over the loss of its prey. That was enough to motivate Gregory to break free of his paralysis. He launched himself into a fast walk, which soon turned into a run. He continually cast glances back over his shoulder to be sure the thing hadn't risen out of the foul water to give chase.

After splashing through the ford, he began his ascent up Berryman's Crest. He soon broke free of the wretched ground mist and halting several feet away, he dropped his bag and bent forward at the waist. There came a brief coughing spell and when it subsided, he came upright trying to pull as much air into his lungs as possible. Keeping a careful eye in the direction from which he came, he waited for the burning in his lungs to cease.

When Gregory determined nothing was in pursuit and he no longer felt physically distressed, he turned his attention to the distant Carter House. Every window was illuminated with eerie light, and in the belvedere, the chandelier blazed.

In less than a minute, it was extinguished, followed by the unearthly light in the dormers, the second-floor windows, and finally, the first floor. The house now became a shadowy mass perched upon Nixie's Bluff, lit only by moonlight. Gregory watched as four pinpoints of lights, exited the house from where he knew the front door would be.

Trouping out onto the lawn, they met with many firefly-like flecks that moved out of the trees to the west. Coming together, they began to dance and swirl, forming different patterns. They then trouped east to the trees and the lights blinked out.

This was the first time Gregory had seen this much activity up on Nixie's Bluff since Benjamin Carter had returned from abroad. He had heard the old man hadn't been seen in Gowan since the evening he arrived on the MA & RI Rambler from Kingsport.

Witnesses said Benjamin had been hustled into the big Pierce Arrow by Kaleb Knight, along with Carter's new bride and three other ladies. Then there was the talk of Kaleb chauffeuring young witches down to McCarthy's. They had come scantily clad and belligerent. The gossip he had overheard on the party line said they had gotten out of the car at one point and played tag like children. Millie Behnke (who had been in the store at the time) told Maddie Clemens, "I seen through the window, even though they was wearing veils, that those girls had faces like hairless pole cats, every one of them!"

Seeing no more activity up at the mansion, Gregory gathered up his satchel and continued up the slope. Breaking the top, he could see the soft radiance produced by the lights of Gowan in the distance and could just make out the well-lit cupola of Sweeny's; a friendly beacon telling him he was almost home.

Sighing with relief, he established an acceptable pace in that direction. As he made his way, the clouds departed and the stars shone with intensity. The crescent moon rode directly above the path in front of him. The road remained level all the way to the town and moving through the Meadowlands he felt happy to be free of the trees. Thoughts of what he may do after arriving home for the evening pushed out the images of his horrifying encounters.

Remembering he had acquired a copy of Mark Twain's, *The Steamboat Race*, he thought he might seek his bed sooner than usual this night in order to get an early start on it. Maybe even treat himself to the bottle of cider that he had secreted away in the pantry. He just hoped there was enough of the distillation remaining to bring this evening's frightening events to satire.

It was then that Gregory felt a slight breeze move against his back. He thought it odd that only the ragged grass at the edges of the road moved while the clover out in the fields remained unaffected. It seemed as if the gust had been funneled up the byway merely to impact him. He chalked it up to some kind of an illusion, but when it happened again, and then persisted, he realized his initial interpretation had been correct.

Stopping, he turned and it washed against his face, ruffling his hair, and nearly lifting his hat. It brought a deep woods smell along with something one would find in proximity to an outside privy. Gregory's sensitive gag reflex brought the taste of chicken soup. Pulling out his handkerchief, he covered his nose and gazed back across the roiling ground mist.

There appeared to be a dark cloud forming above Ghillie's Gate. It blocked out the stars and seemed to be moving his way. It lengthened out into a curlicue as it came corkscrewing through the sky. Then he heard it—an unearthly cackling, punctuated with screeches and maniacal laughter. Behind that, a persistent buzzing drone coupled with the flapping of great wings.

The breeze escalated to a wind, taking the hat from his head to float away into the clover. He watched as the moonlight danced over the dark cloud in specks and spots. It glimmered as it rolled and danced through the air, an unearthly light flashing in countless eyes, their owners' grotesque bodies painted in an oily sheen.

It wasn't a cloud after all, but a flock of horrific fiends. A jolt of fear shot through his body. Dropping his satchel and handkerchief, Gregory turned and broke into a run. His eyes, wide with fear, strayed back over his shoulder and he stuttered out, "This can't be happening."

The terror he felt put wings to his feet as a scream built in his throat. Yet, instead of emitting a dissonant bellow, only a loud grunt could be heard as he was suddenly struck in the lower back. He stumbled from the force of the blow, and as he fought to remain on his feet, he watched his satchel tumble past and roll into the ditch. Someone—or something—had picked it up and thrown it at him as if in jest.

When he was able to recover his equilibrium, he glanced up as the front of the flock passed a mere ten feet above his head. The stench was overpowering and along with what he had first experienced, there were now other assorted smells which, surprisingly, included human sweat.

A whimper escaped his lips and he began to sob as the throng of fluttering and flapping, unclothed humanoids blocked out the moon. Some soared with the feathered wings of birds; others undulated with those of wasp and dragonfly. The worst came in the form of gargoylian beasties sporting the leathery appendages of bats. Every one of them seemed to be staring at him with bulging eyes, their mouths agape in hideous grins as if it was all for sport. He thought to break for the fields, but every time he moved to the edge of the road, they moved with him.

He could turn and run the other way, but he had no idea where he would go. Looking back, he saw the flock stretched out behind him for a great distance. There was nowhere to go but forward.

Gregory knew if he kept up his present pace, he wouldn't make it to the safety of Gowan before he collapsed. The thought to just stop and give up occurred to him, but his fear was too great. His breathing had become ragged and he stumbled more and more as he ran. Forced to slow to a fast jog, he dodged left, then right, muttering, "I can make it, I can make it."

But he was drained and still had half a mile to go. Now in an extreme state of panic, he felt wing tips pummel him as if to hurry him along. An occasional fist dropped down and punched him as the hideous flock rolled and swirled just above his head. The noise was deafening, and he was sure he heard human voices in dispute embedded within the din.

Gregory felt someone tapping his left shoulder, and when he didn't respond, they slapped his head and pushed him hard from behind. He fell forward, his face only inches from the hardpack, before a large hand grabbed him around his neck; its uncut nails scratching his tender skin. It righted him and then lifted him several inches off the ground. Dropping him back on his feet, he hit the roadway in a lurching run.

Cackling laughter filled his ears each time he was battered and it brought a fleeting memory of times in his childhood when the usual mob of boys would chase him daily about the schoolyard.

"Gregory!" something snarled in a loud whisper from behind.

"Gregory Bly!"

There was something familiar in that voice, but in his haggard state, he couldn't sort it out. It was raspy and punctuated with a high-pitched wheeze.

"Look at me, Gregory Bly," it jeered.

He could now feel a presence at the side of his head, and there was a loud buzzing in his ears.

"No! You're not real," Gregory whimpered as he slowed to a tottering walk, holding his hands out in front as if searching for something to hold on to.

"If you can see me—I am real!"

He suddenly recognized the voice and that compelled him to look. A scream broke from his lips as the putrid breath of the boggart he once knew as Benjamin Carter, hit him full in the face. He let go with a staccato of shrieks as simian-like hands caught him under his armpits and hauled him up to be enveloped by the foul cloud of boggart fae. Even in his daze, Gregory knew he was helplessly airborne and gaining altitude.

The thing that had once been Benjamin Carter, flew with Gregory dangling from the sinewy arms that wrapped his chest. It's huge, wasp-like wings droned as it rose higher and higher into the air. Through the chaotic mob of creatures below him, Gregory could just make out the blurring lights of Gowan.

As the flock turned west toward Nixie's Bluff, Gregory's head tilted left and then rolled back on his shoulders. The fiend kept a tight grip on him, and just before Gregory swooned, it turned its grotesque face down to him and with the brute's saliva raining down on his face from blubbery lips, the beast hissed, "Welcome to the Unseelie Court, Mr. Bly."

CHAPTER EIGHT

CORA

II

~

1

Wednesday morning found The Lost Collie Tavern just wrapping up from breakfast. It was after the local farmers had left the tavern and Cora was bussing tables, that the Gowan police car pulled up outside. She didn't like Merlyn Cobb. If the tavern had any kind of window at the front and she had seen, "That fat gobshite!" coming, she would have had Al come forward and she would have retreated into the kitchen. Setting down her basket of dirty dishes, she brushed her hair back and turned to face him.

"Cora," he said, as a greeting.

"Merlyn," she said, as more of a question. "What can I help you with? You know we have our own police here in Grunewyck. Does Chief Conway know you're over here?"

"Easy, Cora, doing my best. Got a missing boy I'm having to deal with right now. So, I don't need any crap from you."

"What missing boy?"

"Vernon Sweeny, disappeared into thin air."

"Sorry to hear. So, what's that got to do with me?"

"Nothing, I'm here as a favor to Doc Bolen, and… too you. It's about Chastity."

"What about Chastity?" Cora said, moving closer to the heavily

174

perspiring man, her brow clouded with concern.

"Has something happened to my sister? Is she alright?"

"Well, in a sense, I'm guessing... it's just, this morning, early, she showed up at the cattle yard and let all the cows loose. Then she had the gall to go up to the library just after Millie unlocked the front door and tried to checkout fifty, or so, books. When Millie tried to get her to change her mind, Chastity dropped them all on the floor and ran over to McCarthy's where she went to taste testing all the apples in the boxes out front."

"And this is something that we need to be concerned about?"

"Well, yes. I mean, I got enough calls at the office, that... you know I just can't ignore it. Especially when she started pulling up her sleeping gown and exposing herself to folks in passing."

"Did you take her home?"

"Nope, took her over to Doc Bolen's office."

"Did the doc check her? What did he say?"

"He said to come over and get you. Thinks maybe it's time to have her committed."

"Committed? All these years my sister's been like this, and now you're talking committal?"

"Not just me, Cora, and not just Doc. The agreement you have with that... would-be nurse maid, Abigail Cunningham, just ain't working. As soon as she leaves, Chastity's out the door and causing trouble for folks. I'm sorry. Gowan has been good about it, but... enough is enough. You're going to have to either take her on yourself and bring her over here or sign the papers. You know if her husband, Henry, was still alive, it would be he who would take care of it. But with him dead and gone, the responsibility falls on next of kin. That be you."

"Merlyn Cobb, if Harvey Matthews was still alive, Chastity wouldn't be going to no nut house. He would have saw to her."

"Yep, just like he always had. But now, he ain't, and the folks are clamoring for something to change. They've had enough of Chastity's shenanigans. I say it's time, and Doc Bolen says it's time. Cora, you have to be thinking what's in the best interest for Chastity. If something bad happens to her, it's all coming back on you. Is that what you, and Al, want?"

"First of all, don't tell me what I have to be thinking, and...Oooo! you just wait here."

With that said, she left him and stomped into the kitchen where her husband was washing dishes. There was an indiscernible exchange of words and Cora returned, appearing defeated. Al came through the door pulling off an apron. Nodding at Merlyn, he said, "Hey, Merlyn."

"Al, how's things?"

"Would have been better if you hadn't showed up, but it's not like I wasn't expecting you."

"Al's way of thinking is the same as doctor Bolen. I can't fight you and the whole town of Gowan, so...let's get going," Cora growled.

"Want me along?" Al asked.

"Naw, you stay here and keep this place going. Call Pearl to come down and help you for the lunch hour, she cooks better than you do, anyway. Our regulars will be getting a treat today, that's for sure."

"Okay, see you when you get back," Al said, sounding somewhat apologetic.

"I'll be calling you before then... from somewhere. If I don't get back tonight, I'm sure Pearl will stay on til the dishes are done for supper. You can tend the bar, that ain't no real task, as you know."

Merlyn walked over and held the door open for Cora. She grabbed her fancy little purse from behind the bar and passed him without a word. Climbing into the Model A, she slammed the door.

"Al," Merlyn said, and touched a finger to the brim of his hat.

"Merlyn," Al said and nodded once before the big man shut the door.

They rode in silence back through the Hollow to Gowan. They stopped at Chastity's place long enough for Cora to pack a bag for her sister even though Merlyn was against it, saying that she wouldn't need it where she was going. Grabbing Chastity's threadbare Raggedy Anne doll that Henry had bought for her when she first started to lose her mind, Cora returned to the patrol car.

They drove to Doc Bolen's office where Cora was met with giggles and hugs as Chastity had no idea of the weight that lay on her sister's shoulders. Doc Bolen explained everything to Cora behind closed doors. Merlyn departed the office, grinning, as if he was glad to be done with it.

It would be Doc Bolen's nurse, twenty-two-year-old, Emily Dickinson doppelganger, Caroline Moore, who would drive the two sisters to Arkham using the Bolen's Rolls Royce as the good doctor couldn't very well leave his patients and the village without its physician.

The trip was long, but Chastity had remained somewhat catatonic for a good portion of it, and when she wasn't, she spent the time exclaiming about all she was observing out the windows. Cora and Caroline exchanged small talk for the first hour and then rode in silence for the second. The drop off at the facility was uneventful and after a short discussion with Dr. Evelyn Peaslee, and her intern (and daughter), Alma, Cora hugged her sister goodbye. Chastity, clutching her doll, barely acknowledged it and didn't seem to notice when Cora left her in the care of the doctor and her assistant.

The ride back was filled with tears and then consolation by Caroline, using her most commonly used phrase: "It's all for the best." After Cora's tears had dried, the conversation fell to gossip about how the Depression and the impending reservoir were only going to make matters worse for the citizens of the Spry River Valley. It was late afternoon when Caroline dropped Cora at Chastity's house.

She stood on the cottage steps watching the Rolls move away up the now dusty street and threw Caroline a single wave. Wanting to take her mind off Chastity, she put her focus on Gregory Bly's cottage just across the street. She hadn't seen him since their talk, and she was starting to wonder.

2

Gregory's father had built the cottage back in the Victorian era and it was the best-looking abode on the north side of the town; next to the grander Sweeny mansion, of course. Cora recalled not having seen the teacher passing that morning as she stood on the Collie's gallery porch. She normally greeted him at that time and he always waved to her as she swept. She felt a pang in her gut and her thoughts went back to that last night she had seen him and how nervous he had been about that lonely walk home. She felt she should have tried harder to convince him to take a room upstairs at The Lost Collie. The worry had been almost unbearable and had only subsided when the news of Chastity pushed it out. She should have said something to Cobb.

Walking over to the Bly cottage, she knocked on the door and when no one answered, she checked and found it locked. Moving around to the back, she looked in windows, but saw no one. The rear door was locked, but she gave it a good shove and it popped open. Stepping into the well-ordered kitchen, she was surprised at how clean everything was.

"Mr. Bly? Gregory Bly?" she called without reply. She moved into the front rooms and the stillness of the inside unnerved her. Forcing herself up the stairs, she checked the two small bedrooms. The bed clothes were impeccable. The grandfather clock, out on the landing, chimed six times, startling her. She hurried back downstairs and departed the same way she came in. Slamming the door, she was able to get it to relatch. Moving around the south side of the cottage, toward the front, she heard, "Cora?"

The old woman shrieked and looked up to see Janey standing in the street, an inquisitive look on her face.

"Oh, Janey, you scared the shite out of me!"

"Sorry, so... everything alright? Over to visit Gregory, are you?"

"Aye, just over for a visit, but..."

"How's he doing? I haven't seen him in a long time."

"He didn't pass by the tavern this morning and he's not inside," Cora said, poking a thumb at the cottage. Walking to the street, she added, "How are you, Janey? How's your mother?"

"Oh, I'm good. Mother's good. Everyone is good, well except for maybe... Gregory?"

"Aye, I'll admit, I am worried. So, what are you up to?"

"Oh, I was going to see Tom, but he was in the bathtub. He invited me in, but, well... you know," Janey said and giggled.

Cora chuckled and winked at her.

"Uh-huh," Janey said, winking back. "So, anyway, I thought I'd go down to the school and maybe do a little prep work. I want to get that place shipshape."

"It's that time, isn't it? Well, I'll be spending the night here at Chastity's. So, another night in Gowan."

"How is your sister?"

"Bad news. Had to get her committed today. Doc Bolen had her sent over to the asylum in Arkham. Long drive, but Caroline drove us, and that Rolls is pretty comfy on a long trip. So, lots of tears, you know. But like Caroline is so fond of saying, it's for the best."

"Yes, but I think that's what every nurse says."

"So, I have to get to cleaning out the house. Probably have to sell it."

"Or wait until the State offers you something for it. I imagine no one's going to want a sunken house unless they like living at the bottom of a reservoir. Maybe a catfish or turtle would take it off your hands?"

Cora had a delayed response, but when Janey giggled, Cora realized the humor and laughed out loud.

"Come with me to the school house, will you? It will give us time to talk. Besides, I don't want to walk back in the dark. I'm sure after I talk to you about what's on my mind, neither of us will want to be alone."

"I can certainly do that. I'll come along and be your protector," Cora said, "Nothing much else for me to do this evening, besides Chastity's place." Linking arms, they walked toward the school house, chatting and carrying on like they had always been the best of friends.

3

Janey and Cora, soon arrived at the path that led to the schoolhouse door. The building sat far back in the trees, well away from the road. It had no playground, so the children played among the ancient tree trunks; the older students usually perched on the benches along the outside wall, exchanging gossip and taunting each other. The bell in the cupola was still functional and Janey actually thrilled at the thought of her first day when she could pull the rope to send its peel resonating.

"Bet you never thought you'd be where you are now, aye?"

"It had always been a wish, but not one I ever thought would come true. I think mostly because I always thought I could do a better job than Miss Durnell."

They exchanged grins as they moved up the path. Taking out her key, Janey unlocked the door and they stepped in. There was a stale odor in the room and dust hung in the air highlighted by the rays of the sun. Durnell must have taken the time to straighten things up on her last day.

A Primer had been placed on each desk appropriate to the year of the student, the younger in the front, the older behind. The remaining were neatly stacked on a shelf.

"Well, we should get some windows open," Cora said and taking it upon herself, she walked around and pushed up every sash. Janey poked her nose in the supply room and then the teacher's quarters with its single bed devoid of linen. She pulled the chain for the toilet just to hear it flush and finding it satisfactory, she smiled and moved to open the windows back there. When she came out, she found Cora reading through a third-grade Primer. It made her think of Gregory Bly who tutored that particular age over in Grunewyck.

"So, you say Gregory wasn't home and you didn't see him on his way to Grunewyck?"

"That's right, didn't pass by this morning. I tried to get him to stop making that trip in the dark, but he was just too proud even though he couldn't hide that he was afraid. Maybe he forced himself because he thought it wasn't manly to be scared of the dark, or… the Hollow."

"Well, in your opinion, Cora, and tell me true, your gut feeling, please? You must be thinking something, with all that's been going on around here. Do you suspect foul play?"

"Aye, foul something, anyway. I've been rolling and rolling this over in my mind. The problem is, there is nothing solid. Most of what I hear comes through the grapevine, so you know how that is. Think about this, we haven't seen your father since his return. I remember, even though I live in Grunewyck, he was a pretty public figure around here. I think a man like Benjamin would have wanted to flaunt his new bride. Showing up daily in town, influencing politics; all of that. With all this talk of the reservoir, you'd think he would be the loudest voice heard… whether for, or against. Now, he's missing, Kaleb Knight is dead, Gregory is missing. Then there's Molly Sharp, and that spinster by the name of Sadie Mills from over Grunewyck, they both dropping out of sight. Colleen Potter's daughter, Lissy, discovered fairy circles in the Hollow, a strange creature in a pond, and another one in the ravine below Nixie's Bluff. Then James Potter is killed by his own automobile, and now, official word from Merlyn Cobb, Vernon Sweeny didn't come home after Kaleb's funeral. I talked with Lissy after her father's burial and she doubled down on that it was a Caoineag that she saw down below Nixie's Bluff."

"That's the banshee, right?"

"Aye, I know, hard for you to believe. Until you see it with your own two eyes, you'll remain a sceptic. Lissy, isn't, that's for certain, and recalling all I saw back when I was a child, well… it's not too hard for me, either."

"Yes, I suppose I would have to see something solid before I could be completely convinced. So, I guess I will need you to find me something, Cora. Show me something. Give me something. I am open minded and I like to believe I think progressively, but… well, you're the expert here."

"And so is Tom, I know this from our talk up at Brenner's. He's the one with the schooling, but he too needs to get on board of looney Cora's fairy train."

"Ah, puh-shah, Cora! We should all get together, the three of us, and hash this out. Maybe make an expedition up to the house and see for ourselves."

"Aye, Merlyn told you not to go up there until he okayed it, but he's taking his sweet time and we can't wait for him. Seems to me that this all funnels back down to Mabel, or Mab, as Merlyn let slip to Nealy Garret, who let slip to Helen Blake, the worst gossip in Gowan. She passed it to Beulah McKay, making it so she could broadcast it across the entire county. Now, for the kicker… are you ready?"

"Oh, my giddy aunt! Cora, tell me, please! You got me squirming under my own skin."

"So, once again, in myth, of course, Mab was the ruler of the dark fae, Queen of Air and Darkness. Some say, the Winter Queen. The story has it, as my grandda told it, Mab was a loving compassionate woman and had been married to Dagda, a Celtic deity. When that marriage ended, she became embittered and corrupted by her own magic. She has always had courtiers, someone my uncle called Cluracan. But I feel he may have been replaced with lesser beings. Woodland animals transformed into handmaidens. Perhaps, the three that showed up outside McCarthy's."

"You know, I remember now, in Shakespeare, ummm… Romeo and

Juliette, Mab was the little midwife, something of a playful spirit?"

"Far from it! Shakespeare had it all wrong. But it wouldn't matter to him, so why should he have cared? I'm sure she'd like for us to think that she's the Shakespeare version, anyway. But she controls the solitary fairies and worse than that, The Unseelie Court."

"Sorry? The Unseelie Court?"

"The terror that flies by night, but more on that later. I have to get back to Chastity's."

"Yes, and I have to get back to Headmost, mother is feeling poorly. I have to check on her. I don't think I'm going to get anything done here today, but there's still time. I'm going to stop and talk to Tom. I want to hear what he has to say. You don't mind, do you?"

"Naw, but just Tom, no one else. Least 'til we know more."

"Help shut these windows, will you? Least we got a little fresh air into this place. I'll come back in the morning."

"Very well."

After shutting the windows and locking the door, they walked to Chastity's cottage. Before they went their separate ways, Janey said, "It's all... kind of exciting, isn't it?"

"Aye, well... and a little scary."

"Can't really have one without the other, can we?"

Cora looked hard at Janey, taking in the woman that the mischievous tomboy had become. "Still fearless as shite, aren't you?"

"Oh, I don't know about that, I..."

The old woman didn't let her finish. Embracing Janey, she kissed her cheek and stepping back, she said, "We'll talk some more, got to go call Al."

Cora walked away disjointedly as if her arthritis was really handing it to her. Janey watched her for a minute, then turning, headed for Brenner's.

ᛟ

After a quick call to Al to tell him she would be spending the night at Chastity's cottage, she rested a bit on the sofa. She would sleep there. Her sisters bed would be more comfortable, but its present condition wasn't suitable for any sane human.

After making and eating a quick supper from what Chastity had on hand, she packed a few boxes, and then sought the sofa to rest her aching joints. It was late and she lay for the longest time in the dark, staring up at the exposed beams of the ceiling and listening to the night noises through the open windows. Sleep kept its distance. Growling out her annoyance, she got up and walked around the parlor because movement helped reduce the ache.

The clocked chimed the hour and Cora saw it was only ten o clock. There would be no alcohol in the house as Harvey and Chastity had always been teetotalers.

"The hell with this."

Leaving by the front door, she headed up to Brenner's. She would need a few rounds of gin to calm her and dull the pain in her knees and hips. If she was careful and left before she drank too much, she could make it back to the cottage in order to pass out on the sofa and not in a ditch.

Cora moved up onto the main boardwalk and stopped outside Brenner's door. Nealy Garret sat in his car in the usual spot in front of McCarthy's. Boots was wrapping things up at the café, the only other business open this late in the evening—besides Brenner's and Zelda's.

She hurried inside as if to avoid detection by Nealy. Sandy Brewster sat on a stool at the bar, obviously drunk. He was going on about how he planned to expand his business. Colin stood, wiping down the bar, pretending to listen. Beth sat at her high desk in the back, a bottle of gin and a glass at her disposal. She worked steadily, pencil in hand. Cora knew her from their school days. Beth had been a whiz at math and everybody believed she would go far. She married Colin right after graduation and became his partner in the tavern. Colin had mentioned time and again how Beth had saved his business. Cora and Beth were comrades in arms, except Cora was the one who owned the Lost Collie when she married Al.

Paul LeBarge was working in the kitchen with the door open and she could see him moving around, stacking pots and pans, wiping down counter tops and occasionally poking his head out the door as if he was expecting someone. The only other person in the tavern was Bessie LaVern who sat alone at a corner table with a glass of beer and tears streaming down her cheeks.

"Well, the lost collie has been found!" Colin said and laughed.

"Colin," Cora said as a greeting, and approaching the bar, she addressed Sandy.

"Mr. Brewster."

"Well, Cora MacLean, get tired of your own place, did you?"

"Naw, Sandy, I've come over to make Colin and Beth an offer for this tavern, thinking about expanding, you know?"

Colin's eyes grew wide and Sandy's mouth dropped open. Beth stood up from her desk and made her way over to them, a scowl on her face.

"Ah, come on, Sandy. I'm just pulling your leg."

"Oh my, Cora, you had my heart racing," Beth said, gulping, her hand on her heart.

"Sorry about that."

"I wouldn't sell, anyway," Colin said flatly and sneered.

Beth glared at him and then leaning in toward Cora, she said in a low tone, "If what I'm hearing through the grapevine has any grain of truth to it, ain't none of us going to have a place very soon. Appears the State wants the Spry River Valley all to itself. I 'spect you would have given us a lot more than they're going to... I was hoping."

"Oh, no, sorry, but that's all gossip," Cora said.

"Well... it is Gowan."

"Aye, 'tis."

Sandy Brewster's face went from inquisitive to sad. Beth had put the kibosh on his future plans to expand by opening her mouth about the reservoir. Bringing his focus to the inside of his beer glass, his eyes glazed. Colin, his lips clamped shut, turned away and feigning dusting the bottles on the back shelf, he watched the others in the mirror.

Cora looked over at Bessie, who was also just staring into her beer glass. She whispered to Beth, "Is that Bessie LaVern, over there?"

"Sure is. All grown up now. She'll be a fine catch for some fella. Came in all a fluster. Ordered a beer, sat down, took one sip and hasn't touched it since. Just been sitting there, crying her eyes out. No one's got up the nerve to go over yet and see if she's okay. She's never been in here before. We used to serve her folks quite often. That is until they got so highfalutin from Roy going to work for the Carters as the factory manager, that my place wasn't good enough for 'em anymore."

Cora, her eyes still on Bessie, said, "You remember they used to live in Grunewyck, right? Then they got that new house built over there at the bottom of Prosper Mountain. Back when ol' Bart Carter sold off some property and folks was at each other's throats to buy up lots just so they could have a place abutting Headmost House. Probably thinking some of that Carter magic might rub off on 'em. I used to see Bessie out playing with the other girls on the Grunewyck Road, jumping rope, hopscotch, and such. Used to play with the Davidson's oldest girl."

"Yeah, I remember when the LaVern's moved here. Like I said, they were coming in here quite often around that time, having a Friday night out, dinner and drinks. Then, they just stopped."

"Hear Bessie's working for Sally Combs up at the clothing store?" Cora said.

"Yep, that's a whole 'nother story. I dare not spread the talk on that matter. Why don't you go over and talk to the girl. You're a whole lot braver than the lot of us. Maybe she'll spill the beans as to what's going on up at Sally's."

Cora looked at Colin's reflection in the mirror, dressed as he always was, white silk shirt, dark waist coat, and sleeve garters. He raised his eyebrows and grinned. She turned and looked at Bessie who now had her head in her hands. It wasn't unlike Cora to bend an ear to people. That was the bartender in her. Dropping five dollars on the bar, she took her bottle and glass and approached the young girl. Beth returned to her desk at the back. Colin turned and watched Cora cross the room as he wiped out glasses, grinning in his usual cynical manner. Sandy Brewster just slowly rotated his glass around and around, his brow still clouded with concern.

5

"Hallo, Bessie."

"Oh, hello, Misses MacLean."

"You can call me, Cora."

"Oh, okay," Bessie said, then sniffed and wiped at her nose with the back of her hand.

"May I sit with you? You look like you could use a friend."

Bessie studied Cora's face for a few seconds and then waved toward the other chair saying, "Sure, yeah... have a chair."

Cora sat and poured a glass of gin. The girl, seemingly embarrassed, returned her eyes to her near full glass of beer, giving Cora a chance to get a good look at her. Bessie wasn't quite as blonde as Janey, her hair a curly version of a bob. She was fortunate to have nearly flawless skin and small pouty lips that hid perfect teeth. The girl's dark blue eyes, when not brimming with tears, were always full of curiosity. Her body was unusually perfect. She was the kind of girl that could make it big in Hollywood, least until she got older and lost her looks. Her manner was reserved, but she wasn't afraid to offer a friendly smile.

"Well, I'll just cut to the chase. What's troubling you, lass? You're much too young and pretty to be over here crying in your beer. Tell me all about it."

"I don't know if I can."

"I think you'll feel better if you get it out, especially after a good cry."

"I'd be asking for trouble if I say a word. This town is just too small. They'd have me crucified by the end of the week."

"That bad, huh? Well, I'm going to ask you to trust me. No judgement. Besides, I'm not from Gowan," Cora said, lowering her voice.

Bessie suddenly picked up her glass and took a long drink; too long, in fact. Setting it down, Cora saw it was half drained and scowled. When she met Bessie's eyes, she smiled in an accepting way and the girl said, "I don't know, I'm pretty sure if I told you everything, I, uh...you know? Well, okay... I think I'm in trouble."

"What, you get yourself pregnant? You can just..."

"No, no, it's worse than that?"

"You murder someone?"

Bessie laughed, and Cora smiled like she hoped Bessie's mood might be improving with her presence. "Listen, Bessie, I'll make you a promise. Whatever you share with me, stays with me. Wouldn't be right to hurt you in any way, shape, or form. You're a young woman with a promising future. It may not be here in Gowan, but promising, none the less."

Bessie drained her glass and set it back on the table. "Mister Brenner, another, please."

"Are you sure? That one went down pretty fast. You might want to…" Colin said, a questioning tone.

"Mister Brenner!" Bessie nearly shouted, the anger in her voice taking Cora by surprise.

Colin said nothing more, filled another glass and brought it over. Bessie pulled a dollar from her small clutch purse and slapped it on the table. Colin exchanged glasses, swiped up the bill, and turned away without a word.

Bessie took a small drink and then staring across the beer glasses' rim at Cora, she said without blinking, "I'm in love."

"Well, how is that trouble? Why, I remember when…" Bessie interrupted with words almost too indiscernible to hear, "…with a woman." Bessie's eyes grew frightened.

"Oh… uh… Sally?" Cora asked in a whisper.

Bessie nodded, and tears spilled from her eyes. She took a long drink from her glass, then set it on an ancient coaster before casting her eyes down to the table top.

"I see what you mean by trouble. You ever consider leaving this town? Maybe college, or… a big city? Maybe Boston?"

"Yes, that is the plan, it's just… just not happening fast enough."

"I'm sorry. But now may be a good time, I mean, with the talk of the reservoir and all. How are your folks treating you? You told them?"

"No, but they suspect something and we had a big fight and they kicked me out. Then I had an argument with Sally because of it. She wanted to go to my house and confess and tell them she was going to take me away with her. They would have called Chief Cobb on her. I'm sure he would arrest her for nothing at all. And now… now I can't find her."

"What? You can't find Sally? What do you mean?"

"I came back to the shop the next morning, the front door was locked, but the back door was wide open and Sally wasn't anywhere, and I checked, too."

"So, she wasn't upstairs, or…"

"No, I checked around town and no one had seen her. I thought she might be over at Boots', but they hadn't seen her either and she wouldn't go off and leave the damn backdoor wide open."

"You said you had a plan to leave? Do you think after the argument she might have packed up and left?"

"No, she wouldn't do that, and not without a suitcase, and surely— not without me."

Bessie began to weep and hid her face in her hands.

"Bessie, I'm going to walk you home, okay?"

"Nope, nope, can't go home," she said and standing, she staggered back and almost knocked over her chair. Cora downed her gin in one gulp, rose, and coming around the table she took the girl's arm and held on until Bessie found her feet.

Cora looked at Colin and then back at Beth. "Well, I think somebody's had enough."

"Uh, yep," Colin said.

"Come on, Bessie, let's step out for some air."

Bessie didn't argue, and Cora helped her out the door. They stood for the longest time on the boardwalk out front with Bessie weaving back and forth. Nealy's usual roost stood vacant.

"You want I walk you up to Sally's? If you can't go home, then… maybe there?"

"Nope, I can't face her right now. If she's there and sees me drunk, she'll just nag me. I might as well just go over there and sleep with the pigs… that's what I am, you know? Just a dirty ol' pig."

"Now, Bessie, you're no pig. You're a beautiful, young woman with a future. There ain't nothing dirty about you."

"I know, I know, thas why Sally loves me so much. That's whatsh she tol me, anyway."

"Bessie, I want you to come home with me. I'm staying at my sister's place just down the street there. She's got a nice, big sofa you can rest on. You'll be safe there."

They began to walk in the direction of Chastity's, Cora trying to keep Bessie moving in a straight line.

"What'd your shister say about a dirty ol' pig wallowing on her nysh, clean sofa?

"Oh, I think Chastity's done saying anything about anything."

188

"Oooo! Chasidy, she's that crazy… oh, sharry, dats my mama talking. I'm so sharry, I…" Bessie stopped her lurching walk, bent over and promptly vomited on the cobblestones. Cora, seeing it coming, kept Bessie in her grip and stepped around behind her to avoid the splatter.

Bessie remained bent over for a minute after rubbing her lips clean with the back of her hand and wiping it on her dress. "Looky, is that pottaydo's? I don't remember eating dat."

"Come, let's get you to the cottage so you can lay down."

"I want to lay over dere, in the gwass, it looks so comfo… comfidable… com… it looks nysh.

"Nope, let's go, just a few more feet."

Cora kept a tight hold on Bessie as she kept up her lurching walk. She moved with her head down and eyes closed like she was walking in her sleep. They finally arrived at the cottage and went inside to the tiny parlor. Cora sat Bessie on the sofa and removed her shoes. Taking the girl's arm in order to position her on her back, Bessie must have thought she wanted her to stand again. After gaining her feet, the girl pulled off her dress, popping a few buttons in the process. Falling back, she allowed Cora to finish the task. Bessie passed out almost immediately and began to snore.

Picking up the dress, Cora lay it over a chair, positioning the girl shoes underneath, then kicking off her own, she took the nearby wingback and settled in for the night. She was asleep in minutes and both women lightly snored together in the dark of the room, the ragged lace curtains waving softly in the cooling breeze.

6

Wolves had been extinct in Massachusetts since the eighteen forties and had anyone been out in the wee hours of the morning and saw the creature moving through the trees on the west side of the cottage district, they would probably be thinking dog, and that maybe, Silby Bishop's German Shepard had gotten loose. If one could have made a closer inspection, they would see it wasn't canine at all. Trotting silently through the trees, the beast zigged and zagged to avoid obstacles and soon came to a halt in the portion of the woods that projected like a tiny peninsula out into Chastity's backyard. The wolf-like creature transformed into something more human and began to sing a siren's song that resonated in the night air.

7

Abigail Cunningham sat with a single candle at her kitchen table. She couldn't sleep because she had failed her obligation to care for Chastity and had worried herself into a tizzy. Her remedy, a warm glass of milk. The mantle clock chimed two and almost as if by prompt, a song rolled out into the early morning air, a childlike voice carried on a cooling breeze. Abigail couldn't afford screens for her windows, but there was no way she could keep them closed. Sheers of cheese cloth were cheaper, and she had made an effort to dress every window with them. It cut down on the mosquitos at night and the flies in the day. Gowan didn't see many thieves or burglars, and Leo Dane was the only man, Gowan knew, who would have the nerve to crawl in through an open window at night. But Abigale kept her bedroom door locked when sleeping and her dead husband's ten-gauge, double barreled coach gun, was always close at hand.

She tiptoed to the window above the dry sink and listened. It was as if someone was singing someone's name. It chilled her and she mumbled, "Ghosts, I 'spect." As much as it frightened her, she still went to the backdoor, quietly pulled the bolt, and opened it just enough to slip through.

Abigaile stood quietly on her tiny gallery porch next to a large pail perched upon a stool with her washboard protruding. She hid behind it and listened. The song was coming from the finger of trees that projected out into Chastity's backyard.

The singing abruptly stopped and the crickets, frogs, and katydids took over. Whoever it was, they must have detected her and even though the gooseflesh rose on her arms, she didn't flee, instead, she stared hard into the dark. The tension of the moment finally became overwhelming and Abigail went back inside, shutting and locking the door.

The singing started again and the woodland creatures grew quiet as if to allow the song to be the only sound to fill the night. Abigail shuddered. Leaving her milk, she hurried to her room, shut the door and locked it. After securing the two windows, she grabbed the coach gun and climbed onto her bed. Pushing herself back into the corner, she waited for whatever was out there to come for her.

8

Abigail hadn't been able to make out the name that traveled ethereally on the breeze, but Bessie could. It started in her dreams, softly, urgently. As she came more awake, it became clearer. Sally was calling her. Her eyes popped open and she sat up abruptly. Cora was in the wingback, deep in sleep. Sliding to the edge of the sofa, Bessie sat for a moment realizing she was dressed only in her pink camisole and tap panties. She had worn no stockings and her shoes were now on the floor. Standing, she walked slowly into the kitchen at the back of the cottage, feeling her way to avoid creating a clamor as she moved through an unfamiliar house. Stopping at a window to listen, the volume of the song increased as if Sally knew she had captured her lover's ear. It was a soothing sound, seductive in its tone. Bessie was drawn to it. Quietly unlocking the backdoor, she stepped barefoot onto the porch.

The song emanated from the trees behind the cottage. A comforting solace enveloped Bessie and she seemed to glide as she moved toward the singer. It was Sally who stood among the trees adorned in a green gown whose sheen vacillated in the dim light of the moon. She reached her arms out to Bessie, who despite her bare feet, failed to heed the pain brought by the rough, forest floor.

Bessie whispered, "Sally," smiled, and reached out to her as she moved, failing to notice the long, claw like finger nails or the yellowish eyes that coldly calculated the distance to the approaching Bessie. Then, with a lightning swipe of her right hand, the fiend opened Bessie's vein. The girl's reaction was indifferent and a few seconds passed before she fell forward into the Sally thing's arms. Catching her, it pushed its lips to Bessie's neck, and began to feed on the rich, red blood.

Cora came awake in a violent start and jumped to her feet. She looked at the sofa where she was sure she had lain Bessie LaVern hours before. Rubbing her eyes, she gazed again at the piece of furniture before walking over and laying her hand on a cushion. It was still warm and spotted with Bessie's perspiration. Looking around the cottage, she found her roommate was nowhere to be seen. There was a chance Bessie had gone to the outhouse. Going into the kitchen, Cora saw the backdoor stood open. Wanting to check on Bessie's condition, she lit the lantern from the table and carrying it outside, she stood, watching, listening. The crickets and katydids were raucous, a multitude of fireflies danced in the air, and a Barred Owl, perched further up the slope, asked, "Who-cooks- for-you? Who-cooks for you-all?"

Opening the door to the privy, Cora held the lantern high. Bessie wasn't in there. Turning away she heard a noise like something falling within the trees.

The adrenalin flowed in and she felt her chest tighten, bringing a pain that radiated down her left arm. She didn't want to go any closer, and the lantern's glow would not reach that far. Forcing herself, she moved hesitantly toward the sound.

"Bessie?" she called.

The insects stopped their racket and for a brief second, Cora could just make out a silhouette standing among the trees. It dropped toward the ground, growled, and then took off at a run up the slope through the ancient trunks. It crashed through thickets, one after another, and above the cracking of twigs, Cora heard it panting.

She gasped and hesitated. But despite her fear, she continued to tiptoe toward the trees. Upon arriving, she peeked around the trunk of a large silver maple and said, "Bessie?" Still nothing.

The glow of the lantern picked up a footprint in the soft loam; one small enough to be the girl's. Cora gulped hard and moved forward, her eyes wide and unblinking.

Her lantern soon picked up the pink of Bessie's underwear. Holding the lamp higher, she saw the girl stretched out on the ground, blood on the front of her camisole, most of it around her neck and chest.

Cora choked back a shriek and rushing to the girl, she grabbed her arm and shook her, calling out her name. Setting the lantern on the ground, she sat her up and shook her again, shouting, "Bessie? Bessie?"

The girl was limp and unresponsive. She was dead as far as Cora could tell, but confusion reigned because, Bessie's face remained pink and tranquil in the lantern light. It was almost as if she hadn't minded at all that her throat had been slashed.

9

The phone rang at Headmost House and Tabby was up and out of bed flying down the stairs in her nightgown and bare feet. She needed to stop the ringing before it woke the house. A few minutes passed and then she was at Janey's door, a candlestick in hand. Lightly tapping, she brought Janey from her bed.

"Tabby, what is it? Has someone died?"

"No, sugar, a woman is on the phone for you. A Missus Cora?"

"Did she say what this is about?"

"No, no, just for you to come talk to her, quick as you can."

Janey walked out of her room, rubbing at her eyes and yawning. "Tabby, what's the hour?"

"Half past two, sugar."

Janey yawned again, mumbled something under her breath, and finding the railing, she haphazardly negotiated the stairs. Tabby followed close behind in case she needed to grab Janey, should she lose her footing. The night was hot and the downstairs windows were closed and locked. The air inside was stifling. Janey's gown was soaked with sweat, leaving nothing to the imagination, making her glad it wasn't Percy who had come to wake her. Picking up the handset from the top of the telephone table, she said, "Hello, Cora? Are you okay?"

"Can you come to Chastity's?"

"What's happened? Are you sick?"

"Naw, but I need you here."

"What's wrong, Cora?"

"Not on the phone... just come, please."

"Okay, well, give me a few minutes, I'll have to get the car out."

"Okay, but please, hurry."

"Give me ten minutes and I'll be there."

She heard the phone click off and then the second, more metallic click of Helen Blake disconnecting. Janey suspected a phone call this early in the morning had brought Helen from her bed, probably hoping for some juicy tidbit of information. The old operator must have been sorely disappointed.

"Do you want Percy to get the car, sugar?"

"No, no, Tabby, I'll be okay. I suspect you will let him know that I have taken it, please?"

"Certainly will."

Janey decided to go sans undergarments and pulled on yesterday's dress, happy that the bob would only require a couple of strokes with a brush. Hurrying down the stairs, Tabby met her at the bottom with the Cadillac's key and Janey's personal flashlight. "Thanks, Tabby, so sorry to have woken you." She started to walk away but Tabby grabbed her arm and spun her around to embrace her. Then releasing Janey, she said, "I don't know what's going on, but I be sure to give you a hug before you go, because, well... something ain't right. But it ain't none my business."

"Thanks, Tabby," was all she said and Tabby let her out the front door. Percy always parked the Cadillac in the circle portion of the drive and it was only garaged in the winter. Climbing in, Janey let off the brake and coasted down toward the gate. When she had rounded the first bend out of sight of the house, she popped the clutch and the engine roared to life. Turning on the headlights, she coasted the rest of the way to the bottom where she stopped just long enough to open the gate.

Janey knew she wouldn't have to worry about Nealy. There was a good chance he had already made his nightly arrest and would be at the office chatting up the drunk for the remainder of his shift. The patrol car wasn't in sight and she gave a sigh of relief. Glancing up at the second floor of the tavern, she was surprised to see Tom's light was still on and wondered if he had fallen asleep reading.

She had no trouble finding Chastity's place as all the windows glowed. Janey went on a little further, then making a U turn, she came back and parked on the street in front of the cottage. There came an unusual sensation; a foreboding. It frightened her a little and she sat in the driver's seat for a few minutes after turning off the car, just studying Chastity's place.

Knocking lightly on the front door, Janey waited. Cora soon cracked a curtain, pulled the bolt, and opened the door just enough for Janey to slip through. Hurriedly throwing the bolt, she turned to Janey.

They stood and stared at each other for a few seconds before Cora threw her arms around Janey and began to sob. Janey embraced her and rubbed her back not saying a word. Cora's sobbing soon subsided and she stepped away, rubbing at her eyes.

"Sorry to have you out, but… something terrible has happened."

"What is it, Cora? Please tell me before I go crazy."

"It's Bessie LaVern."

"What about Bessie?"

"I think she's dead."

"What… what do you mean, you think? She either is or isn't… Cora!"

"I can't tell," Cora groaned.

"Where is she? Is she here in the house?"

"No, come with me. Let me show you."

Taking Janey's hand, Cora led her to the kitchen where she retrieved the lantern from the tabletop. At the bottom of the backsteps, Cora released Janey's hand and turned the lantern's wick as high as she could.

"Follow me," she said, and then explained everything as it had happened. "Now, be ready, this isn't going to be pretty," Cora said as they entered the woods.

The lantern glow lit up Bessie's body and Janey gasped. "Oh, my giddy aunt, there's blood."

Janey thought to pull her flashlight from her pocket but wasn't so sure she wanted to see any more of what lay before her. But curiosity won out and taking it in hand, she shined it on the corpse.

Bessie's camisole was soaked in crimson at the front from the obvious tear in her throat, but there were only a few large spots on the ground. What troubled her even more was that the girl's face remained pink and serene.

"Did you see anything, Cora? What did you see?" Janey said and gulped. Cora had set the lantern on the ground and had stepped back, rubbing her hands up and down her hips. "Look at her face. Do you see her face?"

"Yes, I know… so odd. Did you see what happened? Cora… tell me."

"I think it was some kind of an animal, well… at first a person… that turned into an animal, like a dog, or… a wolf."

"That makes no sense. Besides, Massachusetts doesn't have wolves."

"I know and that's part of what's troubling me."

Janey began to walk around Bessie, shining her light on the ground. "Whatcha looking for?"

"Tracks, wolf tracks... I don't know. Actually, any kind, I guess. It's just... if it was a wolf, you'd think there would be more damage, uh... to her neck."

Janey hoped for prints of bare feet or shoes, but there was only what looked like small hoof prints littering the ground on the opposite side of the body. "Do those look like deer tracks to you?"

Cora leaned over, "I suppose. Haven't ever seen any deer, seen a lot of sheep, though."

"Well, I've seen plenty and those are the tracks of a small deer," Janey said as she moved up the slope, the flashlight directed at the ground. "Now I'm seeing tracks, like a dog, or... a wolf."

"Told you, didn't I?" Cora said, sounding irritated.

"Okay, okay, I believe you, but it still doesn't make any sense. Deer tracks? Wolf tracks?"

"I want to get back inside. What if whatever did that to poor Bessie, is still out there? Maybe watching us, right now."

Janey shined her light around and other then picking up the eyes of an old owl that glided away with a cackle, there was nothing but tree trunks and underbrush. "Shall we take Bessie inside?" Cora asked.

"I don't know, won't we be disturbing a crime scene? If that's what it is."

"Oh, the hell with that, we can just tell Merlyn she was still alive, so we drug her inside and that's where she died."

"Yeah, but she sure doesn't look dead, other than her throat and the blood on her clothes."

"Come and help me grab under an arm. We'll drag her."

Janey didn't argue and they struggled to get Bessie inside. Laying her out on the kitchen floor, they sat, panting and sweating. The clock chimed four, sparking Cora to get up and make sure all the windows were curtained.

Janey leaned forward to look at Bessie and said, "I could have sworn that wound was bigger... uh... longer. Cora took another look and gazing back at Janey, her eyes wide, she said, "Aye, I see what you mean. Hmmm..."

"I think we ought to be calling Chief Cobb. I know Nealy's at the office, but I'd rather it be Cobb who comes."

"One's no better than the other, but if we are going to do that, we need to come up with a story. One that we both know, one we can, ummm... co... uh..."

"Corroborate on?"

"Aye... that."

Cora moved to the water pitcher and poured herself a glass and drank it thirstily. Janey stared up at the ceiling, trying to pull it all together. Thinking they ought to cover Bessie with something, she looked back at the corpse to determine if a table cloth might do, or if something bigger, like a sheet, would work better. She gasped, and Cora said, "What? What is it?'

"Her neck, look at her neck. Oh, my giddy aunt!" Janey said, jumping to her feet, the goose bumps rising on her arms.

The wound was healing right before her eyes. Cora came around the table and inhaled loudly, throwing her hands over her mouth.

"Crivvens! Look at that!"

Collapsing in a chair, Cora's right hand went to her chest. Janey felt frozen in place. Bessie's face still had that serene look about it and Janey figured the girl should have been bluing up by now. That's what she had heard people do when they've stopped breathing for a long time.

"We need to get Chief Cobb down here, so... let's agree that you called me because you wanted help finding her after she walked out of the house. You only trusted me to help. So, if they want to see from where she had come, we can show them. Oh, and we'll mention the tracks before we go out, that way we can say maybe it was dogs, or something, and because she was still alive, we dragged her back inside and she collapsed and died on the kitchen floor."

"Well, they're going to want to know why I called you and not Nealy, and... we can't say that she died. We have to let them decide that she's actually dead, otherwise they may get suspicious."

Janey was listening but still watching Bessie, her neck near fully healed at that point. Cora got up, walked into the parlor, turned around, and came back.

"Did you hear me?"

197

"Yes, I heard you," Janey said, "How are we going to explain where the blood came from. I mean, that cut is pretty much closed?"

Cora stared at the body for a minute before saying, "We can say we thought she might have been bleeding from her mouth. I remember a friend of mine had the consumption and in her last days, it looked a lot like that. Let's hope they think the same."

"They?"

"You know Merlyn's going to drag Doc Bolen out of bed and have him down here."

"Okay, maybe we should change her clothes or something, and maybe just wipe all the blood off, too?"

"Naw, when they go out and look and see what wee bit of blood is out there, we are going to have a tough time explaining why she was clean. Better to leave her as she is. There are going to be enough questions."

"Okay, so... you want to make the call?"

"Aye, I'll get that fat arse out of bed; it'd be my pleasure."

Cora made the call, telling a sleep fogged Merlyn to come on over to Chastity's and he better bring Doc Bolen. Merlyn growled out, "Why the hell can't you be calling Nealy?" But Cora was already hanging up to avoid any conversation that might include Helen.

She and Janey moved out into the parlor so they wouldn't have to look at the supposed dead girl. "What do you thinks going on, Cora? I mean, this just isn't natural. It's not real. That gash in Bessie's throat is completely healed up now. That's not going to happen if she's dead." Janey toyed with the flashlight, watching Cora's face, waiting for a response.

"You want to know what I think?"

"Yes, of course."

"Are you sure, because I'm going to take us clear back to Scotland?"

"Yes, help me make some sense of this because you know what I'm thinking."

"Aye, you're thinking vampire, and... well, you'd be close. But not quite what you know. This ain't no Dracula."

"So... what, then?"

'I'll just say it... Baobhan Sith."

"So, like you told us at Brenner's?"

"Aye, like I said, Dracula wasn't the only vampire."

"But, she's..."

"Aye, I think our Bessie is changing into one."

"So... Mabel, again?"

"Aye, Mab, again?"

"But it wasn't Mab who did this?"

"Naw, but she brought it. Sorry, Janey, but your father was a damn fool and what he wrought on Gowan... and probably the rest of the Spry River Valley, is a... well... so, you want to hear more, or you had enough to think over for now?"

"No, I want to hear more, but... it's so hard to believe. If I hadn't seen, well... So, you mentioned the terror that flies by night. Is this, that?"

"I did mention the Unseelie Court, but this isn't that, either. Like I said, it's Baobhan Sith. But I can tell you about the court, if you like?"

"Certainly."

"Okay, so, my grandda talked of the Unseelie Court when I was a wee lass. Me, my brothers and sisters always thought it was just another way to keep us home and not out gallivanting about the moors after the gloaming. You've heard of the gloaming, yes?"

"Of course, who, in all of the Spry River Valley, hasn't? My grandfather, Uriah, told me all about it when I was still a child living up at Carter House. He used to say, 'Janey, don't get caught out in the gloaming' and then he'd try to scare me by growling like an animal and grabbing me. It was all in fun. He was always teasing me about that and about me going out into the woods where the 'Nixie's were. Sometimes he tried to convince me I was a 'Changeling' and not truly a Carter. My father used to get so mad at him. He was my only source for what we're talking about."

"Just a second," Cora said and getting to her feet, she walked into the kitchen to view Bessie. Turning back toward the parlor, she said, "If it wasn't for the blood on her chin and clothes, you'd think she was still alive. She's still pink."

Janey said nothing, and just nodded, smiling nervously. She didn't want to look. Cora came back to her chair and sat down.

"So... the Unseelie Court?"

"Aye, so... a swarm... for lack of a better word, of flying boggarts, goblins, and buttery spirits. Hobgoblins on the wing. The worst of the Sidhe. They grab up unwary travelers, pulling them up into the swarm, basically kidnapping them to replenish their ranks because they can't breed. We see them at a distance as a dark cloud, unless of course you're a victim and they find you out alone. They are under the control of Mab and her magic. If Mab is here... so is the court. That is, the Mab we knew, and I suspect, the Mab we are soon to meet."

"So, you think, ummm... Gregory?"

"I only suspect, but I imagine if we were to walk the Hollow road at night, we would soon be introduced to the lot of them. They would be difficult to escape from, we would have to have a plan."

"Like a predesignated place to hide so they couldn't grab us?"

"Possibly, but better... we just go on up to Carter House and confront Mab."

"And convince her to leave Gowan? Or... kill her?"

"Can't kill her."

"What? She can't die?"

"Well... right. She's not mortal. But we can banish her. First, we'd have to fight and kill her handmaidens."

"You mean those three women that were seen at McCarthy's?"

"Those weren't women... they were something else."

"So, what then? Shoot them? I can handle a gun and I'm a pretty good shot."

"No, not that easy. Guns are worthless against them."

"Then... what?"

"Iron, or so my granny said. The Sidhe detest iron. Granny said it burns them. So, fae will never possess things made of iron. Chains, and such. My uncle Archibald was a history professor in Edinburgh. He was quite the story teller. Ireland had what they called 'The Mythical Cycle' and it was in that time that the Milesians invaded Ireland and battled the ummm... let's see if I get this right, the... Tuatha De Danann, the lords and kings of the island. They fought with weapons of bronze, while the Milesians fought with weapons of iron. The Tuatha De Danann lost and were driven underground, or off the island to become, forever, Sidhe.

Ever since then, iron has been their bane. We all had beds with wrought iron frames to keep from being snatched and turned into changelings. Uncle Archie said that iron grounds the magic and their power cannot be invoked. We used to wear jewelry made from iron, necklaces, bracelets, and rings. Some were painted, I even had an enameled necklace made of iron. I lost it though."

"So, maybe something to stab them like a knife made of iron? I have never stabbed a soul in my life. It might be hard for me. Punched a few. Knocked a few boys out for dipping my braids in inkwells, but…"

"It won't be the same as stabbing a human being, I can assure you. Perhaps hit them with something iron. You can whip or bind them with chains; iron made chains will hold them."

"But that means we'd have to get close enough to put the chains on them."

"I'm not saying it's going to be easy, Janey. But knowing you as I do, you will do whatever you need to do when the time arises."

"Probably so, but…"

The sound of horse hooves trotting on the road floated in through the window. They got to their feet and moved together to the front door. Merlyn was tying Massy to a tree in the front yard. He then looked the Cadillac over before walking to the door. Cora opened it to allow him in. Janey stepped back into the parlor and waited.

"Cora, what's going on here? I thought we were through with Chastity for a while?"

"We are, Merlyn, you got Chastity right where you wanted her. This… is something else."

"Like I need something else. Got enough going on in a town that's supposed to be quiet."

"Well, we're going to add a wee bit more to your plate. You're a big man, you can handle it," Cora said and smirked.

Merlyn glared at her, his brow clouding. Pushing past her, he came inside to see Janey standing across the room.

"Miss Janey Carter," he said and muttered, "Shit." Summoning some bravado he said with a patriarchal tone, "What are you doing here?"

"Well, Cora and I are friends, Merlyn. She asked me down to comfort her, you know, because of Chastity and all."

She glowered at the big man standing there in his sweaty uniform shirt and bib overalls, his fedora tipped back on his head. Cobb knew better than to get into any kind of an exchange with Janey. He'd had more than a life time of that going clear back to his days as a young officer. He looked back and forth between the two women and then took out a cigar and prepared to light it.

"Merlyn, if you don't mind?" Cora said.

"Well, I do, but it's your house. Don't mind if I chew it, do you?"

"Not at all," Janey said.

"So, what's all the rigamarole? You got another body?"

"Matter of fact, we do," Cora said.

Merlyn's mouth dropped open, and he scratched his forehead. "I was just kidding, Cora. Damn it."

"Well, I'm not," she said and walked past him toward the kitchen. "It's poor Bessie LaVern."

Merlyn followed her in with Janey close behind. Cora pointed to the body, and he gasped. Stepping back, he threw a look at one woman and then the other. "What the hell? What happened to her?"

"Damned if we know," Cora said and went on to tell him their made-up story. Merlyn scratched his head and walked around Bessie a couple of times, leaning down to take a closer look. Janey said nothing until Merlyn asked, "So, Janey, is that true?"

"Certainly is, couldn't have explained it any better. It's all very strange."

"Yes, it is," Merlyn muttered without looking at them. "Where's the telephone?"

Cora directed him to it and he racked the little metal hanger for the handset several times, trying to get Helen, then he said, "Helen, Chief Cobb, wake yourself up and get me Doc." They stood in silence for all of a minute, before Merlyn said, "Doc, Chief Cobb. Need you down at Chastity's right away, we got something here needs your look-see. No, I'll say no more on the phone, just get in that fancy car of yours and git on down here. Okay, see you."

He hung up the phone and said, "Doc's on his way."

Ducking back through the parlor door, the floor boards creaked under his weight. He looked back and said, "So, you dragged her in here?"

"Aye, we did," Cora said, "She was stumbling, but still breathing. We laid her out where you see her, and then she didn't breathe no more."

"Hmmm…" he said and walked back in and looked at the body. "You know… don't look like she's dead. But with all that blood all over her, it… it looks like it came out her mouth. Had a cousin got the consumption once. Got to spitting up blood… he looked like that. I 'spect she had the consumption. But we'll let Doc decide."

Cora turned her back on Merlyn and facing Janey, she winked. Janey maintained her poker face. Turning away to face the open kitchen window, Janey feigned despair and whimpered out, "So terrible, poor Bessie," and turning back, she cast her eyes to the floor and covered them with a hand.

"Well, you ought not to be standing there. Best you get out the room where you can't see her. I'll be out front smoking my cigar."

Merlyn walked out to stand on the porch. Lighting up his cigar, he stood gazing at Massy nibbling grass in the dark under the trees.

Doc Bolen soon arrived in his 1932 Rolls Royce and parked it on the street behind Janey's Cadillac. He hurried up to the porch where he found Chief Cobb standing in the dark behind the glow of his cigar.

"What's the problem, Merlyn?"

The big man leaned down and whispered everything to Doc, who then turned away and went inside. Merlyn followed him. Doc stopped and grinned at the two women standing together in the parlor.

"Hello, Cora…Janey. Where's Bessie?"

"In the kitchen, here, I'll show you," Cora said and led the way. Doc walked around the table, took one look and said, "Arc you sure she's deceased?"

Cora said, "Well, I'm not sure, Doc, that's kind of your department, isn't it?"

"Yep, I looked at her, too, Doc, and I'd say the same, but you're the doctor, you tell us."

"Merlyn… the stogie?" Cora said, sternly.

"Yep," he said and returned to the porch.

Doc Bolen glanced up at the dim light bulb hanging from the ceiling and grabbing a lantern, he turned it up and handed it to Janey, "Please, hold this so I can see what I'm doing."

"Certainly, Doc."

"Sure doesn't look dead. How long you say she's been like this?"

"Been almost two hours since we brought her in from the woods," Cora said, moving closer to Doc, all the while rubbing a hand around the center of her chest.

"Brought her, or… dragged her?"

Cora threw Janey a fleeting glance and said, "Kind of dragged her, she was stumbling, though. I found her out in the woods behind the cottage. I woke up to find her missing from the divan, so I went out to check the privy and I heard her in the trees. I went out there and that's where I found her."

"So… you brought her to this spot?"

"Aye, and she was still breathing, but there was so much blood."

"Merlyn, you want to come in here?" Doc said.

The big man put out his stogie, shoved the remnants into a bib pocket and came back inside. "Merlyn, have Cora take you out back and show you where she found Bessie."

"Lead the way, Cora."

"Janey, you stay and hold the lantern," Doc said.

"Of course, anything to help. Here, Cora, take my flashlight." They exchanged glances before Cora took the light from Janey's hand and then led Merlyn out the back door.

"So, she was out here?" Merlyn asked.

"Yes, right back here."

When they got to the spot, she pointed it out.

"Can I have that light?"

Cora handed it off and Merlyn began moving around, shining the light on the ground. Cora remained silent watching his expressions as he examined the forest floor. "Got big spots of blood here. And look at them prints, looks like deer. Did you see any deer out here?"

"Nope, just Bessie in her underclothes," Cora said, now massaging her left arm.

Merlyn widened his circle of inspection. "Dog prints over here. Running away, it looks like… maybe chasing the deer. You see a dog? Somebody around here have a dog? Looks like a pretty big one?"

"Aye, the Martin's have a dog. It's kind of big."

"Hmmm... Merlyn said and walking back toward the cottage, he kept the flashlight trained on the ground in front of him.

Stopping, he turned and said, "Why do you suppose she came out here?" Cora stopped and looked up at him. "Well, I don't want to suppose anything, Merlyn, maybe she got confused and wandered out here, I don't know. She was drinking beer a wee bit earlier. But I suppose you can speculate just as much as me, aye?"

"I suppose."

They walked back to the cottage, Merlyn still shining the light on the grass. When they reached the outhouse, he examined the paving stones leading from there to the back door. Opening the door to the privy, he said, "I wonder if she just got lost on the way to the crapper?"

"Got me."

"She never been here before, right?"

"As far as I know," Cora said, trying hard to keep the irritation out of her voice. Merlyn turned from the outhouse and stood looking around the yard as Cora, with arms crossed, tapped a foot, sighed, and rolled her eyes.

Janey watched Doc do his business. Rolling Bessie onto her side, he pushed a leg of her panties up to expose a buttock. "Hold that light over here, will you, Janey?"

She did as asked, a scowl forming on her face. Doc pushed his glasses back up on his nose and leaned in close. "What are you looking for there, Doc?" Janey asked.

"Lividity, the blood will settle in the lowest part, and... there is none." He let the panty leg fall and rolled Bessie back. He sat still for a moment scratching his head, looking like he was analyzing. Using his stethoscope, he listened to her chest again. "Odd, so very odd," he said. Standing up, he put the stethoscope back in his bag and snapped it shut. Looking at Janey, he said, "Thanks, Janey, you can put the lantern back on the table, now."

Janey did as he suggested just as Merlyn and Cora came back inside.

"Well, Merlyn, what's new? Deduce anything?"

"Nope, just like these two said. So, what's the word, Doc? Consumption?"

"Well, that's the way I'm leaning. I haven't seen Bessie for years.

Her folks used to bring her into the office every year until she graduated school. But I haven't seen her since. I think we'll have Louis come and pick her up and take her over to his place."

"You want me to call him?" Merlyn asked.

"No, we've given Helen enough trouble for one night. Perhaps one of us should walk down there and roust him out."

"I can do that," the big man said, "But I'm taking Massy. I can ride right up on his big ol' porch and…"

"Uh… no, be best if you just knocked.

"You never were any fun, Doc," he said and left the cottage to mount his mare and race away, hooves clattering on the roadway, much to the dismay of all the northsider's still trying to sleep.

He was back in ten minutes and, five minutes after that, the lights of Louis's truck could be seen coming up the road, ground mist roiling in the headlights. The truck backed up to the front door and parked. Louis and Duncan got out and came up onto the porch.

Doc met them with, "Hello, Louis, how's Prudence taking the news of Vern's disappearance?"

"Oh, you know. Expected her to be more broken up about it. All she did was open her flask, take a long drink, and then push me out and slam the bedroom door in my face. She locked me out. Had to sleep down the hall in the guest bedroom."

"Well, okay… come on in, I'll show you where she's at."

Doc took them into the kitchen and showed them the body. Duncan let out a low whistle and said, "Bessie LaVern, damn, wasn't expecting it to be her. Damn, if she ain't bloodied up all that sexy underwear."

"Why don't you just shut it and go get the soft tarp," Louis said, smacking Duncan on top of his head.

"Ouch! Pa, what…"

"Do it!" Louis said raising his voice, apparently irritated that he was awaken from his beauty sleep. They all moved back into the parlor, Doc relaying some details he wanted Louis to be aware of.

Duncan returned with the tarp and Janey watched him move to the body, and then kneel out of sight behind the table. She saw he was taking his time and a suspicious thought occurred.

Leaving the group, she moved to where she could see him kneeling beside Bessie. He didn't notice because he was so wrapped up in ogling Bessie's bare breasts. He must have slid the slender straps of her camisole down her shoulders for a quick peek before he wrapped her.

"What you doing there, Duncan?" Janey said flatly.

Duncan quickly pulled up the camisole and replaced the straps without a word. He began to work the tarp under the body as the rest of the group came in. Janey made eye contact with Merlyn, who then scowled at the unknowing Duncan.

"What's going on in here, Duncan?" Louis asked.

"Nothing, pa."

"You better have not been doing what I think you were doing."

"I wasn't," Duncan said, giving Janey a look, his eyes pleading. Janey scoffed and shook her head.

"Why don't you get your ass outside and git in the truck," Louis said and grabbing Duncan under an armpit, he hauled him to his feet and directed him toward the front door. Duncan stomped away with an, "Ah, pa."

Louis, with Doc's assistance, wrapped Bessie's body with Merlyn offering suggestions on how they could do it better. They soon had her properly draped and hauled her out to lay in the back of the truck. Gathering on the front lawn, Doc said, "I'll see you down there, Louis," Doc said.

"You sure you don't want a ride?"

"Okay, I'll ride down with you. I don't think Cora will mind if I leave my car out front."

"Not at all."

"Very well, thanks again, ladies," he said and climbed into the truck.

"You drive, Duncan, I'll ride in the back to make sure the body doesn't get molested... anymore," Louis said glaring at his son, who sheepishly pulled his head back inside the truck window. Letting off the brake, he put the truck in reverse, grinding the gears.

Once they were gone, Merlyn moved to Massy and climbed aboard. "Ladies," he said, tipping his hat to Cora and Janey. Then spinning the large mare around, he goaded her with his boot heels and Massy took off, her shoes beating a tattoo on the northside road.

Cora let out a sigh and said, "Whew! Glad that's over. I'm tired as hell and I'm not getting nothing done around here."

"So… what was that they said about Vern?"

"Merlyn said he's gone missing. No one's seen him since the night of Kaleb's funeral."

"I didn't see anything in the paper?"

"I think they're keeping it hush-hush, for now."

"That's horrible. I don't think I'm going to sleep too well for a while. There's too much going on. It's all so very strange. I thought I'd come back from Thayer to a quiet life, and now… all this."

"Well, Janey, thanks so much for coming down here, you should get back to Headmost and at least try for a wee bit more sleep. I've got to call Al and let him know I'm going to be here a little longer, and to be sure to keep Pearl on until I get back."

They got to their feet and embraced, "We'll talk some more later, okay?" Janey said. "We should also get Tom in on this."

"Aye, we should, the three of us can put our heads together and stop this nonsense before Louis gets too much more business."

"Yes, the three of us," Janey said, smiling. Leaving the cottage, she walked out across the lawn toward the Cadillac. Turning one time to wave, she saw Cora rubbing her left arm as she stood watching her go.

10

Janey returned to Headmost and leaving the car in the circle, she went inside. The Snoaks had the house opened up and were already in the kitchen when she poked her head in to greet them. She told them she was going back to bed for a little while. They nodded their understanding with Tabby saying, "Everything okay, sugar?"

"Well… no, but we'll talk later."

"Sleep well, Miss Janey," Percy said.

Janey doubted that was going to happen. Moving quietly up the stairs, she pulled her dress off over her head and dropping it on the floor, she lay naked on her bed. A cooling morning breeze came in the window as she lay staring at the ceiling. A thought crossed her mind and going to her jewelry box, she dug down deep and pulled out a necklace. Its pendant was a nickel sized; white enameled flower made of iron with a little yellow gem at the center. Tiny rust spots showed through where the enamel had chipped. It was a necklace for a little girl, one Janey had since she was five. Hanging it around her neck, she returned to her bed and pulled the sheet over her. Rolling onto her side, she gazed out the window through the parted curtains, fingers caressing the necklace.

She lay for a long time trying to push that picture of a blood covered Bessie out of her head, but more so—the wound that had healed right before her eyes. Finally convincing herself it was more than she could fathom at the moment, she switched her thoughts to Tom and that night in the bandstand. Within a few minutes, she was fast asleep.

11

She woke a little after noon, her brimming bladder crying out for relief. After pulling on her flimsy dressing gown, she dashed down the hall to her mother's toilet closet. The door was locked.

"Mother, are you in there?"

"Yes, sorry, I'm going to be a while, that mulled wine we had last evening, I guess."

Janey hurried back down the hall to the main stairs where she heard Constance holler, "I need to talk to you!"

"Yeah, yeah," Janey said with irritation.

She hoped she wouldn't run into Percy on the main floor, but the car was no longer in the circle. He had probably gone down to McCarthy's for something. She heard Tabby banging around in the kitchen as she took the short hallway that ran from the entry hall to the back door. Exiting the house, she headed for the privy that stood just outside the high brick wall that enclosed the backyard. After unlocking and throwing open the gate, she dashed to the outhouse.

Going inside, she did her usual check for animals, wasps, and black widow spiders. Finding none, she stepped in and pulled the door shut behind her. The handle was wrested from her grip and the door swung open to reveal a grinning Sully Albright, his dungarees and white undershirt spattered with blood. She saw the craziness in his eyes as he shouted, "Ha, got ya! That Tom ain't here to help you now, is he?" Pushing his way inside, the door slammed as his hands closed around Janey's throat, her bladder promptly giving up its contents.

CHAPTER NINE

TOM

II

~

1

Doc Bolen saw the need early in his practice for something of a hospital to be built in Gowan. Hoping to beat Grunewyck to the punch, he had an addition put on the back of his existing office and in it, five separate rooms, each one just big enough for a bed and all the modern conveniences that he could add later.

A common statement, put in varied ways to his wife, Hannah, was how glad he was that he got it completed before 1928, when the Depression hit.

Her response was just as typical, "Oh? There was a Depression? Hardly noticed being it's Gowan and all."

A small nurse's station had been placed where the corridor from the front office took an abrupt left turn and ran along the inside wall, granting access to each individual cubicle. The night nurse would sit there if she had to stay over, then she could take an open bed when they closed down for the day. Doc needed somebody to remain if he had patients, usually his nurse, Caroline, or Hannah.

It had been a while since he had anyone stay overnight, but he was starting to get a feeling that his comfortable evenings, snuggling with Hannah in their own bed, were coming to an end. The law of averages was due to weigh in real soon.

2

Tom arrived at the townhall minutes after Maddie unlocked the door, and then he had to convince her to let him up to talk to Merlyn.

"He hasn't had his coffee yet. He doesn't talk to anybody until then. Come back later."

"He'll see me, and if you won't let me up there, I'll just go around you and go up anyway."

"Okay, your funeral."

Scowling, Maddie nodded back toward the door to the stairwell. Soon Merlyn was gazing wearily up at him from his desk. Taking off his hat, he rubbed his face as if it hurt. "Come on in, Tom, but just so you know, I haven't had my coffee."

"I know, Maddie told me. Chief Cobb, I want to go to Carter House… today."

Merlyn gave him a look like he was going to give Tom a chewing out, but seemed to resign himself and looking beaten, sat back in his chair and said, "I'm running on only a few hours of sleep. It's been a busy night. We've had another person die here in Gowan, but… more of that later."

"Okay, you said a couple days, and we are well past that now. So, what's the word? Can I, or can't I? Because, even if it's can't, I know I can get permission from Constance, or even Janey, for that matter."

"Now, just calm down, Tom. Philip Shannon's got something going and I'm just waiting on him."

"Well, then maybe it's him I ought to be talking to. Maybe he needs a little shove to get him moving."

"Have yourself a seat, Tom. I'm supposing I can share what I already know since you are kin to Kaleb and… since we can't find, or… get in touch with Ben Carter. Only the Carters can tell you if you'll be taking over for Kaleb."

"Okay, so what do you mean you can't find Benjamin Carter?" You went up there, right?"

"Yeah, we did, Shannon and I, but that woman wouldn't let us in. I tried to get a warrant, but Judge Benson said I didn't have enough evidence for that. So, Shannon hired himself an agent to do a little investigating, if you know what I mean?"

"No, I don't know what you mean. Who did he hire?"

"Can't say."

"Do the Carters know?"

"Well, I don't believe so, but I dare not say anything to Constance until we know for sure. If it's bad news, she ain't going to take it very well, and that woman looks like death warmed over. You saw her at Kaleb's funeral, couldn't even stand up. She's liable to keel over if we find out that things aren't so good up there. I tell you right now, they sure didn't look that way. The horses got out and scattered to the wind. The grass on those lawns is practically up to a man's knees. The paints peeling, parts of the house are falling off, and there's these damn big vines growing up the walls. If somebody don't cut them down soon, they're going to cover the whole damn place. We suspect if Ben were there, he wouldn't let it be like that. Somethings fishy, if you know what I mean?"

"Sounds like it to me."

That's the way it went for at least another thirty minutes. Little was learned, but it seemed like it all hinged on what Philip Shannon could share. Tom prodded Merlyn who finally gave in, but not without letting Tom know he was a troublemaker and had been since day one.

Merlyn got up, walked down the hall and yelled from the top of the stairs, "Maddie, get Philip Shannon on the phone."

Tom heard her say, "Okay, Chief," then came the racking of the phone's receiver. "Helen, get me Philip Shannon, Chief Cobb wants him put through, lickety-split. No, I didn't hear that. Bessie LaVern? Who told you? No, well Beulah McKay don't know diddly squat about the truth…"

"Maddie, now!" Merlyn bellowed.

"Okay! Sorry, Helen, Chief Cobb says it's urgent."

It grew quiet for a few seconds before, "He's on, Merlyn."

Merlyn picked up his phone and spoke into it. "Phil, Merlyn here. What's the word on that thing? That's right, Phil, uh… what do you mean you're not ready? Well, I am! So… no, forget it. I'm coming over there and I'm bringing Tom Lynn. If you don't give us what we want, we're going to gang up on you and soak your head in Brenner's well, got me?" Merlyn winked at Tom, who just sat watching with indifference.

The conversation went long winded, leaving Tom to watch the clock. He heard the front door open downstairs and Nealy Garret say, "Hey Maddie, the chief in?"

"Yeah, but he's with someone. You're going to have to wait."

"Wait? What do you mean? It's my office too."

"Wait," she growled.

Well...okay. So, in that case, I got a joke for you. A duck walks into a bar..."

Nealy got through his joke and then laughed. Maddie said nothing and Tom heard what sounded like Nealy pacing.

Merlyn hung up the phone and looking at Tom, he said, "Let's go over there because, come to think of it, I'm tired of waiting too. Merlyn left the room and Tom followed him down the stairs.

"Merlyn, Nealy's down here telling me jokes about ducks."

"I thought I told you to go home and go to bed?"

Nealy whined, "I did, but I couldn't sleep long. Too damn hot."

"You got yourself an electric fan?"

"Nope, but I'm thinking about it."

"Well, if you're going to be here, you might as well do some paperwork or something. You know what? You can call the FBI for me and see if they got anything, yet."

"Sure thing, Chief," Nealy said excitedly and ran up the stairs.

Maddie left her horseshoe shaped counter to disappear into the lady's room and shut the door. The townhall was the first to get working toilets, followed by Doc Bolen's office. Maddie always referred to them as one of the fringe benefits of her job.

"Back, soon," Merlyn hollered with no answer from anyone.

Tom followed the big man in silence as they worked their way across the green, the belltower chiming one o clock. Tom's stomach rumbled and he wondered if maybe he should go to Boots' A Walk Inn for something other than what he was getting at Brenner's. Clyde could whip up a pretty decent steak sandwich. The problem was, Tom's meals at Brenner's came with the room. He was fast running out of money and keeping the room was a drain on it. If he didn't get up to Carter House soon—and it was livable—he was going to have to leave Gowan and that would mean leaving Janey. Her offer to work for Constance at Headmost House was becoming more inviting.

Merlyn began to wheeze as they arrived at Philip Shannon's office. Tom wondered how much longer the big guy could be an actual working police chief and if Gowan offered any kind of pension plan. Beings it was rumored that the state was looking to level most of the towns in the Spry River Valley, Gowan was probably not going to be around to pay Merlyn a single dime for his retirement.

Merlyn held the door for Tom and followed him in. Philip was sitting behind his desk eating a stack of butter and syrup covered pancakes on one of Boots' plates. A cup sat steaming next to the food and Tom caught a hint of whiskey, suspecting it was Irish Coffee. Seeing who was coming in, Philip dropped his *Pep* magazine into an open drawer and pushed it shut with a knee.

"Any good-looking women in there, Phil?"

"Women?" Philip said as if he had no clue what Merlyn was talking about.

"The naked one's in that girly magazine."

Philip ignored him and turned his attention to Tom. "Well, if it isn't Tom Lynn. How are you?"

"Just fine."

"Okay, enough with the howdy do's, you got anything for me, Phil? You sent your so-called agent up, didn't you... to Carter House?"

"Uh, yeah," he said and turned his gaze back to Tom.

"Don't you worry about Tom; he needs to know just as much as me. So... what you got?"

"Yeah, so, I sent my, uh... investigator up..." Merlyn threw a smirk at Tom. "...and he gave me a report. Seems Ben Carter was nowhere to be found. The house was in worse shape than the day we went up. Oh, just a second," Philip said, and opening another desk drawer, he pulled out a manila folder. Pushing his coffee cup aside, he set it on the desk, opened it, and pulled out several sheets of paper. Putting on glasses, he read, "Something about the inside of Carter House looked like it had been ransacked. There were vines and other such things crawling up the wallpaper in every room. It looks like, let's see... oh, okay, seems that Mabel and her cohorts are living in just one room, the master bedroom on the second floor. Leo… uh… my investigator, relayed, and I quote, 'The place was in ruins.' That's all."

"Your, uh… agent, see anyone? Like that woman."

"Mentioned something about seeing them dancing on the front lawn, candles in their hands, and then going off into the woods."

"How many?" Merlyn asked, now leaning on the desk with both hands, trying to read what was written on the papers.

"No more than four of them. Supposedly Ben's wife and those other three. The ones we saw in town that day. The ladies-in-waiting, I think is what everybody is calling them."

"Courtiers," Tom said. "They're courtiers." Merlyn turned and looked at Tom. Philip stared past the big man, giving Tom a look that asked, 'Are you a swellhead, or what?'

Turning back to Shannon, Merlyn asked, "What about the outbuildings? The same?"

"Yep, the same. It sounds like a lost cause."

"Well, I'm just concerned about Benjamin Carter. I still suspect foul play."

"I believe you have just cause for a warrant now, Merlyn. I'm thinking we got enough to safely assume that Benjamin Carter is missing and that there needs to be an investigation. Oh! And here's a little more just cause."

Reaching into the open drawer, Philip pulled out a wadded-up handkerchief. Unwrapping it, he exposed a set of dentures.

"What the hell is that? Someone's teeth?"

"Uh-huh… Benjamin Carter's teeth," Philip said, his eyes wide. "Taken from his dresser top."

"I 'spect Ben Carter wouldn't go anywhere without his teeth."

"That's right. He never would. Benjamin Carter was a vain man and wouldn't leave the house without them," Tom added.

"But somebody forced him against his will," Philip said, looking hard at Merlyn.

"Uh-huh, just what I was thinking," Merlyn said, turning to Tom as if for his two cents worth, but Tom was still preoccupied with the teeth.

"I'll just take those and keep them in evidence." Rewrapping them, Merlyn stuck them into the pocket in the bib of his coveralls next to his well chewed cigar.

"I'll be heading over to Judge Benson's, now. Tom, you heard enough? What you want to do?"

Tom pulled himself from his revery and gazed at Merlyn as if confused. "What? Oh, sorry… yeah, I want to go up there. I want to see for myself—whether you mind or not."

"Okay, have it your way. But just know, I don't approve. You'll be doing this of your own accord. Just let me know what you think about what you see. I have some paperwork of my own I need to get started on. You sure you don't want to wait until I get that warrant and then go up with me?"

"I'll give you 'til the morning, and if no warrant, I'm going up… and I am taking Janey. She has just as much right as anyone and with consent from Constance, we won't be breaking any laws."

"Fair enough. Well, let's git. I'll give you a call over at Brenner's. And Phil, I'll have the Judge call you."

They turned away and headed for the door. Merlyn turned back and said, "I'll be in touch, and keep your pecker in your pants. Don't want no women coming in here and seeing you going at it over that magazine." Merlyn chuckled, and Tom shook his head in disbelief, not looking back.

No sooner did they get the door shut, then Carter's Cadillac came racing down Main Street. Percy was at the wheel, Tabby in the back. Merlyn thought to shout for him to slow down, but Percy beat him to it by hollering, "Chief Cobb, it's Miss Janey, meet us at Doc's!" Squealing around the corner, he whipped up in front of the doctor's office.

Tom threw Merlyn a look of concern and took off running after the car. Merlyn followed, trying with some difficulty to keep up. They watched Tabby help Janey out of the backseat of the car, Percy holding the office door. The two had to drag, more than carry, Janey inside. When Tom arrived, she had already been taken into the exam room. The door was shut and Hannah had them gather in the waiting room. Doc came out of his office, and Hannah whispered something in his ear. Doc turned and said, "Be back with you folks in just a minute," and then disappeared into the exam room; Caroline following. Tom caught a glimpse of Janey stretched out on the table, her face either red from crying, or—from a beating.

Merlyn came in the door, sweating profusely and definitely winded. When his breathing returned to normal, he stood with his hands on his hips, studying everyone in the room.

"Well, Percy Snoaks, what's the story?"

"Well, Chief Cobb, it was that Sully Albright, that maniac that do work over at Brewster's slaughter house. Leese that what Janey say. Got her at the outhouse, he did. Tried to have his way with her. Hit her a couple times and tried to choke her. We know what he wanted... a sex maniac he is, that cow killing bas..."

"Percy!" Tabby said, "Now, you just calm down."

"I can't, Tabby, it's Miss Janey. Damn it! It's Miss Janey!"

"I know, I know, sugar, but you just got to calm down."

Tom felt his ire coming up. He wanted to push his way into the exam room, but he fought the urge and just paced.

"So, you say, Sully Albright? You sure?" Merlyn said.

"Damn right, Chief Cobb, I seen him run off up the mountain, and Miss Janey say so."

"Alright, I best get out there and see if I can find him."

He walked to the front desk and picked up the phone without asking. Hannah started to react to that, but then changed her mind. "Helen, Chief Cobb here, get me hooked up to my office, I want Nealy."

Doc came out, closing the door behind him. "Well, folks we're going to keep Janey overnight for observation. I don't think we'll have to send her up to Aylesbury, but we'll see."

"When can I see her," Tom asked.

"As soon as we get her situated in the back. She's still pretty upset. Thinks she may have passed out. Percy, where's Constance?"

"Still up at the house, shall I bring her."

"No, you just head back and let her know she can see her daughter later this afternoon... or tomorrow morning. Tom, she's been asking for you. So, why don't you stay. Okay, Percy, Tabby, thanks for getting her here. Bring some of her clothes back when you bring Constance, okay?"

"Okay, Doc, but..."

"Come now, Percy, we done here. Let's head on back to the house and tell the Missus."

"Okay, but I don't think…'

"Don't matter what you do or don't think, you helped Miss Janey, and now it's time to go," she said, taking Percy's arm. "Thank you, Doc, we'll see you tomorrow," Tabby said, smiling through her worry.

Tabby hurried Percy to the door. Merlyn hung up the phone and said, "Alright, I guess we're heading out to look for Sully. I'm going over to get Massy and see if that bast… see if Sully's sulking about over there at the slaughter house. Tom, you want to come and help search? We can get you a horse. I know you can ride, so…"

"No, maybe later Chief, I want to see Janey first."

"Okay, then. I'll get Charley and a few others. We form a right good posse—most of the time. Anywho, I'll be back. Got to take a statement from Janey."

With that, he went out. Doc returned to the exam room and before he opened the door to go in, he said, "Have a seat, Tom, going to be a few minutes."

"Okay, Doc, I'll be right here," Tom said, sitting down in a chair against the far wall. Eventually the door to the exam room opened and Tom heard Caroline talking to Janey. Jumping up, he ran over to the admissions desk where he was stopped by Hannah, who said, "It'll be about fifteen minutes, Mr. Lynn. Please, give us that."

"Okay," Tom said, peering around her, trying to get Janey's attention. Caroline had Janey up, out the door, and on her way down the corridor to the back

"Is she going to be alright? Did he… did that son of a bitch, you know, did he, uh… get her?"

"Doc will talk to you in fifteen minutes, you just go have yourself a seat, now. I know you're worried, but give us a little time, Mister Lynn."

Tom moved back to his chair; his level of agitation high. It was longer than fifteen minutes. People came in for their appointments. Tilly Fleming, Ellie's little sister came in for a wasp sting that had her arm swelling. Ross Bailey came in because his hammer had found his thumb while working on a back door for the bakery. Cal Loeffler dashed in with a bloody handkerchief wrapped around a thumb that needed stitches. When Doc finished with them, Tom had stopped steaming and just sat, drained. Doc disappeared into the back and then Caroline came up and said, "You can see her now, Tom. She's asking for you."

Doc reappeared and said, "Caroline, you go on home and take a nap, you'll be here overnight tonight."

Tom saw Caroline smile and hurrying to the closet behind the desk, she took off her nurse's hat and tossed it inside. Grabbing a clutch purse and a magazine off a shelf, she walked past Hannah and said, "Boots' got butter brickle! I'm going to have some with my French toast."

"Back at ten, young lady. Set an alarm," Hannah said.

"See you then," she called as the door closed behind her.

Doc led Tom to the very last room at the end of the back hallway, the only one with a window. They had it shut at the bottom, but the sash was pulled down from the top to let in a cooling breeze. Doc had installed steel screens to keep the mosquitos and horseflies out. "We'll be the only ones drawing blood back there!" he had quipped.

The curtains blew and the rotary fan in the corner oscillated with its repetitive noise. Tom came around one of the many partitions that divided the rooms and seeing Janey, he couldn't help but gasp. The red he saw earlier on her face was the results of a slap, a clear hand print on Janey's left cheek. She reached for him with bandaged hands and he moved into her embrace. Janey began to cry and Tom fought to keep from doing the same.

"I'll leave you two for now," Doc said and returned to the front.

3

Janey needed a minute to compose herself and dry her eyes. There was a noise outside the window and Tom went there to investigate, taking advantage of the moment to wipe his own. Looking out on the village's maintenance building next door, he saw Pennington Parker, the maintenance chief, giving young Ernie Cooper an earful. The boy's head was hanging as he leaned on his rolling trash barrel with its bicycle sized wheels and two different brooms protruding up from the attached rack.

"You alright, Tom?" Janey asked, her voice raspy.

"That's what I should be asking you," he said and came back to sit on the edge of her bed.

"Oh, I'm a little beat up, but that's Sully for you. Never thought he'd go this far. That's why we could never have a thing. The dumb ass had such poor control of his impulses. We were classmates in school, you know?"

"Uh, yeah. So, I'm sorry, but I have to ask… Janey, did he get what he came for?"

"Why? You thinking I'm soiled now, and you're going to have to leave me? Maybe take up with Caroline?" she said and laughed.

"No, no, I…"

"I'm just joshing you, Tom. So, why? If he did, are you going to kill him?"

"Well…" he said and getting up to peer around the partition to be sure no one had come in, he turned back to her, his hands in his pockets.

"If I have to."

His eyes met Janey's and for a few seconds they remained locked. In a tone, lower than Tom's and hardly discernible, she said, "I still might, if I catch him in the right place at the right time."

Tom just smiled and Janey took a drink of water from the glass on the nightstand.

"So, tell me what went down, how'd you get him to let go?"

"Just like the creeps at Bournemouth, a knee to the gonads. He dropped like a rock and fell out the door. Percy was in the backyard and saw us over the fence. He gave a shout, and I heard Sully run off behind the outhouse into the trees. He'd nearly got my dressing gown ripped off of me and all I could think was, I am going to get fucked, whether I like it or not… oops, sorry! And right there on that toilet seat."

"That's what I was afraid of happening."

"So, anyway," Janey said, "I want to talk about something else. I was with Cora last night. Something more terrible than this business with Sully has happened. Bessie LaVern died last night out behind Chastity Matthew's place. The circumstances were, uh… unusual."

"You sure you want to talk about that, right now? Don't you think you should rest?"

"No, I don't," Janey said, nearly losing her voice completely. She glared and Tom gave her a submissive expression.

"Okay, so, listen up me bucko because I can't say it twice. We have to go up to Carter House and meet this woman. Cora told me all kinds of things that I'm having a hard time believing. All this about the dark fairies, the Winter Queen, and the Unseelie Court."

"The Unseelie Court? Here in Massachusetts? I mean, I know about the Unseelie Court. I studied it a bit over in Amherst. But that fairy tale is one from…"

"Scotland?"

"Ummm… yes."

"Where is Cora from?"

"If I remember correctly… Scotland?"

"Yes, and where did my father meet his not so blushing, gold-digging bride?"

"The same place?"

"Yes, and so, you may have heard that Mabel may not be who she appears to be?"

"Okay, yes, so, who is she? Chief Cobb said she told him and Shannon to call her Mab. So, is that who Cora thinks she may be?"

"Yes. So, anyway, did you talk to shyster Shannon?"

"We were just leaving his place when we saw the Cadillac come by."

"So, what did you learn?"

"Carter House is in shambles and your father, is… uh, missing."

"Oh, well, that is something, but I'm not surprised. He had it coming, but all the more reason for us to intervene. So… Mab, this Winter Queen. A bitter temptress presiding over the solitary fairies and the Unseelie Court."

Tom sat with his mouth gaping, his brain obviously in turmoil. Not knowing what else to say, he said, "And you believed all that? Cora's an alcoholic, Janey. Do you think we can trust her?"

"I felt like I could, she was convincing. She told me a girl by the name of Lissy Potter, from over Grunewyck, had a banshee experience down in the ravine below Nixie's Bluff, and may have seen a… uh… oh yeah, a Grindylow in the Hollow, and definitely, a fairy circle."

"All that? Little girls like to tell tall tales, as you may know," Tom said, raising his eyebrows.

"Yes, like I haven't heard that all my life," Janey grumbled.

"Sorry."

"Lissy's father died that very night on the street in front of their store."

"Oh... uh... So, that's how the myth goes if I remember correctly. The washer woman at the ford, washing the shirt stained with blood."

"Uh-huh, and now all these people are missing or dead. Bessie was my convincing moment. Honestly, Tom, I don't know what else to think."

"Who's missing?"

"Oh, you haven't heard? Gregory Bly, Vern Sweeny, Sally Combs..."

"Sally?"

"Yes, Sally... now let me finish. My father... Oh! Molly Sharp and Sadie Mills over in Grunewyck."

"Where'd they all go, and in such a short time? I mean... okay, don't answer that."

"That's right, Tom, use that educated brain of yours. What does the Unseelie Court do?"

"Kidnaps folks on the road to replenish their ranks?"

"That's right, and who calls them to rise and fly?"

"Uh... Mab?"

"Very good, you get a gold star from the teacher, but since I don't have any with me, you get a kiss instead."

Tom leaned over and they indulged in a slow passionate kiss, then pulling back he said, "So, what are we going to do about this if it's true? What can we do against magic? This hocus-pocus?"

"Think about it. What do fairies detest the most, besides getting interrupted in their fairy business, anyway? That one thing?"

"If I remember correctly, it's iron."

"Yes, so we need to get some. I have this," she said and pulled her necklace out of her gown. "I have had it since I was a little girl, belonged to my grandmother. Nineteenth century. Made of iron, enameled white with a gem stone in the center."

Tom reached out and touched it. "Sure is an ugly thing."

"Yes, but it's the real McCoy. Cora told me all about what her folks did back in Scotland when she was a kid. I guess it's not hard to believe when you're raised in that kind of culture, huh?"

"Okay, so I should start collecting things made of iron to take with us when we go up to the house."

"We need chain, short lengths that we can handle easily. Cora said it will ground the magic, or something like that. Then, they can be killed."

"Killed?"

"Yes, what did you think? That we're going to have them all down to Headmost for dinner? I can assure you, Tom, it won't be like killing a human being. But I want you to go down and talk with Cora, maybe have her come up. She'll fill you in. That woman has a plan."

"When?"

"Tonight, or… now!"

"But I wanted to…"

"No, I may be in here one more day, Doc said. I want to be ready when I'm done with this place. My mother has a gun. I want to have it with me… just in case."

"A gun?"

"Yes, a derringer, forty-one caliber, if I remember correctly."

"You think that's going to help?"

"You never know, best to be prepared."

They heard the front door open and a familiar voice called out, "Where's my girl! Where's my Janey."

Their eyes met and together said, "Constance." Tom moved to the chair by the window. They heard Hannah talking low and then the shuffling sound moving down the hallway to Janey's room with the familiar tapping of Constance Carter's fancy cane on the floor.

"Your mother has arrived," Hannah said loudly from down the hall.

Janey rolled her eyes. "Now's a good time to go see Cora. Come back later tonight. I suspect mother will be gone by then."

"Okay," Tom said and quickly moving to the bed, they kissed. "See you later," he said, winked, and turning he almost ran into Constance coming around the divider. "Constance, how are you?" he said, moving out of her way.

"How am I? How am I? How do you think I am? My only child is attacked on my property by a cow killing ruffian, and you want to know how I am?"

"A cow killing ruffian that got a knee to the gonads!" Janey sang out, her voice cracking at the end.

"Janey! Now's not the time for such humor," Constance said, scowling.

"Oh, mother! We need to laugh about it or we'll all go crazy."

Tom departed the office without another word, grinning to himself. Percy was out front, wiping down the Cadillac, obviously trying to expend his pent-up energy.

"Need yourself a ride, Mister Lynn?"

"Oh, no thanks, Percy, I can walk. And... it's Tom."

"Okay, Mister Tom."

"Did you bring Janey clean clothes?"

"Oh, no, sorry Mister Tom. Missus Constance was hurrying me so, I done forgot."

"Thank you, anyway, Percy. See you later."

Tom walked to Main Street, his stomach rumbling. He realized how hungry he was. He would eat first before going down to see Cora, maybe take a nap. She still didn't know of the attack on Janey, and as soon as he told her, she would want to see her new friend immediately. He couldn't wait to get some food and the thought of that steak sandwich nearly put wings to his feet.

ң

Duncan Sweeny snuck downstairs into the basement prep room, the smell of formaldehyde heavy in the air. He was used to it. He often complained that it was permanently imbedded in his mucus membranes and could smell it even when not home. Louis was upstairs on the second floor, loudly arguing with Prudence about her drinking, but it was really about his missing twin brother. They would be at it for a while, so there was still time for him to get another look before his father came down or the soon expected county coroner showed up.

The tall, white curtained divider, used to conceal any corpse that lay on the table, was still in place. It hid the prep tables and the door that led up a short set of steps to the backyard where they brought the bodies in. The divider would keep him from being seen by anyone entering the room from the front. He could have Bessie dressed before they came in.

He was no longer allowed to be in the room when they cut the clothing off the female corpses. Louis had counted on Vern to take over

224

the business after he passed. He didn't trust Duncan other than to clean up, start the incinerator, burn dead folk's clothes, drive the truck, and dig graves.

One time Duncan had talked Vern into switching roles, hoping his father wouldn't notice the difference. Louis had been working on Carla Buck, an eighteen-year-old farmer's daughter from outside the village. She had fallen to her death from the hayloft in the Buck's barn and broken her neck. So, she looked like she was just lying there asleep on Louis Sweeny's table.

Duncan, acting as Vern, was assisting his father who was cutting off Carla's clothes. She was left to lay naked on the cold enamel surface for a long time. Duncan had become aroused and couldn't hide the bulge at his crotch. His father had turned to ask for something and noticed. Discovering that it wasn't Vern at his side, he slapped Duncan silly. Calling Vern down, the other brother admitted the truth and took the blame. There had been a terrible shouting match while the poor girl lay in her birthday suit, her pale blue eyes wide open but not seeing the spectacle unfolding before her.

Duncan stopped outside the curtain and listened. Louis and Prudence were still going at it, his father growing louder by the minute. He backed around the end of the divider in order to keep his eyes on the stairway door. When he felt the coast was clear, he turned and two things happened. He got an unexpected rush of adrenaline and his mouth dropped open to emit an involuntary groan.

The table was empty.

Bessie was nowhere to be seen. The sheet still draped the table, but her blood caked camisole lay on the floor. Her tap panties lay closer to the exit at the back. The door hung open. Duncan began to tremble. The girl had looked so alive when they brought her in, but not so much that they expected she could just get up and walk away. Duncan ran.

Coming up the stairs, he rushed down the central hallway toward the front door. Doctor Nelson had just turned the doorknob to come in, sending Duncan into the tiny room under the main stairwell. He quietly shut the door and burrowed into the piles of sheets they stored there. Covering his head, he shuddered violently, and found he couldn't control the tears that leaked from his eyes.

225

5

Tom arrived at Chastity's close to sunset, his nap having gone a little long. The cloudy day had grown considerably darker, leaving him to believe a storm might be in the making. Walking across the cottage's front lawn, he caught the silhouette of Cora passing a window. Moving up on the porch, he knocked and waited. Cora came, peered through the ragged curtain that covered the small window in the door and seeing it was him, she grinned and opened up.

"Tom! What a surprise! Didn't expect you to come calling. Come on in."

"Thanks. Janey sent me down. Said we should talk."

"Aye, I can just bet what about. You heard about Bessie, right?"

"Yes, I suppose that would be a good place to start. Chief Cobb has, in a roundabout way, okayed an expedition up to Carter House."

"Speaking of Carters, where's our Janey? Thought she'd be with you."

"Well, that's the bad news, ummm..."

Cora's eyes went wide, her mouth formed a small 'O' and then puckered.

"Oh, don't tell me, was it..."

"No, no, seems Sully Albright wasn't too happy about seeing her with me and tried to have his way with her. Attacked her at the outhouse up at Headmost. We suspect his goal was rape, but all he got for his trouble was a knee to the jewels."

"So, where's Janey now?"

"She's up in Doc's rooms. She got slapped around a bit and Sully nearly choked the life out of her, but... well, Doc wants her there for a day or two."

"Of course, he does. A nice little venture he's got going. We should go see her; I've had enough of this packing."

"Janey would like for us to come late. Her mother, Constance, was up there. Thought it might be best to remain clear until mama's gone home."

"Aye, okay, would you like some tea? I've got the kettle on."

"Thank you, yes. Janey wants you to tell me what you told her about this Mab, and I'm supposed to tell you what I know. Unfortunately, your

226

knowledge is through experience, mine… is all book learning."

"I'm sure we can put our heads together on this and come up with some kind of an answer. Have a seat, I'll get the tea."

Tom noticed that Cora now wore an old, dark colored motif style necklace, and when her right hand wasn't lightly rubbing her chest, her fingers were resting on the necklace. He waited while she puttered around the kitchen, and when she returned with two cups and handed him one, he said, "Interesting necklace, looks old."

"Aye, tis, belonged to my grandmother. Chastity inherited it from her. I just now found it. So, I suppose you know the purpose of iron in our situation?"

"If I remember correctly, fairies detest the stuff. Burns them and grounds their magic, correct?"

"Aye, that's the best way to put it."

"Cora, if it weren't for my experience as a kid up on Parson's Ridge, I'd have a tough time believing all this."

"Of course, it's not science. There is nothing to support it. Not an everyday occurrence here in America and not really a part of the culture. What do we know of it? The things our ancestors brought from the old country… Scotland, Ireland, England? Here in America, it's the Indian myths and legends. Something my brother was just bonkers about. You know? The Wendigo, and the… oh what was it, oh! The Skin Walker. The Navajo's Coyote. Ask anybody here about fairies and they'll laugh and probably bring up wee winged sprites flitting about the garden, or that Tinker Bell from that J. M. Barrie fella's play… and book. Aye, I read it once. I want to level with you now, Tom. I grew up in the fairy culture, my experience is not the same as yours. What's happening is not something… from here, but it's a good place for Mab to start when it comes to nonbelievers. We were just the unlucky ones who hit the jackpot when Benjamin Carter hooked up and brought her back to Gowan. I am sure she tricked him, cast some spell over him. He was the perfect candidate. He has money, property, and influence. I believe it was a fresh start for a goddess whose fire was smoldering. No one believes anymore, not now, not in the twentieth century. This is the perfect situation for her. Now, I hear she is telling people to call her by her real name. Merlyn Cobb and Philip Shannon being two of them.

Well, Mab was the Queen of Air and Darkness, a bitter bitch, the Winter Queen, and ruler of the dark fae—the dangerous ones, and… the Unseelie Court."

"Yes, Janey mentioned that. A cloud of um… boggarts, flying around at night, attacking travelers on lonely roads. I touched on that in Amherst, but no more than a week's worth, so to speak. And now you're saying they might be here and that this Mabel, uh… Mab, brought them?"

"Aye, conjured them, more like it. Once the ball gets rolling and they increase their ranks, all she has to do is sit back and watch it happen while sporting a wicked smile. People are coming up missing, Tom. Gregory Bly for one. Stopped showing up for his evening meal, was absent from his students and the Collie. He was tutoring daily over in Grunewyck. Saw him twice every weekday, going to and from. The grapevine says he's nowhere to be seen. His cottage across the street is empty. No lights on, no comings and goings."

"Well, maybe he just wanted to get away? I heard his mother died about a year ago and that he got a little weird afterward."

"Of course, who doesn't. Grief is like that, and those two were pretty close. But other than moping about and bending people's ears, he kept working, kept teaching. Tried for that teacher's job here in Gowan, but Maddie doesn't like him. She probably stood in his way. Now with the talk of this reservoir, there is no promise in it. No promise in anything in the Spry River Valley, for that matter."

"Okay, so… give me something besides Gregory Bly. Convince me. What about my uncle? Do you suppose that's what drove him to run? Then there's Bessie? What about Bessie?"

"What about Bessie? Okay, do you need to hear that Janey and I dragged her scantily clad body out of the trees out back to lay her out on the kitchen floor, her throat torn open and nary a drop of blood coursing through her? Do you need to hear how Janey and I stood right there and watched that open wound heal as if by magic? And the girl never looking like she was actually dead. That's right, Tom. Janey and I cooked up a story for Merlyn Cobb and Doc Bolen. He'd have us over in that holding cell if we told him what had actually happened. Probably charge us with murdering the poor girl."

Tom said, "Janey never said anything," then looking up at the ceiling, he pressed an index finger to his lips.

"That's why she sent you down here. Unless ol' Beulah's standing outside the window, listening, I suspect it will stay between us."

"Yes, certainly. So... what do we do, now?"

"We are going to have to go up to Carter House and pay this Mab a visit. We should simply act curious, ummm... inquisitive I think is the word, aye? Just family members concerned about Benjamín. If we come off threatening, we all become a target, you, me, Janey... It's better Mab has her sights set on all of humankind rather than just the three of us."

The room had grown quite dark and Cora lit a nearby lamp. "Think it's going to storm? Been a long time since it's gotten this dark this early on a summer evening. I still remember that hurricane that hit New Bedford back in '04. Rained like the dickens here, thought it would never end. Anyway, hold on a second, I'll be right back."

Cora got up, stumbled, then bent her stooped frame straight. "Damn, getting stiff in my old age," she said. Tom watched her massage her left arm, then picking up the lantern, she moved into the bedroom. She was gone less than a minute and came out carrying a time worn bracelet. "Here, take this and put it on, no argument."

"What is it?"

"It's a bracelet, Chastity's. You might need it."

"It's for a girl, Cora."

"Don't be ridiculous, Tom, put it on."

"Is it iron?"

"Yes, of course, and you know why you're going to have to push your manliness aside and wear it, right?"

"I do, now," Tom said and took the bracelet from Cora's outstretched hand. It was heavy and etched with spirals. Slipping it on, he hid it beneath the cuff of his shirt sleeve.

"It may get rusty and leave a mark on your wrist, but that's better than the alternative."

"I hear you," he said and grinned up at her. "So, what do you think the outcome should be to this whole affair? Should we have Chief Cobb arrest them? Tar and feather the lot of them and run them out of town, or... are we going to have to commit murder?"

"It won't be murder, like I said, they're not human. Her so called, 'ladies in waiting' are there to protect her. Probably animals transformed into human-like creatures. And just like that Dracula story, she can take control of unprotected humans to have them do her bidding. Namely, that Renfield character, Dracula's underling."

"What? You're kidding?"

"Naw, I'm not. Mab can knight a human to become her Winter Knight. Someone noble enough to defend her. A human who wouldn't be susceptible to iron the way she is. He would have to be put down just like any other human. We may not be able to get to her, though… kill her, I mean. Sadly, we can only banish her, send her somewhere else to start over with someone else. That shouldn't stop us from trying. So, we need to stick with iron. Bind them with it, ground their magic, and maybe, drive an iron made knife into their guts. We can always distract them by dumping sugar or salt in their sight, as my granny used to say. They'll have to stop and count every grain. I've never done it, but that's supposed to be the trick to take the fae's attention off you so you can get some iron on them. May not work with Mab, but most certainly with her minions. Sadly, she may call others."

"Like?"

"Redcaps, Jack in Irons, or even the Baobhan Sith, the creature we think might have taken Bessie."

"Okay, so you told us about the vampire woman, but what about this… Jack in Irons?"

"You must have read about him in your studies? A large human like creature, uglier than sin, maybe a giant, fond of knocking the heads off of men so he can hang them from his belt? Known to attack folks in lonely places."

"Sounds rather horrific… that ever happen back in Scotland?"

"Well, there were cases of men found without their heads. Jack's a rarity, though, but Mab can call him, nonetheless."

"So, speaking of iron, Art the blacksmith has tons of it. He's also tried his hand at sword making. Well, least back when I was a boy, he did. Wonder if he still has the one's he made still sitting around the place."

"Swords would be good, but hard to explain to people in passing.

Knives would be better if you want to do some stabbing. You can hide them. But once you've stabbed one, don't pull the knife out. I don't know what to expect, afterwards. Don't know if they just die like human beings or disappear in a puff of smoke. That's when you can reclaim your blade for the next."

"That's just it, what if I need that knife to fight off another?"

"Well, bring two! Tom, it's all guessing. I've heard all kinds of things. Don't know if they need to be bound with it, or simply touched. We won't know until it actually happens. That's why we need to always have a piece of iron on our person. I truly think chaining them should be our goal. So, stop thinking human. Think more... fairy tale. We'll have to approach them in a tame way. Like, babes in the woods. Get close and strike quick. We'll have to be clever. Once we have them grounded and mortalized, then... burn down the house."

"Burn the house? With them inside?"

"Yes, of course. Why not?"

"I don't know, it may be hard to do. Like burning witches at the stake."

"Perhaps we could get Reverend Hale to light the match? He's commented often how he's descended from those amadants down in Salem who burned innocent women back in the sixteen hundreds."

"Do you think he could help? Maybe if we convinced him they were witches?"

"He's probably already thinking that, if he's got an ear to the grapevine, namely... Helen Blake. Good chance he already has a plan in place. We could talk to him, kind of beat around the bush about our concerns. Substitute the word, witch, for fairy?"

"Perhaps. You know him better than I do. Think you could pull it off?"

"I think it would be easy enough. More tea?"

"Some, but I want to get back up to Janey. Want to come?"

Cora had been standing all this time, rubbing her left arm as if she was in a little pain, once even grimacing as if it had become unbearable. "Yes, I want to see how she's doing. I'll get the tea."

After taking Tom's cup, she grabbed hers and retreated into the kitchen where she lit another lamp. The phone rang, startling Tom. He

231

heard Cora gasp as if it had frightened her too. He heard the click of the hanger for the earpiece and, "Hello? Oh, Al. How things going over there? Keeping up? Good. And Pearl? Aye, she's a big help. Making a wee bit of progress here. Chastity didn't have much. Got most of her clothes in some old boxes. Probably going to have to get some help. I can ask a few people here. Okay, so… yeah, maybe tomorrow, or the next day. I can get a bath here, but I need a change of clothes, starting to smell like an old lady. What's that? I am an old lady? Yeah, okay, ha-ha. Aye, see you soon... old man."

Tom heard her hang up the phone, followed by the clank of the tea cups. Cora reappeared in the door, smiled and said, "That was Al, he…" she stopped talking and stood listening.

"Did you hear that?"

"What?"

"Shush! Listen."

Tom perked his ears, not really sure what he was supposed to be listening for.

"There it is again. Out back… somebody's out there, Tom," she whispered.

Moving across the room, she handed him both cups. "Take these and stay here, act like we're still drinking tea and talking," she said under her breath. Tom noticed she was sweating profusely; a lot more than he was.

"Stay here, I want to take a peek."

Tom thought to argue, or offer to go in her place, but she was already in the kitchen, picking up the lantern. Stopping to look out the window in the door, she then opened it and stepped out. Tom leaned forward from his seat and peered around the parlor doorjamb.

Out in the backyard, fireflies filled the air. Crickets and katydids were raising a ruckus and a Whip-poor-will began to pipe. Tom talked loudly to no one, a tea cup in each hand. It was difficult to stay put, but Cora had her reasons for it, and he didn't want to intrude—yet.

6

Cora was all the way down the back steps when she realized that maybe it wasn't such a good idea after all. She stood peering around in the dark, seeing only as far as the glow of the lantern would allow. Shadows writhed, making her wonder if they actually weren't something else. Something alive. The clouds roiled overhead and she found herself waiting for the lightening and the first crack of thunder.

A memory flooded in from her girlhood back in Scotland. Her father had sent her out to retrieve a lantern that she had left behind in an outbuilding. She didn't want to go, so she argued. "Send Charlie," she had said, he was braver, and lads didn't mind. Her father said, no, it was her mistake, she had to own up to it. "Let me take a candle." He had denied her that. Her fear would be her punishment. It hadn't gone well; something had been in there that wasn't a sheep. She didn't wait around to see what it might be, and grabbing the lantern, she fled. In the morning, one of the sheep had been found dead, its throat torn out.

The little girl inside her must have believed she could conquer her fear if she faced whatever the dark held. Moving out to the middle of the tiny back yard, she held the lantern high and turned slowly in a circle, leaning forward, staring intently. She soon faced the base of the mountain and the light of the lantern picked up three pairs of glowing yellow eyes.

One of them sang her name, soft and inviting, the evening breeze presenting it to her in a seductive manner. She was drawn to it, but she remained glued to the spot where she stood, fighting the urge to submit completely. In her head, the words, "Don't go!" practically screamed at her. Then, a squeaky voice came from the shadows on her right, "Go to them, Cora, you're no brave lass so as to resist their call."

Cora started to turn toward the voice that she thought rats might sound like if they could speak. Her eyes soon took in a woman with the face of a polecat; sans fur. Her pointed ears poked through thick, black hair that hung to her waist. It grinned mischievously, showing tiny pointed teeth.

"Hail, Cora, I am NicTaghan. My queen has sent me so I may help you in ending the woes of a mortal life. The stink of death is upon you. You are closer to the veil, then you know."

The different scents of the woodlands filled Cora's nose and then a strange lassitude enveloped her body. She felt herself falling into a stupor. NicTaghan was casting a spell, a magic that would help bring

233

Cora to what she knew were the Baobhan Sith, waiting in the trees.

NicTaghan place her clawed hand on the small of Cora's back to usher her forth. The handmaiden found resistance. So, sliding her fingers up the old woman's back to her neck, she contacted the iron motif protruding from her victim's collar. Sparks flew, causing the dark of the small yard to fill with a fleeting, brilliant white light. It illuminated the fiends standing within the trees showing creatures that had once been, Molly Sharp, Bessie LaVern, and Sally Combs. All three dropped down simultaneously to morph into wolf-like creatures that sped away up the slope.

Mab's handmaiden emitted a shriek that was abruptly cut short when she transformed into a small, silver cloud that rose above Cora's head. Reversing direction, it fell to the grass as a large ball of ice to shatter upon the ground. The frozen vapor fell away to reveal a large and confused looking pine marten. Giving Cora a loud, angry hiss, it sped away into the shrubbery leaving a trail of smoke behind and the smell of singed fur.

Cora, free from her lassitude, did the very thing she had done that night in the sheep shed and fled toward the cottage. She didn't get far before a crushing pain enveloped her chest and radiated down her left arm. She wasn't aware she had dropped the lantern, or that she had barely avoided splitting her skull on a stone paver.

7

Two of Chastity's best tea cups hit the Persian rug that centered the parlor precisely at the same time that the flash of light pierced the dark behind the cottage. It took Tom three seconds to move from his seat to the back door. There, he saw the lantern laying on the lawn, still burning, and Cora, on her side, unmoving.

"Cora," he shouted and not bothering to use the steps, he leapt over the balustrade to land lightly on the grass. Running to her, he righted the lantern before rolling her onto her back. Cora's breathing was shallow and erratic. Picking up the lantern to get a closer look at her face, Tom saw something gleaming in the grass. Another gold bauble. After quickly shoving it into his pocket, he checked Cora's pulse and finding one, he picked her up like she was a child and ran for the doctor's.

CHAPTER TEN

GOWAN

III

~

1

The town of Gowan knew all about the gloaming. That magical time of day that ushered the sun to bed so it could allow in the darkness. It wasn't unusual. As infants, human beings become aware that at some point, within a twenty-four-hour period, darkness would settle on the land.

It wouldn't be until much later in their lives that they would learn about a different, but very relative, kind of darkness that settles in the heart. The type kept hidden to avoid judgement and persecution. A darkness that grows over time to become deep seated by adulthood. A condition fed by injustice, rejection, selfishness, envy, greed, hate, and prolonged suffering; the kind brought about by one's inability to cope with their own fragility.

Some of the townsfolk feared what lay in their hearts. They did everything to hide it by putting on airs in order to present a pristine image. The people closest to them felt it was a personal responsibility to defend their fellow humans by making declarations like, "But Alfie Jewel is a good man, and he takes care of his family." Yet, in the back of everybody's mind, where the truth usually goes to fester, they all knew that good ol' Alfie beat his wife and children weekly in order to keep them inline. Dahlia O'Brian fell right in there with Alfie. One of her defenders was overheard saying, "Dahlia is as kind as they come, how can you say that about that poor woman?" The thing is, nobody ever bothered to check why the high number of stray cats that she took in, to house and feed, never rose above eight. Not one villager ever witnessed the collection of tortured carcasses she collected from her basement floor and secretly dumped into the Spry River off the lower foot bridge in the wee hours of the morning.

On the other side of the fence, there were those who weren't afraid to lay their hearts bare to expose the darkness within. Folks who were necessary to the community. A small knot of people who were considered, by many, to be acceptable as the lesser of the evils. A group that contained people like, Sully Albright, who often expressed glee in driving a sledge hammer between the eyes of any sheep, pig, or steer. Then there was Nealy Garret, who would rather shoot you than argue. He had done it enough times in his career that aiming his beloved Colt .44 at a perpetrator always brought him to arousal. No one ever got close enough to see the crazy gleam in his eyes (or the bulging at his crotch) when he pulled that trigger, leaving any witness to wonder if they had actually seen, or simply imagined, the fleeting smirk on Nealy's face when the body hit the floor.

There were those who drove the darkness, town folk like Beulah McKay, Helen Blake, Audrey LaVern, Mary McCarthey, and a few others, all artisans at crafting words to spread hate, create doubt, and ignite jealousy throughout the village. A practice they believed harmless, like the use of… opium laden Laudinum for their nerves, mercury-based Calomel for the upset stomach, the occasional sampling of cocaine infused Vin Mariani wine stashed away in their cellars, or the use of their cherished lead and cadmium laden dishes inherited from their mothers.

If you weren't already thinking unkind thoughts about your neighbor, exposure to this troupe of scandalmongers would most certainly prime the pump.

Howard Dent, the banker, the second most powerful man in Gowan next to Benjamin Carter, secretly paid his clerk, Vivian Bishop, to perform certain carnal acts after he had shooed away all the other employees for the evening.

Then there was the notorious Tip Thomas, who lured sweet young things from Boston with promises of fame and fortune as Zelda's premiere act. Girls that would soon find themselves suffering Tip's sexual depravity on a daily basis before being turned over to the roadhouse clientele. His small harem of working girls, under threat of being found floating face down in Whip-poor-will Hollow, knew the consequences for not keeping their mouths shut.

Toward the other end of the scale, one could find Danny Billings, too timid to have a girlfriend, seated at a north window in the attic of the train station, utilizing his father's navy issued binoculars to spy on the judge's daughter, April. Nine o' clock never failed to bring the girl to her bedroom to cavort about in various stages of undress, curtains left wide open, as if she longed for her adolescent form to be adored by any set of prying eyes.

Philip Shannon's nefarious activity wasn't just limited to Gowan but stretched clear to the east coast and as high as state government. But there was never any solid evidence of his guilt and even though often ridiculed, nobody in his hometown wanted to open that can of worms. Philip was a clever man with a narcissism that left him to think he was superior to the people he served. He was secretly creating a mountain of wealth and there were very few souls in Gowan who hadn't, in some way, contributed to that.

Gowanites considered Duncan Sweeny to be too simple minded to be of any threat. However, the young widow Southwick, who had taken him as a lover, would never know that the things he did with her, he had secretly practiced on a multitude of deceased female corpses over a decade as they lay cooling on the embalming table of an inattentive father.

Yes, the town folks knew about the darkness that they perpetrated on each other. It was a shared thing, just like the darkness that the gloaming brought. What the majority of them didn't know, and were soon to find out, was that there was another kind of darkness that would soon be brought by that mystical time of day, a malevolence that had already befallen a credulous few, and like the twisted hand of the boogeyman reaching from the shadow, would soon touch them too.

2

Sam Shoats knew there was something very wrong. Things were happening that didn't make sense. On clear evenings, he used to stop and watch the sunset, often lingering into the afterglow. Yet now, he worked with urgency to complete his chores in order to return to the house and put himself behind locked doors. His recent purchase of a surplus model 1903 Springfield rifle, brought him a satisfying degree of comfort. It would do what his shotgun couldn't; reach out across that meadow with its .30-06 round to devastate all it touched.

"Try to steal my milk, now, you heathens," Sam growled, standing at the south fence, the barrel of his new rifle resting on the top rail as he adjusted the rear sight for distance. He fired off a couple of rounds, taking out a tiny tree branch here and there, making sure he could hit his intended target. Accomplishing his task and bolstering his piece of mind, he returned to his abode.

He stuck the rifle in the corner behind the backdoor, hesitated, picked it up again and pulled the bolt back until he could detect the gleam of the brass cartridge within the receiver. Yes, Sam was ready. After returning the rifle to its designated spot, he joined a somewhat impatient Aileen at the supper table.

3

Danny Billings often sat alone on the edge of the station platform after the last train had come and gone. He was waiting for nine o clock to roll around and the lighting of a certain upstairs window at the Judge's house. Until then, he would sit and enjoy the gloaming that brought the nearby woods alive with a nightly chorus of owl, fox, coyote, and Whip-poor-will.

One past evening, a wolf had howled from atop Mount Ovis directly above where the steel rails curved around its base. He had risen to his feet to listen. Danny had heard that Massachusetts' no longer had wolves and wondered if he had made a great find. The air continued to darken as he paced back and forth along the wooden platform trying to catch a glimpse. Then someone called his name, or more like—sang it. It had been so subtle he feared he was just hearing things. But it persisted, growing louder and louder by the minute. It sounded as if it came from the trees, but any attempt to spot the source was thwarted by the shadows. Part of him wanted to jump off the platform and go over there, but another part said, "Don't you dare!" Being a young man of reason, Danny backed his way to the door, his excitement now turning to fear. Entering the ticket booth from the inside, he stood watching, now protected by glass and wood. Things didn't feel right, and he was damned if he was going to go out into those trees to discover the source of that song.

4

One of Percy Snoaks's responsibilities was to light the chandelier in the cupola at Headmost House. He was getting old and sometimes didn't remember. The lady of the manor never checked, though, and Janey didn't care. If she wanted it lit, she would do it herself. She never questioned Percy. The lamp lighting was also the time he set aside to slip out onto the roof and watch the sun go to bed for the night. He would often gaze at Carter House in the distance, reminiscing about the old days. As of late, there had been a nightly reoccurrence of a dark cloud rising from the Hollow in the area of Ghillie's Gate. It resembled a flock of birds, insects, or—something worse. Spiraling up into the night sky it would soon disappear into the indigo void. For some reason, it struck fear in his heart. Something wicked had taken root in Gowan, and Percy Snoaks believed they were all going to be made to suffer for the sins of Benjamin Carter.

5

Nealy Garret craved the night; it was his time to prowl, a given opportunity to hunt and apprehend his prey. He enjoyed the snicker of the tightening handcuffs and forcing his victim into the back of the car. Nealy wanted to be the man to take over when Merlyn Cobb retired. He had quietly commented to those he knew, who didn't like Merlyn, that no person who sported that amount of weight would ever live to retirement age.

Sully Albright, the cow killer of Gowan, had escaped into the trees behind Headmost House. Nealy knew this, and without thinking too hard on the matter, had a damn good idea where Sully would go.

Ten minutes after Merlyn left the office to return home for a quick bite before going out to gather men to hunt for Sully, the phone rang at the police office. It was an annoyed Merlyn. He had just sat down for his supper when Tip Thomas called. Sully Albright had just stumbled through the door, clutching his crotch, and swearing up a storm.

Nealy entered Zelda's; gun drawn. It wasn't quite the busy time, but when the present clientele saw the large, .44 Colt, pointed at Sully's back, they parted like butter to a hot knife.

"Sully Albright, you're under arrest," the officer shouted. The revolver held six rounds, but Sully knew full well it would take only one of them to blow his arm clean off, and Nealy looked nervous. Sully didn't resist. Nealy escorted him out to the car in cuffs, the officer scowling as if dismayed over Sully not trying to escape, or better yet, attack him.

Nealy booked Sully just like he did the nightly drunks. Merlyn stopped in and stood watching. Once Sully was behind bars and the cell locked, the Chief walked over and glared. Sully couldn't hold his stare and cast his eyes to the floor. "That was a stupid thing you did, Mr. Albright. Of all people, Janey Carter? You're going to serve time for this. Probably over in Springfield."

"Innocent until proven guilty," Sully muttered.

"Yeah, since when?" Merlyn said and laughed. "Maybe I should accidently-on-purpose unlock that door. You'll escape and somebody will have to shoot you."

Sully looked past Merlyn to Nealy, who leaned against the wall behind the desk, his right hand caressing the wooden grips of his revolver, a wicked grin plastered on his face.

"Keep a close eye on him, hey, Nealy? I'm going back home."

"About time for patrol, Chief. Am I going to have to sit here all night?"

Merlyn squinted an eye at Nealy and pulled up his dungarees, only to have them slip back down.

"No, you just do what you always do, just don't make any unnecessary arrests until we get this shit heel out of here. You called the sheriff, right?"

"I'll do that this minute," Nealy said and hurriedly sat down at the desk, clicking the receiver to call up Helen.

"Fat ass," Sully mumbled as Merlyn closed the office door. Nealy cast him a malicious glance and pulling his Colt, he lay it on the desk, the muzzle pointed toward his prisoner.

6

Roy LaVern lay in his bed, staring at the ceiling. In the summer months the gloaming was bedtime for him and his wife, Audrey, who now lay beside him, all cried-out, enough so she could finally fall asleep. Taking to his bed after a long day at work and a good supper in his belly was always something to look forward to. But not this night.

He was able to comfort his wife in her grief, but not himself. Inwardly, he was boiling. His only daughter, dead at eighteen. Bessie had a promising future—just not in Gowan. Then she got mixed up with that Sally Combs and it all changed. So much for Paris and the girls dream to become a fashion designer. The Depression had an effect on the factory, but as a manager, he would be the last to go. They had to cut the work force by a third. He had been charged with the task of telling the workers. If they had to lose any more employees, the factory would have to close. He actually worked for Benjamin Carter, now. And before him, Bartholomew. He thought when Bartholomew died, he would lose his job. But Benjamin had kept him on and in an interview after the loss of his brother, the elder Carter praised Roy and told him to keep up the good work. When the layoffs came, he still feared for his job and it left him mean tempered. Roosevelts New Deal had helped—somewhat. But that wasn't going to change what was coming and not even the Carter's could stop the state from building their reservoir.

Rumor had it, the workers who lost their jobs were signing up to become Woodpeckers for the demolition companies. He and Audrey had been planning for Bessie's future, and his position at the basket factory had allowed them to save. Then Merlyn Cobb showed up at their door. Bessie was dead. That was followed by Louis Sweeny calling to report that the body had been misplaced. Funeral services had to be postponed. How do you misplace a body? Roy was on the verge of exploding.

Getting out of the bed, he paced the room. Looking out a window he could see Headmost House. The light in the cupola was lit and there was only a dim glow at the parlor window. Moving to the front of the bedroom, Roy looked out on the town. He could see Sally's shop. It was her fault.

He had heard all the rumors and he believed them. Sally was some kind of a devil. Bessie had only been allowed to work there because she had begged and pleaded. It would be a good place to start before she sailed off for Paris, she had said. Then graduation came, the last class for that old spinster Harriet Durnell. By midsummer, Bessie began to spend random nights away from home. She had used her best friend, Lyla McKenzie, from Grunewyck, as an excuse. Slumber parties, late movies at the York theater up in Athol, and other such things. However, one morning after she had supposedly been at a slumber party, she was seen having breakfast with Sally at Boots' A Walk Inn.

Roy would have most certainly passed his daughter bicycling back to Gowan that morning if she had been where she was supposed to be. There was no way he could have missed her. Audrey had worked hard to calm him down, saying, "You have no proof, Roy. Don't go off halfcocked 'til you do." Now his daughter's dead body was hanging in limbo somewhere, probably stolen by graverobbers right out of the mortuary. They hadn't even been able to say their goodbyes.

Removing his next day's trousers and shirt from the clothes butler in the corner, he dressed as soundlessly as possible. Quietly closing the bedroom door on the way out, he padded down the narrow stairs. Finding his boots, he pulled them on and then fumbling around in the top drawer of the entry hall sideboard, he pulled out his army issued S&W revolver from his service days in World War One. He was going down to the dress shop, wake that woman, and give her a piece of his mind.

7

Tom looked in on Janey at the hospital. She was asleep, so he woke her with a gentle touch on her shoulder. Rubbing her eyes she appeared to not recognize him. Then it sunk in and they embraced, kissing. Tom pulled back, to stand and just gaze at her. The marks on her throat and the small cut on her cheek brought an inner fury. He felt the tears welling, so he turned away and went to sit in the chair.

Janey remained sitting up and said with a smile, "So... you're a sight for sore eyes—literally—sore eyes." Then touching her split lip, she winced. It triggered Tom to start imagining all the things he was going to do to Sully.

"Just so you know, Sully was arrested. Nealy caught him at Zelda's having a beer."

"It's just all so surreal. He and I used to be friends and classmates; we ran around together for years."

"Yeah, I remember."

"Now this. Before he started to choke me, he did mention how you weren't there to protect me. He tried to rip off my dressing gown and open his fly at the same time. I suppose he thought I was going to just stand there and take it. He must have forgotten who I was. Back in the day, we'd trade blow for blow in arguments, with him always being the first to hit, usually trying to punch me in the stomach. But... I was the one to always finish them. I should have taken it as a sign that our relationship was not a good one and that I'd best steer clear. Oh well."

"Yeah, so he's over in the holding cell waiting for the sheriff's man to come around and collect him. I was thinking about going over there and taking a look at him, and... maybe taunting him through the bars."

"Yes, and then you'd be in there with him. You know Nealy doesn't like you, right?"

"Yeah, I know. I can dream, though, can't I?"

"You can... and you do," she said and chuckled. "So, did you go down and talk with Cora?"

"I did, but... are you ready for something that might make it all worse?

"Oh, no, Tom! What now?"

"Cora is just down the hall in room one."

"No! What happened?"

"Doc thinks heart attack. She's sleeping right now. He says it was a mild one. But that most certainly opens the door for the next—which may not be so."

"Oh my," Janey said as tears rolled down her cheeks. She put her face in her hands and Tom got up from his chair and walked over, sat, and draped an arm over her shoulders. She leaned her head against his chest. After a minute, she wiped her eyes, and blinking up at him, she asked, "So, you were there, right? When it happened?"

"Yes, but it's a strange story. Cora went out back because she heard a noise. She asked me to stay put. I didn't want too because my gut said go with her. But I also wanted to accommodate. It was a bad decision."

"Did she call out to you when it happened? How'd you know?"

"The strangest thing… there was a flash of light, a lot like a flashbulb on a camera. I couldn't stay put any longer and ran out there. I picked her up and carried her all the way here on the run. I think it's the hardest thing I've ever done."

"And, the noblest. That's quite a jaunt." Janey took his hand and squeezed it, looking admirably up into his face.

"Oh, and I found this." Taking the bauble from his pocket, he rolled it around in his fingertips in front of her face. It was warm to the touch; almost hot.

"Oh, no, it's just like the other one, except the symbol is different. You don't suppose…"

"I do suppose, one of Mab's vassals was out there, or… all of them."

Janey got a chill and looked toward the small window. "Close that curtain, huh, Tom. I can't bear that they might be outside right now."

"I don't think they are."

"Well… I think they can very well be. So, please?"

"Whatever you wish."

Janey took the bauble to study it while Tom pulled the curtain, then laid it on her nightstand and said, "So, they came for her. Why? How do they know her?"

"I think that moment you two had with Bessie triggered their interest. The fair folk don't like humans meddling in their affairs."

"So, did you see them?"

"No, it was just Cora out there. I didn't waste anytime looking. I just picked her up and ran. No time to think," Tom said and shrugged.

"Why didn't they take her, or… whatever they do?"

"Purely speculation on my part, but I think one of them touched Cora's necklace. Some kind of… what do they call it…? Oh… motif necklace, I think. Made of thin, sculpted iron. A thing left over from the Victorian Era. There was still a whiff of rather rancid smoke in the air and the necklace itself had a singed mark on it where the metal had bubbled for a second."

"So, Cora took her own advice. Good for her. And the smell? I mean, what did it smell like?"

"Burnt hair," Tom said, crinkling up his nose in disgust.

"So, they did try to take her?"

"Yeah, and got a hell of a surprise. You'd think they would have detected it right off."

"You'd think. Cora said, as children, they used to sleep in beds with iron frames so they wouldn't be taken. You know, the whole Changeling thing? You'd think they could sense it, but maybe its presence also deprives them of that."

Tom picked up the bauble and put it back in his jacket pocket before returning to his seat on the bed.

"What are you going to do with it?"

"I don't know, but right now it's a little too warm for my trouser pocket. So, I'll keep it in my jacket where there's a couple layers of insulation. Hey, you suppose Mab's handmaiden burnt up when she touched the iron, and then dropped it?"

"Perhaps, certainly would be in our favor if she had. I'm sure Cora could tell us more when she wakes up. So, Mab may be down to just two of them, now? Probably even more angry with us than before. Cora said they were probably conjured from animals. I wonder how long it takes to make a human sized creature from a field mouse?"

"I don't know, but if it takes a long time to cultivate a new one, that's in our favor, too. She still controls all the solitary fairies, regardless how many minions she has. It's just she loses the intimacy of having ladies-in-waiting. If she lost them all, she would be alone up there. Grindylow and banshees, don't make for great bed fellows."

"So, we could hurt her if we eliminate her handmaidens? There would be no one to do her bidding. No one to protect her," Janey said, her face growing thoughtful.

"That's what Cora said, but also, Mab can knight a human to become her, uh… Winter Knight? I think that's what she said. Someone honorable."

"So, somebody who could, uh… be killed by normal methods. So, like that Renfield."

"That's what Cora said. Except, maybe more powerful and like I said, honorable. Renfield was kind of a pantywaist, if I remember correctly."

"Weak, but deceitfully clever."

"Something else… I think we have to keep in mind every minute. We are in more danger now than ever before. I don't mean Gowan, I mean, you, me, and anyone close to us."

"So, my mother? Tabby? Percy?"

"Yes, I suspect she has already eliminated Ben, and Uncle Kaleb is dead."

"So, I need to warn mother. I need to call the house and have them leave Gowan. Percy can drive them in the Cadillac. They can go to the house in Salem, and…"

"And that may not be far enough. Nowhere, may be far enough."

"Then what? What can we do?"

Tom raised his hands in a shrug and said, "Plain and simple, we need to banish her. Leave nothing for her here. Send her back to Scotland."

8

Nealy returned to the office, greasy paper bag in hand, an order from Boots' that was just closing up when Nealy popped in for Sully's dinner. Steak sandwich and fried potatoes. Nealy hated playing jailer. He had been checking his watch constantly, hoping more time had passed and the sheriff's deputy would be showing up soon. Sully wouldn't talk to him, he just lay on the cot, sometimes showing his stupid grin. A look that said, 'Just give me a chance. Make some stupid mistake, and I'm out of here.'

Setting the sack on the desk, Nealy walked over to pour a cup of coffee for his inmate. Half way across the room he stopped and turned back. Sully was on the floor, face down. He looked dead.

"Sully!" he yelled. When he didn't move, Nealy walked over to stand at the bars. "Sully Albright! Wake your ass up." Still nothing. Nealy couldn't tell if he was breathing or not. He moved around to the cell door for a closer look. Sully was too still to be faking it, yet Nealy hesitated. "Sully, get off the floor and get back on your damn cot, hear me?" He picked up the bag of food and tossed it through the bars. It landed on Sully between his shoulder blades and then slid to the floor.

Nealy felt panic and he thought to call Merlyn, but how would that look? No, he had to handle this himself. He might have to go and get Doc Bolen, but that might be putting Doc in danger. Until he could determine if it was a medical emergency or not, he'd best not call.

"Sully!" he shouted again and still no answer. He'd have to go in. Taking the key ring off the hook, he unlocked the cell door. Pulling out the Colt, he walked in and stopping just short of Sully, he poked him with a toe.

The cow killer moved like lightning. Rolling over he grabbed Nealy's foot and threw it up in the air while coming to his feet. The Colt went off, the bullet disintegrating when it hit the plaster wall above the cot. Nealy fell back against the bars, still trying to point his gun at his attacker. Sully was too strong and grabbing the gun with his left hand, he sent a haymaker to Nealy's jaw. The officer's head snapped back, bounced off the bars, and he collapsed to the floor.

Sully now held the gun pointed at the officer and cocked it like he was going to shoot him. Then turning away, he uncocked it, grabbed the lunch bag, and pulled out the sandwich. Pocketing the revolver, he closed the cell door, locking Nealy inside.

"Let's see how you like it, lawman." Taking a bite of the sandwich, he expressed his approval with a, "Yum, still making a good steak sandwich, hey, Clyde?" Moving to the office door Sully opened it to peek through the crack. Seeing the coast was clear, he took the backstairs and slipping out the door at the bottom, he ran for the trees, unseen, except by a pair of dark, beady eyes watching from a nearby thicket.

9

Danny Billings had Thursday evening free; the returning train had no passengers for Gowan. So, with a long whistle, it passed on through without stopping. The engineer would make Brimfield early.

Locking his room, he left the station and was soon walking north on

Ovis Street. Ignoring April's place altogether, he took in all the other big houses of the prominent business folks of Gowan. With the talk of a reservoir, he knew all of them would be gone in a couple years. Danny had made it clear to others that it saddened him to think his town was going to be wiped off the face of the map. By the time he married (if he ever did) this place would be but a memory. His only hope was that there hadn't been an official announcement, so it was all just talk. When the news came, Cap McKendry would be sure to plaster it across the front page of the Gowan Gazette. The railroad would reroute the train on new tracks, probably somewhere to the west, above the rim of the valley. Hadley, most likely. There was a chance that he could move there and be first in line for the station agent's position at a new station. The thought thrilled him. He would have to act soon.

Danny's lifelong dream was to work the south station in Boston. Maybe serve as a conductor on any one of the big-name railroads like New York, New England, or Colony. Paul LeBarge told him, "You're just procrastinating. You should just go now and not look back. You don't have to wait until the water of the Spry River's lapping at the station door." Danny was surprised that Paul even knew the word 'procrastinating'.

He decided to cut through the open space between the doctor's office and the town maintenance shop and then walk across the lawn behind city hall. That gave him a straight shot to the cemetery. There was enough light still in the sky to visit his mother's grave. His father was still alive and living over in Bournemouth. Danny never went there; he didn't care. The old man had abandoned them shortly after giving Danny the pocket watch. His mother had been working as a maid in Otis Loeffler's house for nearly twenty years and died shortly after her husband left her.

Danny stopped to look at Loeffler's big Gothic Revival styled house sitting next door to Doc Bolen's. He wished he could still see his mother through the windows as she worked. He had never been allowed to visit her while she did. Some nights she never came home, leaving Danny to fare for himself. The Depression always had him and her worrying that the butcher shop may fail and close, leaving the Loeffler's penniless.

Isabelle Billings had passed away in that big house. Stroked out in

248

the kitchen. Danny had not been allowed to see her until she lay cold and sheet covered on the table at Sweeny's. The Loffler's had always been nice to his mother and had paid for her funeral, offering Danny a place to live because the cottage would have to go back to the bank. He was fortunate enough to have his job, so he declined and moved into the back room at the station. Danny loved living at the station but missed his mother something terrible.

Climbing over the short, rusty, cast-iron fence, he made his way to her grave. Out of the corner of his eye he thought he saw somebody moving through the trees at the base of the mountain. Just a flash of a white shirt moving north, and then, gone. Five seconds later, two large brown cocklebur covered horses broke from the tree line as if frightened by the bearer of the white shirt. He watched them run through the cottage backyards and when they got close, he hollered at them. Upon seeing Danny, they turned back toward the mountain side and disappeared once again into the trees. "Gonna have to tell Nealy about that, I guess," he muttered to himself.

Danny turned his attention back to the headstone and began to pull the weeds around its base, revealing: Isabelle Billings-Mother and Wife, 1872-1934. The marker was made of sandstone, so it was cheap. Marble or granite would have been better, but free is free. Besides, it wasn't going to stay there for long. Danny had heard that graveyards had to be dug up and the bodies transferred to another cemetery. He had asked Gil if he thought the pine box would still be in good enough shape to be moved. "I 'spect so, Danny boy. You probably get to pick where you want your ma reburied. Aylesbury be a good place. They have a right fine cemtary up there." Danny agreed.

Now, sitting back on his calves, he gazed at the headstone and said, "Hi, ma, it's Danny. Yeah, I know you know. Who else would it be, right?" The tears came. His ol' man would have beat him if he saw Danny crying. Like watching sunsets, it wasn't manly.

The breeze picked up and changed directions briefly, with it came the odor of something rank. He'd once come across a raccoon with its head caught in the crotch of a tree, an unfortunate accident for the little critter. It must have died of hunger, which means it had been there a long time before breathing its last. The smell he was smelling was a lot like that—just worse. Danny wiped his eyes and getting to his feet, he worked his way back toward the trees and the direction from which the breeze had come. The closer he came to the woods, the stronger it got. Stopping, he wondered to himself if he really wanted to see what it was. He could just turn around and head up to the café or Brenner's. Yet Danny knew he'd be wondering all night if he didn't get at least a peek.

Moving into the trees, Danny halted when the stench became unbearable. Walking in ever widening circles, he came upon an uprooted tree that had blown down in a storm. It was old and its root ball was massive. Its fall had left a crater the size of Liam McClary's wagon. Stepping around the trunk, he peeked between the roots. The smell hit him full in the face and he backed away, retching. When he recovered, he moved upwind and peeked again.

There was a dead body in there. It was caked with blood. The shirt was ripped open at the chest and the ribcage lay exposed. The throat was a mass of maggots and what had been a large flap of skin hung away like a lid left open. Clouds of flies rose and fell. Danny held his breath and tried to make out the face, but the state of decay offered no revelation. It was the shock of yellow hair that gave it away. Only Vernon and Duncan Sweeny had hair like that. Something had killed him and pushed him inside that hole. Stepping back, he vomited, then taking control of himself, he hightailed it for the police office.

When Caroline left her station to go out front, Janey got out of her bed and walked down the hall to Cora's. The old woman was partially awake, her eyes following Janey as she came in. "Cora, I heard you were here."

The old woman reached out to Janey and a tear rolled out of her left eye. Janey took her hand and held it.

"You're going to get better; I just know it."

She gave Janey a half smile and croaked out, "Aye, I'm a tough old bird."

"So true."

"Did you talk to Tom?"

"Yes, he was here. Went back to Brenner's for his supper. Coming back later."

Cora rasped out, "Did he tell you everything?"

"I believe so. So, you had a heart attack, I hear?"

"Oh… it's been coming for a long time. Kind of stupid of me to ignore it."

"Well, maybe you can tell me later. I probably should leave you to your rest."

"No, I want you here. No telling what tomorrow will bring."

"Tom said he found you out back of Chastity's and carried you here on the run."

"Such a sweet man, don't let him go, Janey Carter. Aye, like a fool I went out back in the dark, by myself, no less. Made him wait in the parlor, talking out loud to no one. Wanted to keep them thinking I was still in there. The Baobhan Sith were waiting for me in the trees, then…" Cora stopped gasped and gave a shuddering breath as she exhaled.

"Cora, maybe…"

"NO! I have to say it. I heard a noise and started to turn back toward the house. One of those… women… if you want to call them that, put her hand on me. I guess she hadn't sensed the iron necklace under the collar of my dress. Then snap, a flash of light, and a sound like fat cooking in the skillet. I remember… a bright, little cloud of mist rising up, then it dropped and shattered like ice, leaving a pole cat on the grass."

"Okay, okay, just rest, try to breathe."

Cora gave Janey a half smile and then opened her mouth wider to pull in more air. After a couple deep breaths, she said, "That's one down."

"That's what Tom and I thought. He found one of those gold baubles afterwards." Cora only nodded.

"I'm going to let you rest. Doc's releasing me tonight and I need to go home. I need a bath and a talk with my mother. We'll chat later."

Cora nodded and Janey squeezed her hand before returning to her own bed. Caroline came down the corridor and seeing Janey walking back to her room, said, "Everything okay, Miss Carter?"

Looking back, Janey forced a smile and said, "Oh, everything's just dandy."

251

¶

Like Danny Billings, Paul LeBarge had the night off. Colin said to take a day and not worry about anything. Paul now lay naked next to a just as naked Ellie Fleming. He had crawled in through her bedroom window; by invitation of course. They had met at the café for several days straight and then she had invited him over. He arrived just after dark. A second-floor sash came open and a slim arm came out to summon him in. Climbing the trellis, he rolled through the window headfirst and righting himself, he saw her standing there in a filmy, sleeveless dressing gown, a candle on a table highlighting her curves from behind. It's not what he expected. He thought there would be just talk and maybe a kiss. But she began to disrobe him and that kiss— became many. He resisted at first, but she had persuaded him. It was the first time for both of them, and the love making had been awkward. He was worried her folks would hear, but her father was away, looking for work in another town. Her mother, after a few too many sherries, lay passed out on a sofa in the parlor.

Ellie rolled to face him and they embraced. He said, "You want to do it again?" Ellie just grinned, she was already preparing for a second go. Afterwards, Paul dozed off and jerking awake, he sat bolt upright and said, "Gotta go, Ellie, can't fall asleep here.

"Oh, it'll be alright," she said and sitting up she grinned as the sheet fell away to expose her small breasts. Paul didn't respond, instead he crawled out of the bed and dressed, his dry clothing absorbing the sweat from his body. Ellie got up and put on her dressing gown. The room was stifling and now smelled of sex. She met him at the open window and they embraced. That's when the door burst open and Ambrose Fleming appeared, his eyes glinting in the lantern light, his fists clenching.

"Pa, I thought… I thought…"

"Yeah, I know you thought. You were supposed to think that."

"Pa, this is Paul, he's my new boyfriend, he..."

Ambrose moved fast and hit Paul with an uppercut that nearly sent him out the window. Ellie fell back onto the floor with a thump. The last thing in Paul's ears was her scream as her father kicked him and he swooned into darkness.

12

Sully Albright had holed up in a tiny cave he knew on the east slope of Parson's Ridge just south of Nixie's Bluff. When night came and his eyes adjusted to the dark, he worked his way down into the Hollow. Skirting the swampier portions, he returned to the Grunewyck Road beyond the fording place, swaggering as he walked, sometimes singing vulgar songs under his breath. Moving up the rise, he prepared to deal with the tight hairpin curves that wound around the little hillocks that lay before him. It had been dark for about an hour, but the only thing Sully felt he had to be concerned about was the presence of the working men returning to Gowan from Grunewyck.

If any one of them saw him, word would get out and Chief Cobb would surely know where to start looking. Instead of staying on the road, he passed over the first hillock, pushing his way through the small conifers and thickets that dotted the mammoth, grassy mound. Sully stopped and peeked through the trees to make sure no one was on the road, then walking down the slope to the hardpack, he crossed and started up the next.

He thought of stopping at the Lost Collie and grabbing a beer. He could always stay overnight in one of the upstairs rooms. There was still a day's pay in his pocket, and Al, having been a bootlegger back in the twenties, would ignore that the law was looking for his guest as long as there was money coming his way.

Reaching the top of the next hillock he stopped, scanned the road through the branches of a small pine and then stepped out. Halfway down, something rustled in the brush on the other side of the road. Sully stopped and thought to run back, but didn't like the idea of retreating from something that might simply be a racoon or opossum.

The insects stopped their noise and the Whip-poor-wills that had been piping, since he arrived in the Hollow, did the same. Now in complete silence, he thought maybe to go over and try to find out what the noise was. Walking to the edge of the road, he peered into the trees beyond. The woods were dense there, and the shadows wavered within, but the low hanging clouds reflected ambient light back to the earth, making it easier to see.

"Who's there? Come on out, you coward, ol' Sully's waiting for you."

Something big moved his way. Branches cracked, the underbrush snapped and popped, and the tops of the smaller saplings bent outward. There came the rattle of chains and Sully said to himself, "Sounds like a damn cow. Probably escaped a farm somewhere. Wish I had my damn hammer."

Finding a section of heavy branch about as long and as big around as his arm, he grinned and said, "This will do just fine." He waited; the thick branch poised to strike; his eyes focused on the spot where he thought the cows head would emerge.

An overpowering stench filled his nose just before the undergrowth parted. Instead of a cow's head, Sully stared straight into the dead eyes of a human one. It was one of many that hung by their hair from a wide leather belt. A look of shock crossed his face and he shouted, "What the…" as his eyes traveled up the giant that stood before him. Bronze chains draped its body over a tunic of filthy fur and in its right hand a massive club, the business end adorned with spikes.

Sully locked eyes with the beast as he struggled to pull the Colt from his pocket. Something in the creature's eyes hypnotized him, and before he could utter another word, his head was parted from his shoulders by someone who swung a meaner club than he.

The beast pulled Sully's head from the spikes of his club and gazed into the fast-glazing eyes with their look of surprise. Blood dripped from the ragged point of separation at the neck and ran down the giant's arm. Grunting with satisfaction, the beast tied Sully's greasy, dark hair to his belt to hang with the others, and then shambled back into the trees. The woodland creatures resumed their raucous song as if it were just another typical night in the Hollow.

Janey couldn't sleep and was laying in her bed reading an old copy of *Collier's* when Caroline came in.

"Phone call, Janey."

"Who is it? My mother? It's late."

"Uh, no, it's Tom."

"Oh, that makes sense. He probably can't sleep either."

Janey rose from her bed and followed the nurse to the day desk. Picking up the phone by its cylindrical shaft, she held the mouth piece at her lips and the cone shaped speaker to her ear.

"Tom?"

"Yes, Janey, just wanted to share some news. Sully Albright has escaped. I don't think you're in any real danger. He was seen crossing the Meadowlands toward Whip-poor-will Hollow. Hopefully they will catch him before the morning."

"How'd that happen? Our infamous Nealy Garret not staying on top of things?"

"I don't know for sure, but he got himself knocked out for his troubles. Danny Billings found Nealy out cold in the jail cell. He called Chief Cobb, who is putting together yet another posse. He's asked me to join. I haven't given him an answer yet. He's also got the state police on it."

"Well, if you go, be careful. That man's killed one too many cows and may have gone off the deep end. Just be careful."

"I will. So, how's Cora? Awake yet?"

"Oh, somewhat. We had a short talk, but she's in no shape for conversation. What she did tell me was, well... sort of good news. It was one of Mab's minions who met her in the backyard down at Chastity's cottage. Cora said it turned into a pole cat and ran away. The necklace did its job."

"So, we are down to two. What do you suppose Mab will do if she loses them all?"

"Don't know, Cora doesn't think she'll use any of the solitary fairies. So, the hope is, she'll go away."

"Okay, well, we probably shouldn't be talking about this over the phone, there are too many other ears. I'll see you soon."

"Okay, come as soon as you can. I so want to be out of here. See no sense in staying. Oh, and Tom..."

"Yes?"

"I love you."

The telephone line was silent for a second, before Tom said, "I love you too, Janey."

She slowly hung up the phone and placed it back on the desk.

Looking up at Caroline, the nurse grinned. "Not a word, Caroline," Janey said, trying to hide her own grin.

"Not me you have to worry about, Janey. I am sure Helen is already on the grapevine with the news. So, Sully has escaped?"

"Yes, sadly. They're going after him. Merlyn's rounding up a search party."

"So, what's this about fairies?"

"Oh, nothing, uh… Tom's writing a book about folklore and fairies. Cora's the expert you know… that's all."

"Oh, uh… okay," Caroline said, suspicion clouding her brow.

"Back to bed," Janey said and walked away, "When will Doc be back? I want to check out."

"Soon, I'm pretty sure he'll let you go."

"Okay, good. Going to check on Cora."

"Thanks, my feet are killing me and it's not even midnight yet."

Janey looked around Cora's curtain and saw she was still asleep. Returning to her own room, she pulled back the window curtain to peer into the dark. A chill climbed her spine, and letting the curtain fall back, she got into bed and rolled over to face the wall. For the first time, in a long time, she felt afraid.

Up at the other end of town, Helen was already in a conversation with Reverend Hale. Soon a small bag was packed and set at the doorway that opened from his rooms into the nave. Taking a freshly opened bottle of whiskey with him to his bed, he sat propped up on his pillows, drinking, planning, and waiting for the dawn.

म्

Roy LaVern stood outside Sally's clothing store, trying to see inside. The shop was dark and no lights had been lit. Stepping back to the outside edge of the boardwalk, he gazed up toward the unlit windows of Sally's rooms. He felt the weight of the pistol in his pocket and gave it a pat. Bringing the revolver had been an impulsive move, but the loss of his only daughter had taken him there. He could always use grief as a reason for doing away with Sally. A look of uncertainty crossed his face. "Maybe I'll just knock her around a bit," he muttered to himself.

Moving around to the rear of the store, he checked the backdoor and finding it unlocked, he stepped inside, stopped, and listened. Nothing. He tiptoed onto the display floor with only the sound of crickets outside and a passing car. Going to the stairway door, Roy found it open and went up. The smell of stew or soup coupled with perfume and dirty laundry filled the air. He moved around, trying not to bump into anything. He found the bedroom and the unmade bed with no one in it. Clothing lay draped over furniture and scattered over the floor, some of it, Bessie's.

"No one home," he said, his words sounding strange in the quiet room. "Boots', most likely." Sally hadn't been welcomed much of anywhere else except for McCarthy's, and Zelda's wasn't her style. Roy returned to the first floor and exited the back door. As he stepped off the porch someone called out to him, an almost indiscernible, but familiar voice in the dark. Then, "I'm here daddy." He stared at the old carriage house at the back of the property. "Daddy, I'm here, daddy," came again. Tears filled his eyes and blurred his vision. "Bessie?" escaped his lips, "Bessie, is that you?"

The walk-through door swung slowly open to reveal a dark interior. Somebody stood just inside. Roy stopped and tried to wipe the moisture from his eyes but the emotion was too strong. Whoever was in there, stepped back against the rail fence that separated the stable from the carriage park.

"Bessie, darling, are you in there?"

"Here, daddy, here. Come, help me."

Roy stumbled inside. The shadow became a silhouette backed by an open overhead door on the street side of the carriage house. Moving forward, he blubbered, "Bessie?" Stopping a few feet away, the smell of forest loam, pond water, and decaying wood, filled his nose, overriding an older smell of horse manure and musty straw.

An automobile turned onto Ovis Street, its headlamps flashing through the cracks in the walls and illuminating the shadow person for a second. The picture that traveled from Roy's eyes to his brain, said, yes, it was Bessie. She was adorned in a long-sleeved green dress that dragged on the straw, but her eyes were yellow, almost animal like, unblinking. Roy looked as if in a trance, hypnotized by what he saw through tear filled eyes.

Bessie moved toward him a few steps, the sound of small hooves echoing on the wood floor. He raised his arms to embrace her and sobbed, "They told me you were dead."

"Yes, foolish mortals…"

Roy never felt the creature's inch long fingernails slice through his neck. Grabbing his arms, it flung him to the floor and fell on him much like a panther on its prey, relishing the blood spouting from his neck as it mauled his chest.

Lissy lay asleep in her bed, her sleeveless chemise soaked with sweat. She had gone to bed early; much to her mother's surprise. School was supposed to start in less than a month. So, for Colleen Potter, it only made sense.

She was dreaming that a great wind was blowing outside and was deciding whether to open a window, or not. In her dream, she found herself standing there, her hands on the sash. Throwing it up, the wind came in so strong it blew her back to her bed.

Lissy awoke, sleep fogged thoughts whirling in her head. About the time she realized it had been a dream, a breeze did cool her sweltering body. There came what sounded like small hooves scampering across the bare wood of the floor. She remained unmoving, opening her eyes just a crack. The window had been secured before getting into bed. It was now wide open.

The *clack-clack!* of whatever it was, came again. Rotating her eyeballs toward the corner without moving her head, she could just discern a dark figure standing in the shadow next to her vanity. It whispered her name, a seductive utterance that caused Lissy to shudder. The adrenaline flowed, and her mind cleared for all of a minute before it began to cloud up again, a strange lethargy taking over her body.

Lissy fought her descent into pleasant oblivion. The urge to flee the room and holler for her mother was strong, but she feared whatever was over there would grab her from behind before she even got to the door.

Summoning up all her courage, she whispered to the shadow, "What do you want?"

A voice from the abyss said, "Why… I want you, Melissa Potter.

Lissy? Join us and have that sister you've always wanted."

The shadow began to move toward her at a snail's pace, tiny clack after tiny clack as the silhouette loomed larger. Lissy closed her eyes and tears began to roll out onto her cheeks. She tried to remember all Cora MacLean had told her the day of her father's funeral. There had been so much, and Lissy hadn't been in any state of mind to receive instruction. Her recent experience at the Hollow was enough to eliminate any skepticism, though. Now, some fiend had come for her, and she was all alone.

The so called 'temper' that she was continually chastised for, welled up, and she didn't resist. It cleared her head and pushed away the fear. Lissy waited, motionless, and even though she wept, she also seethed. Her body seemed to vibrate as the clacking and the swishing of the kirtle clad visitor moved closer. A certain odor soon enveloped her. It was the smell of the forest, toadstools, and decaying leaves.

Lissy raised an eyelid just slightly to view the figure that now stood over her and she stifled a scream. The passing of a cloud brought the moon through the window and she saw it had the face of Molly Sharp. Long finger nails gleamed as one of its hands rose slowly toward the ceiling. The Molly thing grinned, showing a mouth full of long, sharp teeth, and she whispered seductively, "Oh, Lissy… so sweet, so sweet."

Lissy began to shake uncontrollably as she watched the drool drip from the creature's chin. Its glowing snake eyes closed halfway as if already relishing the upcoming feast. The beast began a light keening, a noise that was soon cut short by an iron made, three toothed hair comb piercing its throat. For Lissy it had been like stabbing cooking lard.

The Molly thing slapped its long slender fingers over the protruding comb and glared at Lissy who now stood on the mattress, the semblance of a war cry waning from her lips, a noise Colleen Potter would later describe to Lennea Trask as sounding like the squall of a wildcat.

The vampire began to dissolve right before Lissy's eyes with a sound like frying bacon. Disintegrating into a cloud of smoke and ash, it swirled out the window, leaving the comb behind. Lissy ran after it and slamming down the sash, she locked it. Returning to her bed, she picked up the comb and sat on the edge of the mattress, rocking back and forth, sobbing.

16

The door burst open, and Lissy's mother stood in the opening, a candlestick in her hand. "Heaven forbid, Melissa Potter, what is going on in here?"

When Colleen wasn't looking, Lissy hid the comb under her pillow.

"Answer me! What was that noise? I thought I heard you scream."

"Just a bad dream, mama."

"Oh my god, you scared the bejeezus out of me."

"I'm sorry."

"Was it about your pa? I know I've been having a few of those myself. Was it your, pa?" Lissy said nothing.

Colleen sat down next to her daughter and put an arm over her shoulders. Lissy leaned into her mother and wrapping her arms around her waist, she pushed her face into Colleens breast and whimpered.

"There, there, darling," Colleen said as she patted Lissy's arm. "It's all okay, now. Hush! It was just a nightmare. Just a silly ol' nightmare. It's over now."

Lissy squeezed her mother for a brief moment and then relaxed, the look on her face betraying her doubt. It was far from over.

CHAPTER ELEVEN

JANEY

IV

~

1

Janey stood in a room full of fog, the water vapor swirling. Hands came out of the mist and grabbed her throat. She felt her mother's derringer in her hand and bringing it up, she pointed it into the fog and pulled the trigger.

Coming awake in a panic, the magazine she had been reading slid to the floor. There was an argument going on down the hall; it was Tom's voice and he was getting loud. He was having a row with Caroline about visiting hours and Janey figured it must be well after ten o clock. Then came Doc, quietly interjecting, "It's alright, he can stay, just calm down. Go get yourself some coffee out front and let me talk to Tom. Go on now, I'll take care of this."

Not wanting to let the good doctor escape without requesting her release, Janey got out of bed. Feeling lightheaded, she remained sitting until the moment passed. Getting up a little slower, she slapped down the hallway in her bare feet.

Tom and Doc Bolen appeared, stopping at the vacant nurse's station where Doc checked paperwork on a clipboard. Janey went to Tom and embraced him from the side, not allowing him to turn.

"Awake now, are you? Thought you were tucked in for the night," he said.

Doc nodded and smiled at Janey before stepping into Cora's cubicle to leave the curtain open while he listened to Cora's chest with his stethoscope. Cora appeared to remain asleep throughout the process. Janey quickly stole a kiss from Tom before anyone could put their eyes on them.

Turning back, Doc said, "Janey. How are you? Still looking a little pale. Caroline says you been talking about going home? I suppose that would be alright. I want to check you one more time just for good measure."

His face was its usual pleasant, somewhat inquisitive, self. Janey smiled, "Yeah, Doc, I've had enough of this place, no offense. Just don't think I need to be here."

"Okay, very well. You have people at home that can look after you. You've had no life-threatening injuries, even though it could have most certainly been worse. Luckily your knee came in handy. Your sleeping gown was in rather terrible shape, so we scrapped it. Can somebody bring you clothes, so you don't have to go home in our gown? Maybe Percy, when he comes to pick you up?"

Janey looked down at her muslin johnny gown that they had given her and smiled at everybody, saying, "Not the height of fashion, is it?"

2

Cora's eyes opened and the old woman watched the three of them with some semblance of a grin on her face.

"Oh! Cora, you're awake."

"Aye, seems I'm still alive," she said as Janey moved in for an embrace.

"Why thank you, darling. That's so nice."

Doc said, "Yes, we pulled you out of this one, Cora. Being it's your first, with a little rest, there's a good chance, you'll get better. We'll be keeping you on bromides for a little while. You can stay as long as you wish. If you want to go home, we might have to give it a week before we pack you into a car and send you over to Grunewyck. Hannah has called Al and filled him in. She says he told her as soon as things settle, he'll come. But he knows, too, that you may have to stay through next week. I've used up one of my four bottles of oxygen, but I'll have Liam stop and grab the empty and pick up some more on his run over to Springfield. Damn, I wish that man would get himself a truck instead of humping it with that wagon. You'd think he was living in the nineteenth century."

"Naw, I don't need it," Cora said and laying the oxygen mask on the night stand next to her bed, she grinned.

"Stubborn woman," Doc said. "Probably what kept her alive. Looking at the others, he smirked.

"So, what happened down there, Cora," Janey asked, sitting on the edge of the bed.

Cora looked at Tom and then to Janey to make sure they saw her eyes travel over to Doc, who was now wrapping the hose to the oxygen tank. He suddenly stopped and turned to the old woman and then looking back at Janey and Tom, he said, "What's up? You don't want to tell the story? Cora? You feeling winded?"

"Naw, Doc, nothing like that, it's just…well…"

Tom, who had been standing silent, piped up, "It's an odd tale, Doc."

"Why's that? Just a run-of-the-mill heart attack from what I can tell. Plain and simple."

"Not so much that, as what caused it."

Doc looked at Cora with that half smile, then at Janey who was doing her best to maintain her poker face. She looked at Tom and shrugged, "Tell him, Tom. Tell him what you know. Save Cora her breath."

Tom sought Cora's permission and when she nodded, he turned to Doc, who had set down the coil of hose and was now facing them.

"Well, Doc, you know the story of Bessie, right?"

"Yes, I do, and also that Vern Sweeny's decomposed body was discovered in the woods just west of the cemetery. Danny Billings found him, torn to shreds. I went down to sedate poor Prudence, but the woman was three sheets to the wind and didn't seem to have a clue what was happening. Now Bessie's body is missing. Sally Combs is missing. Gregory Bly, too. Possibly… your own father, Janey. Had you heard? So, yes, I know there is something going on around here. There's the talk of young Lissy Potter, over in Grunewyck, having had some kind of a run in with a banshee at Nixie's Bluff. Then her father, James Potter, dies that very evening. So, tell me what you know, Tom...Janey?"

Janey responded flatly, "We suspect that my father's new bride is behind it all."

"You mean, like she's some kind of a mob boss? Perhaps kidnapping and executing people in the valley for the state in order to move their reservoir project along?" Doc chuckled and smiled at their somber faces.

"Uh...no, Doc, something worse, something, uh... more supernatural," Tom said.

"Well, no doubt you're aware I'm a man of science. I'm going to have a tough time believing in ghosts and goblins and all that."

"That's just what Mabel wants, skeptics. We were no different, at first. Some things have happened, things that can't be explained."

"So, Gowan has a boogeymen flitting about? Don't tell me this Mabel is the queen of the fairies and she's unleashed them into the Spry River Valley?"

No one else was laughing, and looking around at each other they then focused on Doc who was now squinting at Cora. No longer smiling, he said in a monotone, "What happened down there at Chastity's, Cora?"

She drew a long breath and looked toward the oxygen tank as if maybe she had been mistaken about needing it.

"There was a noise out back of the cottage, so I made Tom stay in his chair and I went out there. Those so-called witches everyone is gossiping about, the ones that came down to McCarthy's? Well, they ain't witches. They are, uh... handmaidens, Mabel's, or... Mab's, ladies in waiting. They do her bidding. There were three, I suspect there are now just two. One of them was out there and grabbed me. She touched my necklace, and just like that, poof!"

"Kind of like a flash bulb," Tom interjected.

"Aye, kind of like that. The next thing I know, I'm waking up here in your makeshift hospital, Doc."

Ignoring the comment about his hospital, Doc Bolen said, "Poof? You mean, disappeared?"

"Naw, I meant it turned into a frozen cloud of mist and then... well..." Cora said, now irritable.

"How could that be?"

"Don't know, and don't ask if it could have been my condition that brought it."

"Yes, and I saw the flash from inside the house."

"And then there is… Bessie," Janey said.

"What about, Bessie?"

"Her throat had been cut like someone had slashed her with a knife, not a big cut, mind you, just a few inches to open up a vein."

"But there was no cut. I looked at her myself. You saw me do it."

"Exactly," Janey said, the expression on her face sincere enough to cause Doc to cast his eyes to the floor, an index finger on his lips.

"I'm having a tough time rationalizing this," he said.

"Stop that, now, just listen to what I'm saying," Cora pled.

Doc walked away without a word and went out front. He said something to Caroline and then came the sound of the closing of his office door.

3

The room went silent for a minute and then growing impatient, Cora whispered, "Where's he off to?"

"Sounded like his office," Janey said, lowering her voice in an attempt to avoid Caroline's ears.

Tom looked over his shoulder at the sleepy Caroline, who now sat at the front desk, sipping her coffee. "Think it might have been a bad idea to bring Doc into this?" he whispered, looking at the other two in turn.

"Not doing so, would have just been ignoring what's coming," Cora said. "It's like this damn reservoir, it's going to get worse before it gets better. People need to know, especially if we are going to take some kind of action against Mab. The reservoir we can't stop, that's already a done deal. But I believe with this Mab—we can. The thing is, she may become moot if her domain becomes a big lake. She's the Queen of Air and Darkness, not water."

"Oh, I beg to differ," Tom said, "She controls the solitary water fairies, Grindylow, Kelpies, etcetera. I suspect not much will change. As long as Carter House remains her castle, she can still wreak havoc on towns like Brimfield, Gilbertsham, Packard, and Hardwyck. I could go on, but you get the point, right?"

"Okay…" Cora said, closing her eyes and taking a deep breath.

"Yes, we can't just walk away. We may not be able to kill her, but we can displace her. I think we should try, regardless," Janey said, her eyes leaving Tom and moving to Cora who was starting to look paler by the minute.

They heard Doc's office door open and he reappeared at the front desk. "Caroline, I plan on being here awhile. You can head on home, or have Hannah make you up a bed over at the house."

"Okay, Doc," she said and looking back at the three of them, she smirked before disappearing from their sight. Doc locked the front door after Caroline departed and returned to the group.

"Okay, so, I'm going to pretend like it's all true and say, what's next? How do we get that woman gone? I suspect… sorry, Janey, that she's already dealt with Ben. Sadly, that still leaves Constance, and you, my dear. I fear you are in danger, too. Might be best if you left town. Do you still have that house over in Salem?"

"You know about High Gable?"

"Um… yes… it was years back. I received an invitation from your father for Hannah, and I, to spend a weekend with him and a few other, so called, 'important people' from the Spry River valley. Some kind of money-making venture, I reckon. We declined, but the return address on the envelope supported my belief that Ben had a few other properties, in other towns, besides Gowan."

He turned, looked at Cora, and said, "Cora, you're looking a little peaked, I think you should get some sleep. Janey, I want to get you checked out and on your way home. You are going to have to convince Constance to pack up and make arrangements to have whatever personal property you want hauled out of Headmost to some place far away. Somewhere you won't be such a threat to… what did you call her? Mab? Tom, you should go with them. You're from Salem, right?"

"That's right, but we have work to do here. Something's got to be done about that woman. I'm not much on backing down from a fight."

They talked for another hour. Doc, even though previously stating his reluctance, went along as if everything the other three had experienced was the undeniable truth. To Janey, it was obviously

266

apparent that he was just humoring them. She thought he just might need an experience of his own, and perhaps, they could see he got one.

ᚻ

Doc surprised them by changing the subject to talk about a telephone call he had gotten earlier from Philip Shannon about the reservoir and that it was definite, the state was going to take the valley. Nobody was surprised. Tom hugged Janey and said, "You know where to find me." He then departed for Brenner's and some much-needed sleep. Doc convinced Janey to remain until at least sunrise, and she returned to her bed to mull over all she had learned and to let Cora get some rest. Not one of them got a whole lot of sleep.

ᚱ

Janey woke at three o clock Friday morning from another bad dream. She was itching to go home. She had called several times the evening before to have Percy bring her some clothes, but Helen said she couldn't get through. Janey left her bed and padded to the desk to find a groggy Hannah.

"I want to go home, Hannah."

"Janey, it's three in the morning. Couldn't you at least wait til sunrise?"

"Nope, I'm going, even if I have to walk there in this johnny gown and bare feet."

"Okay, okay, just a second, I might have something."

Going to a closet in the hallway, Hannah looked back as if to size up Janey and then reaching in she took out a drop waisted dress on a hanger and offered it to her.

"What's this?" she asked.

"A spare, just-in-case dress."

"You mean... a dead person's dress?"

Hannah scowled and said, "It's been laundered. Do you want it or not?"

Janey took it, looked it over, held it to her body to size it, and said, "Fine, beggars can't be choosers, I guess."

She returned to her room, pulled the curtain, and changed into the dress. It was two sizes too big, but acceptable. It would be the second time she traversed the town without underwear and bare feet, but she was sure Doc didn't keep those things on hand. The dress was pretty with its small, red blossoms on a yellow background. It made her wonder if she had seen it on anybody she knew in the past and if it had come from Sally's.

Returning to the front, she was met by a bleary-eyed Doc who had sacked out in his office for a few hours. "Are you sure I can't convince you to stay?"

"Nope, I've had it up to here," she said, tapping the top of her head. "I'm going. I want to sleep in my own bed."

Glancing at Hannah, they exchanged looks, then turning back to Janey, he said, "Okay, I'll run you home. Just let me go to the house and get the car. Hannah, you got the helm for a while, I'm running Janey home."

Janey followed him. He turned, somewhat surprised, when he realized she was.

"I'll walk with you, Doc. I'm just itching to get out of here."

"You don't have to; I can bring the car around."

"No, no, I've had enough of that in my lifetime. Got to do something, I'm going stir crazy."

"Okay, suit yourself."

They walked in the dark toward Doc's house and turning to Janey, he said, "Janey, I have to say it again, I'm having a tough time getting this whole affair through my head. But I suppose if I were in your shoes, Tom's, or Cora's, I could accept it more readily."

"It's not over yet, Doc. If things keep going as they are, I am sure you will have your own experience soon enough. Just bear with us a little longer. Can you do that? Not that I want something to happen, just seems naïve to believe it won't."

"Okay, I hear you. Now I'm wondering if this thing is, perhaps, too big for us? Does Merlyn know anything about what's going on?"

"Well, it's my understanding he was one of the first to meet Mab, known as Mabel at that time. From what I saw, he was a little worried. Then there's the rest, Bessie, and Lissy, and... well, you've already heard that part."

They had arrived at Doc's house and climbed into his Rolls Royce. He started it up, backed out of the short driveway, and headed back toward Main Street. Passing the office, Hannah came running out, waving frantically. Doc slammed on the brakes, nearly putting Janey on the floor. Leaning out the window, he said, "What's wrong? Is it Cora?"

"No, Cora's sleeping. It was a phone call. Bruce Nelson wants you down at Sweeny's. Something about a body found out in the Hollow. I asked who, but he said for you to just come on down there, he didn't want to talk on the phone."

"It's three fifteen in the morning, for Pete's sake! Doesn't anybody just sleep anymore? Okay, call him back, tell him I'm on my way. No, wait, don't call. I don't want to give Helen anymore for the grapevine. I'll just head down."

"I'll get back inside, got to make another pot of coffee."

Doc looked at Janey, "Want to come with me to Sweeny's?"

"Yes, I'll come along," Janey said, her eyes still on the retreating Hannah.

"Might get gruesome. Are you sure?"

"Certainly, let's go and get it over with."

"Okay, but..."

"Relax, Doc. I'm a big girl now."

Doc just grinned at her and accelerated away. Janey felt a slight jolt of adrenaline and wondered who now lay on the table at the mortuary. If this kept up, there wouldn't be anybody left in Gowan to flee the coming flood.

6

Doc drove by Sweeny's. Every light in the place was lit, including the cupola. There were several cars parked there, a model A with County Coroner stenciled on the side, and another with 'SHERIFF' in bold, white letters on black paint. Doc made a U-turn and parked behind them.

They were soon walking across the lawn to the front door. Glancing up, Janey could see Prudence in her dressing gown, sitting in a chair at what she assumed was the bedroom window. The old woman wasn't looking at them, and Janey could have sworn she saw her tip a flask.

"You'd think Louis could have put in a walkway after all these years.

269

Damn well know he's got the money to do it. Always was a penny pincher. I suspect that Prudence is up there drowning her sorrows over Vern. Did I tell you Danny Billings found his remains up in the woods behind the cemetery? They suspect homicide, pretty torn up, I heard. Oh! Sorry…"

"Doc, you have to get over it. It's me, Janey. Nothing makes me burn more than a man thinking because I'm a woman that…"

"Okay, sorry. Just trying to be polite."

The screen door swung open and Duncan appeared. After a few seconds of looking Janey up and down, he said, "Downstairs, you know the way, right, Doc?"

"I do, thanks Duncan."

Janey smiled at the boy. "Hello, Duncan. Missing your school days, yet? If you'd had one more year, I'd be your teacher."

"The schools done. You won't be teaching no one, no how. Reservoir's coming. The word's official, pa said so."

"Yeah, I heard. What a shame."

Duncan closed the door and stood watching Janey's undulating backside as she walked away. He had shared with Vern, once, that Janey had one of the finest bottoms ever to move through Gowan. Janey tossed a glance back over her shoulder, but Duncan was already retreating into the parlor.

The door to the basement stood open and she followed Doc down the stairs. There was the smell of cigar in her nose along with embalming fluid. She could see the boots and shoes of all the men present through the opening at the bottom of the long, white curtain-like partition.

Coming around the open end, Louis said "Doc, sorry to bother you, just needed you to come down and have a look-see since it's your territory, and I would like someone to concur. Oh, who's this? Janey Carter? Why are you here?"

Janey grinned at Louis, Bruce Nelson, and the man with the silver star pinned to his chest. They all looked at her like she was an intruder. "Janey was with me when I got the call, she agreed to come along."

"No place for a woman," the Sheriff said, tapping the ashes from his cigar onto the spotless floor. Sticking it back in his mouth, he squinted at her with one eye.

270

"Sheriff, you may not know Janey Carter?"

"Carters? Yeah, I know. Big wigs here in Gowan. Enough said." Turning away, he walked over to stand at the head of the table.

"So, Louis, what... or who, do we have here?" Doc said.

"Well," Louis said and moving to the table, he glanced once at Janey before saying, "Coming off," before whipping the sheet from the body. It wasn't just Janey who flinched at the sight of the headless corpse. Doc gulped, the Sheriff exhaled a great amount of tobacco smoke and took a step back. Janey smirked, not only because she had reacted no differently than they, but also because the clothing on the body told her it was a headless Sully Albright.

Only Louis and Bruce moved closer to examine the corpse. Bruce sighed and said, "Gentleman, and lady, we presume this is a one, Sully Albright."

"I have to agree," Janey said, "Those were the clothes he was wearing when he attacked me."

"Well, so you came in handy, after all," the sheriff said, grinning maliciously.

"Thank you, Janey," Bruce said, and scowling at the sheriff, he moved up to examine the neck area.

"Looks like Sully's head was ripped from his body. The fact that the wound is so ragged, would attest to that. Something hit him with tremendous force."

"Ever seen anything like that?" Louis asked Bruce.

"Just once, on a farm north of Grunewyck. Matt Hayness, didn't duck quick enough when a boom loaded with stones swung his way. I suspected he wasn't going to need that new foundation built after all. Took his head clean off, well, not clean..."

"So, this is Sully Albright?" Doc said.

"Yep," Sheriff said, "Seems he lost his head over the deal."

The big man laughed, but the rest just stood staring. "A Sheriff joke... sorry. So... anywho, he was found out in the Hollow by a couple of Gowan factory men out drinking late at the Lost Collie. I think he must have pumped out every last drop of blood onto the roadway. Couldn't find the head, though. Got a couple of men out there still looking. Thinking I'm going to have to call it a homicide."

"Anyone call Chief Cobb?"

"Wasn't in, talked with Nealy," Louis said. "Told me Merlyn was going out again this morning with his posse to track down Sully. I'm guessing he can forget all about that."

"Sheriff, think you could ring up the police office and tell them they don't need to resume the manhunt? I'm sure Nealy can go find Merlyn and give him the news."

"Sure thing, Doc. Mister Sweeny, you got a phone down here?"

"No, you'll have to go upstairs and use the one in the entry hall."

Letting out a long sigh, coupled with a stream of tobacco smoke, he adjusted the gun belt under his large belly, shook his head, and walked away.

"So, how you progressing on Vern? Anything?" Doc asked.

Casting his eyes to the floor for a second, Louis rubbed his face as if he was having a tough time containing his despair.

"Sorry, I guess it could have waited."

"No, no," Louis said, "The autopsy is complete, Bruce here thought he might have been murdered and then mutilated."

Bruce, in his professional manner, stated, "Vern bled out from multiple wounds in his throat and chest. Made me want to think he had been attacked by some wild animal. A big cat, or… well, something with claws. Oddly, there should have been more blood present at the scene."

"What about a wolf?" Janey said. "Cora thought she saw a wolf in the woods behind Chastity's cottage."

"I don't know. Looked more like claw marks than teeth. Besides, haven't been wolves in these parts since Adam."

"Haven't been any cougars either, unless a tiger or a lion has escaped from the circus. Hear anything about a tiger escape?" Janey said with a degree of sarcasm.

"Well, uh, no…" Bruce said, looking at her now like he wished she hadn't come after all. She and Doc exchanged looks and something passed between them. "So, where is Vern's body?" Doc said, putting his focus on Louis who was wiping his eyes with a dirty white handkerchief.

"Got him in the cold room, set for cremation, why?"

"I'd like a look at him… just to say I did."

"Well, he's prepped, not sure what looking at him is going to do for you?"

"Humor me," Doc said, his usual inquisitive face now projecting an assertiveness that couldn't be denied.

Louis sighed and said, "Right through that door. Drawer number two, help yourself."

"Thank you," Doc said and turned away to open the door in the wall behind him. Janey remained with Bruce and Louis who were doing their best to avoid eye contact. Finally, Louis said, "How's your ma? Her and Prudence used to talk all the time. But that was before her move to Headmost. I 'spect having to leave her very own home because of your father's new wife, has been a little hard on her."

Janey heard the drawer in the other room roll out and Doc's wingtips moving around the tile floor. She finally made eye contact with Louis who looked like he wished he had never asked the question. "My mother's fine, Mr. Sweeny. How is Prudence? She must be taking Vern's death kind of hard? I imagine you all are."

Louis nodded and a stray tear rolled out of a watery grey eye. Bruce looked away as if something on the floor had caught his attention. Janey felt it had been tit for tat and then the roll and slam of the drawer in the other room startled them. They all looked that direction as Doc came into view. "Well, if I'm not needed here anymore, I think I'll get Janey home. Janey? Shall we?"

"Certainly," she said and joined him before heading up the stairs. "Good morning, Louis. My best to Prudence. Dr. Nelson, same to you," she added over her shoulder before following Doc up to the first floor.

They met the Sheriff in the hall, still on the phone. Janey caught a glimpse of Duncan in his night shirt, peering around the door jamb of the parlor. When they stopped to speak to the lawman, the boy came out and stood beside them as if he too wanted to hear what the Sheriff had to say. He kept throwing glances at the side of Janey's face and neck, sometimes sniffing as if he was trying to catch her scent. His eyes soon traveled down to her unsupported breasts and Janey crossed her arms, turning away to look at a large portrait on the wall.

"Well, got Nealy on the phone here," the Sheriff said as he sat on the edge of a table in the hall, "Said he can see through the window where

Chief Cobb has gathered a group of men and they are standing around the belltower with flashlights and lanterns."

"Starting early, I guess," Doc said as the grandfather clock chimed four. "Okay, then, well, maybe we'll see them on the way to Janey's house. Then we can confirm that they are aware. Just to help out," Doc said.

The sheriff looked at Doc like he was trying to figure out if he was really trying to help, or perhaps, didn't trust him to do his job.

"Well, I'm heading downstairs to let Louis and Bruce know what Nealy said. Then I'm going out to the Hollow and see what I can do about helping my deputies find Sully's noggin. Probably have better luck after the sun comes up. You want to come along, Doctor Bolen? Could use an extra hand. I know it's police work and all, but helping is helping, right?"

"Thanks, but no. I'm beat and I feel like I could use a little more shut eye."

"Didn't think so," the Sheriff said, a smug look on his face. Turning to Duncan he said, "What you looking at, snot nose?" Duncan shrank away, turned, and retreated into the kitchen.

"Good day, Sheriff," Janey said and walked to the front door without looking back. "Miss Carter," he said, tipping his hat as he watched her retreating backside over his shoulder. Then looking down at Doc, he winked, and mumbled, "Quite the looker, huh, Doctor Bolen?"

"Good day, Sheriff," Doc said, frowning. Turning away he followed Janey to the car.

Once inside the Rolls, Janey said, "Glad that's over with."

"Yes, a dead body can be unnerving."

"It was more the live ones. Especially that Sheriff. Take me home, will you, Doc? I need a comfortable bed."

"Certainly. So, seems Sully got his just reward, but the question still stands—how?"

"Rather a gruesome way to die, having one's head ripped off."

"Yes, true, but I'm still stumped. Maybe he got hit by a car. But there was no other damage. Hard to believe just his head got hit and not the rest of him."

"No sense in trying to rationalize this, Doc. With the forces at play, it's got to be something we are not going to think of."

Doc started the car and pulled away to roll slowly up Main Street. "So… are you convinced yet that there's something going on that is unexplainable?"

"Well, Janey, I suppose. Like I said, believe it or not—I'll stick with you until I do make some sense of it."

Janey glanced at him in the dim light of the car's interior. She figured he must be almost seventy years old. His white hair always seemed immaculate, his brass framed glasses granting him a look of distinction. His white doctor's coat, an article of his profession, was ever present, even when he left the office for a meal at Boots' or an evening at Brenner's. He was always on call and he never seemed to mind. To Janey, his life had always seemed to be in constant motion.

"So, Doc, what are you going to do when the reservoir takes us from our beloved Gowan? Retirement?"

"I'll be one of the last to go, I imagine. Got to be with my patients until the end. As soon as the last name in the filing cabinet has flown the coop, then perhaps Hannah and I will be off to the Cape. Got a summer home there. Think I'm going to do some fishing, maybe a little consulting. Been a doctor all my adult life going clear back before the turn of the century. And you? What of you? I see you got a serious attachment to Tom. Do you think it might go somewhere?"

"There is always teaching, I can teach anywhere. That's what I went to Thayer for. As for Tom, I can only hope for the best. My mother doesn't like him much. We might have to tiptoe around her for a while. He's from Salem and still has a few relatives there. So… we will see."

"We most certainly will."

They rolled up to the group of men now standing in the street just outside the green. Tom stood with Merlyn and several other familiar faces, all looking like they needed coffee.

"Well, looks like Nealy caught them before they could head out," Doc said, stopping the car. Tom walked over and leaned in the window. "So, you've heard? Or should I say, 'seen'?"

"Yes, so much for that," Doc said.

Janey took Tom's hand and they exchanged looks. "So, what are you doing up at this hour?" he said.

"Was going home, had enough of hospital beds, Doc was kind enough to release me. But first I had to go down and identify Sully."

"Sounds like he got what he deserved, yes? Deader than a door nail, Nealy says?"

"Yes, but we are going to have to talk about that, the three of us. It was rather a peculiar way to die."

"So, what now?" Tom asked.

"I'm going home to bed," Janey said.

"Can I come?"

Janey squeezed Tom's hand, and Doc threw them a look of disbelief and then grinned.

"Just kidding," Tom said, winking. The men on the walk started to disperse. Charley Bates Jr. headed over to the slaughter house, complaining to Cal Loeffler, who went with him, that he hoped what Sandy had said about him taking Sully's place was just a joke.

Phil Shannon stood alone watching the three of them at the car. Merlyn, not saying anything, looked up at the sky as if studying the coming dawn, his hat in his hands. Nealy came and spoke briefly with him. Merlyn shrugged, put on his hat, and headed toward home. Nealy then walked over to the Rolls and nudged Tom out of the way to address Doc through the open window.

"You got a look at the body, huh, Doc? Well, can't say he didn't deserve it. Hey, did you see my gun? Was my gun on him? He took my Colt, you know? I bought and paid for that gun with my own money, now I 'spect it's lost. Where'd they find him? Somewhere out in the Hollow, I know, but…"

"No, there was no gun. But the Sheriff went back out there. You might go and find him and he could show you where it might be. If Sully still had it, that is."

"Oh? Well, good. I'm gonna go ask the Chief. Otherwise, he's gonna make me haul around a shotgun. Damn things are a nuisance. Gonna go ask."

"You do that, Nealy," Doc said.

Nealy took off in a run after Merlyn. Doc and Tom both shook their heads. Janey remembered when her and Nealy were in school. He had been bullied severely and she suspected that is what drove him to

276

become a policeman.

"Okay, Doc, I'm ready for home."

Tom leaned in further and they exchanged a quick kiss. When he stepped back, she told him that she loved him by forming the words with her lips, but not making a sound. He responded in kind. Doc smirked and looked away.

7

The dawn was giving way to sunrise when Tabby met Janey at the front door. She gave the loaner dress the 'once over' and then embraced her.

"Are you okay, sugar? Sorry we couldn't get down to Doc's last evenin', the Missus, she was just too confounded by this whole goings on. She didn't want us to leave her alone."

"That's okay, Tabby. I'm home now and going to bed."

"Do you want a bath? I'll draw you a cool bath."

"Would you, please? That would be wonderful. Where's Percy?"

"He's out back getting wood for the oven. Janey leaned right, so she could see down the short corridor that led to the back door. Percy was coming out of the woodshed with an armload of wood and she thought she heard him singing.

"Okay, I'll be in my room. If you can let me know when the bath is ready? And not too warm, okay?"

"Okay, Sugar," Tabby said and patted Janey on the shoulder.

Reaching the top of the stairs, Janey saw light leaking out of the bottom of her mother's door. Constance was awake. Janey accidently creaked a floor board and heard, "Janey, dear, come in here and see your mother."

Janey opened the door, stepped in, and smiled at Constance who now lay on top of her blankets. She had a book in her hands, but Janey couldn't see the title.

"Mother, how are you?" Janey asked, noting that Constance looked even paler than usual. "Oh... not getting any better, I'm afraid. Getting harder and harder to catch my breath these days. The question is... how are you? Did Doc take good care of you? Such a terrible thing to happen to my child. Where did you get that horrid dress? I don't remember you having that one. Looks like Susanna Plinth's. She fell down and hit her

277

head last year. Waited too long to go to Doc's. When she showed up her head was swollen and they had to cut her hat off. She always wore a hat, you know? So, died right there on Doc's exam table not two minutes after they got a gown on her."

Janey shuddered and started to speak, but Constance interrupted.

"Well, they got Sully down at the police office, I hear. I suppose there will be a hearing."

"No, mother. I guess the word hasn't gotten around yet, least not to Beulah McKay."

"What word's that?"

"Sully Albright is dead."

"What? No? Who killed him? Don't tell me... Tom? I figured he'd kill him as revenge for you. They've always hated each other."

"It was more Sully hated Tom, but... no, it wasn't Tom. Sully's body was found out in the Hollow, but the sheriff did say it was murder."

"Oh? Where'd you see the sheriff?"

"It doesn't matter, I'm going to take a quick bath and then I'm going to bed." Not even ten minutes with Constance and Janey had all she could bear.

"Should still be some hot water left in the tank, Percy's got the fire going."

"Wonderful," was all she said and leaned in to kiss Constance. A peculiar odor filled her nose when she got close. The redolence of old people nearing their last days. Something more imagined then real, she guessed. Perhaps recognition fueled by one's own experienced subconscious mind. The ambiguous smell of death. She looked close at her mother's face. It was there in her eyes.

Janey felt a weighty sadness envelope her and she struggled to maintain her composure. "I'll be back," she said as she moved toward the door.

Taking the doorknob in hand, she smiled back over her shoulder. Constance was watching her intently, a strange light in her eyes. "I may not have heard about Sully, but I did hear about the reservoir. It's coming, for sure. It's the end. I think—the end of everything."

"Well, there is always the house in Salem."

"I'm never leaving Gowan."

A fleeting feeling of confusion came over Janey followed by a moment of clarity when she grasped her mother's meaning. She smiled again as the tears welled, and stepping out, she pulled the door shut as if closing another chapter on her life.

8

Janey lay in her bed, staring at the ceiling, waiting for sleep. She spent no more than ten minutes in the bath with a bar of soap. Just enough to get the stink off her body. The cast iron flower necklace still hung around her neck. It would remain there every day, all day, until this business with Mab was through—or herself, dead.

The room was starting to heat up even though the sun had not completely broken the horizon. The lace curtains rippled in the morning breeze at the open windows. She had placed two cast iron bookends in the shape of elephants on each one. Her hope was that they would ward off any attempt to enter by anything not human. Having open windows on the second floor, even without a trellis, was risky business these days.

She thought back on Cora's mention of how her and the rest of her family were now targets. Constance never slept with open windows as she believed that sleeping exposed to the outside air could bring illness. Tabby and Percy, up under the roof, were just the opposite. Janey hoped that because the Snoaks weren't kin, they would be spared by Mab.

Janey wondered if fairies could pass through solid objects. She thought to ask Tom, but she doubted they could. They weren't ghosts or specters, so were still subject to the laws of physics. It was just the magic. Janey had locked her door and placed the key close by. She itched to climb the stairs to the cupola and view Carter House. She feared that if she put her eyes on that place, Mab would detect her and know from where she watched.

They were still going to have to go up to Nixie's Bluff, or at least, her and Tom. They couldn't just waltz in, appearing all innocent, like originally planned. They were past that now. It was apparent with Cora's attack that they were now known. When they went up there, they would be going into battle and would have to be prepared. She thought about who might be trusted to come along. Cora was out of the question. Tom was a definite, and perhaps, Doc. Merlyn would just try to take control by invoking his authority. So, he too would have to be left behind.

Janey had to think about it some more, and while she did, images of Sully without his head kept creeping in. What could have happened out there in the Hollow that could have caused such an injury? A shudder moved over her like a thousand little spiders. She tried to push that picture out of her head for the millionth time.

It would be another half an hour before exhaustion would override it, but even in sleep, the nightmares found her. The one that would haunt her throughout the following day was of her standing in a room full of people she knew. Constance had been seated next to Beulah McKay. They had been talking loudly when Constance said, "Yes, you're right, no rest for the wicked." When Janey looked her way, the room went quiet and she found they were all glaring at her. She came up out of her deep sleep with a start and opening her eyes for a minute, she realized it was just a dream. Rolling over onto her side, she mumbled in a sleep-soaked voice, "You want to see wicked? I'll show you wicked," and then fell back into slumber.

9

Sheriff Pete Mowry stood in Whip-poor-will Hollow, scratching his head and eyeing his model A where it sat nose deep in the swamp. Steam bubbled up from a ruptured radiator and rose into the dark air. He was sure his men had heard the car leave the road and hit the tree. The same one that had also saved him from plunging to the bottom of the swamp. What perplexed him more, though, was why a small black pony had rocketed from the brush, crossed the road in front of the Ford, and then disappeared into the trees on the other side.

The sheriff didn't normally swerve for animals, but hitting a pony with his car was unconceivable. Pete bent forward and gazed into the thickets, looking for any movement to tell him where the pony had gone. There was none. The frogs, crickets, and katydids, had resumed their riparian chorus. Whip-poor-wills piped from different locations and a fox barked (sounding more like a shriek) as if asking, 'Why are you here?'

He could hear his men working just around the tight hairpin turn that he was getting ready to make just before the accident. In his haste to retreat from the partially submerged car, he had left his flashlight behind. He wasn't going back into the muck to retrieve it. Pete and his deputies rarely came into the Hollow. There was just no need. The times he had to come, he'd always had one kind of an eerie experience or another. "Always feels like I'm being watched," he had once commented to his deputy.

Pete turned and looked toward Nixie's Bluff. The silhouette of the belvedere at Carter House was just visible above the tree tops. He had heard things about Benjamin Carter taking a new bride in a foreign land and the trouble that had begun upon their return. Word had come to his office, from Philip Shannon, that he suspected Carter was missing and perhaps he and his deputies could keep their eyes peeled. Pete chose not to act until Shannon could show proof that Carter was missing and not simply away on some business venture. There was also the grapevine, but Pete didn't pay much attention to that. Shaking his head and sighing, he turned and headed down the road to where his men were still canvasing the woods for Sully's head.

The sun was trying hard to show itself, but the clouds thickened and a light, misting rain began to fall. Pete's two men, Deputy Stanly Weston and special deputy, Arliss Balch, had placed lanterns around the blood-soaked ground where the body had been found. Pete saw his men emerging from the tree line on the north side of the road and hollered, "Hey there!"

"That you, Sheriff?" Weston shouted, "Where's your car?"

"Yep, got run off the road up around the bend," the big man said and tramped over.

"What the hell by? Ain't seen no cars come through since we got here."

"Ah, shut it, Arliss. It weren't no car. Someone's damn pony got loose and run out in front of me. I'm half sunk in the swamp."

Arliss cast his eyes down, he knew better than to question Pete Mowry. If he wanted a position like Stan, as a full-fledged deputy, he was going to have to kowtow to Pete's every whim.

Stan said, "How the hell we gonna get back, Sheriff? Arliss and I been out here all night, and we're beat."

"Well, we are either going to have to pull the damn thing out or walk back to Grunewyck. Maybe get ol' man Davidson to come down here with a tractor and hook a cable."

"Knew we should have brought the horses," Arliss said, turning to Stan, who just shrugged and looked at Pete.

"We're walking back," Pete said." So just git the fool idea out of your head, Arliss. You just gather up those lanterns and turn off them damn flashlights. They're too damned expensive to be leaving on whilst you not using 'em. You fellas find Albright's head?"

"Hell, no," Stan said, flicking off his light and sticking it in his pocket. "Couldn't have rolled all that far, for criminy sake. Found a Colt revolver, though." Stan started to hand it to Pete, who said, "Just hang on to that. Might belong to that idiot officer Cobb's got working for him."

Stan then attempted to turnover the revolver to Arliss, saying, "Here, you carry it."

"Now, dammit, I said, you!" Pete growled. "If you don't want the weight, give him your flashlight, but you keep the gun, hear me?" Stan shrugged, nodded and replacing his flashlight with the revolver, he handed the light to Arliss who was already overburdened with lanterns and his own flashlight.

Arliss huffed, but keeping his eyes off of Pete, he rearranged everything before turning away from the other two, obviously fuming.

Stan said, "So, we looked damn near everywhere and no head of any kind. I think we're done here, Sheriff, I truly do. Besides, this place gives me the creeps. Been hearing all kinds of weird things that don't make no sense, and..."

"Like what?" Pete asked, looking from Stan to Arliss and then back.

"Well, like... something big was moving around back in there. Then there come enough splashing to make a man think the world's biggest damn catfish was having a heyday."

Arliss turned back, but keeping his eyes cast to the road, added, "Yeah, and it's been sounding like there's a crowd of people back in there having a gathering and talking their damn fool heads off. And then there was...

"What the hell is that, there? Take a gander up that away," Stan said and pointed.

The other two turned to look. A dark cloud appeared to be corkscrewing up from the area of Ghillie's Gate, slightly contrasting against the overcast. It was moving their way.

"And what the hell is that noise?" Arliss said, shaking his head as if trying to dislodge the roaring, flapping, and buzzing like resonance that filled his ears. The cloud began to twist as it moved across the underside of the clouds.

"What, for god's sake, is that?" Pete said.

"I don't know, Sheriff, but I don't feel like sticking around to find out."

"Well, where the hell we gonna go out here?"

"In the direction it ain't," Pete said and turned to find himself alone as the other two were already hightailing it up the road toward Grunewyck. Pete hadn't run in a long time, but the impulse was too great to remain. He soon found himself closing the gap between him and his deputies. Pulling his hog leg from its holster, he fired it back over his shoulder into the noisy cloud that was fast closing. There came a cackling laugh as if a gun fired in its direction, was a ridiculous gesture. Stan, hearing Pete's gun go off, pulled the Colt from his pocket and mimicked his boss.

"Hey! You idiot! I'm back here! You damn well better keep that barrel pointed skyward," Pete said, now wheezing. Arliss dumped the lanterns and grabbing a flashlight in each hand, increased the gap between him and the others.

It became apparent that the cloud was actually a flock of frightening creatures. It lowered to undulate within eight feet of Pete's head. The hog leg came up again but was smacked from his hand before he could pull the trigger. His hat was knocked from his head, and then two large hands took a hold of him and he was lifted skyward. The good sheriff began to swear and when he turned his face up to direct his profanity toward whatever held him, his steady stream of expletives changed to a scream.

A multitude of glistening bodies, with glowing eyes and gaping mouths, laughed and jeered as if in a state of glee over Pete's futile struggles. Stanly was next to be taken and had been able to get off one more ineffective shot before the Colt was wrenched from his hand.

Stanley screamed a lot more than Pete but mostly because of the pummeling he was receiving as he was passed from boggart to boggart.

Arliss proved to be a little harder to catch as he zig-zagged down the road, slipping out of large simian hands several times. A last-ditch effort to make for the trees almost proved fruitful, but one of the larger denizens of the Unseelie Court, with its buzzing insect like wings, put serious effort into capturing the hysterical man.

Racing past the rest, it came in low and wrapping its long slender arms around the runner's waist, it squeezed Arliss so hard it took the wind right out of him. The deputy dropped the lights and swooned before he could even start screaming.

The vast flock of bogey fae began to rise higher and higher, finally melting into the clouds overhead, every grotesque mouth voicing their mirth at having captured three mortals all in one swoop.

Thirteen-year-old Martin Davidson, who had been out preparing for an early morning fishing trip, was stepping from his father's storage shed and heard raucous laughter emanating from the clouds over the Hollow. Goosebumps rose on his arms and his hair stood on end. Not waiting to see what it might be, he hightailed it for the house, dropping his pole and coffee can full of worms. Bursting through the door, he met his mother and threw his arms around her, pushing his face against her chest.

"My oh my! Martin! What's got into you, you're as white as a sheet?"

Martin lied, "Some big animal, in the bushes outside, ma."

She scoffed and said, "Ain't nothing around here big enough to eat a boy your size." She tousled his hair with a chuckle and continued on with her morning tasks.

Martin would never share the incident with anyone until years later, and then it would be retained in his memory as one of those things that he could never be sure about. He would use it as a tall-tale to share with his drinking buddies at a tavern in Ipswich, the town where the Davidson family would start a new life on a new farm before the year was out.

Tom sat alone at a table in Brenner's, his breakfast half eaten. He never voiced his disappointment over the disbanding of the posse to Chief

Cobb or anyone else. He had a plan to somehow divert the group of men to Carter House, giving him an opportunity to look over the property and perhaps confront the occupants. With Cora bedridden, that left Janey, and possibly, Doc. Tom knew he could always go up there alone; he had all the knowledge he needed to do what needed to be done. He didn't want Janey to go, there was no sense putting her at risk. If Mab already had a target on Janey's back, taking his newfound love into that woman's lair would be a bad idea. He could always tell her what happened afterwards. If he didn't survive, none of it would matter anyway.

He wanted something more than his iron bracelet standing between him and Mab's troupe. A trip to the blacksmith should offer something. He could concoct a story to tell Art Jones about his memories of how the blacksmith had toyed with sword making back in the day, and then offer to buy one for the sake of nostalgia. Something to have as a keepsake for a town that was soon to become extinct. He would have to figure out a way to carry it. Walking around with a sword would surely attract attention. There was also the chain idea, he could grab a couple of short lengths while there.

Tom finished his eggs and bacon, then sat looking around the room. Beth appeared to be dozing at her desk, and Colin was busy behind the bar doing his last-minute checks for the morning and writing occasionally on a pad of paper. He glanced up and saw Tom watching.

"Anything else, Tom? Maybe pancakes? We have pancakes. More coffee?"

"No, Colin, completely full up."

"Okay then."

Colin came over and took the plate, cup, and silverware.

"You're doing some hard thinking over here, Tom."

"Yes, got a lot on my mind."

"Most of the town does. Gowan's one of the unluckies. You heard about the reservoir, right?"

"Certainly, another chapter closing. We knew it was coming, though, right?"

"Well, I think everybody felt there was a slight chance that maybe…"

Beth called out, "Paul's not up yet."

285

"Nope, but I'm damn well aware. I had to cook breakfast, if you remember?"

She shook her head as if in disbelief and made her way to Tom's table. In a low tone, she said to Tom, "Poor Paul, old man Fleming, Ellie's pa, worked him over good last night. Caught him and Ellie in her bed, you know? Poor fella, could barely walk when he got back here. I was afraid Fleming would follow him down and make trouble, but I guess he must have been pretty satisfied with what he had doled out up at their place."

"What about Ellie? Must be kind of embarrassing for her if the word is getting around. She might not want to show her face at the café," Tom said.

"If she doesn't show, Boots is going to start pulling out what hair he has left. Might have to hire a temporary, but I suspect it won't matter after tomorrow night's meeting at the townhall. A good many people will start packing up to head to higher ground."

"But there's still time, right? I suspect the Woodpeckers will need a place to eat and sleep, and... drink. They'll save the café, this tavern, Fiske's boarding house, Doc's office, and, uh... Zelda's, for last. Might be wise for you all to hang on until the last minute, make some extra revenue before you have to pack it in," Tom said, and looking at Beth, he could see the wheels turning.

She leaned slightly toward him and said, "You know... that bastard, Shannon, was supposed to have told the mayor and council back in March, but he was sitting on it. Probably scheming a way to make a profit from it. There are a few asking for his scalp. Gave my cousin a call up in North Athol, you know? Up at the far end of the valley? Said they have already started flattening buildings there. I was putting in an order for supplies down at Gibb's Ford where I get my whiskey and Kelly O'Brian, he's the proprietor down there, told me they've already got half the town gone and it would have to be my last order. I'd have to get my whiskey somewheres else. The demolition company is doing just what you said, saving the tavern and inn for last so them Woodpeckers can have a place to stay and drink while they knock the town down around them."

"Sad news. I guess this will be the last time I come to Gowan."

Colin said, "Yeah, they's working from both ends of the valley, gonna meet up right here. Good idea to wait, I suppose. I 'spect Beth and I will hang on 'til the very end. I know Boots will too, once he gets wind of it... the idea, that is. Make a few more bucks before we have to skedaddle. Could probably put five to a room, upstairs, with eight rooms, that's, uh... forty men, I believe, can sleep here. Gonna need some more help, though. Think I'll ask Charley Bates Jr., maybe Danny Billings, or Cal Loffler, to stick around after the butcher shop and the slaughter house close down. Sandy's already talking about getting out before the end of the year, and Otis, the same. Gonna have to pack my cold cellar full of pork and beef before they do, just so I can hold out until the end. Hey, how about you? Want a job? You got nothing going, right? Gonna head back to Salem soon, I'm imagining? Hell, you're only sticking around because of Janey... oh, sorry. That's just rumor."

Tom looked him square in the face, not sure how to react. It was true, after Kaleb's death there was nothing for him to do around Gowan. He was down to his last few dollars. He could react to Colin being nosey, or he could hold off losing his temper and see what the bartender had to offer.

"Well, Colin, wouldn't you stick around for that reason?" he said, locking eyes with the older man.

"You darn tootin' I would. Nothing wrong with it. If I was young and single and Janey Carter took a shine to me, well... you're a lucky man, Tom."

"I suppose I am. So... what about that job?"

"Oh... interested? You'd be second to Paul, if you start tomorrow. He's not much on bossing people around, though. So, don't worry about that. Room and board, plus a few dollars a day. We'll move you over to number one, which is the smallest with a bed, a dresser, and a chair. Looks out on our house on Ovis Street. Sorry, no balcony. But you can climb out onto the roof of the kitchen, if you a mind to?"

"Sounds like you got yourself a man. When do I start?"

"Tomorrow, if you like?"

"Okay. It's my last 'paid for day' in number ten."

"That's fine, that's fine."

"I've got some other business needs attending to this morning, though," Tom said, looking first at Beth and then Colin.

"That's okay," Colin said with Beth adding, "That's fine with me, too. I can get you on the books and we can get your personables moved over. How you feel about tossing out drunks? Doesn't happen much, but I've got to know if I can look to you for that?"

"Not a problem, I can throw a bad drunk out if need be. But like you said, doesn't happen much from what I see."

"Good. So, let's go back and wake Paul and let him know," Colin said.

"Couldn't that wait?" Tom asked.

"He's got to be up soon, anyway," Colin said. "We got two rooms occupied right now. Some feller sacked out in number two. He's here for the meeting. Come from the demolition company. Gonna explain to the town folks what they can expect. Then there's Mrs. Osborn and Claudia, her baby, down from Dunwich. She's in number three. The infant might wake you crying in the night. So, be ready. Seems... Elizabeth, that's her name, got into a row with her husband, Joe, on the train to Aylesbury. She snuck off the train here and left him thinking she was still on board. I 'spect he got quite a surprise when he went looking. Probably walked the train from one end to the other. Anyhow, let's go on back and roust that lazy bones, Paul."

Tom followed Colin and Beth into a small hallway at the back. Beth kept right on going out to the outhouse. Tom and Colin stopped at a door in the wall on their left, right across from the back entrance to the kitchen. Colin knocked but there was no answer. He knocked again and called, "Paul, you in there?" Tom waited for Paul to swing the door open, bruised, bleary eyed, and angry. Nothing happened. Colin pushed the door open. It was dark, but Tom could see the bed in the corner. The blankets were a mess, but there was no one in it. "Damn," Colin muttered and switched on the ceiling light, confirming the room was empty. It was a good-sized space with a dresser and a wardrobe, a couple of chairs and a washstand in the corner. All the drawers in the dresser were pulled out and one of the wardrobe doors hung open. They were both empty.

"Damn it all to hell, Paul, you..." Colin said.

Walking to the bed he picked up a small piece of folded paper, left

288

on top of the pile of bedding. Flipping it open, he eyed it for a second and then handed it to Tom. "Read this, will you? I can't"

Tom looked at Colin, shrugged, and took the note. "So, you can't read… and he doesn't write worth a damn." It was Colin's turn to shrug, a scowl on his face.

Colin and Beth,

So sorry to have to leave you in a lerch, but I can't let no man beat on me for no good reason. I've took off, me and Ellie are gettin married. Wer leaving Gowan, maybe go down to Springfild or even Bosten. Can't say for sure, but anywheres ol' man Fleming can't find us or I'm sure   he'll try to hall Ellie back home even tho shes of a good age to be doin so. Yood think sheed be abel to live her own life. I hope her leavin is hard on him. Serves him right. Don't worry bout me. I've been savin all the money you had paid me and Ellie has her savins too.

Thanks for all you done for me, you been like my ma and pa all these years.

See ya,

Paul

"Well, Colin, looks like you're down a man?"

"Can't say as if I blame him. He's an orphan, you know. Surprised he stuck around as long as he did. So… how you feel about starting tonight?"

"As long as I can have this morning off. Should be back by evening."

"Okay, I've got to tell Beth."

"Certainly," Tom said as they walked out of the room. Colin, closing the door, said, "We'll move you down tonight. Looks like you get the big room now." He stuck out his hand and they shook on it.

"Be right back. If you could just take up a position behind the bar, that'd be great. Help yourself to a drink, if you like."

Tom nodded and went to stand behind the bar, looking as if he didn't know where to start. He had to come up with a reason to tell Janey why he took the tavern job instead of going to work for Constance. Even though he loved Janey, and truly liked the Snoaks, he just couldn't have Constance bossing him around.

The place grew quiet with the exception of the raucous snores rolling down out of room number two. Turning, he looked at himself in the big mirror. He noticed his face was haggard and he had a few new grey hairs. His blue eyes traveled down to the cheap iron bracelet on his left wrist and took in the spirals cut into the metal. Pouring himself a cup of coffee, he toasted himself in the mirror and said, "Here's to killing bad fairies."

11

Tom swept the entire tavern floor and organized the chairs and tables. When done, he informed Colin upon his return that he was heading out to take care of his afore mentioned business.

"That's fine, Beth and I will take care of things until you get back."

"Already on it," Beth said, now standing in the door of the kitchen, tying on an apron.

"Be back soon," Tom said and walked out.

Heading up the boardwalk toward the blacksmith's, he saw the McCarthy's were already setting up their outside display of produce boxes along with a rack of corn brooms.

"Hello, Tom," Mary said. "You hear about the reservoir? Gonna be a big meeting. You gonna come?"

"Not sure just yet, Mary. Doesn't affect me much. I'll probably be heading back to Salem soon. Feel bad for you folks, though. What are you going to do?"

Silas stepped out of the front door carrying a small sandwich board to set next to the crates. "Well, we know we're not going to get what we want for our place. We're looking at a store over in Hadley. The present owners are closing up shop due to poor health and we got a bid in to buy it. Much bigger town, probably better for business. Folks over there will have to go clear to Amherst for their groceries if somebody doesn't buy the store and reopen. I 'spect they'll be damned happy to see us if we get it."

"Well, good for you. You got a lot of goods to haul."

"Liam McClary and some of his fellow teamsters are looking to be hired for the job. Heard they're chomping at the bit."

"Okay, guess I'll see you tonight?" Tom said and gave them a short wave before turning to head down the boardwalk.

"Good day to you, Tom," the McCarthy's said in unison before returning to their work.

12

Tom passed Sally's shop, and arriving at the corner, he found all the doors to the blacksmith's closed. It was unusual because even in the dead of winter, the smithy would have the big front door wide open along with a few windows. If a person ever wanted to go somewhere in Gowan to get warm, it would be there. No hammer rang at the forge and Tom noticed Art Jone's sign no longer swung from its bracket. So much for his idea. He hadn't thought it through well enough and he chastised himself for that. The swords had been a good idea, but if Cora had escaped with the protection of a mere necklace, then his bracelet might be enough. That was the logic that sent him on his way.

CHAPTER TWELVE

LISSY

II

~

1

L issy, still feeling the effects of her late-night encounter, searched their store to find items she would need for her quest. She had spent a good portion of the morning trying to go unnoticed while she did, hoping to be out of there by noon and on her way to Carter House. She was going to burn it to the ground.

If that woman had claimed the old mansion as her castle, Lissy was going to see to it that she was deprived. Colleen Potter was busy, as usual, and she never asked Lissy to help even once. The girl suspected it was because the more work her mother had, the less she would dwell on the loss of her husband.

Slipping out the back door, Lissy took the alley to Pickett Street and made her way out of town to the west. Passing the Grunewyck train station, she crossed the tracks and walked through the small prairie that bordered the woods. Owen Curtis, the station agent, would share later that Lissy appeared to be on some kind of a mission. The first thing he noticed about the teenaged girl was the way her hair was done up, requiring one of those long-toothed hair combs to hold it in place. Then there was the way she moved, an almost angry, stomping kind of walk. And finally, the flour sack hanging by its drawstring over her shoulder. Owen would always wonder what was in that sack. If he had been privy to its contents, he would have seen a box of kitchen matches, a small, corked bottle of kerosene, a candle, two short lengths of iron chain, and a flask of drinking water. Along with those, an apple, a small wedge of cheddar cheese, and a hunk of homemade bread, all wrapped in cheese cloth.

Lissy walked a dirt path that paralleled the Scottsburg Road, which ran out of the west end of town, up the slope and then curved north. It would take her up to the ridge, ending at an abandoned farm. There, it intersected with a more prominent trail that ran along the ridge, all the way to Mount Ovis. Lissy didn't need to go that far. She would leave it where a smaller one branched off and led to the back side of the apple orchard at Carter House.

Stopping briefly, Lissy checked to make sure the iron made butcher's knives, wrapped in heavy canvas, weren't poking through the sack. They were two of the very same knives her father had been duped into buying years before. He wasn't the only one in the valley that had been a victim of a grifting cutlery peddler. He was a smooth-talking, slick haired man who convinced many good folks that these knives were the wave of the future. A very short one, that's for sure.

The manufacturer went belly up and their corps of salesmen, who had invested heavily in the company to get into the game, were left penniless. Grifters being grifted. Out of desperation, they began to push the knives that they had been saddled with, on the unsuspecting residents of the Spry River Valley.

The set James Potter had purchased was left to sit, rusting in the display window with hopes someone would take them off his hands for a mere pittance. Lissy had helped herself to two of the eight. She thought to take them all, but feared the weight would drag her down and she would have to dump them before she was even half way to Carter House. Two was more than enough.

She stepped into the trees and finding the well-worn trail, she picked up her pace. The day remained cloudy, but the misting rain had stopped for the moment. The day was warming up.

By the time Lissy had reached the back boundary line of the Carter's property, she had sweated through her dress. She had hoped to wear suspendered dungarees and one of her father's linen shirts, but her mother was having them laundered. She had to settle for a simple, knee length, brown frock. Her lace up clodhopper boots were suitable for walking, and wearing a pair of good, thick socks, she wouldn't suffer blisters.

The upside was, the dress would allow her freedom of movement, the down side—climbing, jumping and running, would expose that, besides her boots and socks, she wore nothing else. "Who would be around to notice?" she said, when making her decision.

Lissy had gotten into trouble for losing what her mother said, was one of the girl's best pair of knickers on her last excursion into the Hollow. Because she might have to run, she wasn't going to do it in urine-soaked underpants. Lissie made a point of letting her mother know that she didn't like girl things. The frilly, lacey things that girls were forced to wear. All the clothes that women had to wear that men didn't. It wasn't fair. She openly made fun of elderly local women who still sported corsets and wore bonnets. Lissy willingly accepted the single slap across the cheek from her mother as dues for such behavior. Lissy was content to be in trousers and button front shirts every day of any year.

Colleen started lecturing her on the matter. "It's not lady like. Your tomboy days are over, missy, time to start acting and dressing like a lady." Lissy's response: "But… I don't want to be a lady!" That got her sent to her room without supper where she quietly destroyed her very best dress and then hid it, fully expecting to be beaten once it was discovered.

Leaving the main trail at the fork, Lissy walked the seventy-five plus yards to a small pile of boulders next to a large pool of water at the end of the footpath. Climbing up on top, she could see the house through the apple trees. The grass of the once well-manicured lawn was now up to about her knee. The apples hadn't been harvested and most of them had fallen to rot upon the ground. The open door to the orchard tenders shack swung back and forth in the breeze. Two horses, one white, the other brown, moved lazily from the tree line to graze on the uncut grass as a single hawk circled just below the clouds.

Wanting to get a look at the front of the house, Lissy returned to the main trail and continued south. She went as far as the bluff and when she came to an opening in the trees, she gazed down into the ravine at the pool of water where she had seen the washer woman.

The rock where the crone had kneeled, sat empty. Lissy was glad for that, but shivered anyway. She could also see the lane that led in from the Grunewyck road, the covered bridge, and the gargoyle statues that guarded it. Finding a fallen tree trunk to sit on, she looked back toward the front of Carter House, watched, and waited.

Lissy hoped Mab would make an appearance, or any one of those handmaidens. She doubted they would, though, the gloaming wouldn't come for many hours. She suspected the occupants would remain hidden until then. That's why she was determined to go inside. Fear mixed with her excitement, but that was okay. She had come for a fight and she wasn't leaving without one.

Setting her bag on the ground, she scrounged around inside and pulled out one of the two short lengths of chain. They had been created for the farmers in the area as a general use item. Her father had purchased a barrel of the two-footers from Art Jones. For some reason they had sold like hotcakes on a Sunday morning. Lissy had yet to determine why.

Taking the short length of chain by one end, she swung it above her head. It whistled and clanked, leaving her to wonder if she could get close enough to strangle Mab with it. She reckoned she could throw it and send it spinning to wrap around an arm or leg. Probably not a good idea, though. Doing that meant she would have to retrieve it if she missed, which, would put herself in more peril.

Wrapping an end around each hand, she stretched it out at face level and then practiced wrapping it around an imaginary throat. Movement caught her eye, and looking past the chain, she saw a man approaching the covered bridge on the lane.

He wore black slacks with a white shirt, but no tie. A black suit jacket, hooked by an index finger, was slung over a shoulder. She didn't know him and wondered if he might be that Tom Lynn she had heard was spending so much time with her new teacher. "What are you up to, mister Lynn?" she mumbled to herself.

It troubled her that he was coming right up the road in plain sight. Somebody would surely see him. She could see no weapons and wondered how he planned to defend himself. Did he know he would need iron to defeat the creatures in that house? Lissy decided she was going to have to stop him before he got there.

She would try to catch him at the mouth of the bridge. Speed was of the essence. He was still far enough away that she could make it in time. Pulling the second chain from her bag, she dropped it into the front pocket of her dress. Then removing the knives, she unwrapped them, stuffed the canvas wrap back inside the sack and lay the knives on top of the other items for easy access. Slinging the bag over her shoulder, she slid off the log and ran like the wind.

2

Lissy crossed the property out beyond the orchard, out of sight of the house, using the trees and thickets as cover as she came down the hill on the opposite side of the lane. She could occasionally see the man through breaks in the undergrowth as she moved down the slope. He had stopped under the natural stone bridge and was looking up toward the house. After putting on his jacket, he moved into the trees. Working her way through a thicket, she popped out into a small clearing and met him face to face.

"What… Who are you?" the man sputtered. "What are you doing here?"

"Are you Tom Lynn?" Lissy asked defiantly.

"I am. The nephew of Kaleb Knight, the caretaker of Carter House."

"Well, then… I'm Melissa Potter. Lissy… from Grunewyck."

Tom looked her up and down in her plain brown dress and studied her freckled face.

"How do you know me?" he asked.

"You know Cora, right? Runs the Lost Collie tavern? She told me. Your uncle's dead, now, right?"

"Yes, but why are you here? This is no place for you. There might be danger here."

"And why is this no place for me, when it's some place for you? Isn't this just as dangerous for a man as a girl? You think you will fare better against what's in that house than I will?

"Just like Janey," he muttered under his breath, admiration in his eyes.

"What did you say?"

"Nothing, sorry. So, what is it... you think is in there?" Tom asked, his eyes straying to Carter House before coming back to Lissy's, which not only looked ferocious, but were now glinting.

"There's a woman in that house. Well... maybe not a real woman. Not a human woman, anyway. A woman making people think that she is... when she's not."

"And what is it you're going to do about that pretend woman in that house?"

"I'm going to burn her and that house to ashes. You going to help me?"

"I think we should at least present ourselves proper and meet her. Then, perhaps, we can send her on her way."

"Meeting her is out of the question. Sending her on her way, well... I'm all for that. But if you're not quick about it, she will use her magic on you, and you... won't be you, anymore, Mister Tom Lynn. So, don't be ridiculous. She knows who we are, and she'll just play along until she gets us where she wants us. Then it will be too late for me and you. She's already sent something my way, and she'll be sending something your way, too... and Miss Carter's."

Tom stood in disbelief at hearing this young girl's words. Whatever innocence young girls carried into their adolescence—Lissy Potter didn't. Childhood had abandoned her, and the tempered harshness of adulthood now lingered behind those angry eyes. Then the tears began to leak from the corners, and she nearly shouted, "She killed my father! Now, I'm going to kill her! Are you going to help me, or not?"

Upon completion of her statement, she plopped down onto her backside in the weeds and began to sob into her free hand. Tom crouched in front of her and said, "You should forget about this. Go home, be with your mother, she needs you. Time will take care of it."

Lissy stopped sobbing, and looking up into his face, she asked again, "Are you going to help me, or are you going to try to stop me? Because if you try to stop me..."

She was quick. Her hand snaked into the bag and came out holding one of the iron made knives. Pushing the tip within inches of Tom's throat, she watched as his eyes went wide, and the hand that had reached for her, froze in the air.

"Okay, I'll help... I'll help."

The knife went back into the bag. Tom duckwalked backwards and stood up. Lissy's dress had ridden up almost to her hips, exposing her thighs. Realizing this, she jumped to her feet and looking away, she brushed down her dress.

"I'm sorry, I really don't want to hurt you, Mister Lynn, but I'm going up there. You either come with me or go someplace else. I don't need to even go inside to set this place on fire, but I think that would work better. She won't have no place to be. I'm going to destroy her castle. She can take her bad fairy friends and go back where she came from. But I'm not going to leave here until she comes running out, and if she burns up, fine. If she comes out, I'm going to stick her with my knife. And, well... if she gets me first, then... so be it."

That stern look remained. This wasn't false bravado. Tom had seen obsessive behavior before. Men trying to complete tasks that were obviously too overwhelming for one man. Undertakings that eventually killed them and put them into the written word as legends. Steel driving John Henry being one, Casey Jones another.

"Okay, where do we start?" he said.

"Um... well, we are just going in that backdoor. You'll be my lookout while I start the fire, and then we'll leave. We can wait on the lawn until they come out. I know there are three others' in there that are going to try to protect her."

"Only two, now."

"Only two? How do you know?"

"Because one tried to get Cora, but she got it instead."

"Cora got one?" Lissy grinned, sniffed, and rubbed the tears from her face. "Good, that's one in our favor. Come on, let's go," Lissy said and moving past Tom, she marched up the driveway. "It's not the gloaming yet, so they are probably sleeping. They don't like to come out in the sunlight or out in the open. So, I think we won't have a problem until we get inside where there's no light."

Tom followed Lissy, the look on his face pensive like he wanted to say something. Perhaps try harder to talk her out of it. They soon came to the top of the lane and were now level with the house and the back porch. Lissy never slowed in her self-destructive march. Tom stopped and said, "Lissy, stop. Just one minute."

"No, we have to keep going. There can't be any second thoughts. If we stop and think… we'll just try to talk ourselves out of it. Are you coming?"

Tom touched the bracelet with a fingertip and said, "Okay, right behind you."

Moving onto the back porch, Lissy saw the door was open just a crack. It made her shudder. They were expected. She wanted to stop and peek inside, but instead, she kicked the door as hard as she could. Stepping over the threshold, she looked around. It was steamy, and condensation floated in the air as light mist. The room was dim, but her eyes were quick to adjust. She felt Tom come up behind her, and glancing back for a second, she studied his face. He gave her a nervous grin. Turning back, she moved farther into what had been a kitchen, but now looked more like a greenhouse.

The air was stifling. Lissy noticed the moss growing on the walls and floor. There were crickets and katydids moving over it, quieting their noise in the presence of the intruders. Some kind of a bird flapped through and exited the open door. Lissy's heart rose in her throat and she threw a hand over her mouth.

She looked back at Tom again. He raised his eyebrows and put a finger to his lips as if to hush her and then grinned like it was all for play. She could hear other birds in the house. A large bat fluttered past the open doorway that led into the dining room. It then returned before rising up to the ten-foot-high ceiling, lost from sight. Poking her head in she saw only the large table remained, all the other furniture had been removed. A frog began to croak but Lissy creaked a floor board and it halted its enquiry.

Walking over to the table, she set her bag on top as quietly as she could and turned to Tom, whispering, "Good a place as any. I brought things that we can use, like chains, and well… you already saw the knife. Take what you like. All except the kerosene and matches, they're mine." She stepped out of the way, so Tom could look inside.

"Okay," he said and walked over to inspect the contents of the bag.

"This is where I want to do it… set the fire, I mean. The curtains look like they will burn quite nicely."

"Well, I'd like to look around first, if you don't mind? Maybe go upstairs? Doesn't seem like anybody's home."

"Oh, they're here; can't you feel them?"

The insects that had begun their chorus back in the kitchen, suddenly ceased their noise and a rather regal voice emanated from nowhere in particular.

"Aye, we're still here."

Lissy looked surprised, and spinning around, she pushed her hands behind her back to hide the chain. Tom spun around, knocking Lissy's bag to the floor in the process.

Standing in the center of the kitchen was a rather elegant looking woman dressed in an unusual looking gown of green, plum, and gold that billowed on the floor. Her long white hair hung loose and was adorned by a narrow band of gold that she wore like a crown. Her face was young, but expressionless, her nose celestial, and her eyes changed from green to obsidian.

The woman wasn't much taller than Lissy and she stood with her hands clasped as if waiting. The backstairs door into the kitchen creaked open and one of her handmaidens stepped out to sneer at them. From the left-hand corner of the dining room, just a few feet away, the one with the white patch materialized from shadow; giggling. It padded out of the room to stand next to the regal one that Lissy assumed was Mab.

She remembered the two from the first time she had laid eyes on them down in the woods. But now, there were only two, both standing a head taller than their queen. Tom stepped closer to Lissy and their dark beady eyes tracked him, each making a brief hissing noise, before stepping in front of Mab. One stuck out her tongue at him, crossed her eyes, and then grinned. The other giggled, opening her mouth to show small, sharp teeth.

Lissy felt herself begin to panic; something she hadn't anticipated. She had felt so bold coming there, but now, in the face of the enemy, she wanted to flee.

"Run, Tom!" she yelled, and grabbing at his wrist, she pulled in an attempt to get him to follow her. She lost her grip, but fled anyway, moving through the front parlor and out into the entry hall by the front door. She stopped to see a large hall tree had fallen over to block what would have been her exit out. Realizing there was something in her chain free hand, her eyes fell on Tom's iron bracelet. She had pulled it off by accident.

"Tom," she yelled. Nothing.

They hadn't chased her, so peeking back around the door jamb, she saw Tom stood as if hypnotized, one of Mab's hands stretched out toward him. A strange language filled the air. Mab had captured him and Lissy believed it was her fault.

The smallest handmaiden with the white patch scampered into the dining room. Lissy turned to run up the staircase and heard it squeak out, "Don't run, my sweet, come to me. Come to NicNeas, let us talk, maybe we can be friends, aye?"

Lissy bounded up the stairs and found the condition of the second floor the same as the first. Checking doors as she ran down the hall, she realized too late that she had passed the one that held the stairs that lead up to the third floor and the belvedere where she could climb out onto the roof. There was still a chance she could slip out a window and climb down the heavier vines.

Arriving at the door at the end of the hallway, she threw it open to discover it was the master bedroom. It was not like the rest of the house. The large canopy bed, its headboard against the far wall, was made up, and sleeping pallets lay on the floor, one on each side and at the foot of the bed. The windows in that room were also covered in ivy on the outside, making that space rather murky.

Lissy moved behind the door and pushed herself against the wall, shielded on the right by a tall dresser. She tried to control her breathing, but her lungs burned, her mouth felt dry, and bile had risen into her throat. Tom's bracelet was still in her hand. She dropped it in a pocket, becoming angry at herself for being so reckless.

"Where are you, my dear? Don't you want to play with me? Come out and play with me," the squeaky voice said; now in the corridor. Lissy shivered. She imagined that is what small animals would talk like if they could. "Come out and play with NicNeas, things have grown dull for me in this big house."

301

Lissy remained as still as she could, trying hard not to fidget. There was a chanting coming up through the floor and she feared all was lost for Tom Lynn. She let the chain uncoil from her hand, and maintaining a hold on one end, she wrapped the other around her left, leaving a good fourteen inches between them. Then stretching it out like she had practiced, she crouched slightly and waited for NicNeas.

Fear filled seconds turned into nerve racking minutes. Then came the slightest sound of claws scratching the floor.

"I can smell you, lass. Such a pleasant scent you have. Are you in my lady's chamber? Do you want to take the place of NicTaghan? You could be our sister; NicDobhran and I. My lady would hold you in high regard. Come to me, wee un. Come be NicNeas's sister."

Lissy felt another dose of adrenaline course in when she detected motion through the crack of the door. Stretching the chain across her chest, she mouthed the words, "Be brave, be brave."

NicNeas moved out past the door, still creeping toward the bed. It was like she couldn't sense Lissy, and the girl wondered if, perhaps, the presence of the iron was shielding her. When Nicneas was half way to the bed and started to bend forward to look underneath, Lissy quietly moved out from behind the door and pounced. Pushing the chain against the back of Nicneas' neck, she drove the handmaiden to the floor. There came an animal like shriek, the chained glowed like an ember where it touched Nicneas, and the smell of burning hair rose to Lissy's nose. There came a flash of light and a loud pop that caused Lissy to reel backwards and land on her bottom, her legs splayed out in front.

She watched with amazement as a colorful cloud of mist, the size of a large watermelon, rose slowly toward the ceiling. Upon reaching the plaster, it transformed into a ball of ice and dropped to shatter on the floor. A bewildered looking weasel appeared at the point of impact, a wisp of white smoke rising from the back of its neck. It hissed at her and then rocketed out through the broken window.

As Lissy got to her feet, a long mournful howl resonated up through the boards of the floor. NicDobhran mourning the loss of NicNeas. Despite what had happened, the chanting continued. Following NicNeas, Lissy moved to the window and looked out. Seeing the yard was free from danger, she climbed down one of the bigger vines. At the bottom she dropped the last five feet and found herself back on her bottom.

She thought hard about going back inside to liberate Tom, but felt she needed help. Rising to her feet, she ran down the lane, hoping to find somebody who would come back with her.

Had Lissy attempted to return to the kitchen to rescue Tom, she would have witnessed her companion in a trance-like state, down on one knee, his head bowed toward Mab. She would have seen the ice sword in the Winter Queen's hand, the blade resting on Tom's shoulder as she spoke ancient words. But the most spectacular thing of all—snow falling in the kitchen of Carter House on a hot, summer day.

3

By the time Lissy had made the Grunewyck Road, the clouds had thickened. Day became night, the thunder rolled, and lightening flashed. The storm didn't seem normal, it had come in too fast. "Mab's doings," Lissy muttered.

Thunderstorms didn't normally bother Lissy, they intrigued her, much to her mother's dismay. Colleen Potter would shout at her to get inside, but Lissy resisted. Now, she did wish there was a place to retreat into.

Standing in the road, looking toward Grunewyck, Lissy thought to run home like the last time, but that meant going back through the Hollow. The feeling in her gut said she would never make it. Gowan was closer.

She felt the weight of the chain in her dress pocket. If there was going to be more running, that would be a problem. Leaving the bracelet, she removed the chain and tied it around her waist.

Lightening flashed, revealing what looked like a dark funnel cloud touching down in the area of Ghillie's Gate. Lissy watched, mesmerized, hoping it would move toward the northeast as most tornados do. With each lightning flash, the tail hanging from the clouds seemed to be growing smaller until it pulled up into the clouds completely.

Lissy took off at a jog toward Gowan, looking back on occasion to make sure the tornado wasn't reforming. A lull came in the wind and she felt the first smattering of rain drops. Without the wind in her ears, she also heard strange laughing and cackling, a resonance backed by a consistent buzzing emanating from the clouds overhead.

The hair prickled on her arms and the bile rose in her throat—it wasn't a funnel cloud, after all. It hadn't been coming down when she first saw it; it had been going up. Whatever it had been, was now concealed in the storm clouds overhead.

It was a straight shot to the northside of the village and she did it as fast as she could. The buzzing was getting louder and she dared not look back. Sweeny's funeral parlor soon came into sight. "Great," she said, "The last thing I'm going to see before I die is the place you go after you do."

Lissy milked every ounce of strength she had to go faster. Looking back once, she saw the flock of boggarts undulating in and out of the clouds. They were nearly on her. When they dropped into view, she saw the gaping, tooth filled grins and flashing eyes. The lightning, even though bringing more weirdness to an already weird situation, was helping her keep track of the flock of hobgoblins. Lissy felt her second dose of adrenaline course into her bloodstream, and with it, came her second wind.

She had less than a quarter of a mile before she would make the tree line and the school house. The lightning flashed, the thunder rolled, and glancing back, Lissy watched long, greenish, muscular arms drop from the low hanging clouds behind her. An involuntary whimper escaped her lips as she imagined large, clawed hands grabbing her under the arms and lifting her into the sky.

Remembering the chain in her hand, she raised it above her head and began to twirl it. The wind had picked up drastically, and her weapon began to whistle. One of the dangling arms came too close and the chain severed it just above the wrist. An earsplitting scream filled the air and Lissy watched a large, green hand tumble past, the severed end cauterized and smoking. The airborne beast burst into a bloody mist; its amputated hand doing the same.

Even though capable of moving faster than Lissy could run, the flock seemed to balk at the sight of one of their own meeting its end. Rolling upward, the flock disappeared into the rain swollen clouds.

Lissy broke from the road and into the meadow. She stumbled briefly before gaining her footing. Her speed slowed because of the softness of the ground, but she now knew, without a doubt, the iron-made chain would work just as Cora had said; better, in fact.

The flock had resumed its forward motion, but remained just behind her as if its leaders weren't sure what to do. "They're waiting for you to fall down," she panted out. Yet even if she did and dropped the one chain, they still couldn't touch her because of the other wrapping her waist. Then, she was in the trees.

Lissy could hear the beasts crashing through branches, raining leaves and debris down on her as she serpentined through the ancient oaks. The rain came harder, soaking her to the skin. Her lungs burned and she began to lurch and bounce off of tree trunks. Arriving at the front steps of the schoolhouse, she used the last of her energy to leap onto the front stoop. She hit the door running and the force of her body knocked it open, ripping the latch from the wood.

Somersaulting inside, she rolled onto her feet, spun, and slammed it shut. Dropping the thick wooden bar into heavy metal brackets, she secured the door. Then putting her back to it, she slid down to the floor. Something hit it from the outside, her head banging lightly against the panel. What sounded like fists, pounded on the door. The buzzing was louder now, and she could hear unearthly voices in debate. The banging on the door soon stopped and the flock of boggarts moved up and out of the trees where they circled the school house, cloaked by the clouds.

Archie Bennet, who lived next door, like Lissy, loved to be out in thunderstorms. His mother had told him to remain inside or else he just might regret it. Archie's muttered response was that he wished he didn't have to listen to her nagging anymore. His wish was granted and he was plucked from his backyard to be lifted into the roiling clouds, screaming like he had always made fun of his little sister for doing.

Lissy, hearing the boy's screams, opened a shutter to peer out. She got a two second shot of the boy's kicking legs before he disappeared into the dark, swirling vapor above the trees. Lissy shrieked and slammed the shutter closed. Then running across the room, she dived into the opening under the teacher's desk. Hugging her knees, she rocked back and forth, trembling.

She didn't know the boy taken by the skyborne fiends, but the sight of it had pushed her to the edge. That could have easily been her up there. There came a bout of lightheadedness followed by a flash of lightning. The thunderclap that came after was so loud it caused everything to shake and Lissy to faint away.

Startling awake sometime later, she impulsively pushed her chain out to block the opening, preventing any trespassing boggart from gaining access to her hiding place.

The sun was out and its rays worked their way in through the cracks around the front door. Lissy crawled out of her hiding place under the desk and stood in the middle of the room, just listening. She could hear voices, but the buzzing and flapping had ceased. Peeking through a crack in a shutter at the front, she saw people dragging tree out of the road and righting things that had been blown over. The Unseelie Court was gone and Mab's storm had subsided. Unbarring the door, she stepped out onto the front stoop and scanned the sky, her eyes eventually falling on Carter House in the distance.

A man moved through the nearby trees, picking up clothing ripped from a nearby clothesline. He saw Lissy and hollered, "Good thing you got inside there, missy, that was a doozy of a storm. I think it might have been a tornader. Are you okay?"

"Uh-huh," she muttered as she passed him on her way to the road. The shock was wearing off, but she knew it wasn't the end. There would be more to come. She needed to find somebody to help her. That somebody was probably Miss Carter. Cora told her that she lived in a place called Headmost House up on the northside of Prosper Mountain. Balling up the chain to hide it in her hand, she began to trot in that direction.

A woman stood in the street, calling out, "Archie! You, Archie! Where are you? When I get my hands on you…" She saw Lissy and called out to her, "Do you know my boy, Archie? Archie Bennet? Have you seen him?"

Lissy shook her head no, trying not to make eye contact. The screams that brought her to the school house window still rang inside her head. She knew what had happened to Archie, but his ma would never believe it. Lissy just kept moving.

CHAPTER THIRTEEN

ALDO HALE

~

1

everend Aldo Hale walked toward Gowan, lost in thought. His horse had thrown a shoe and he couldn't get anyone of his parishioners to loan him their car. He had stopped by the Lost Collie to see Cora, but Al had informed him of her situation, then asked the Reverend if he wanted a drink. Aldo knew full well it would cut into his time but he couldn't resist a double whiskey. Standing at the tiny bar, he brooded about the walk to Gowan. He had witches on his mind and felt he was solely responsible for bringing about their demise.

Reaching the ford at the ravine about an hour later, he had caught sight of a man moving out of the covered bridge in the distance and up the hill to Carter House. "What are you up to, mister?" he said to himself.

Aldo's plan was to gather several able-bodied men to accompany him to Nixie's Bluff and get permission from Constance or Janey Carter, to go up there. He thought to stop by Doc's and speak with Cora. They didn't like each other much, but she might shed some light on some things he was curious about. Aldo soon lost sight of the man, so pushing onward, he trudged up Berryman's Crest.

A bank of clouds rolled in rather quickly as he entered the cottage district and he picked up his pace. He just made the front door of Doc's office when the rain began to come down. He greeted a bleary-eyed Hannah with a smile and a howdy as she moved to the window to look outside. The door to the exam room was shut and he could hear Doc talking with a patient inside.

"Hello, Nurse Bolen, I'm here to visit Cora MacLean, is she awake?"

"Well, if it isn't Reverend Aldo Hale. How's life?"

"Could be better. Would you check and see if Cora is awake? I'd like to talk to her."

"Certainly, Reverend. Wait here, please."

He watched Hannah make her way around the night nurse's station, and pulling a curtain aside, he heard, "Oh, good, you're awake."

"Well, it's still daylight out, you know, or is it? Getting kind of dark. Anyway, haven't even had my supper yet. Too early to be tucked in for the night. When is Doc going to let me out of here?"

"A few more days, Cora, then you can go home and rest there. You have a visitor, by the way."

"Is it Janey or Tom? Been waiting."

"Nope, it's Reverend Hale. Here to save your soul, I imagine."

"Hell, I should be the one to save his. Well... send him back. I'm up for a fight, anyway."

"No fighting. Not good for you anymore, Cora. Here let me take your temp." Hannah stuck the thermometer between Cora's lips, waited the prescribed amount of time, pulled it out, read it, smiled and said, "Okay, I'll send him back."

"You do that."

Hannah returned to the front and said, "Go on back, Reverend. She says she's ready for a tussle. Please, don't oblige her. Remember, she's had a heart attack."

"Oh, you don't need to pity me, I can't oblige it," Cora hollered, "Come on back here, you old charlatan."

Hannah nodded toward the back and Aldo smiled, adjusted his collar, and strolled that way.

Cora watched him come, his black trousers and jacket covered in dust. His long graying hair was swept straight back from his forehead, his goatee showing greyer than what was on top. She didn't attend his sermons because she couldn't abide his view on things. Outside, the wind picked up and the room grew even darker. Hannah turned on the lights and smiled at Cora as she moved through, ignoring the Reverend.

"Hello, Cora. How you feeling?" Heard you had a heart attack. Sorry, been a while since we talked. Stopped into the Collie and spoke with Al, said you were here. So, I walked over."

"You mean Al didn't run you out with a shotgun?"

"Uh… no, he was rather cordial, actually."

"So, probably in one of his better moods. Most likely because I haven't been around to nag him. What do you want, Aldo? You came all this way, so… must be important."

"Well, rumor has it…"

"You mean, the grapevine? Or should I say, Helen Blake?"

"Say whatever you want, but I'm not here to fight, and you're not supposed too."

"Aye, take advantage of an old woman when she's down. So, what is it that brings you? Your place is over in Grunewyck."

Hale looked back over his shoulder and not seeing Hannah, he walked away and checked the other beds to see if they were empty. Returning to Cora, he said, "I want to talk about Carter House… and those witches."

"Witches? There are witches?"

"Why, yes, four of them, living up at Carter House. You trying to josh me? You know to whom I refer."

"I don't know of any witches."

"You know of three who came down in Carter's automobile. Then there's their leader, who… no one's ever seen. Well, except for maybe Chief Cobb and that shyster, Shannon."

"Playing too much into it, Reverend. It's been blown all out of proportion through that gossip you're so fond of."

"Then, who are they, if not demon spawn?"

"You really want to know? Or do you want to go on believing they're witches so you can have someone to burn at the stake?"

"Burn at the stake?"

"I know your history, Reverend. I know where you come from. I know from your fire and brimstone sermons that you couldn't want more than to make a name for yourself by rooting out witches in the twentieth century. Tell me I'm wrong?"

"I'm sorry you see me in such a strange light. We don't burn people at the stake, anymore."

"Then what you going to do? Have them arrested? Run them out of town on a rail; tarred and feathered?"

"There are things that can be done, but I wouldn't go as far as to incriminate myself by sharing them. I came here to learn what you know, hoping it would help me eradicate those devils. I was kind of counting on you to help me. I just want to know what you know."

"Are you sure about that? Because I can assure you, it's not what you think. You just might be out of your league on this."

"Out of my league? Nothing a good scripture reading can't cure."

"You're wrong there, Aldo."

"How do you know?"

"The very reason I'm in here. I guess you can say... even I didn't have the heart for it."

"Nothing that God can't put asunder."

"You can chant scripture 'til your blue in the face and all you're going to do is annoy them... just like you do, me."

"So... what do you know?"

"That they ain't witches. They be fae... plain and simple. That there's the Queen of Air and Darkness along with her handmaidens."

A grin formed his lips and he said, "You're telling me they is fairies? Like, Peter Pan, or those folks from Shakespeare, what was that...oh, Midsummer Night's Dream." He sneered and shook his head.

"No, those were trooping fairies, the Seelie Court. They might have a good laugh at your expense, but this is the Unseelies we're dealing with... the dark Sidhe. We are dealing with Mab... and she's no milk toast."

"So, how do you know this?"

"First, aren't you going to ask me how I know there is only three, not four?"

"Very well?"

"Because it was one of them dark haired, ferret faced bitches that came for me at Chastity's just two minutes before my ticker decided to take a holiday."

"So, she attacked you?"

"I 'spect that was her goal, but she got her hands on something she shouldn't have."

"You killed her? How?"

"Nope, it was all by accident."

"So, tell me?"

"Iron, plain and simple. They can't abide it. Supposed to ground their magic and cast them into mortality for whatever amount of time it's present. But it looks like it does more than that. That imp touched my necklace and dissolved into a cloud, and then into a polecat that took off like a streak, hissing up a storm."

Cora picked up her Victorian era necklace from her nightstand and showed him. Aldo's face remained expressionless. His eyes narrowed and he said, "Iron, huh? Sounds like codswallop to me."

"Believe what you want, Reverend. But if you're thinking about facing off with that... that woman, you may want to bring some along. Maybe a pry bar, or better yet... a frying pan."

"This should be enough," he said and pulled a small, wooden crucifix, slung on a leather thong, out of his shirt collar, and then a well-worn pocket-sized version of the Geneva Bible from inside his jacket.

"Well! There's an oldie, for you."

"A distant relative's. Got passed down through the years."

"I suppose it has John Hales signature inside the cover?" Cora chuckled. It was her turn to shake her head.

"And if it does?"

"Won't do you no good. Well, unless you throw it at her."

"Good enough for me... and my work."

"Believe what you want, Reverend, but heed my word, I've told you all you need to know. If you don't act on it, well... it's your funeral."

"I'm going to gather me some good, strong men, and go on up to that house and drag those... whatever they are, out by their hair, and, well... then we'll see."

"You came here to find out what I know. You have. Now, I'm tired and I need to rest. You're just wasting your time here. There is nothing you can do."

Growing angry, Aldo stuffed his book back inside his jacket and said, "We'll see about that," and stomped out. Cora turned her face to the side and nestled into her pillow, whispering, "Yes, we will."

311

CHAPTER FOURTEEN

GOWAN

IV

~

1

People were already gathering at the townhall for the meeting even though they would be waiting an hour or more before the start. There was talk about resistance, but most of that was quashed as it was too late for such nonsense, Philip Shannon had saw to that. The main topic of conversation, though, was the unexpected storm that had rolled through, possibly spawning a tornado that most confessed they never saw hide nor hair of. The air on the wet grass of the green was somber as the inhabitants gathered like they had for one hundred and fifteen years. The first one, a year of excitement about the future of their new town, and now, the last, would be about its end.

There was some talk of the missing and the dead. "Was it illness?" one man asked. "Maybe suicide?" another conveyed, "Mayhaps those poor folk couldn't bear losing their home or their beloved town." A few of the attendees present knew some degree of the truth, but they weren't talking.

Nealy stood at the back of the crowd, just watching and listening to the talk. Merlyn had dropped out of sight, but he had been a bear lately and Nealy was happy to be free of him. He understood the pressure his boss was under with all the work that had boiled up, starting with the disappearance of Benjamin Carter and the deaths of Vern Sweeny,

Kaleb Knight, Bessie LaVern, and Sully Albright. Along with them, the now missing sheriff and his two deputies. Merlyn had been charged with retrieving the sheriff's car out of the Hollow and it now sat behind the townhall waiting on the state boys to look it over.

Nealy heard someone walking fast like they were afraid they might be late for the meeting. Turning, he watched Lissy Potter heading up the center of Main Street, a chain belt wrapping her waist. She stopped briefly to watch the crowd, her hands on her hips.

"What you suppose is going on there?" Nealy said, pointing. Sandy Brewster turned to look and watched Lissy. "Just a girl running up the street, Nealy. Ain't a crime, you know."

"I know that, but she had a chain wrapped around her waist. Don't you think that's kind of odd. Like she's wearing it for a belt even though she's got a dress on."

"Looks like that Potter girl from over Grunewyck. I knew her pa. Had the general store. He was killed not too long ago. I imagine she's gone a bit touched because of it."

"I know who she is, dammit! But... what the hell is she doing?"

Philip Shannon appeared on the porch of the town hall. Having dragged a lectern from inside, he placed it center stage and began to lay out papers he had removed from his satchel, taking Nealy and Sandy's attention away from Lissy. Another man came out who nobody knew, said something to Philip and they returned inside. Lissy, not caring what Philip had to say, turned and walked away.

2

Young Hugh Swinerton was late for the meeting, mostly because he had waited out the storm. Whatever amount of money the state was paying for properties in the Spry River Valley was more than acceptable to him. His farm, just a mile north of Shoat's dairy, had failed. He had inherited it from his father. Since he wasn't actually farming anymore, he was just living in a dilapidated house on an overgrown property that wasn't worth the cost of a piss pot. He never married, mostly because no one would have him. But it's not like he had never tried. The only way he could ever get a woman to even look at him was because he had forked over good money. His regular visits to Zelda's had lasted until the money had run out. Now, with only a quarter in his pocket, he made his way up the west side of Parson's Ridge. He would have to cut through Benjamin Carter's property to get to the Grunewyck Road.

Topping the ridge, he made haste through the woods and came out in the orchard behind Carter House. Stopping, he looked around and not seeing anyone, he hurried through in order to pass behind the stable to find the path that ran from the natural stone bridge to Ghillies Gate. He wasn't even half way there when he heard the sound of horse hooves coming fast. A tall man, dressed all in white with black, knee-high riding boots, appeared astride what Hugh knew was an Arabian stallion. He had always wanted one as a kid but all he ever got was resistance from his father. "There are more important things to get done around here than riding horses!"

The man on the white horse charged him. Hugh turned and ran back the way he had come, but he was no match for the horse. Looking back once, he shouted, "No, I was just... wait, please, I..." Those were Hugh Swinerton's last words before the horse ran him down. Lurching to his feet, now severely concussed, Hugh stood with a perplexed look on his face. The pounding of horse hooves came again from behind and a strong hand latched onto Hugh's collar to drag him across the yard, the toes of his shabby boots skipping over the ground. His screams lasted until he was tossed headfirst into the well, impacting the wall inside. Plunging to the bottom, there followed a heavy splash and then a chorus of mirthful cackling. The tall man smirked and turned his horse to ride nonchalantly away as if he hadn't a care in the world.

3

"Miss Janey, you got yourself a visitor," Tabby announced to Janey as she sat with Constance at the dining room table having their meal.

Constance scowled at Tabby and then at Janey before turning her attention back to her maid, saying, "We're eating now, you go tell them to come back later."

"Mother, I'll handle this. It's my guest, not yours. Who is it, Tabby? Tom?"

"No, Miss Janey, you best come look for yourself. She on the front porch."

Janey cast a look at Constance and then getting up, she followed Tabby to the front door. Stopping just short of the vestibule, she stepped aside to allow Janey to pass by.

The young girl on the front porch turned to face Janey. Her eyes were sad, and tears leaked from their corners. Her hair was a bird's nest, and a three toothed comb floated among the golden-brown strands. There were freckles, but they were hardly discernable from the dirt. Her nose had been running and there was a tiny bit of dried blood on her chin. The knee length brown dress was filthy and torn. The most unusual thing—the iron chain that wrapped her waist. Janey knew who she was without having to be introduced.

"Lissy? Lissy Potter?" Janey said as she pushed through the door. A whimper escaped the girl's lips, followed by, "Miss Carter?"

Janey said, "Yes, why?"

Lissy pulled something from her pocket and handed it to her. Janey took it and saw it was the bracelet Tom had been wearing. "Tom's?" she asked. Lissy nodded just once before breaking down completely and throwing herself into Janey's arms.

Janey accepted her, not needing to be told that something bad had gone down. A terrible ache formed in her chest and her own tears began to flow right along with Lissy's as Tabby stood nearby, perplexed. They remained entangled in each other's arms for a long time, forging a bond that, unbeknownst to them, would last a lifetime.

ℍ

Lissy had been allowed to clean up with Tabby's assistance, using the Snoaks' water basin in the mudroom as Constance didn't allow strangers into her bath. Janey then took Lissy up to her room and rummaging through her armoire she found an old dress from when she was close to Lissy's age. "Here, take this. It's old but it's clean and you can keep it." Lissy didn't argue, and untying the chain from her waist, she let it fall. Then grabbing the collar of the old brown dress, she pulled it off over her head.

The expression on Janey's face was a cross between concern and disapproval as she eyed the maturing body of her new friend standing before her in only clodhopper boots and thick gray socks.

"I have some underwear that would fit you nicely. You're at an age where you shouldn't be going without. How about it?"

"No, thank you. You ever had to run in wet underwear, Miss Carter?"

"Yes, actually."

Lissy face became like stone and she added harshly, "Underwear that was wet because you pissed yourself?"

"Oh! Well, no."

"Well, good for you, because it ain't no picnic."

Janey said no more as if deciding she shouldn't have spoken at all. Changing the subject, she said, "Shall we do your hair?" and offered the chair at her vanity.

Lissy's face softened and she smiled, "Will you help me? I can never seem to get it right."

"Certainly."

Sitting down in the chair Janey had offered, Lissy studied herself in the mirror. Janey removed the comb and after handing it to the girl, began to brush out her tangled locks. Lissy's expression became tranquil and she seemed to be enjoying the attention.

Having had years of experience attending socials and other gatherings, Janey fashioned Lissy's hair in a most stately manner. When she finished, the girl returned the comb to her hair, skewering the well secured bun at the back of her head.

They were soon out back in the garden having tea and chatting. Tabby watched from the backdoor, a smile on her face. Constance studied the two from her chair in the small conservatory; her best China cup in her hand and a scowl on her face.

"You see those chains, Tabby? What do you suppose that's about? Odd, don't you think?" Tabby just smiled, shrugged, and returned to the kitchen.

Constance had also questioned Janey, "What were those tears for?"

Janey lied, "We are all just really sad about Cora, is all."

"Another person you hardly know," Constance said and shuffled back into the dining room. She was unable to attend the meeting at the townhall. So, she had sent Percy to listen and report back. She had mentioned to Tabby that she felt her world was fast approaching extinction and that she wouldn't live to see the first building to come down in Gowan. She also expressed her worry about Janey's future, saying she found some comfort in that her girl would always have High Gable House in Salem to shelter in, even though it was a bit smaller than Headmost and a great deal older. Benjamin had purchased it the year Janey was born. Then he moved himself into the old Gothic Revival to remain until Janey's third year of life before returning home.

Constance watched the two out in the back yard talking. She knew that Lissy was supposed to be one of Janey's students; but the start of school had been delayed; probably forever. She told Beulah McKay that Janey wasn't going to get her dream job after all. Beulah, on a more positive note told her there would, more than likely, be need for a school teacher down in Salem. Constance responded with, "Well, you know, Janey doesn't need a job. She says it's a matter of principle. You know what I say? Nonsense, that's what I say."

Constance watched the girl reach out and place her hand on Janey's. In less than a minute Janey was on her feet and pacing back and forth, stopping on occasion to gaze at Lissy, who was still talking.

"Tabby! Tabby, come here," Constance called, but Tabby didn't come right away. She was going to send her maid to find out what the fuss was all about. She waited impatiently, listening for Tabby's footfalls.

𝄐

Janey stood in disbelief, Lissy watching her, appearing as if awaiting a beating for opening her big mouth.

"So… Tom may still be alive? Are you absolutely sure, Lissy?"

"Yes, Miss Carter. They did something to him, not sure what, but he didn't come out of that house and I was too scared to go back in. I'm sorry," the girl said with a whimper.

"It's okay, Lissy, not your fault."

Janey returned to her chair and minutes passed with her and Lissy sitting in silence. Janey was pondering her next move. A hand went to her flower necklace with its chipped white enamel as she contemplated.

"What are we going to do, Miss Carter?"

"First of all, please, call me Janey. I will never be Miss Carter to you. Second, I think we need to get out of here for a while. Too many ears.

317

Let's go."

Tabby, having answered Constance's call, now exited the backdoor at a fast walk, but when she arrived at the small table all she found was lukewarm cups of tea and the back gate swinging slowly back and forth in the evening breeze.

Janey and Lissy made their way down the path behind Headmost and walking the fence line between her house and the property to the east, they found their way down to Railroad Street and then Main. Going to the blacksmith's shop they saw all the doors and shutters were closed. Janey tried the door and found it unlocked. The two of them slipped inside.

"Why are we here, Miss… Janey? There's no one here? It's dark and it smells bad?"

Janey touched the chain wrapped around the girl's waist and said, "For that."

Grinning at Lissy, she moved to a shelf, found a lantern and after lighting it she began her search. They soon found the area where Art Jones stored his finished items. Many things had been placed in oak barrels for bulk sales. Plow shares, pieces of iron fencing, horse shoes at seventy-five cents for a dozen, axe heads, assorted tools, and—rolls of chain. Next to them, a barrel with a tag that read, 'For Liam-Delivery-Potter's General Store: Precut Chain Lengths.'

"These were for us… my folks, I mean," Lissy said.

Glancing into the dark interior, Janey sighed. The barrel looked empty. Anger flashed in her eyes. "Not anymore," she growled and kicked the barrel. It fell over and rolled away, something rattling inside.

Lissy chased after it and when it stopped moving, she reached into the mouth of the barrel and said, "Well… there's one left."

She held it up for Janey to see. The look of dismay left Janey's face and taking the chain from Lissy, she said to the absent blacksmith, "Well, Art, it looks like you were able to cut at least one more before you left us."

Finding an old rag, she wiped it clean of oil. Then wrapping it around her fist, she continued her search. While she looked, Lissy said, "I suppose if those flying hobgoblins come after us, this would be a good place to hide, huh?" Janey chuckled and said, "Yeah, there's enough iron in the place to keep even the nastiest of fairies away."

They came upon different components for picket fences made of iron. There were long, narrow flats for rails, and assorted sized rods for pickets. The shortest were about eighteen inches in length; almost too long to be concealed. Janey took two of them anyway.

Moving to the grindstone, she had Lissy crank while she sharpened one end of each picket. Setting them to cool, she walked over to Art's closet-like office. There was a note tacked just below the window in the door that read:

Gone to my sister's over in Warton. She's taken sick. Don't know when I'll be back, if ever.

Art

"Hmmm..." was all Janey said, and when she turned away, Lissy did a quick read before following. Retrieving the rods, Janey handed one to Lissy. "Take this and keep it behind your back. Try not to poke a hole in my dress, huh?"

"My dress... now," Lissy said and stuck out her tongue.

"Just teasing," Janey said and chuckled before moving toward the front door, blowing out the lantern on the way. Leaving it on the floor, she poked her head out and seeing no one, she stepped through.

"Wait! Don't leave me in here alone," Lissy yelled and ran out, grabbing Janey's arm.

They were soon walking north in the middle of the street. All the shops were closed except for Brenner's and Boots'. Biddy and Clyde stood at the empty café' window, waving at the two as they passed. Boots had gone down to the meeting and his employees were getting a much-needed break. Beth Brenner sat on a large wooden box at the front of the tavern, a beer in one hand and a cigarette in the other.

"If you're going to the meeting, you might be a little too late. Colin will be back with the news, soon enough. If you want to sit here with me, you're more than welcome."

"Oh, no thanks, Beth, we've got something else to do. Maybe we'll stop and check on our way back."

"Okay, we'll be here, I'm guessing. Good gracious, we're going to have to move! All these years and it's just pack up and get the hell out. Oh well, see you later."

Janey was trying to come up with a plan but kept drawing a blank. She needed help, but Tom was out of the picture now. A talk with Cora was in order.

Lissy wouldn't give up the two chains wrapping her waist, but Janey convinced her to give up her picket. They lay them and Janey's chain in a patch of weeds by the door and went inside the doctor's office.

They found the front desk vacant, but moving back toward the hospital addition, they ran into Caroline coming down the corridor carrying a dirty plate, silverware, and a glass.

"Janey! Here to see Cora?"

"Yes, may we?"

"Who's your friend?" Caroline asked, smiling at Lissy.

"This is Lissy, one of my students. She's also a friend of Cora's from over in Grunewyck."

"Well, okay, so… Cora's just had her supper and she needs to rest. Please keep it short."

"Will do," Janey said

The curtain was drawn and as they approached, Janey announced their presence by calling out, "Cora?"

"Still breathing. Come on in."

Janey pulled back the curtain and saw Cora sitting up in bed, smiling. "Well, Melissa Potter, come all this way to see your friend, Cora?"

"Lissy, just Lissy, and… well… yeah."

Janey said, "She has something to tell you, Cora. It's bad news, but you should know. I can't keep it to myself, sorry."

"Oh, just tell me. If it kills me, it kills me."

"Better not be killing anybody back there," Caroline shouted from the front desk.

"Caroline, my dear, could you please move out of earshot so I can visit with my friends?"

"Now, Cora…"

"Now, Cora, nothing. Can't you go into Doc's office and shut the door? Take your magazines and go."

"I will, but only so I don't upset you. You don't need any upsetting. This reservoir thing is enough, let alone the other things that are going on around here."

320

Janey turned and watched Caroline pick up several magazines and move out of sight. Upon the closing of the doctor's office door, Janey said, "Lissy, tell her everything you told me."

Lissy told Cora what had transpired up at Carter House. When she got to the part about Tom, Cora gasped, groaned, and shook her head in dismay. Lissy started to go into it a second time, only from a different angle, but Janey stopped her. The girl covered her mouth, blushing. Sitting in a chair, she remained quiet, her eyes moving back and forth between the two women.

Janey handed her the bracelet. Cora inhaled sharply, took it from her, looked it over and slipped it on her own wrist. Obviously dismayed, she said, "I should mention something now that Mab has taken Tom. She could very well turn him into her Winter Knight. That way she can have a noble mortal to do her bidding. Iron won't have the same effect on him as it does on Mab, but he can still be killed by normal means."

"Killed? We are going to have to kill him?" Janey said with a look of terror.

"I'm sorry, Janey. I know how you feel about him. I, too, found him likable, but there will be a time for grieving later. He's hers, now. Her's until he dies. Tom's a serious threat to us. The one thing in our favor is, it takes a while for him to develop his mantle."

"His mantle?" Janey asked, as Lissy slid forward on her chair to take in Cora's every word.

"Yes, his role, the thing that will soon make him nearly impervious. If we wait too long, we may not be able to kill him. She's probably already knighted him and he has his power now. Don't hesitate to do what needs doing."

Janey stood watching, listening. "I'm not sure I can kill Tom, or any other human for that matter."

"I'm sure you will do what needs doing. Now, there should be more than just the two of you, though. Maybe Chief Cobb, or Nealy. Perhaps… Doc?"

"Where should I go?" echoed in the corridor. Janey turned to see Doc coming their way. They hadn't heard him come in. She looked back to Cora who had put on her poker face and when Doc entered the room, he studied them, one at a time. Seeing Lissy, he said, "Melissa Potter, sorry about your daddy. How are you?"

"Lissy, I like, Lissy."

"Okay, Lissy, what brings you to Gowan?"

"I came to see Cora."

"Very well, so… what's going on? And, as I said… who needs to go where?"

"Remember what we talked about earlier? Carter House? Mab?" Cora said.

"Yes, I do," he said, "Still having a tough time getting it through my head, though."

"Well, she's taken Tom. That woman… that Mab," Janey said with fire in her eyes.

"What? She's taken Tom? Tom Lynn? Took him where? How'd she do that?"

"He went up there by himself, Lissy was already there. She saw the whole thing and was able to get away."

Doc looked at Lissy, who just sat, nodding her head, wide eyed.

"Well, I'll be damned. Are you sure?"

"As sure as snow in a blizzard," Cora said, "We are going to need you to help us, Doc. Tom and I are out of the picture, Janey needs to go to Carter House, mostly because it's still her home… so to speak. That in itself carries some power. We could ask Lissy not to go, but I don't think there's any stopping her."

"That's right!" Lissy said jumping up. "You're going to have to lock me up, cause I'll go, anyway. You can't stop me. I got a score to settle."

Doc sighed and rubbed his forehead. "I guess I'll be going with you. I got to see this for myself. I need to get a look at this Mab."

"What have you got for protection?" Cora asked Janey.

"Short iron chains and a couple iron rods."

"What are you talking about?" Doc asked, confusion clouding his brow.

"Iron," Cora said. "It grounds the magic and makes them mortal. In my case, it changed one back to what it was before."

"Same here! Burns them good, too!" Lissy added, "I took one of them women… Well, turned her into something else… that, uh… Nick Neese or something like that."

322

"She had a name?" Doc asked.

"Uh-huh, she told me it before I jumped on her. Had the strangest face, something like a pole cat without fur. She even had pointy ears like I seen on them Christmas elves."

"You jumped on her?" Janey said.

"Yeah, she turned into a weasel, I think it was… and jumped out the window."

Lissy was grinning like she had been out burning ants with a magnifying glass and succeeded in annihilating the whole nest. The other three just stared at her, perplexed, as if they were all wondering where the fear was that most girls Lissy's age would have. Cora went to grinning. "We got the makings of a hero among us," she said, nodding toward Lissy who looked from one to the other with an expression that went from glee to doubt.

Doc studied Lissy and her chain belt as if she might be just a bit touched in the head. Returning to her chair, Lissy pulled the hem of her dress down over her knees. She was grinning again, watching the other three intently.

"We should head up there, now," Doc said, "I'll go get my car, you two, meet me out front. Cora… try to get some rest."

"Aye, and how much rest do you reckon I'm going to get, laying here thinking about what's happening to you up at that house? It might be best you wait 'til tomorrow and do this in the daylight. But then again, if I was in your shoes, I don't think I could wait, either."

"If we don't come back, you go ahead and have Caroline call Chief Cobb and he'll gather a posse."

"Like that's going to do any good," Cora said flatly.

Doc walked out, and they heard him chat briefly with Caroline. Janey hugged Cora as if it may be for the last time. Lissy jumped in for her share and Cora kissed her on the top of her head like it was some kind of a blessing.

Caroline came back and looked in on Cora. They all grinned at her like little children caught in the midst of a prank.

"I don't know what you're up to, but…"

Janey and Lissy hurriedly left the room, grinning. Cora said, "Pull my curtain, will you, Caroline? Doc says I need to rest." Then fluffing up her pillow, she pretended to sleep. Caroline let out with a "Humph!" closed the curtain and returned to her desk. Picking up the phone, she racked the receiver and said, "Helen, it's Caroline, get me Beulah on the line, will you."

6

Janey and Lissy collected their iron and piled into Doc's car. Janey lay her picket on the seat beside her and then wrapped her chain around a hand. Lissy sat in the back, fondling her iron rod, a faraway look in her eyes. Doc glanced at her in the rearview mirror but said nothing. All three were soon gawking at the large crowd of town folk gathered for the meeting. Nealy was now on the porch, standing next to Philip Shannon. He held a short, double-barreled scattergun, its butt plate resting on his hip, the muzzle pointed above the heads of the attendees. Merlyn was nowhere in sight. The majority of the citizens present knew Nealy wouldn't think twice about using his shotgun and that kept them all in check.

Janey exchanged glances with Doc and he said, "Looks like things are heating up about the reservoir."

"Yes, if they only knew what we know. They might think differently. I mean, better to get out of Gowan while they're still alive."

"You mean... what we presume," Doc said, still showing his skepticism.

Lissy said from the back seat, "If I'm right, presume means—just guessing," "...and there's no presume.... It's real, and it's happening."

He looked at Janey and then in the mirror to see the anger in Lissy's face. Janey looked back to see Lissy, now leaning forward in her seat, her head cocked to one side, glaring at the both of them.

Knowing what the teen had been through, she empathized. "It's going to be okay, Lissy. Doc will know soon enough. Then I'm sure you won't hear any more maybes."

"It's not going to be okay... least not 'til that woman's gone, and if that means dead, well... You will see Doc, you will see." Slamming herself back in the seat, she pushed herself into the corner, grumbling as she fingered the sharp point of her picket.

"I'm sorry, Lissy. It's just, I'm a man of science and it's difficult to believe in magic. I just need convincing. I am sure as soon as I see it, then there will be no question." He glanced in the mirror again but Lissy didn't respond as she sat staring out the window at the passing cottages. Janey's face had become thoughtful, her eyes on the chained wrapped hand in her lap.

A hundred or so feet beyond Berryman's Crest, Doc said, "Who in the hell is that, now?"

Janey looked up to see a tall person standing in the middle of the road in the light mist, looking up toward Carter House. Lissy slid to the middle of the backseat and leaned forward for a better look. When they got close, they saw it was Aldo Hale.

Doc said, "It's the Reverend. What the hell is he doing over here?"

Now grinning, Janey said, "I think I know, and it's the same reason we're going up to Carter House. Cora mentioned that he believes there are witches up there. I bet he's thinking he's going to vanquish them. Maybe have them arrested and then hanged in the town square like his relatives did all those years ago in Salem."

"Stupid," Lissy muttered.

Aldo turned, walked to the Rolls, and stopping outside the window, he leaned down to look inside.

"What's going on, Reverend?"

"Well, hello, Doctor Bolen, and Janey Carter! Just the person I wanted to see."

Turning his eyes to Lissy, he smiled and said, "Well, hello, little one. I know you. Haven't seen you in church lately. Not since your daddy died. Sorry about your daddy."

The girl said nothing and just glared. Janey looked back to see Lissy's eyes glittering and suspected she didn't like Aldo Hale. She really couldn't blame Lissy; not too many people did.

"So, where are you folks off to this evening?"

"I'm giving Janey a ride up to Carter House to save her a walk. I…"

"Very good, that's just what I wanted to talk to you about. I don't know why you're going, but there's witches up there and you might be in for a heap of trouble if you do."

Lissy spat out, "Ain't witches!"

The Reverend glared at her through the window. "I'm supposing you're thinking, like Cora, that they's fairies," he laughed and added, "Well, whatever they are, they need to be stopped. Miss Carter, I would like for you to give me permission to go up there and face those demons."

Pulling a small bible from his jacket he presented it to them. Janey looked at Doc and he shrugged. "Well, okay, you have my permission, but I think you're in for more than you are bargaining for, Reverend."

Aldo said nothing and pulled open the back door to climb inside. Lissy slid away to the far corner. The Reverend glanced at the metal rod and asked, "What you got there, Miss Potter?"

"Something for sticking bad things with."

"You thinking about sticking them witches with that?"

"I'm telling you, they ain't witches," she said, "They're fairies, bad fairies! Believe me, I know! They got Tom Lynn, and…" A sob broke from her lips and laying her rod alongside her leg, she covered her face and turned away.

"They got Tom Lynn?" Aldo asked, his eyes traveling to Janey and then Doc.

"That's the story," Doc said, "We haven't seen him around, and Lissy tells us he was taken by Mab."

"He's one of them, now, and… and it's my fault," Lissy blubbered out.

"One of who? Are you sure?"

"That's what the girl said and we're taking her word for it," Doc said.

"Well, that sticker won't do you as much good as this," the Reverend said, pulling out his little wooden cross on its leather thong. "It's the lord's work I'm doing, and…"

Janey looked back and locked eyes with Aldo. "Oh, my giddy aunt! Let's just drop it for now, no need to upset Lissy any more than she already is. You got your permission, so… just hush up about it. If you can't, then I'll take that permission back and you can just get out of this car, right now."

Lissy looked at Aldo, a sneer on her tear covered face.

"Yes um," was all the Reverend said.

Doc put the car in gear and started to move but then stopped abruptly and glared out the windshield, saying "Now, who in the hell is that?"

7

Merlyn sat upon Massy in the meadow just west of the Grunewyck Road. The freak storm had left the clover wet and the big horse was soaked to the knees. Merlyn had positioned himself just short of the tree line that was the south border of the Carter's property. The horse pawed and chewed at the clover while Merlyn watched the house up on the bluff. It was fast becoming the gloaming and he felt an urgent need to be gone.

He could see that some kind of ivy nearly covered the entire house. The grass in the lawns was three times longer than when he and Shannon had been there. Judge Benson had, again, denied him his search warrant.

The Chief had a serious decision to make and before he turned Massey for home, it had to be either yes or no. So, his mission this day had been purely reconnaissance. He just wanted to see who might be coming or going up on the bluff. It was during this reconnoiter that he had watched a rider, clad all in white, riding a just as white horse slowly around the property. He saw nothing to confirm the gender, but something about the way they rode told him it was a man; someone experienced with horses.

Lately, Merlyn had been thinking about chucking it all. He could just leave it to Nealy and get the hell out of Gowan. The job had become somewhat overwhelming and he wasn't getting paid for all the extra work. Too many dead, too many missing; including the county sheriff and his men.

Mayor Willy Wilton didn't want to talk to him about all of that right now; he had his own issues with the reservoir. But he had promised Merlyn that they would get together at a later time. Helen had orders not to put Merlyn through when he called, and his knocks on the front door of the Wilton's big house that sat just west of Headmost, went unanswered.

As Merlyn sat upon Massy in that field, considering all the pros and cons, he decided it was a yes. "Deerfield, here I come," he muttered to himself.

It was his boyhood home, and it was far enough away to not be affected by the reservoir. His brother, most likely, would take him in. He had nothing to gain by staying in Gowan. His house belonged to the town. There was no money coming to him from a property sale. When the demolition company's Woodpeckers arrived with their hammers, wrecking bars, and dynamite, he would be long gone. "To hell with Mayor Wilton and his pissant town," he muttered, watching the man on the white horse move out of sight behind the Carter's carriage house.

The sound of an automobile rolled across the field and Merlyn watched as Doc Bolen's car stopped just short of the lane leading to Carter House. The headlights picked up a figure walking out of the perpetual mist of the Hollow. It looked like Reverend Hale, his all-black ensemble, bolstering Merlyn's presumption. Hale walked over to stand next to the car, apparently talking to whomever was inside. Then he climbed in. Not even thirty seconds passed before a truck moving at a high rate of speed careened around a bend and then splashed through the water of the ford.

The Rolls started to move, then stopped abruptly. Three people got out with the Reverend and moved to the side of the road, the oncoming vehicle obviously a concern. They were Doc Bolen in his white coat, a teenaged girl, and a woman, who was, without a doubt, Janey Carter.

"Well, Janey Carter. What you up to?" Merlyn said to no one.

They stood talking amongst themselves watching the oncoming vehicle. When the truck's lights fell on them, it slowed and then stopped a hundred or so feet short.

Merlyn recognized the truck from Potter's General Store. Someone who looked like Colleen Potter got out and stomped up the incline toward the others, waving her arms and shouting. Stopping, she put her hands on her hips and hollered what sounded like, "You come here. You're going home with me, right now."

Merlyn grinned and mumbled, "Must be Melissa."

He watched Lissy shirk away and then sidling over, she wrapped her arms around Janey's waist. Colleen walked over and tried to peel Lissy loose. Janey threw up her arms as if surrendering, doing her best to not interfere.

Merlyn would have normally intervened at this point, but his mission was a secret. If this was going to be his last few hours on the job before he departed Gowan, he wouldn't want to make any work for himself. Merlyn just wanted to fade away—quietly. He remained still, trying to keep Massy from fidgeting and giving away their position.

Colleen got Lissy's arms free, but then she broke and ran up the road a short distance. Stopping, she stood defiant, yelling, "I ain't going!" When Colleen attempted to approach, Lissy ran a little further. Janey and Doc appeared to be trying to reason with Colleen as the Reverend stood by, just watching. Janey walked over and attempted to put a hand on Colleen's shoulder, but the older woman slapped it away and Janey recoiled. The Reverend stepped in to assist, but Colleen shook a finger in his face, and screeched what sounded like, "I don't need no trouble from you, Reverend Hale." Then she turned and stomped back to the truck.

Climbing in, she slammed the door. After much maneuvering, she got it turned around and sped back the way she had come, the water in the ford rooster-tailing as the vehicle passed through.

Merlyn brought his eyes back to the four. Lissy had returned to the others and was now embracing Janey. The Reverend stood behind them as if he too consoled the girl. They stood for some time before they all climbed back into the car and headed up the lane toward Carter House.

The sun had dropped below the ridge, and Merlyn shuddered. Turning Massey away, he headed back to Gowan. He would stop at his house, pack up a few important things, and then skedaddle around to the eastern side of Mount Lillie after crossing the ramshackle foot bridge that spanned the Spry River. From there, south to Gilberton where he would spend the night at the boarding house, and leaving before dawn, he would start that long ride to Deerfield; never to return.

8

Colleen Potter was furious. Driving recklessly back through the Hollow to Grunewyck, she muttered to herself, her hands white-knuckled on the wheel. She had received an offer for the store, a mere two hundred and fifty dollars. A life time of supplying the town with general merchandise and now she was being forced out. The Woodpeckers were already occupying the boarding houses in the town and a base camp had been set up in Holgraves big hay field on the northeast side of the village.

All the merchandise would have to be sold. Lissy was supposed to help her pack up. But the girl had always been stubborn, like her father.

Colleen would have to call her brother to come down from Danton and help. They didn't get along well and he would expect at least a fourth of what the store had in stock as payment. She would have called the sheriff to come and get Lissy, but he had disappeared along with both his men. There was always Chief Conway to help her force Lissy home, but she would have to find him first, and it seemed he had been quite busy as of late.

People were being found dead under all kinds of unusual circumstances and some weren't being found at all. There had been state policemen prowling around asking questions. Now her own daughter was acting strangely. Ever since that night of her dream, she had been acting aloof like she had something else more important to do than the usual teenage girl things, or to help her mother. Now she was found with Aldo Hale, Janey Carter, and Doctor Bolen, standing out on the Grunewyck Road. Colleen would find Chief Conway, or Lyle Beasley, his officer, and they would go back to Gowan and force Lissy home.

Colleen was driving too fast for the hairpin turns in the Hollow and losing traction, the truck slid off the road and went nose down an embankment where it slammed into a tree. The radiator sent a geyser of steam skyward, the engine rattled for a minute and then quit. She wouldn't be able to start it, unless she could pull it back from the tree to reach the crank.

She howled at the ceiling of the car and pounded on the steering wheel. Trying to calm herself, she sat staring into the dark waters of the Hollow through the cracked windshield.

All the usual noises of the place had stopped, but as she sat there realizing how stupid it was for her to be in the Hollow at sundown, she heard them start up again. First the frogs, then the crickets and katydids. They were followed by the cackles and calls of owls, and finally, the Whip-poor-wills. She was going to have to walk home.

Climbing out of the truck, she slammed the door, a sound that seemed to announce 'The End'. She looked back at the truck, the white logo on the door declaring, 'Potter's General Store'

"Not anymore," she muttered.

Turning away, she climbed the short slope up to the road, slipping a couple of times in the process. Catching herself, she said, "Shit, shit,

shit." It had been a long time since she had used profanity.

By the time Colleen got to the bend in the road, her eyes had adjusted to the dimming light. It was the gloaming. Afterglow painted the western sky, the moon now peeking through the trees behind her. Other sounds came to Colleen's ears as she walked, strange ones that she couldn't identify. She wasn't alone. Something moved through the brush. Something big.

Colleen gasped, stopped, and waited, a hand covering her mouth. She was almost to the bend where the road would straighten out to take her north to the Lost Collie. Twigs snapped and the undergrowth crackled. The noise was now behind her. She spun around, a partially muted scream escaping her lips.

There was a heavy panting noise coming from the trees, and then a small black pony stepped out onto the road, making all the usual horse noises. It was Samson, Lissy's pony. It stood looking at Colleen for a minute or so, then a soft knicker escaped its lips as if it recognized her.

"Samson, how'd you get loose? And what are you doing way out here?" It took a couple of steps toward her and knickered again. She would just ride him back. Walking to the pony, she grabbed its mane with her left hand and swung her right leg over its back. The pony didn't resist. "You couldn't have showed at a better time, little boy."

Before she married James, Colleen had been a farm girl. She still retained all of her riding skills. It had been a while since she had ridden, but Samson wouldn't be too much trouble.

The beast stood for a minute, staring down the road toward Grunewyck. "Well? Shall we?" she said and gave him a little kick.

The pony started to move, just stepping slowly. After about twenty or so feet, Colleen began to realize that there were certain things about this animal that didn't meet the makeup of Lissy's pony. Riding upon its back, the pony seemed bigger. It didn't move like Samson. It was when the creature looked back at her and she saw its eyes glowed red in the dark, that Colleen tried to jump off. She was caught in the mane somehow, the hair tightening around her hands. The beast rose up on its back legs, spun around, and lunged back the way from which it had come.

"Whoa, you, whoa," Colleen hollered, but the pony only moved faster.

Instead of sticking to the road, it went over the top of the hillock. Crossing the road on the other side, it plunged into the underbrush. Throwing back its head, it let go with a high pitched, maniacal whinny and tore through the trees.

Colleen had to remain low and centered on its back to avoid getting her brains bashed out on passing tree trunks, or worse yet, decapitated by a low hanging branch. The pony's speed was almost blinding now. There came a brief two seconds to acknowledge the glimmer of the moonlight glinting on the surface of a pond that opened up before her.

Colleen's scream was cut short as the water closed over her head. Slipping from the strange creature's back, she was towed along, her body spiraling, the mane, now more like tentacles, tightened on her wrists.

The pony was intentionally pushing itself toward the bottom, its legs making long, deliberate strokes. The last thing Colleen saw before she opened her mouth and the cold, green water flowed in, was the beast looking back at her with those glowing red eyes and a wicked, human-like grin.

9

"Suppose we park the car and walk up? Maybe we can sneak up on her?" Doc said, peering through the windshield at the house, its dark bulk contrasted by the twilit sky. They had stopped just short of the covered bridge to peer at Carter House through an opening in the trees.

"She knows we're here," Janey said. "There will be no sneaking. You might as well just pull up to the carriage house and turn the car around so we can make a quick escape."

In the dim light, neither Aldo, Doc, or Janey had seen the eyes of the closest gargoyle come alive for a few seconds—but Lissy had. Sitting at just the right angle, she caught the slight gleam brought by the ambient light reflecting off the black, moist eyes of the statue. Then they were stone again, leaving no evidence they had ever changed. She gasped and shirked back in her seat. The other three looked at her and Janey asked, "What is it?"

"The gargoyles, they have eyes."

"What do you mean?" Aldo asked, his whiskey breath washing over her.

"Of course they have eyes," Doc said.

"No, I mean… real eyes."

They all looked at each other and then back at Lissy, who said flatly, "Janey's right, Mab knows we're here."

The two men turned their faces back to the house. Janey's remained locked on Lissy's and something passed between them. Giving Lissy a slight smile, she turned to Doc and said, "Shall we?"

Doc put the car in gear and it rolled slowly through the bridge and up the hill. Arriving at the carriage house, he did what Janey had suggested. Facing the Rolls down the hill, he set the brake and shut it off. The headlights went out and the darkness enveloped them. They sat still for a few seconds as if waiting for something to happen.

"Dark, huh?" Doc said, "Guess we should have brought lanterns or something."

"There may still be some in the stable. My father kept them in the tack room. We should check. Oh, and take this," she said, handing Doc the iron picket. "You might need it."

"How does it work? Do I just stab them?"

"You don't need to; you can just touch them with it like it's a magic wand and that will do the trick. Right, Lissy?"

"That's right," she said. "But… you can stab them, if you want. I'm going to stab them. That's what I did with that Molly Sharp thing. But you'd have to wait for them to dissolve before you get the rod back."

Lissy then offered her iron picket to Aldo, "Here, you can have mine. I still have the chains."

"So… what about Molly Sharp?" Aldo asked.

"Nothing. Forget it. Do you want this rod, or not?"

"No need, I have this," Aldo said and held up the tiny bible, the little wooden cross clamped under his thumb against the cover.

"All right, have it your way," Lissy said. Scoffing, she turned away to look out the window at the dark, vine covered house.

They remained in the car, nobody wanting to make the first move to get out. The danger of the situation was becoming real.

Janey, being a natural born leader, opened her door and climbed out.

Lissy was right there with her. Aldo was next, but Doc stayed in his seat.

Janey leaned down and looked in the window. The old man was studying the iron rod in his hands.

"Coming, Doc?"

"Ummm… yeah, sorry. Starting to have regrets," he said. Despite the dark, she could see the fear in his eyes. He was the only one who didn't have a dog in the fight.

"So, convinced yet?"

"Getting there. You just might be braver than me, Janey Carter."

"I have my doubts. Hell, Lissy just might be braver than the whole lot of us," she said and looked at the girl who now stood beside her. Lissy smirked slightly as she studied the carriage house.

"Well, shall we?" Janey said and walked to the stable door.

It stood open and the gloom lay heavy within. Janey reached inside reluctantly like she feared that something might grab her. Finding the button, she pushed it and was surprised to find electricity still lit the fixtures that ran down the aisle between the stalls. The stable was electrified long before most of the house. Janey was not surprised that the horses held precedence over her and her mother. Her father had always been that way.

The other three followed her into the tack room. Pulling soot covered lanterns from the shelf, she handed one to each of them. Lissy declined. "I want both my hands, free," she said flatly.

"Have it your way," Janey said, opening a small drawer beneath the shelf to pull out a box of matches. After lighting each wick, they moved back outside to stand together, studying the mansion.

"We should burn it," Lissy said, looking at Janey, "Like… right now!"

"Not so quick. Remember, I used to live here. I was born here… So, I don't think I could." Looking at the other three, she shrugged and said to Lissy, "Probably a good thing you don't have a lantern, after all." There was no response.

"What's next? Shall we go knock and see if anyone's home?" Doc said.

Janey walked toward the back porch holding her lantern high with her left hand. Lissy stayed close enough to jostle her at every step. Aldo forced his way past them, his bible pushed out in front, his lantern the same. He muttered, "… I shall fear no evil…"

Doc, having taken up the rear, shook his head in disbelief.

Aldo pushed open the door and Janey stepped up behind him, the light of their lanterns barely penetrating the gloom inside. Vines had grown in through the windows and climbed the wallpaper. The room appeared ransacked; the floor littered with kitchen debris.

The Reverend took one step over the threshold and his action was immediately followed by a low grunt from the shadows. Something whistled through the air, catching the Reverend's lantern in the process and knocking it from his hand.

Janey and Lissy shrieked. Doc shouted, "What the hell?" as Aldo fell onto his backside. A rather antiquated looking bronze axe head, designed more for battle than cutting wood, had buried itself in the door jamb.

A large, almost portly man, with dark warty skin, grinned at them from the dark room. His eyes were large and bulging, his nose almost nonexistent. On his head he wore a blood red hat, almost like Santa Claus' without the white fur trim. A dark, furry waistcoat, cinched by a wide leather belt, covered his upper body.

There was wicked glee in his eyes as he tried to work the axe from the wood. Janey wasted no time drawing her chain covered fist back to strike the creature. Lissy beat her to it by driving her iron rod into the beast's belly, it's sharp point penetrating the fiend without resistance.

A strange, cackling shriek burst from its lips. It bared its rotten looking teeth as if to bite Janey, but then swirled up into a cloud of smokey vapor and floated away into the dining room leaving Lissy's iron rod to clatter to the floor.

The beast's axe, still stuck in the door frame, dissolved into a pile of sand and blew away. The only evidence that there had been an attack was the damage to the door jamb.

Helping Aldo to his feet, Janey turned to Doc and said, "Convinced?"

"Very much so. I think I need to stop thinking in terms of logic and reason."

Janey noticed he was very pale in the lamplight and his hands were shaking. "You alright, Doc? Maybe we should go back to Gowan?"

"No, no, press on. I was a medic in World War One, you know? I can handle it. Press on."

"Yes, let's get in there," Lissy said, and after grabbing up her picket, she pushed past them into the kitchen.

They were down to two lanterns now, with the Reverend's laying broken on the floor, spilling kerosene out the wick port. Janey moved to the center of the kitchen and held her lamp as high as she could.

A chorus of squeaking and cackling echoed throughout the house. The crickets, katydids, and Whip-poor-wills were raising a ruckus, while somewhere an owl called.

Doc said, "I think I'll stay here and guard the backdoor."

Janey glanced at him but said nothing. Her heart was beating in a way that was not at all familiar. Moving into the next room, she followed Lissy. Aldo remained in the open doorway.

The dining room was free of threats, as was the front parlor, but woodland smells filled the space along with some that were obviously human.

The two walked through into the entry hall to gaze down the back hallway that led to the second parlor, Benjamin's study, and the back staircase. Doc's lantern played through the bottom of the closed kitchen door at the far end creating weird shadows as he paced.

The Reverend soon joined Janey and Lissy, causing them to startle. "You okay, Doctor Bolen?" he called back.

"So far, so good," Doc said, the tone of his voice telling them differently.

"I'll check the rooms back there. What are they?" Aldo said, pointing down the corridor.

"The second parlor, my father's study, and the last door on the right; the back staircase. Okay, so... Lissy and I'll go upstairs."

"Very good," he said and walked away into the dark corridor, holding his bible like a shield.

Janey and Lissy moved slowly up the main stairs. There was activity in the vines that had all but eradicated the once extravagant wallpapers. The lanterns glow picked up random sets of tiny eyes peering at them from the foliage, but when they stopped to investigate, they found nothing but stalks and leaves. Janey was still in awe of the change from the house she once knew. From extravagant mansion to dilapidated pile.

The upper floor was noisier than the first. Hundreds of insects raucously resonated, birds flitted and fluttered, some chirping out their discontent at being disturbed. The call of a barred owl came down from the third floor through the open stairway door, its, "Who cooks for you? Who cooks for you, all?" a haunting baritone descending from the gloom. A mist was building in the hallway, making it hard to see what lay ahead.

A subtle cackling and squeaking came with the mist, backed by what sounded like a dirge being sung. There seemed to always be endless activity just outside the lanterns glow.

Janey found her old bedroom, and peeling back the vines, she forced the door open. Her and Lissy stood staring in, the room's condition no different than the rest. Water could be heard dripping and something rustled under her old bed. A heaviness settled in her chest. Nothing was salvageable. Only memories, now. Closing the door, they turned toward the master bedroom.

The corridor grew cold and the stairs leading up to the third floor creaked. Turning back, Janey watched Tom Lynn step out into the mist. He was now dressed in a loose white shirt tucked in tight crème-colored trousers. His hair was longer and combed straight back from his forehead. The oddest thing of all—it was almost as white as snow, contrasting his black, knee-high riding boots.

Janey smiled and said, "Tom! Oh, Tom. You're alright."

He said nothing. The mist swirled and thickened, hiding him from her sight. The next time she saw him, he was closer, but not where she thought he would be. She glanced at Lissy, who stood unmoving, staring, her mouth agape. Janey stepped away like she was going to meet her lover. The cloud thickened and swirled again. Then he was there, right in front of her. "Oh, Tom, I…" was all she got out before icy cold hands closed around her throat.

She stared into his expressionless face and glazed eyes. His grip tightened as he lifted her off the floor. Dropping her chain and the lantern, she grabbed his arms and struggled to free herself. From the corner of her eye, she watched Lissy step from the heavy mist and strike Tom several times on his arm with the picket, shouting, "You let go of her."

It had no effect and without relaxing his hold on Janey's neck, he kicked Lissy, sending her flying backwards with a grunt. Giggles and gleeful cackles emanated from the dark rooms and foliage.

Tom carried Janey to the wall and pushing her up against the vine covered paper, he endeavored to crush her windpipe. Janey was losing consciousness, her breath now coming in gasps and wheezes. Her arms dangled as she hung like a rag doll from Tom's grip.

Her right hand soon began to grope in the pocket at the front of her dress. Pulling it free, she cocked her mother's derringer and pushing the muzzle against the chest of the man she had once held dear, she pulled the trigger.

The sound of the forty-one-caliber round was deafening in the hallway. It was followed by an inhuman scream that seemed to emanate out of thin air. Tom relaxed his grip and the mist dissolved away. The corridor immediately filled with birds and small animals fleeing in all directions.

It took Tom nearly ten seconds to collapse. It was in the last two seconds of that ten that a look of recognition filled his eyes before he collapsed to the floor, a crimson stain spreading over the front of his shirt. Janey watched in horror as a wisp of smoke floated up from the bullet hole in Tom's chest, a death rattle in his throat.

Janey slid down the wall, her legs splaying out in front. The lantern had landed flat on its bottom but remained lit even though its glass chimney had shattered. Lissy came to her, clutching her stomach, a pain filled look on her face. Skirting the broken glass, she got down on the floor and embraced Janey, both of them weeping as the man they once knew as Tom Lynn, bled out on the filthy floor of the hallway.

Aldo Hale opened the library door and hit the light switch. Five of the bulbs on the chandelier exploded, leaving only one. Aldo nearly screamed in fear, and ducking back, he watched sparks and pieces of glass fall to the floor.

A minute passed before he reentered the room under the light of that single bulb. There was nothing of interest, just the usual desk, chairs, small tables and other assorted items. It wasn't quite as crowded with flora like the other rooms.

Catching his reflection in the huge, dust covered mirror above the fireplace, caused him to gasp in fear. Then shaking his head, he chuckled to himself.

Working his way around the furniture, he walked to the mirror and studied his haggard looking face. Just as he was ready to return to the hallway, letters began to form in the dust on the glass. They came, one at a time. He watched, amazed, finding it difficult to believe it was actually happening. When the words were complete, he read: 'For what do you quest, charlatan?' His eyes went wide and catching movement behind him, he spun around.

A rather stately looking woman materialized from the shadows, her clothing somewhat medieval in appearance. A slim gold band wrapped her forehead and her long, platinum colored hair cast a glow.

In a rather regal sounding voice that didn't seem to come from her, but from the air above his head, Aldo heard, "Well, pulpiteer, you have come to pay me homage? A Christian in my castle?" Her mouth didn't move, but the words still came.

"Who are you?" he asked. "Are you the witch that presides here?"

She laughed and said, "Witch? You came seeking witches? I'm sorry to disappoint you. But there are no witches here... pretender."

"Then who are you? What pagan monstrosity are you?" he said, his hand slipping inside his shirt.

"I am Mab, but if you are a seeker of witches, then you won't know me. Perhaps you should go down to Salem. There, you may find what you seek."

His hand slowly withdrew his little wooden crucifix and pushed it out toward her. Mav's laughter seemed to emanate from the walls and ceiling, followed by a single word that he didn't understand. From a shadow in the corner, someone stepped out to stand behind Mab. It was one of the witches that had been seen in town.

NicDobhran paced back and forth behind Mab, her mouth open in a grin, her small sharp teeth gleaming. Her tiny black eyes vacillated red and green in the dim light. Her face was frightening. It wasn't human, but yet, it was. She moved lithely, a strange panting noise coming from her mouth.

"And who is this? Another witch for me to vanquish?" he said with false bravado.

Mab and NicDobhran laughed together and the handmaiden came around her queen and moved between Aldo and the door. He yanked the cross from his neck, breaking the thin leather thong. Pushing it toward her, he began to speak scripture, his voice droning, his eyes glued to NicDobhran. She didn't backup, instead she crouched and moved slowly toward him. Mab remained unmoving, watching them, a smirk upon her lips.

"You think that is going to do you any good, here? What do you think I am? Some character from that Irishman's tale of Dracul? You might have bettered yourself and read that fool Yeats's book of the Sidhe. You would have been better prepared," she said.

A noise came from the corridor, the sound of a door opening and slow steps moving their way. The door was open a few inches and the glow of a lantern showed through the opening. Mab moved her hand ever so slightly and in less than a second, NicDobhran was there, slamming the door shut. Aldo jumped and gasped.

The door knob rattled and Doc said, "Aldo, are you okay? Reverend?"

A raspy giggle escaped NicDobhran's lips as she continued her frightening slink toward a trembling Aldo Hale. Mab began to chant and his scripture reading developed a frantic tone. His attempt was in vain. Mab ended her chant with one shouted word. The single, working light bulb above his head popped, showering him with glass. The room went dark and he was unable to see his adversaries. Backing away from the approaching handmaiden, he held his cross high in the general direction he thought she might be.

A strange lassitude began overtaking him as he moved. Tripping over a chair, he dropped his bible. Turning, Aldo stumbled toward the window. NicDobhran grabbed his jacket collar with one clawed hand and pants belt with the other, to propel him head first through the glass.

Aldo, his face bloodied, never felt the pain of hitting the ground, he just somersaulted across the lawn and rolling onto his feet, he stood up. His eyesight began to cloud and within seconds he had lost it altogether.

Aldo Hale was now blind.

Moving into a stumbling walk, he tumbled over the short stone wall that separated the lawn from the lane. Aldo zig-zagged down the hill, whimpering as he went. From the window behind him, he heard a squeaky giggle and the words, "Leave this place, charlatan, you have no power here. Walk the never-ending walk of the smitten. Wander without end."

Aldo didn't look back, nor could he have if he wanted too. Arriving at the covered bridge, he missed the opening completely and toppled head first down the path that led into the ravine. Falling into the deep pool at the bottom, he splashed about, trying to stand. NicDobhran watched until he was out of sight and then spiraling up into a shaft of silver light, she shot away like a tiny comet toward Gowan.

11

Doc, now back in the kitchen, heard two things almost simultaneously, a gunshot upstairs and the breaking of glass as Aldo Hale was tossed out of the library window. They were followed by what sounded like an artillery round passing overhead and he froze, paralyzed with fear.

Bernard Theodore Bolen had never been known as a coward in the days before the First World War, but he had returned from France a changed man. Years of flashbacks and nightmares took their toll. His medical training in the army had brought him to his present profession, but it was his wife, Hannah, who brought him stability. He moved through life, carefully, linearly, and always with Hannah to fall back on.

He gasped and a slight "Agh!" escaped his lips when Lissy burst into the kitchen and hollered, "Tom tried to kill Janey, but she shot him."

Doc turned and looked at the girl. His lantern lit up her face and he could see she was serious. Janey soon lurched through the doorway, the derringer in one hand, the still glowing lantern, minus its glass chimney, in the other. Her dress was splattered with what looked like blood

"Is that true, Janey? Lissy says you killed Tom."

She rasped out, "Yes, I shot him. But... it wasn't Tom... anymore."

"Are you sure he's dead?"

"Yes, I checked his pulse... all that blood..."

"Maybe I should go up there and..."

341

"No," Janey said and coughed, "I need to go. We need to go!"

He set down his lantern and moved to her. Taking the derringer from her hand, he checked to be sure the hammer wasn't cocked. Then dropping it into her pocket, it clanked against the chain that lay coiled in there.

"Where's the Reverend?" Lissy asked.

They both turned to look at the girl and Doc said, "Still in the library, uh... I presume."

Lissy picked up Doc's lantern, walked to the library door, opened it and peeked in. Doc watched from the kitchen door and said, "That was locked a minute ago."

"He's not in here," Lissy said and returned to the kitchen.

Doc went to Janey and ushered her outside. Lissy passed them and ran around the corner of the house. Stopping at the library window, she held the lantern high and saw broken glass in the flattened grass below it.

Janey and Doc came around the corner and she said, "There's blood."

Doc said, "There was a crash after the shot. Maybe he tried to escape and left by the window?"

Janey, placed a hand to her throat and croaked, "We need to get out of here... and we should go now."

"But, what about Tom?" Doc said nervously.

"Forget about Tom, he's dead," Janey whispered, tears rolling down her cheeks.

Lissy groaned, "He's Mab's now, and besides, he tried to strangle Janey. Leave him and let's go."

"Janey..." Doc said, giving her an inquisitive look.

"Leave her alone, Doc. She can't talk. Let's go or we're going to be next," Lissy said, doing a fast walk to the car and climbing inside.

Doc helped Janey to the Rolls and then got in himself. With Lissy in the back seat he started it up and they sped down the hill.

"We need to be looking for the Reverend, he might be on the road."

"Take me home, Doc, my mother needs me," Janey rasped.

"I want to take you to my office and look at your throat, Tom may have done some serious damage..."

"Doc!" Lissy shouted, "Did you hear her? Do it." He threw Lissy a scowl in the mirror, but abided Janey's wish.

They rode in silence from that point, Janey with her face in her hands, Lissy quietly looking out into the darkness, and Doc, still searching the road for Aldo Hale.

12

Constance Carter stood in the bay window of the drawing room at Headmost House watching the town below. She feared for her daughter, and if the gossip had been anything close to being true, Carter House was no longer a fit place to be. She thought to climb up to the cupola, but it had been a long time since she'd tread those stairs. Old age had brought obesity and the melancholia that came with a separation. Climbing just one staircase to go to her room was all she could handle in a day's time. She relied heavily on Tabby and Percy to see that things were taken care of in parts of the house where she didn't traverse.

Tabby was in the kitchen preparing a late supper and Percy had taken a trip to the outhouse. Constance crossed the entry hall and entered the front parlor. After a moment of reflection, she moved through the door that connected it to the library. Shuffling through without stopping, she came out at the back of the entry hall under the open gallery that connected the rooms on the second floor. Nervously rubbing her hands together, she stood watching down the corridor that led to the backstairs. Tabby always left the kitchen door to that hallway propped open in the hot months and her shadow played over the carpet runner that ran its length.

A sound like gusting wind came from her right and Constance turned to look down the short passageway that led to the back door. It stood open, the screen door allowing in the occasional cooling breeze.

"Is someone there?" she called out, "Percy?" He would have had a lantern, but she saw none. She kept her focus on that area, the sound of Tabby working in the background. There came a whistling moan like wind up under the eaves and taking a few steps into that passageway, Constance watched a thick, swirling cloud of mist roll out from the open mudroom door on the right. It quickly dissipated, revealing what looked like a woman with long black hair. She stood as a silhouette in front of the open back door, panting like an animal and emitting little squeaks and chirps. Then she grinned and Constance could see the gleam of sharp little teeth. Her breath caught in her throat and the matriarch of the Carter Empire wheezed out, "Who are you? What do you want?" No response.

The woman began to move toward her and when the dim light of the wall sconces washed over the woman, her eyes flashed an evil green luminance.

"Tell me who you are this instant, or I'll call the police."

"Missus?" she heard Tabby call from the kitchen, 'Missus, you alright?"

NicDobhran now had a tight grip on her wrist and was towing her toward the back door. "What are you doing?" was the last thing she was able to utter before NicDobhran pulled her through the door and out onto the gallery porch. Yanking Constance with the strength of ten men, she sent her flying. Missing the back steps completely, Janey's mother hit the pavers ten feet out with a bone breaking thud.

Mab's handmaiden was the only one present to hear the snapping of Constance's neck along with her final exhalation. Had Tabby arrived five seconds sooner to investigate the slamming of the back screen door, she too would have been witness to the murder of her lady.

A wicked laugh escaped NicDobhran's mouth as she spiraled up into a silver ribbon of light to rocket away into the clouds forming overhead, Tabby's scream following close behind.

"Keep your eyes peeled, girls, we may see the Reverend."

"Fuck the Reverend, Doc, get me home," Janey said, her voice full of gravel.

Doc looked at her with dismay but said nothing. When the car passed over Berryman's Crest, it picked up speed. The wind was increasing, thick clouds began to fill the sky, and lightning flashed.

"Looks like another storm," Doc said.

"Yeah, Mab's storm. Something bad is going to happen and she doesn't want anybody to see it coming," Lissy said from the back seat.

"How do you know that?" Doc asked, glancing at Lissy in the mirror.

"That's what she did when she tried to catch me. She'll send that...

that Unseelie Court out, inside a storm. That way no one will see 'em."

"So, you think her and that... that minion of hers have gone to Headmost?" Doc asked Janey.

"Well, maybe not Mab, but... that minion, yes. Could we please go faster?"

Doc accelerated, racing past the school, the funeral home, and the cottages. He didn't hear what he had construed earlier as an artillery shell hurtling back toward Carter House because of the booming thunder. The glowing ball of light, thought to be fast-moving St. Elmo's Fire by those who saw it, soon disappeared into the clouds.

Arriving at the village green, they saw a vast crowd still gathered there despite the increasing wind and lightning. The lights at the front of the townhall shone and numerous lanterns could be seen swinging from the hands of the attendees. They could see Shannon still speaking from the porch, officer Nealy beside him with that shotgun.

"So, you think it's the handmaiden that we will be confronting at Headmost?" Doc said. Janey just nodded with a grunt.

"Nick Dovron, the last one. I put a stop to that one they called Nick Neese. Turned back into a weasel, it did. So... I know I can stop the one that's left," Lissy said, stroking the chain that wrapped her hand. Janey looked over her shoulder, sniffed and forced a smile for her companion, her eyes still wet with tears. Doc said nothing as he piloted the Rolls through Gowan, a look of dismay on his face.

ᚺ

Helen sat at a window in her room at the back of the telephone house, sipping ice tea. The increasing storm driven wind through the opening was cooling. Tilting her head back, she closed her eyes and let it flow over her. There came the smell of rain and lightning played across the top of Mt. Ovis.

News of the reservoir had been constant. She had heard every conversation that had passed over the lines. There would be nothing left for a woman her age after they closed the telephone exchange in Gowan. The company may offer some kind of a severance package, but it wouldn't be much. For her, life as she knew it, was over. She would have to take the train to West Brookfield and move in with her older sister, Marilyn. They had angrily split after the death of their youngest sister, Emma, murdered at age thirteen.

Helen and Marilyn blamed each other, and the bad feelings never ended. Helen still missed Emma something terrible and her little sister was on her mind a lot lately. She would call Marilyn in the morning and try to reconcile.

Helen and Emma had been close even though there was a good eight years between them. It was because Helen had left her young charge to go and meet a boy all those years ago, that there had not been anyone home to watch over her. Marilyn had specifically told Helen to stay inside and keep the windows and doors locked. She hadn't, and Emma had left the house to wander the meadows in the moonlight. They had searched for almost an entire day before finding the girl's naked body in the shallow creek that ran at the back of their property. Strangulation with evidence of rape, the Sheriff had said. The killer was never caught.

Putting down her glass of tea, she crossed her arms on the windowsill and rested her chin on them. She studied the big houses on Ovis St. All the windows were dark. Most everyone was at the meeting.

A tear ran down her cheek and she said loudly to the air, "Oh, Emma, your Helen misses you so much. I am so sorry I left you."

There came a scampering and scratching sound on the porch just below the window. This was followed by squeaks, chirps, and miniscule laughs. Helen leaned out for a look but her vision was poor and her eyeglasses were in the other room. She went out to stand on the back porch, wiping the tears from her cheeks. Scanning the area, she failed to see the small shadows speeding away in the dark, hidden by the foliage of the vegetable garden. That included the ones that squeezed in under the porch to gather below her feet.

She moved down the steps and looked around, an inquisitive expression on her face. After a minute, she turned to go back inside. That's when she heard someone call her name. It sounded like Emma. It seemed to be coming from the shrubbery around Henry Blanchett's house.

Helen moved that way at a fast walk, calling Emma's name. Finding no one, she listened intently through the rumble of distant thunder. Then it came again, a barely perceptible, "Helen," emanating from behind

Henry's house.

"I'm here Emma," she said and hurried into the backyard of the tailor's abode. Still no one. "Oh, Emma, if it's you, please come out. Don't make me chase you," she said wearily.

"Helen, here. I'm here," came from within the trees.

This continued for several minutes, Helen responding with Emma's name as she picked her way through the woods and up the east slope of Mt. Ovis. She began to show signs of agitation and muttered as she pushed her way through thickets and underbrush. "Please, Emma, I'm old now. This is too hard for me, please…" Stopping about a quarter of a mile from the top, Helen wheezed and trembled from the exertion.

"Oh, Helen," came again, now clear and close. She turned toward the direction of the sound and in the ambient light reflecting from the low hanging clouds, she picked up movement. It was in an open area where many walnut trees had been cut at the turn of the century to become woodwork for some of the local architecture.

"Emma? Is that you?" she said watching a shape move through the field of stumps. She hurried in that direction but soon lost sight of whatever it was.

"Emma, please."

Lightning spiderwebbed across the underside of the clouds, illuminating a racoon sized bogle lounging atop one of the decaying protrusions. It had large black eyes and a Cheshire Cat grin full of large, terrifying teeth. Helen gasped and covered her mouth. In that last second just before the woods fell back into darkness, the bogle fae, mockingly mimicked in a child's voice, "Oh, Helen, do you still miss me?"

Then they were on her.

As they swarmed over her body, she began to scream and run up the slope, pulling and tossing small, furry fiends every which way. They bit and clawed her. They got inside her dress and did unspeakable things to parts of her body that nobody talks about in public. They squeaked and screeched, a multitude of tiny voices taunting her by saying, "Helen!" over and over again. She fell many times, almost suffocating under the mob of odorific, fur covered bodies, but she got up each time and continued her blind, panic stricken run up the mountain.

Helen soon reached the top of Mt. Ovis, her energy nearly spent. Her shrieks were replaced with wheezing and coughing, but the persistent little bogles showed no mercy. Her forward motion became a stumbling run and Gowan's long time purveyor of lies and hateful gossip, promptly ran right off of Mt. Ovis's west precipice.

Most of the bogles jumped free before Helen's three-hundred-foot freefall to the boulder strewn woods below. A few of the beasts rode her down, gleefully shrieking like children on a Coney Island rollercoaster. Upon impact, the fiends jumped free, rolled, and getting to their feet, fled into the trees. Sadly, Helen Blake did not.

Sliding a short way down the slope, her limp, bloody body wedged into an open space under a pile of boulders never to be found.

Doc's Rolls Royce shot through the gate and up the drive of Headmost House. The Carter's Cadillac sat in its usual place. The house was dark all except for a light in the parlor. Doc stopped on the opposite side of the fountain and Janey was out of the car before he had time to set the parking brake. Leaving her iron picket on the floor of the Rolls, Janey kept the chain. Lissy followed suit, leaving Doc to fumble his way out of the car.

Janey was halfway to the porch when the screen door burst open and a blubbering Tabby came flying out to embrace her.

"Where's my mother, Tabby?" she rasped.

"Oh, sugar, you is too late. It's terrible, just terrible. The Missus, she fall down the backstairs. Oh, Miss Janey, I'm so sorry."

Janey broke free of Tabby's arms and ran up the steps into the house. Lissy gave chase, avoiding Tabby who reached out to her as well. Doc met Tabby and taking her shoulders, set the woman down on the front steps. She put her face in her hands and began to sob uncontrollably while Doc tried to console her.

Janey found Percy in the parlor. They had brought Constance inside and laid her on her back on the settee. Percy sat with his head in his hands and when Janey burst in, he looked up; his face wet with tears.

"Nothing we could do, Miss Janey, nothing, nothing at all," he said, rising to his feet. "We needs to call the doctor."

"He's just outside," Janey sobbed out as she knelt beside Constance.

"Oh, mother…" she said, noticing the odd angle of Constance's head, knowing without needing to be told. Her mother's neck was broken. She had just lost Tom, and now, her mother. She lay the side of her face on her mother's crossed arms and began to weep. Percy moved past Lissy and went out to retrieve Doc.

When Doc came in, Janey moved out of his way to sit on the couch with Tabby. Percy brought another lantern and held it high while Doc examined Constance.

"So, what happened here?"

Tabby went into detail about how she was in the kitchen preparing dinner and she thought she heard talking on the back porch. She figured Constance had been talking to Percy, but he was still in a dash from the outhouse when she found Constance down on the pavers, her head bent under her body.

Doc's face showed he was thinking hard about the subject and then said, "Tabby, I need for you to show me where you found her. Please, as soon as you can compose yourself."

Tabby didn't wait, and Percy led them to the back, carrying the lantern. They gathered on the back porch to watch Tabby walk down the steps. Stopping several feet out on the narrow walkway, she said, "Right heres, Doc."

Doc Bolen walked down and paced out the distance, counting under his breath, and stopping next to Tabby, he looked back at the porch and then at Janey who had come down to stand at the bottom of the steps.

"Can I speak to you, Janey? Um… in private?"

"Sure, Doc," she said, rubbing at her eyes.

"Thanks, Tabby," he said, "You can go back inside."

Janey followed Doc to the large ceramic bird bath to stand in the dark and the rising wind. Putting his back to the house and the others, he started to speak, realizing too late that Lissy had followed them.

"Just, Miss Carter."

"I want to hear too," Lissy said defiantly, crossing her arms and glaring.

"Now, Lissy…"

"It's okay, Doc. She wants to hear, so… let her hear. I don't think you're going to save her innocence. I believe that is long gone."

Janey reached out and putting her hand on Lissy's shoulder, she drew the girl over to her side.

Doc scowled and said, "Okay, then. Have it your way. I just wanted to say... there is no way your mother could have fallen down those back steps and landed that far from the porch. I think she was thrown."

"I knew it," Lissy crowed.

"By who... who would have... not Tabby or Percy?"

"No, I think this is Mab's work. Or more likely, this, NicDobhran."

"Yeah, her," Lissy added.

They stood in silence for a moment, lost in thought. Janey felt her ire coming up, the fire of revenge rising inside. It was something she hadn't felt since she was Lissy's age. Trying hard to control her voice, she said, "So, like we talked about earlier, with all the Carter's out of the way, there will be no one to contest Mab's presence at Carter House, yes?"

"Yes, exactly. I think you are in grave danger, Janey. As vulgar as it may sound, I'll say it bluntly: you're next. Running away won't do you any good. Until she's annihilated the Carters of Gowan, she's not going to stop. You can no longer expect this to be a legal matter. There is nothing Shannon can do for you. It appears it's down to her taking your life."

"Well, what about the reservoir, she must know about the reservoir. It's certainly going to take out Carter House."

"It doesn't seem likely, or at least... that's what I think. It sits too high on the side of the ridge and I suspect nobody is going to get close enough who doesn't know, uh... the conventions of the fairies? Not that I know anything other than what Cora has said. Namely, the rule of iron. I suspect anyone who goes up there, unprepared, will be dealt with. So, Carter House will remain. Only you, Janey, still breathing, pose any real threat. Mab probably figures she will never get any peace while you're still alive. And, it won't end there. She can still terrorize the countryside beyond the shores of the reservoir. The water will serve as a great moat around Mab's castle. Well, at least on three sides. The north side of the property will grant access because Parson's Ridge runs higher than the bluff and I can only imagine what any trespasser may encounter on the trek in."

"We are going to have to go back up there, aren't we?" Janey said.

"Afraid so, we are going to have to somehow trick her into letting us get close enough to use some of that iron on her."

"Good," Lissy muttered, "I'm ready."

They both looked down at the girl as she stood fondling the chain in her hands, an eager look on her face.

"Sounds like you have something of a death wish, there, girl," Doc said.

"Yeah, call it what you want. Just because I'm only a kid, doesn't mean nothing."

"Okay, shall we get on with it, then? Sorry about your mother, Janey. I suppose I better call Sweeny and have them send someone up."

"What about Tabby and Percy?"

"What about them?"

"Should they stay? What if something does happen to me, then what?"

"Well, maybe we should wait and see."

"No, I'll take care of it. They're my responsibility, now."

"Okay, very well. Shall we?" Doc said and motioned for them to return to the porch.

Doc came into the house last, struggling to get the screen door shut against the gusting winds. Turbulent clouds filled the sky for as far as they could see, reflecting what ambient light Gowan could send up to them. Doc took Percy aside and began to explain what they were going to do with Constance's remains. Janey left them to it and directed Tabby and Lissy into the library; shutting the door between it and the parlor. Tabby hit the small brown button in its brass back plate and the little chandelier glowed dim, barely reaching the perimeters of the large room. Picking up the phone, Janey clicked the receiver three times and waited. When nothing happened, she repeated it. Helen never answered. Janey felt a coldness fill her gut. Helen never missed a call, her dedication to her position had always been first and foremost. So, why now?

"No one's answering."

"That's odd, Miss Janey," Tabby said, "That Helen, she don't never miss a call."

"Yes, I know," Janey said, weariness in her voice. Sitting down in an overstuffed chair, she appeared to ponder the situation, her eyes cast to the floor. Lissy leaned with her back against the fireplace, a fierceness in her face as opposed to Tabby's pleading expression, both watching the new matriarch of Headmost House.

Janey's love for the Snoaks had produced a need to take care of them. If something happened to her, they would lose it all and be out on the street. She didn't know what agreement her father had with Philip Shannon, or if there was a will laying out how the Snoaks would be provided for. They couldn't be left out in the cold. If she were to act to provide safe harbor for Tabby and Percy, the attorney must never know.

Getting to her feet, Janey placed her chain on the billiard's table and then moved to a large pastoral painting in a gold frame. Slipping her fingers underneath an edge of the gilded surround, she pulled. The picture swung away from the wall with a *click!* exposing a wall safe. Janey had often practiced opening it on her childhood visits, and even with those years behind her, she got it on her first try.

There wasn't much in there; a ledger, a set of keys, and a heavy, white canvas sack with The Bank of Gowan stenciled on its side. Janey could hardly control her glee. Both her and Constance knew that Benjamin, having anticipated the stock market crash of 1929, had taken a large portion of cash from the Gowan bank, and cached it at Carter House as a 'just in case'. The money never went back to the bank.

Janey could always count on her mother's greed. If the cash was still on the premises when she received her notice to vacate her treasured Carter House, it wouldn't be there afterwards. Luckily for them, Uncle Bart was never good about keeping his wall safe, or the combination, a secret.

Setting the bag down on the table, she examined the ring of keys. Each one was labeled and finding the one tagged 'High Gable' she removed it. Then taking one thousand dollars from the bag, she put it and the remaining keys in the pocket occupied by the derringer. Pulling out a leather satchel from under uncle Bart's desk, she put the rest of the money inside. Lissy watched, her eyes wide as if having never seen so much money all in one place.

Strapping the satchel shut, Janey turned and set it on the billiards table along with the single key. The pocket door between the two rooms slid open and Doc poked his head in, "Okay, we're done in here. Did you get Sweeny's?"

"No, Helen didn't answer. Somethings wrong, Doc."

"Yes, that is unusual. We might have to stop down there when we leave. I have to go back to the office for a minute and check in with Hannah, she'll be worried sick."

"Before we go, I need to talk with Percy and Tabby."

"Yes, Miss Janey?" Tabby said.

"Get Percy and meet me in the kitchen. Doc, if you don't mind, this will be private. If you and Lissy could wait here?"

"Oh, certainly," Doc said as Lissy frowned and huffed her dismay.

Janey picked up the satchel and key, then left the room. Tabby got Percy and his lantern and they went into the kitchen.

"Close the door, Percy," Janey said flatly.

"Yes, miss," he said. Both he and Tabby had the look of worry in their faces and were obviously preparing for bad news.

"Sit down, please."

They did so, but reluctantly. Years of servitude had conditioned them to be prepared to be of service at a moment's notice. That they were directed to sit at the 'big table' had caused a mental quandary. It wasn't proper.

"Please," Janey said, and pointed to the chairs across from her.

Tabby took Percy's hand, her eyes filling with fear.

"I'm only going to go over this once. So, don't ask me to repeat it. It's plain and simple. I want you two to pack your clothes, one suitcase apiece. Take this satchel and this key, get in that Cadillac, and drive down to High Gable in Salem. When you arrive, open up the house and prepare for my arrival."

She slid the key across to Percy, "Here's the key. Find a safe place in the house and stash this satchel. There should be enough money in there to last for quite some time; probably for the rest of your lives if you are frugal. It may be a year or more before I can come, but... go on living your lives as if I were there. If... if I don't show, you keep that money... and the house, for yourselves."

Tabby gasped. Percy said, "Now, Miss Janey, I..."

"No argument, Percy. You do as I say. It's for your own good. I want that house open and ready when I arrive. The same for the car. I know you can take care of it; you have always done a good job. It's yours now, Percy."

"Now, Miss Janey, that ain't my…"

Janey pointed a finger at him, "It is, now, Percy Snoaks. Enough said. You will leave tonight. Gowan is no longer a safe place. You don't stop until you've reached Marlborough. Don't get out of the car until then. We are going to leave and head over to Doc's office. When I come back, I don't want to see you here. Lock up Headmost, all except for the front door. Leave my mother where she lay."

"What about the dinner, Sugar. I cooked you and Missus a dinner."

"Help yourself. Eat what you want or take as much as you can with you. It's a long drive to Salem."

"But…"

"Percy! No more, you heard me."

Janey stood and Tabby came to her. They embraced for a long time. Janey kissed Tabby's cheek and the old woman returned it. Tabby stepped back and Janey looked at Percy. Their eyes met. She could see he was fighting the tears. When he rose to his feet, she embraced him. He squeezed her back and then pulling free, he turned away to rub at his eyes.

"When I get back to Headmost, you best be gone. When I get to Salem, I expect that house to be open and waiting. Be sure to make up a room for Lissy. Hear me?"

The couple just nodded, both of them wiping their eyes. Janey left the kitchen and as soon as the door shut, she heard the rattle of dishes and assumed they were preparing their meal. Janey walked into the library and Doc looked up from a board of checkers that he and Lissy had been playing.

"Time to go?" he asked

"I want to change my clothes, then we'll go."

"Good," said Lissy, "I was losing anyway."

"What about Percy and Tabby?"

"They're fine," Janey said and made a face that conveyed, 'Don't ask again.'

Janey took ten minutes to wash Tom's blood from her hands and face, change her clothes, and then head out the front door on her way to the car, with Doc and Lissy trailing behind.

The first stop was the telephone house. There was no real place to park. So, Doc left the Rolls on the street and after knocking for several minutes, they moved around the little building to the back door and found it open. The three of them searched inside and found no one. Helen, too, had vanished without a word.

16

They shut the back door and returned to the car. "We'll have to report this to Merlyn," Doc said.

"Good luck with that."

"What do you mean?"

"Merlyn's got his hands so full, he'll put it on the bottom of his list and never get to it. So... like I said, good luck."

Doc said nothing and looked in the mirror at Lissy who was humming *Ring Around The Rosie*. She finished the song by singing out the last verse, "...ashes, ashes, we all fall down." Catching Docs eyes reflected in the mirror, she turned her gaze out of the window and started humming the song again from the beginning.

The dark clouds still swirled and a light rain pattered. Turning the corner at Slaughterhouse Lane, Doc parked the Rolls in front of his office. They hadn't even gotten the doors open when a sobbing Caroline ran out wringing her hands.

"She's passed, Doc, she's gone... Cora's..."

Doc pushed past her. Janey took Caroline in an embrace and tried to sooth her. Lissy, standing in the open door of the office, began to weep.

"Janey, you, and Lissy, remain in the waiting room please," Doc said as he hurried away. They didn't argue.

Hannah met Doc in the hallway carrying a stethoscope. Blocking Doc's path, she said, "Cora's gone, Bernie."

Doc took the scope from her and continued. Shoving the curtain aside, he saw Cora was sitting up, her eyes closed. Her face was alabaster, her lips now slack and blue. He listened to her heart. There was no sound. Hannah came and stood at the foot of the bed, her demeanor calm from years of having mortality shoved in her face.

"Caroline came to the house to get me. We couldn't get through to Helen, so we couldn't call anyone. Caroline said she was at the desk when she heard Cora kind of groan and then there was a thumping sound. When she got in here, she saw Cora must have been arching her back from the pain and then just collapsed, hitting the headboard."

Doc, with his hand on Cora's shoulder, said, "I suspect it was that fatal heart attack I was so concerned about. She may have known it was coming but wasn't going to say anything. I think she's known for a long time."

Hannah said, "Somebody's going to have to tell Al. Suppose you could drive over to the Lost Collie and get him to come? Maybe stop at Sweeny's on the way and have Louis bring the truck?"

"I suppose I should, he's not going to know unless somebody does." Then lowering his voice, he added, "Be a good opportunity to get Lissy home to Grunewyck and her mother."

"I think she's going to fight you on that. She won't want to leave Janey. I can tell."

Doc just shrugged and returned to the waiting room with Hannah following. "Let's head out, Janey. Hannah, can you and Caroline prepare Cora for when Louis arrives?"

"Certainly, done it a thousand times."

"Then, maybe you or Caroline can get over to the townhall and tell Nealy that Helen is missing. He could go on over to Iris's place and have her head to the telephone house. She can take over until Helen comes back. Can't keep trying to get along without a phone. Okay, Janey, Lissy, shall we get on the road?"

Janey hugged Caroline and kissed her cheek. Then, with Lissy's hand still in hers, she towed the girl out the door. Lissy looked back and sobbed, "I didn't get to see her."

"Later, Lissy," Janey said, "Let Hannah and Caroline do their job. We can say goodbye at the wake."

"What if they don't have one?"

"Don't worry, I'll see to it that they do."

Lissy wrapped Janey's waist with an arm and leaned against her as they walked. That made it harder on Janey, who just wanted to get the hell out of there. Too many deaths in too short a time was too much.

356

¶

Aldo Hale crawled out of the pool of deep water below Nixie's Bluff and began stumbling through the woods, bumping into trees, and tripping over fallen logs. The briers and brambles clawed at him as if they didn't want him to leave. He finally made it to the Meadowlands, now babbling, as he trudged through the ankle high clover. The wind had picked up considerably and thunder rolled in the distance. The light sprinkle that began to fall couldn't make him any wetter than he already was. His vision had partially returned and he could see a small glow in the distance. "Sweeny's," he whimpered, and headed that way.

The light went out within minutes of him seeing it, but Aldo had found the road where it curved west before turning south for a straight shot into Gowan. He tried to shout for help but only a meager croak escaped his lips. Mab had stolen his voice as well.

Moving along the hardpack, he lurched from side to side. What ambient light Gowan gave off, showed as a dim glow in the fog that was Aldo's sight. He picked up his pace as if it had given him hope. At one point he shambled too far to the left and tripped over a tuft of grass. Falling, he rolled down into the meadow on the opposite side of the road.

Scrambling to his feet, he croaked his dismay at the sky and began walking in circles. Stopping, he rubbed his eyes and blinked several times. A small sphere of light appeared in the distance at about waist height, moving erratically left. "A lantern," he said in less than a whisper. He tried to call out, but it did him no good.

He moved toward it in a fast-lurching walk, not a clue if it might be a Will-O-The-Wisp he pursued, or worse yet, that he had only a short distance to go before walking off the undercut bank, at a highly turbulent bend, of the Spry River.

Louis Sweeny, having just extinguished the cupola chandelier for the last time, stood in the dark looking north toward the Hollow. He had always kept it burning for the late returning workers making their way home from Grunewyck. After thirty plus years as Gowan's mortician, the lamp would no longer shine from the rooftop of the old house.

He was in a state of despair because the town meeting had not gone well. There had been nothing to learn other than to show up in the morning and collect the meager check from the state for his property. It had been mostly debates, discussions and arguments. Shannon had wasted over an hour apologizing for Massachusetts and Boston's need for water. When asked how much the state was going to give them for their properties, the answer had brought outrage. The usual peaceful citizens of Gowan soon became an unruly mob.

"There's no way I'm starting from the beginning. My days of making the dead look pretty for their graves are over," Louis had said to Levi Tilman as they stood in the crowd.

"What about that boy of yours? What he gonna do?"

Louis didn't have a good answer, so he said, "Don't rightly know, Levi. He's too damn lazy to work, but he probably don't care, one way or the other."

Lightning flashed and through the dusty glass Louis thought he saw someone wondering east through the clover fields of the Meadowlands. When his eyes readjusted to the dark, he could just make out the figure, stumbling and staggering as they moved toward the river. Whoever they were, they were tall and dressed all in black. "Reverend Hale," Louis said to himself. "Probably drunk as usual. Gonna find himself head first in the river the way he's going. Guess I'd better go save his holy ass."

He dashed down the stairs and in passing his bedroom, he saw Prudence, sitting on the edge of their bed, a flask in her hand and tears on her face. A large suitcase lay open behind her.

Stepping in, he said, "I think the Reverend is drunk and has lost his way. I seen him out there in the meadow. I'm going to check on him."

Prudence stood, raised her silver flask and said, "To the drunks!" and after a lengthy drink, she promptly pushed him out of the room and slammed the door in his face.

Louis hurried down the stairs calling for Duncan to come and join him, but his son didn't answer. The young Sweeny was too far away to hear. That's because he was down at Widow Southwick's cottage. Only a few folks knew of his torrid affair with a woman ten years his senior. Penelope's husband had been killed in an accident at the box plant and she had never remarried. Duncan was glad for it.

Because Penelope always drew her shades at night, neither her nor Duncan would see Louis enter the road at a run, heading for the Meadowlands. She needed protection from prying eyes, especially from her neighbor, Abigale Cunningham.

Louis was fast running out of breath, rasping and wheezing as he moved. He stopped once and thought to call out to the Reverend, but he couldn't draw enough air to do it. Slowing his pace, he began an awkward jog, the light sprinkle soaking his jacket.

The clouds hung even more ragged than before, and Louis felt the rainwater entering his collar and running down his neck and back. When he finally caught Aldo, he grabbed him by the arm. Aldo shrieked.

"Reverend, it's me, Louis. Are you alright? What's wrong, what are you doing out here?"

Aldo grabbed him back and croaked out what sounded like, "I can't see, I'm blinded. That woman has blinded me."

"What woman?" Louis shouted in his face. "You need to come with me, I'll walk you back to the house. You damn near got to the river. What if you'd a fell in?" Aldo responded with something indiscernible.

Louis turned him around to lead him back to the mortuary. They hadn't gone more than ten feet before a raucous clambering resonated above their heads. Louis looked up to see the clouds open up and a flock of airborne goblins swirl down.

"What's that noise?" Aldo rasped. Instead of an answer, he heard Louis scream and felt himself being pulled up into the air. Louis continued to scream and released his hold on Aldo, who fell only a few feet before something caught him.

A large, sinewy, and somewhat greasy arm, wrapped Aldo's chest. He felt himself moving skyward. His vision and voice returned and he said, "Praise be! It must be the angels, and they have healed me." Turning his gaze skyward he saw that it wasn't angels after all, and like Louis, he too began to scream.

Prudence stood at the window of her bedroom watching Louis run up the road and out into the meadow. She could just make out Aldo Hale as he staggered through the field toward the river, his white collar allowing her to track him. It was no more than a few minutes after Louis made contact with Aldo, that she watched what looked like a dark funnel drop from the clouds and pick them up. She stared for a moment; her alcohol clouded brain not sure how to react.

Several minutes passed before she pulled the shade, took another long drink from her flask, and then shuffled back to her bed. She began to pack her suitcase, mumbling to herself.

"Damn tornaders, God damned tornaders," she said, slurring her words. "California, here I come..." she sang. "Where there ain't no damn tornaders!" Chuckling to herself, she took another swig of bourbon.

18

Doc drove north on the Main Street, the windshield wipers slapping. Lissy now sat in the front seat between him and Janey. Halfway through the cottage district, he said, "Janey, now that I thought about it, I'm going to drop you at Sweeny's and you can tell them to get the truck and go on up to Headmost House. I think it be best that you accompany Louis. Lissy and I will head over and tell Al about Cora."

"I want to stay with Janey," Lissy said.

"No, I don't think that's a good idea, Lissy. Janey has business that she best do alone. Besides, you'd be better off at home with your mother."

Lissy threw Doc a wicked glare and pushed up against Janey, "No! I'm not going home. I want to stay with Janey! I'm going to Carter House."

Doc patted her arm and tried to reason with her. "Lissy, you should be home with your mother. She has a lot of work to do in getting ready for your move."

Janey sat with a look of concern on her face. She knew what Doc was trying to do, but she felt it was a little too late to protect Lissy's innocence. There was no going back or wiping out the memories of what Lissy had already experienced.

"Janey, please, tell him. I have to go. I have to do this. I need to see that woman burn."

"Lissy, I agree with Doc, you should be with your mother at a time like this. Leave Mab to us."

"If you take me home, I'll just come back. Only I'll be by myself and if they get me, I know you will feel bad. Do you want that?"

A thoughtful look crossed Janey's face, conveying to Lissy that she wasn't really all too keen on Doc's plan.

360

He piped up, "There's no time for this, Janey. I'll be back around to meet with you and Louis here at the funeral home once you get Constance transported down here. Then we'll decide what we are going to do about Mab."

He stopped the car in front of Sweeny's and Janey opened the door to get out. Doc gently closed a hand around Lissy's left arm and began to pull her toward him. She resisted, but Janey shut the door and stepped away from the car. Lissy began to whimper and tried to reach the door handle, but Doc held her fast. Janey, standing outside in the rain, said, "I'm sorry," her face full of pity.

Doc sped away, watching Janey in the mirror and then brought his eyes back to the road. Letting go of Lissy, she slid to the door and began to cry. She threw Doc a glare and when he looked her direction, she blubbered out, "Damn you, Doc. Damn you."

Doc Bolen's face conveyed all it needed to tell Lissy that her words hurt. But he was the kind of man who would suffer a life time of serious regret if Lissy should lose her life because of him.

The Rolls picked up speed, and bouncing over Berryman's Crest, they roared down the hill and splashed through the water at the ford. He had to brake hard for the hairpin turns and nearly lost control several times. Lissy hung on, glowering through the windshield, her freckled cheeks wet with tears.

The last of the hairpin turns was coming up and they soon came upon Colleen Potters black truck, nose down in the water off to their right. Doc hit the brakes and it was all Lissy could do to keep from slamming into the dashboard.

They sat looking at the truck and then at each other with a, 'What's going on?' look.

"Isn't that your truck… the store's truck?"

Lissy just nodded. Doc put on the parking brake and looking hard down the road, he saw a line of cars parked along the shoulder. Some faced south as if they had come from Grunewyck, the remaining, he recognized as owned by residents of Gowan.

He watched Otis Loffler who stepped out of the underbrush, a lantern in his hand, his son Cal, walking behind him. Both men were soaking wet and covered in leaves and burrs.

"Hey, Doc, come to help?"

"What's going on, Otis?"

"Blaine Wilson, he came across the Potter's truck and went into the town and told Chief Conway. Colleen wasn't at the store and no one's seen her for some time. So, they organized a search party. His officer, you know, Lyle? He come over to Gowan and got a few of us to come help. That damn Nealy said he was too busy. Sandy Brewster's in there with Charley Bates Jr., Cecil Walker, and a few others, plus a whole bunch over from Grunewyck. Some of those fella's I don't know."

Otis ducked down and looked at Lissy, and in the light of the lantern, recognition came into his eyes.

"Why, you're that Potter girl, ain't you? That's your pa's truck, ain't it? Girl, I don't think you want to be here. If we find your ma in that swamp, you may not like what you see. So... why you here, Doc?"

"Cora MacLean died tonight, I'm on my way to inform Al and take Miss Potter home."

"Oh! Sad news. Well, you won't have to go far to tell Al, he's in there, too. Pearl's holding down the fort at the Collie." Looking back at the scattered group of men moving through the trees, Otis hollered, "Al! You, Al! Come on out here."

"No, it's okay, Otis, I'll tell him myself," Doc said and climbed out of the Rolls. Looking back through the window after closing the door, he said to Lissy, "I'll be back in a minute. You just sit tight. I'm an old man and I don't want to have to be chasing you all over. Okay?" Lissy acknowledged his command by scootching down in the seat and crossing her arms, a pout on her face.

"Hey, got something here," someone yelled out.

"What's that?" Cal hollered back?

"Found something... where's the Chief? Chief Conway, where you?"

"Over here, you fool. What you got?"

"We hooked her; she was down deep."

Lissy began to weep for the umpteenth time, trying hard to keep the memories from flooding in. She couldn't stop them and dropping the chain into her lap, she put her face in her hands and cried. Doc shook his head and sighed as he gazed through the window.

362

"I guess were going to need you in there, after all, Doc," Otis said, and putting a hand on the small of Doc's back, he gently ushered him into the trees.

19

Lissy could hear the men talking and shouting. There was a lot of splashing, then it all quieted. There was a discussion going on and somebody mentioned her name. In the quiet of the moment, she could hear the wildlife, it was getting louder by the second. The crickets and katydids increased their volume and tempo. Owls cackled and called, foxes barked, and somewhere a coyote yapped. The Whip-poor-wills began to pipe, and not just one or two, but, hundreds.

There came an all too familiar noise from the sky above the car. That cackling and screeching she had experienced on her run to the schoolhouse. The wind increased and the clouds began to roil. There was a whooshing noise and a clatter as Lissy watched the Unseelie Court come straight down and break into the trees. Branches and leaves flew every which way as if there had been an explosion. Mab's court of winged goblins began harvesting men like they were raspberries in an open glade.

Lissy watched in horror as screaming men were being carried off into the swirling clouds. It didn't escape her that one of them was Doc, his coat flashing white as it rose up into the sky. A gasp escaped her lips, followed by a whimper. A part of the flock broke away and headed for the Rolls.

"They know I'm here," she said, panic in her voice.

Frantically rolling up the window, she locked the doors as they circled above the car. It sounded as if they were quarreling.

"They're fighting over me," she said aloud, almost shrieking it. Bending down to look at them through the windshield, she added, "Got to get out of here."

As if having heard her, the fiends all laughed at her ridiculous notion and swirled closer.

James Potter had taught his daughter to drive at age twelve. The Rolls wasn't the truck, but driving was driving. She slid behind the wheel, giving the controls a once-over. One of the beasts hit the roof with a fist, spurring her to hurry.

There came a loud buzzing like a giant hornet hovering close. Turning to look out of her window, her eyes met those of a hovering boggart at the glass. The hair rose on her arms and the back of her neck as she choked back a shriek.

"Well, if it isn't little Lissy Potter," it said in a squeaky growl. It was Gregory Bly. "Come on out of there, little one. Come on out and join us."

"Fuck you," she screamed, and slamming the stick shift into reverse, she popped the clutch and floored it. The fiend that had been Gregory Bly rose up and hovered, watching Lissy race backwards. She slammed on the brakes at the curve, causing the car to spin and face south. She found first gear and sped away toward Gowan, grinding through the gears as she went. The Gregory thing muttered, "A later time, Lissy Potter," and turning, he flew away to join the others for easier pickings.

20

Janey came up onto the porch at Sweeny's and knocked on the door several times. No one answered. Stepping into the entry hall, she said loudly, "Hello, Mr. Sweeny? Louis?" Her voice had improved. If she talked in a monotone, she could keep it from breaking.

Moving into the front parlor, she looked around. No one there. Returning to the hallway, she stood, listening. The floor creaked above her head. Someone was upstairs. Walking to the bottom of the stairway, she gazed up to the lighted landing at the top.

"Hello? Is someone there?"

The creaking stopped. "Hello? Who's up there? It's Janey, Janey Carter. Louis, is that you?"

The creaking started again; someone was coming. Janey waited and soon Prudence shuffled to the top of the stairs. She was dressed in her usual black dress and lace cap. Janey marveled at how much Prudence, like Constance, resembled Queen Victoria of Britian. Janey didn't like Prudence, but not many people did. She was a cantankerous lush and Janey had never seen her sober.

"What'dyouwant?" Prudence said, slurring.

"I'm looking for Louis? I need his help. My... my mother died, I..."

Prudence's reaction was indifferent, but she did manage a, "Shorry to hear it."

"Prudence, is Louis here? Where's Louis?"

"Tornader got him, so… shorry… weer closed fer bishness. You'll have to go shomewhere else."

"A tornado got him? What do you mean?"

"Go away, weer closed. Get out of my howsh."

"But, I…" Janey said and started up the stairs."

"Donchew come up here! Get out!"

"Prudence, where's Duncan? Can I talk to Duncan?"

"Why? Chew want to fornicate with him, too? Damn floozies, coming around… I said, get out, or I'm calling the law."

Janey backed down the stairs, stood for a minute glaring at Prudence who produced a flask, drank from it, and glared back.

Leaving the house, Janey walked out to the road and stopped to stand at the edge of the lawn in the rain. She looked around as if she wasn't sure where to go next. She didn't just want to leave her mother's body on a couch at Headmost. She decided to wait for Doc. Maybe he could go inside and talk some sense into the alcoholic Prudence.

Grunewyck had a funeral home, but with the reservoir coming, Janey didn't know if maybe they too had closed their doors. She began to walk south. When she arrived at a driveway just one cottage up from Chastity's, she had to jump back to avoid getting hit by a car that came speeding out, no headlamps lit.

Penelope Southwick's derelict Model T flew by and bounced out onto the road. Penelope was at the wheel, totally indifferent to Janey's presence. Duncan Sweeny grinned and waved from the passenger seat. The headlamps came on and the old car sputtered and coughed one time before picking up speed. There were two large suit cases strapped to the back. The car clattered all the way through town and turned right at Railroad Street. Penelope was obviously abandoning Gowan and she was taking Duncan with her.

A second motor noise caught Janey's ear, and turning back, she watched another car approach. It had come up out of the Hollow and appeared to be swerving as it came. Janey recognized the sound of Doc's Rolls and stepping into the roadway, she waved her hands for the car to stop. When the headlights lit her up, it slowed, and then lurched to a halt a good hundred feet back. The engine died and the car lunged forward, the driver slamming on the brakes. There was only one person in the car—and it wasn't Doc.

Janey ran up to the driver's side window and stood looking through the glass at a weeping Lissy Potter. The girl just sat looking back, her face distorted by grief. Stuttering sobs poured from the girl's mouth as Janey opened the door. "What's going on? Where's Doc, Lissy? What happened?"

Lissy launched herself into Janey's arms and they stood in a drizzle-soaked embrace.

"There, there, Lissy. It's going to be okay," Janey cooed, even though her face expressed doubt. When a few minutes passed, Janey stepped back from the girl and held her at arm's length.

"Lissy, where's Doc? What happened to Doc?"

"They got him," she said, and wiped her nose with the back of a hand, "I think they got my mom, too."

"Who got them? Mab? Was it Mab?"

"It was those flying goblins, they got Doc and a whole bunch of others over in the Hollow. My mom's dead, Janey. My mom's drown..."

"How do you know?"

"I saw her, they took her outta the swamp... the truck was... the truck was in the ditch. What we going to do, Janey? They're killing everybody."

Janey stood stunned, at a loss for words. She was almost too numb already to feel too much for Doc. The time to cry would come later, right now there was a task at hand. The rain matted their hair and began to run down their faces. It brought Janey out of her stupor and she said, "Let's get in the car before we catch our death."

Lissy climbed back in and slid across the front seat. Janey followed and after closing the door, she turned off the headlamps. They just sat, listening to the loud purr of the engine and staring out of the rain splattered windshield. Within minutes men began to appear, passing the car in groups, couples, and singles. Some had their jackets pulled up over their heads.

The meeting was over. The talk they heard, as the disgruntled Gowanites passed them, wasn't pleasant. The men looked in the windows as they moved by and all Janey could do was wave halfheartedly, a false smile plastered on her face. Ross Bailey, the local carpenter, approached. Recognizing the car, he stopped and said, "Doc?" before looking hard enough to see it wasn't. "Well, you ain't Doc," he said through the glass.

Janey rolled down the window. "Hello, Ross."

"Well, Janey Carter… where's Doc? This is Doc's car, right?"

"Yep, he's letting me borrow it for a moment."

"Oh, I see," he said suspiciously because Doc never lent his Rolls to anyone. But because it was Janey Carter, the good doctor may have made an exception. "Looks like it's got a hell of a dent in the roof there…"

"Yeah, a big tree branch… So, how was the meeting?" she said, trying to be cordial.

"Well, Janey… we're done. Gowans done, and so's Grunewyck… and a dozen other towns around here, matter of factly. Not like we didn't know. We ain't getting diddly for our properties. That shyster Shannon must be making a pretty penny, though, I'm sure of it. Dark dealings, I say. They going to be here next week. The demolition companies. This place will be swarming with Woodpeckers before you know it. They're already setting up camps all over the valley. Seen a demolition shed north of here on the main highway just south of Aylesbury at Scottsburg. I 'spect they is going to be dynamiting some things. Won't that be a sight? I was up that way, building a fence for the Holgraves, I 'spect you don't know them? Anyway, got to go to townhall tomorrow and sign over my place. Been in Gowan all my damn life, and now this. Maybe I'll head down to Brimfield, my brothers got a shop down there for making furniture, or I could get work as a Woodpecker, just not so sure I'll feel good about knocking down my town. Hey, who you got in there with you?"

Lissy tried to smile. "Hey, you're that Potter girl, James's kid. Sorry to hear about your pa. How's your ma taking it? Not good, I imagine."

The teen just looked away and sniffed. Ross looked perplexed and said, "Well, got to get out of this rain, ain't nothing but a sprinkle, but even that'll soak you to the skin. If you know what I mean? Got to git home and start packing. I'll get my check and then I'm on the road. Oh, well... good night, folks," Ross said and turned away toward his cottage. Janey wanted to tell him to be careful on his walk but didn't want to have to explain why. Forty-five years of walking around Gowan with never a thought to any danger, and if she hollered out it would most certainly bring him back to the window, prolonging the situation. She just wanted to get out of there.

"Sorry, about your mother, Lissy," she said, gazing at the girl. Even though there were tears, the look of fierce determination remained.

"Well, I'm sorry about yours, too. We're kind of in the same boat, ain't we?" Lissy said matter of factly. "We got to... we got to get her, Janey. We got to get that Mab."

"It might be better to just quit while we're still breathing."

"No, we got to get her. Somehow, someway. You're smart, right? You're a teacher, you can figure something out."

Janey just looked at Lissy, not knowing what to say. The look on her face said she was flattered, but that didn't change much of anything. She knew where Tom, Doc, Reverend Hale, and all the others went wrong. None of them believed enough in the iron.

Janey's hand strayed to the flower hanging on the chain around her neck. Lissy's comb still remained in her hair and a chain was still wrapped around her waist.

Pulling her own chain from her pocket, it rattled against the derringer. Leaning forward in her seat, Janey fashioned her own chain belt. Then glancing at Lissy, she saw the girl smile for the first time in days.

"I have to go to Headmost; I need to get some things."

"We need to go to Carter House!" Lissy lamented. "And finish this! We can get her; I just know we can."

"Headmost, first," Janey said staunchly, "Then... Carter House. We need to be strategic about this or we are going to lose."

"Okay," Lissy said with a sigh and pushed loose strands of hair from her face.

Janey turned on the headlamps, and after putting the car in gear, they rolled away toward Headmost House.

21

Beulah McKay stood in her kitchen, finishing off a chicken drumstick. Clad in her dressing gown, she was ready for bed, but couldn't resist the refrigerated leftover fried chicken from Boots'. The day had been too quiet and now her main resource for the grapevine, Helen, wasn't picking up. The evening was warm, every window sash was up, and the sound of the dripping rain filled the air. With the chicken gone, there was no sense in staying awake any longer. Clutching at a hip, she groaned and turned toward her bedroom. Old age was no picnic.

An evening breeze found its way inside, and with it, she thought she heard someone call her name. It's conveyance was melodic. Beulah cocked an ear and waited. She was the only one on Ovis Street that didn't own a business over on Main, but still resided with the Gowan elite.

She had inherited the Queen Anne style house, as well as the money her father had accumulated over his lifetime. It had all come from his carpetbagging and Reconstruction shams. He had made a good life for her. Then her husband, Cedric Adian McKay, made his share, but lost most of it in the 1929 Crash. He had always paid his debts though, and even though he had hung himself in the cellar, he had left her a small fortune safely housed in the Gowan Bank. Beulah never had to do a speck of work. There were people for that. Her presence in the town was beneficial for many of Gowan's citizens who lived a life of servitude. Beulah no longer allowed her housekeeper, cook, or gardener to reside within her abode. She didn't trust them not to rob her blind.

Her name floated in again through the window, only this time, louder. It emanated from the yard behind the house, punctuated by the sound of rainwater rattling in the downspouts. Grabbing her cane, Beulah shuffled to the window next to the backdoor.

There it was again! It sounded a lot like Sophillia Garford, her maid. She had not shown up for work in the last two days. Beulah had collared little Gus Baylor on Main Street and gave him a quarter to run down to the Garford cottage and retrieve Sophillia. He came back to report that even though the place was wide open, neither Sophillia or her husband, Zachariah, were there. He also included that he had opened the cellar door for a look, but it stunk to high heaven, so he didn't go down there.

"Well, what basement doesn't stink?" she had asked him rather cynically.

"Never smelt one like that before," Gus said and demanded another quarter, which Beulah promptly refused. He had stomped his foot in anger and dashed away, only to stop and holler, "You old cow," and then promptly blew her a raspberry, before continuing.

Beulah opened the door and stepped out onto the stoop. Someone was standing just inside the back gate in the shadow.

"Who's that? Sophillia, is that you? What is this? Some kind of prank?"

"Beulah."

"Where you been? Come on up here. Where'd you get that horrid green dress?"

Sophillia began to move slowly toward the back porch.

"You better have a good excuse for not showing up. Come on up here out of the rain, you're going to catch your death."

The figure suddenly shot forward, little hooves clattering on the wet pavers of the back walkway. For perhaps, all of five seconds, Beulah saw Sophillia's face, and then—she saw something else. Contrary to her statement, it was actually Beulah, who caught her death.

22

Danny Billings wasn't sleeping well. He kept having flashbacks of finding Vern Sweeny's mutilated body. In one of his nightmares, Vern actually spoke to him through a bloody mouth and Danny came awake with a shriek. Tossing and turning in the sweltering heat of his little room, he wanted to open all his windows, but his perpetual fear of ruffians showing up from Zelda's and crawling inside, wouldn't allow it. On most hot nights, he would have climbed out a dormer window to sleep on one of the attic balconies, but the rain kept him inside. "Maybe I'll head up to Brenner's for a beer, or two," he mumbled to himself as a car full of loud and obnoxious drunks passed on its way down to Main Street.

Swinging his legs out, he sat on the edge of his cot. The squeaking of the frame seemed to trigger a noise just outside his door in the waiting room. It was a scampering sound, like big rats. Peeking through the key hole brought no gratification. He would have to go out there.

Unlocking the door, Danny stepped out in only his station agent trousers. He expected to find someone sacking out on one of the benches waiting for the morning train. As much as he hated the idea, he was going to have to explain that the last train had come this evening and from now on, passengers would have to catch it over in Hadley.

Something skittered along the far wall accompanied by squeaky laughter. That should have been enough to send any reasonable person to cower behind locked doors. But Danny was known for being pigheaded, and instead, he crept over, hoping to get a peek at whatever it was.

Shadows moved along the base of the wall across the room. Raccoon sized silhouettes, cackled, hissed, and screeched in little voices. The far door Gil used for hauling out the mail and other cargo, swung open and slammed shut.

Picking his way between the benches to the door, Danny poked his nose out and listened. When he didn't hear any more, he stepped out onto the platform.

The rain was light but steady. Whip-poor-wills began to pipe from the woods. Taking a few more steps out toward the tracks, he looked south toward Hill Road, but saw no one.

There came an overpowering stench and turning to look north, he found a hulk of what looked like a man standing within five feet of him. There was a grunt and a bronze battle axe cleaved Danny's head from his shoulders. His body dropped like a stone as his noggin bounced on the rain slick boards before rolling off onto the tracks.

Small, dark shadows boiled out from beneath the platform, squeaking and chirping. The little imps began to kick Danny's head around like a ball, working their way across the cinders, the steel rails, and then between the outbuildings on the other side. One of them grabbed it up by its bloody locks and letting go with a squeaking laugh, it made for the trees, the other bogle fae in hot pursuit.

The brutish creature with his axe, stood quiet on the platform watching them go, then pushing the handle of its weapon under an arm, it removed the red, crusty cap from its misshapen head. Bending down, it used it to sop up the blood that had pooled around Danny's still quivering shoulders, soaking it more crimson than it already was. The beast placed it back on its head, red rivulets running through its short mangey hair and down the slate grey skin of its warty face. Blowing a gob of green snot from its large, misshapen nose, it grunted, grinned, and jumped off the platform to follow the bogles with a waddling gait.

23

Sam Shoats had just returned home from the town meeting. He had hoped his dairy would fall outside the area designated for the reservoir—but no such luck. His property was just inside the shoreline on the western side of Parson's Ridge.

He was seething and cut loose with a few good swear words on the way home, sometimes pounding the dashboard with a fist. A couple hundred dollars for an entire dairy and all the land around it. Ridiculous! Pulling up in front of the house, he saw not a light was lit. He'd had to milk his cows in a hurry in order to get into town for the meeting. Then, to hear nothing but cow flop from that shyster Shannon's mouth. He hadn't had time for Aileen's supper and she had been furious.

Walking to the barn for a last-minute check, he opened the door and stepped inside. Something was wrong, the barn was too quiet. Lighting a lantern, he held it high. The cows were no longer inside and the large sliding door in the far wall stood open.

"Damn it all to hell, what now?" he growled.

Sam stomped across to the door but came to an abrupt halt. Someone was following him. Spinning around he saw nothing, but there was a twittering, squeaking sound like little animals would make. Something scrambled just out of sight.

"Who's there? Who's that?" he yelled. The noise stopped, but as soon as he turned back, it came again, almost like a stampede of small animals on the hard packed dirt of the aisle. Sam never got the chance to turn a second time before they swarmed him. Small creatures, no bigger than badgers, soon covered him from head to foot. He dropped the lantern and tried to pull one loose, but to no avail.

They nipped him, pulled his hair, beat him with tiny fists, and scratched him with sharp little claws. One pulled off his cap and moved up to sit on his head. It donned the dairyman's headwear and then cackled gleefully before biting a hunk out of Sam's ear and jumping to the floor. Another one had latched onto his nose, the stench of the imp's breath filling his nostrils as it gnawed away. He pulled it loose, taking a chunk of his nose with it when he threw it against the wall.

They got inside his clothes, and one's head popped out of his collar at the front to shriek into his face. Sam whirled and shouted, trying to pull the little bogles off. Tearing one loose, he flung it across the aisle, but it landed spryly atop a railing and jumped back to sink its teeth into his arm. They all piled on at once and the weight of them took him to the floor where Sam twisted, rolled, and shrieked

Squeaky laughter filled the barn as they attempted to suffocate him. He bit one that had pressed itself against his face. It screeched and launching itself off, it caught a support column and swung by a hand, mocking him and making faces.

Sam was able to gain his feet, but the mob of bogles remained in place and he staggered around, bumping into things, crushing some of the little beasts who promptly burst into brown odorific gas. Stumbling out the door, he fell into the mud of the yard. A pain blossomed in his chest and radiated down his left arm. He vomited bile and the little fiends jumped clear, forming a circle around his prostrate body, to cackle, hiss, and squeak. He rolled onto his left side and his eyes found the house. He tried to shout, "Aileen," but it only came as a loud groan, and then, Sam Shoats departed his world to go and meet his ancestors.

Had he been able to actually shout her name as intended, Aileen would never have heard him. She too had suffered the onslaught of the dark fae and the fall down the cellar stairs had broken her back and her left hip. Unable to breathe properly, she expired sometime after midnight. Her body and Sam's wouldn't be discovered until Wilbur Meany, the milkman, showed up at sunrise to load his truck.

Tip Thomas surveyed the front room at Zelda's from behind the bar. There were only two people in the place and he asked himself out loud, "What the hell's going on?" He had expected a crowd, mostly property owners coming in with complaints against the state and their "Town killing reservoir."

He didn't go to the meeting. His deal was already done. R.J. Brown, the owner of R.J. Brown's Merrimac Demolition & Lumber Co. had already purchased the roadhouse and hired a few people, including a couple bartenders, to work the place until they had to knock it down.

Brown had given Beth Brenner, Boots McKay, the McCarthys, and Belinda Fiske the same deal. Their establishments would be the last to go. R.J. Brown's brother, Ulysses P. Brown, had done the same over in Grunewyck. They would meet in the middle, so to speak, and finalize their venture by taking down Carter House and all its outbuildings.

"The state don't require it, but they offered me and Ulysses an extra two thousand if we bulldozed Carter House as well. I'm starting with the towns of Pellington and Dunham first, though, and then Gowan," Brown had said. Tip didn't give two shits; he'd be long gone by then.

He had stepped out front on the porch earlier, looking to see if anyone was coming to the roadhouse to make this evening worthwhile. He saw the young widow, Penelope Southwick, pass by in her old model T.

Someone was with her, a someone that looked a lot like Louis Sweeny's boy. Tip knew all about the affair. An older woman with a teenaged boy. He figured Duncan must feel like he had hit the jackpot with that woman. Penelope was known as a 'real looker'. Her and the boy had come to Zelda's often in the afternoon, probably because nobody they knew would be there. It was their safe place and Tip had worked hard to keep it that way.

What happened at Zelda's, stayed at Zelda's. When Merlyn Cobb came poking around, he would get nothing but lies. There had been two suitcases strapped to the back end of that car. "Leaving town with your lover, hey, Penelope?" Tip said to the wet evening air.

He had pocketed two thousand dollars cash money for the roadhouse. A heap more than anyone else was going to get—except for Philip Shannon, who he knew was going to reap a small fortune from helping kill towns like Gowan and Grunewyck.

Tip packed up a crate of beer bottles, and going through the kitchen, he headed for the back stoop. Sadie Giles, the cook, sat in her apron, reading a newer copy of *Picture Play* magazine and smoking a filterless Camel. Looking up, she grinned.

"You might as well go up to your room, Sadie. I'll call you if I need you. Looks like pickings are slim tonight."

"If you don't mind, boss, I'd like to stay. Not much going on up there, neither. I'd like a beer… if it's all the same to you?"

"Help yourself," he replied and stepped out.

After setting the crate with the others, he walked out to the back fence, leaned with his arms on the top and stood listening to the Spry River. He was going to miss the place. His sister and her husband had a tavern down in Thornhill. There was a need for a night time bartender. He liked them enough to say yes. They had a passel of kids to look out for and had hounded him to come down and help. It was time.

As he stood listening to the flowing water and other night sounds, he heard a kind of keening wail that began to crescendo, drop off, and then start again. It sounded like it was coming from the gravel bar just five hundred or so yards to the south where it had formed under the Long Bridge Road overpass.

He thought of a tale his mother had told him about when she was a child and they lived in Kiedler, England. Her father, a forester, had died in a ghastly accident. They had suffered a night filled with such a noise just before his demise. Tip now shuddered.

Normally, he would have gone down to investigate. The large caliber, double barreled, pocket pistol that he always carried usually inspired confidence. But the wailing wasn't of this earth.

Sadie came to the backdoor, flicked her cigarette butt away and hollered out to him, "What the hell was that, boss? Sounds like it's coming from the river?"

"Don't know… wildcat, maybe."

"Twern't no wildcat, boss, that sount like a woman. 'Spose somcone's needing help?"

"You want to go down and find out?" he said, turning with a scowl.

"Oh no, not me. I'm a coward."

"Well, then, shut your mouth. I could go down there… but I ain't."

The wailing gradually died away and the insects began again. Somewhere over on the other side of the Spry River, Whip-poor-wills began to call. Their piping sounded like breathing. He held his breath for a few seconds and they stopped. When he started in again—so did they. Another shudder coursed through his body as the words of his father rolled into his brain, "Them Whip-poor-wills, they'll steal your soul when you die if you're not a good man. So… be a good man, Tip."

"You, okay, boss?"

"Why don't you go get that beer you were yakking on about and leave me be?" he said, glaring from the dark as the drizzle turned into a light rain.

"Hey, Tip," came from the balcony behind him. He looked up to see Lily Peters leaning out over the railing, a pink parasol being held over her curler filled hair. Her dressing gown hung open and her large breasts were no longer contained.

"Roof's still leaking, I can hear it dripping. It's turning the plaster brown, you know?"

"You can't wait 'til a clearer a day to harp on me about that?"

"Well, I tried that. Seems it did no good."

"'Spose you'd like for me to get up there and fix it right this very minute?"

"Might do some good... mayhaps?"

Tip knew about the shingle that hung at a cockeyed angle. One nail would put it right, then that might stop Lily's bitching. She was one of the older occupants of the upper floor. She didn't bring as much revenue because of it. Didn't matter anymore, she was somebody else's problem. Tip started to worry that if there was ceiling damage, it might create problems with Brown and he might have to give back some of the money. One single nail was all it would take to solve the problem. One simple nail to solve all his ills.

"Well, boss, what's it gonna be?"

"Why don't you just shut up and get back inside? I'll be up in a minute; got to go and find my hammer. Then I'll fix it, and maybe... you too."

Lily sneered, stuck out her tongue, and muttered, "You can kiss my lily-white, well-shaped fanny, you old coot." Chuckling, she climbed back in her window to sit at her vanity and smoke another cigarette. She didn't like Tip much; never had. But the money had been good in the early days, so she put up with him. Zelda's was a step up from Ruthie's Roadhouse just outside of Greenfield. She heard it had burned down in '32. Lily had told the conveyor of the news that she hoped Ruthie had been inside at the time.

Tip found his hammer in the outbuilding behind the roadhouse and went up the stairs. Throwing open Lily's door he said, "Found it, and as soon as I'm done pounding this nail, I'm coming back down and pounding you."

"Promises, promises."

He shook his hammer at her and she took a long drag of her cigarette and blew the smoke at him. Leaving the door open, he moved across the hall and up the stairs that took him to the rooms up under the roof. Going into Ivy Pilsen's (she had already flown the coop) he opened the window in the dormer and climbed out.

The cedar shakes were slick with rain. He had second thoughts about the task he had put off for so long. But Brown would be here in the morning, and if he didn't do it now, he would surely forget.

Sticking the hammer and nail in a back pocket, he reached up and took a hold of the dormer ridge and walked himself up. Finding his footing, he crawled to the peak and looked over. The shake was just out of reach on the other side. He was going to have to lean over, hold the nail with one hand and pound with the other.

"I hate you and your big, saggy tits, Lily Peters," he muttered.

When he finally got to the top and lay over the metal cap that ran the length of the ridge, he found he could just reach it. Pulling out his hammer and nail, he went to work. Sadly, for him, the nail bent and he had to pry it straight. That's what cost him.

Overreaching, he felt himself going. The old cedar shakes were too slimy to get a grip and he somersaulted down the back slope. Missing the balcony by a foot, he fell the two stories, crushing two crates of beer bottles with his back. Tip never screamed. Just a single, "Shit,' had slipped his lips as he realized there was no getting out of this one. Only Lily had heard him go.

There was the thumping on the roof, then the abrupt silence as Tip began his tumbling freefall, followed by the crash of bottles. Lily sat opened mouth for a few seconds, not sure what to do. She was glad the infernal wailing from the riverbank had stopped, but now the Whip-poor-wills were making a rather horrifying clatter as the flock flapped east.

Getting up, Lily walked to the window and closed it. Returning to the chair at her vanity, she pulled her robe closed and retied the belt.

Then, taking an opium pipe from a drawer, she lit up.

She smirked at herself in the mirror and then looking back toward the window, through a cloud of smoke, she muttered, "Serves you right, you old bastard."

The clouds roiled across the dark sky, and on occasion, what many of the survivors would later refer to as a tornado, dropped down to take an unwary traveler, or two, from the open byways. The shower ended, and the wind began to gust across the valley and through the Hollow where a line of ownerless cars sat parked alongside the road.

Up on Nixie's Bluff, Mab stood in the unlit belvedere of Carter House, her laugh heard only by NicDobhran, who paced back and forth, grinning, waiting for her queen to raise her hand. When she did, they both transformed into two, thin, shimmering shafts of light and out through the open window they went, soaring through the sky like two spectral arrows; the Unseelie Court swirling above.

24

Nealy had two drunks in custody. They complained that Nealy just wanted to arrest somebody for the hell of it. But they knew better than argue when Nealy had a gun in his hand. The little ten-gauge double barrel wasn't going to argue; its word was final. Lawrence Brackenbury and Jeffery Lowthrop, were two single men who worked the basket factory over in Grunewyck. The two Zelda's regulars sat in the cell glaring at the officer as he tried to get a hold of Merlyn. The line remained dead no matter how many times he racked the forked shaped receiver. He was going to have to go to Merlyn's house and roust him out.

In all the years he had lived in Gowan, Helen had never been absent from her post and if she didn't answer, then Iris Hazelton, the operator's second, was supposed to. The whole evening had been weird and then the talk of the numerous tornados that supposedly touched down out in the Meadowlands and other places in the valley. It had been a strange storm. Dark clouds with ragged fingers hanging down, rotated, as the lightning played through them like mischievous spirits.

"You boy's behave yourselves; I have to leave."

"Hey, Nealy. What you holding us for?"

"Disturbing the peace."

"Well, we weren't the only ones. You got no right to hold us," Lawrence said.

"Yeah, no right to hold us," Jeffery added.

"Well, we'll see what Chief Cobb says about that. Just stay put, I'll be back in a minute."

Unloading the shotgun, Nealy stuck it in a rack and dropped the shells into a drawer. Then taking a key hidden under a police officers' training manual, he unlocked the bottom most one and pulled it open. There were several revolvers inside, all somewhat antiquated. They were Merlyn's personal collection. Off limits. Taking a Remington of the same caliber as his missing Colt, he loaded it from the ammo loops in his belt and shoved it into his holster. Smirking to himself, he stepped out the door, followed by the grumbles of his prisoners.

Nealy was glad the green was now empty of angry citizens; he didn't want to field questions he didn't have an answer for. Stopping at Main Street, he stood oblivious to the sprinkle of rain that was fast soaking his hat. His ears filled with a raucous noise much like the crowd at the baseball games he occasionally attended over in Springfield. It seemed to be coming from straight above him, but the rain wouldn't allow any prolonged search of the clouds.

He no sooner turned his attention back to the street when two whitish streaks zipped by overhead, whistling like cannonballs. They seemed to have targeted Prosper Mountain, except there was no resulting impact.

The noise in the clouds soon waned, leaving Nealy with a scowl on his face. Looking around for someone to converse with about the strange affair, he saw a couple under an umbrella carrying a lantern, walking away up the boardwalk on the opposite side. He was in the midst of his usual swagger down the middle of the street when lights lit him up from behind. Stepping to the boardwalk, he watched the Bolen's Rolls Royce move past.

Doc would certainly be somebody he could pump for information, but it wasn't Doc in the driver's seat; it was Janey Carter. There was some girl in the passenger seat and she was watching him intently.

"Well, Janey Carter, why you driving Doc's car?" he said to himself.

Nealy watched the Rolls turn into the lane of Headmost House and disappear under the canopy of leaves. He'd check that out later, right now he had to get over to Merlyn's place.

He walked across the street, deciding to pass around the north side of the slaughterhouse instead of stumbling his way between buildings. Merlyn's abode was the first one on the north end of Lillie Street. Angus McGowan had taken possession of the house after the lumbermill mysteriously burnt to the ground and Harlan Prosper, the owner, abandon it for Boston. Rather than condemn the place and tear it down, the town council decreed the old Greek Revival would house Gowan's chief of police.

Passing the stable on the northside of Brewster's place, Nealy glanced in and was surprised to see Massy was not in her stall. It was odd that Merlyn would have her out so late.

The cows began to low when the officer came around the corner. There should have been no cows in the holding corral. Charley Bates Jr. should have run them out to the pasture so their noise wouldn't keep the citizens of the town awake. One more thing to cause Nealy to believe that things weren't right in Gowan.

26

The Cadillac was gone when Janey pulled in. "Good," she said, parking the Rolls on the exit side of the turn-around.

"What's good?" Lissy asked, wrapping her chain around her open hand.

"I'll tell you later," Janey said and turned off the car. They sat in silence, looking at the house. The curtains had been closed and Percy had left no lights burning. The rain had ceased, but the wind had picked up. The old Italianate's boxy style looked frightenedly ominous against the back drop of the century old trees. Janey was having second thoughts about going inside. Looking up toward the cupola, she couldn't help but notice the clouds were low enough to almost be touching the metal finial that projected from its peak.

The unusual looking clouds would have only been a passing interest to most, but Janey knew it was Mab's work, done to hide the Unseelie Court. Leaving the iron pickets, they climbed out of the Rolls.

"We need a light. I'm not going in there without one. My tummy's telling me something ain't right here, Janey. There's something dangerous."

"Check the glove box, see if Doc has a flashlight."

Lissy did and found a two celled, Yale unit. "Got one!" she said and turned it on. The flashlight didn't light right away, but shaking it brought results. Janey said, "Okay, turn it off now and give it to me." Lissy did as told and waited.

"Well, let's get in there. Looks like Percy and Tabby have gone. So, there shouldn't be any one inside, well… except for…"

"Who?"

"It doesn't matter. Are you ready?"

Lissy checked the chain wrapping her waist to make sure it was secure, followed by the one binding her hand. Grinning nervously up at Janey, she said, "I'm ready."

"Once we get inside, I'll turn on the lights. We might have to light lanterns, but I'm sure Percy would have left them in their usual places. I want to pack a bag and then we'll lock up and leave. It will be safer if we don't stay in Gowan tonight. Maybe we'll drive down to Brimfield and stay in the boarding house. We'll come back in the daylight. I have to talk to Philip Shannon about some business and then I should probably head down to Salem. Is there anyone at home for you? Do you need to go there? Grandmother, or grandfather? Aunt or uncle?"

"No, nobody. They'd just put me in an orphanage, anyway. Besides, I want to stay with you. Can't I just stay with you?" Lissy pleaded.

"We'll talk more about that. Right now, let's get this business done and get out of here."

"Ain't we going to Carter House and get that Mab? I don't want to go anywhere until we try at least one more time."

"It might be best if we just try to get away while we can still draw a breath. Don't you think?"

"Janey, she's not going to stop until you are dead. You heard Cora. You're in the way. She'll send those… those things, no matter where you go. I just… I just want to be there when she does, so… so I can protect you. Please?"

Janey's face displayed an obvious admiration for the girl, and then something akin to a love light showed in her eyes; like a sister for a sister, or a mother for a daughter. Janey fought back a sob and moved to embrace Lissy. They met halfway and held each other for a few minutes before Janey kissed the top of Lissy's head and pulled back, her hands resting on Lissy's shoulders. Tears glistened in their eyes as they studied each other in the dark. Janey smiled and said, "Well, let's get inside. We'll talk some more about what we are going to do."

They approached the front door as if expecting to be ambushed. Lissy stayed right with Janey, who found it surprising how Lissy, with her hero like stance, brought comfort. Turning the knob, Janey pushed the front door open and stood waiting. When nothing happened, she stepped through the vestibule and into the entry hall. Lissy pushed past her and stood at its center, looking, and listening. Then moving to each door, she gazed into the rooms for a few seconds before disappearing into the kitchen.

Janey didn't want to look in the parlor where Constance lay wrapped in linen sheets, but she forced herself. The lamp was off, so Constance only came as a dark shadow on the settee. It felt so odd that she had been talking with her mother just the day before, and now, she was gone forever.

She followed Lissy and found her still in the kitchen, peeking around the door jamb into the back corridor. Janey believed she knew what Lissy was feeling now. The desire for revenge was growing. When Janey was a teen, the need to get back at the classroom bully was almost always overpowering. Then there was the irresistible desire to prank Miss Durnell every time she unjustifiably blamed 'that Carter girl' for one thing or another, and then punished her for it. By her senior year, Janey had grown quite desperate for graduation and the day she'd be free of, "The old hag!"

Janey felt Lissy looking and turned to meet her eyes. Lissy started to speak when there came just the slightest noise from above their heads. Something had fallen to the floor in cousin Bertie's room, something tiny like a cuff link or a tie tack. They both looked up at the ceiling and then back at each other, eyes wide. Lissy whispered, "Hear that?"

"My cousin's old room. Nobody's been in there for years. They left it just like it was the day he died."

"Who could it be? Mab?"

"Perhaps... we should leave," Janey said.

"No, we should go up there. I know it's scary and all, but we have to."

"Okay," Janey said, defying logic by resisting the urge to flee in the face of a more powerful foe.

They tiptoed out of the kitchen, across the narrow corridor, and up the backstairs. They stopped at the top and studied the closed door on their right. Constance's bedroom was right across the hall from cousin Bertie's. Janey turned on the flashlight but pushed the lens against her dress to hide the beam as they tiptoed to the door.

Janey moved to the hinge side and waited. Lissy stopped on the other and prepared to turn the knob. When Janey nodded the go-ahead, Lissy turned it and threw it open. Janey stepped back in case something or someone should leap out. Lissy didn't hesitate and jumping inside, yelled, "Hah!" Her actions surprised Janey, and she had to stifle a gasp.

Stepping up behind Lissy, she shined the light around. There was no one but them. Lissy hit the light switch, but the bulb in the ceiling lamp didn't illuminate. They walked deeper into the room and looked around. Neither missed the large, gold class ring, commemorating Bertie's graduation from Wentworth, laying on the floor. It should have been centered on the dresser along with the other memorabilia.

"You see that?" Lissy said.

"Yeah, I see it. Bertie's class ring, the one they gave him the day before he drown goofing off with his classmates in the Concord River."

Lissy bent to pick it up and Janey nearly shouted, "No, just leave it." Lissy jerked her hand back and scowled at Janey.

"Sorry, I..." was all Janey got out when Lissy's eyes abruptly moved from her to a shadowy corner of the room. "Someone's in here with us... we just can't see 'em." Adopting an even more defensive stance, Janey watched the chain roll off Lissy's hand to swing free.

Janey shuddered and hurrying toward the door, she grabbed Lissy's arm and towed her along. The girl didn't resist, but when Janey shut the door, Lissy said, "Why'd you do that?"

"Lissy, hear my words because I don't want to say it again. I need to pack a suitcase so we can get the hell out of here. That's the goal, not fighting."

"But... we have them. We got iron and they know it. So, when they try to grab us..."

"Well, until they try, I'm going to go pack a suitcase. No argument. If you want to be with me, then there will be times you will have to listen to me for your own good. Got me?"

"Yeah, I got ya," Lissy said, casting her eyes to the floor.

"Okay, good."

Janey walked away, sorry for her words. Those were her folks words, something they would have said. Now, regrettably, she was saying them too.

Lissy followed Janey, walking backwards to keep her eye on Bertie's room. Janey went into her bedroom and when Lissy was inside, she shut and locked the door. Tapping the button for the ceiling lamp brought illumination. She turned to Lissy and said, "I don't think they can go through solid things. They're not like ghosts. I think, like us, they need openings like doors and windows. They might be able to come through the key hole or under the door, but if you keep an eye out while I pack, it will take them a few seconds to materialize and we'll see them doing it. I suppose it will be much like when they dematerialize. What I'm trying to say is, they have to..."

"I understand, just watch for the weird mist, right?"

"Yes, that will do."

Janey opened the armoire and started picking out dresses and laying them on the bed in an urgent manner. "I still have some of my old clothes in my trunk. Dresses that would fit you. Do you want them?"

"I suppose, well... maybe one or two."

"Okay, so, when I'm done with mine, I'll look."

Lissy kept a keen eye on the door while Janey worked. When she had chosen a couple plain dresses, underwear, and some stockings, she turned to the trunk and pulling out clothes, she held up what she thought might fit Lissy. They were about the same size when Janey was fourteen, except Lissy wasn't as big busted. She could grow into them.

"Okay, that's two, do you want more?"

"Two's fine. With the one I've got on, that's three. Should do me."

"What about underwear?"

"I don't need no underwear."

384

"What about when you get your time of the month? You're going to need underwear. You... are... getting your time of the month, right?"

Lissy looked embarrassed, and staring at the floor, she mumbled, "Yes, one year now."

"Okay, so a couple pairs," Janey said and pulled out some silk Cami knickers with laced leg openings. She looked at Lissy who made a face.

"Probably not what your used to wearing, huh?"

"Kind of fancy, if you ask me."

"But... you'll wear them, right?"

"Not right now, I won't. Maybe after this is all over and I don't have to be running away from scary things and pissing myself by accident."

Janey grinned and laid them on the bed. "Well, maybe a chemise, or a slip, or two. Maybe some stockings? I have some stockings that are still in pretty good shape."

"Don't need none of that."

Janey looked at Lissy's high laced clodhoppers.

"I'll pack a few just in case."

"Whatever you want... they're your clothes."

Janey rolled her eyes, shook her head and smirked. Lissy appeared impatient, like she was annoyed that the situation might be too much like spending time with schoolmates at their houses, trying on new clothes, ribbons, and bows. Boring.

Janey pulled a fine leather suitcase from beneath the bed and filled it with the clothing. Then after adding some items like perfume and other things from her vanity, she strapped the lid shut and took one last look around the room. Lissy tapped her foot, growing more aggravated.

"Shall we?" Janey said.

Lissy sighed with relief, "About time."

Moving to the door, Lissy stopped and listened. After peeking through the key hole, she looked at Janey and said, "I don't see any... thing, out there."

Unlocking the door, she stuck her head out and then headed in a fast walk for the top of the main staircase. Janey turned off the light and followed, the flashlight beam playing over the walls and furniture. The newel lamps lit their way back down into the entry hall.

"So, when do we go back up to Carter House?" Lissy asked.

"Tomorrow. Let's just get out of town for the night, get some rest, and come back then. I'm so tired, I just want to sleep. Also, I need to find someone to come get my mother. Maybe someone from Brimfield."

"What about that, Sweeny? He's the... ummm... funeral man, right?"

"Well, the strange thing is, he wasn't there. Only his wife, Prudence. She told me he got sucked up into a tornado. Didn't make any sense to me, but she wasn't going to be of any help, so I left. That's when you came."

"A tornado?"

"Yes, that's what she said. I think she was drunk and maybe hallucinating. Does you no good to argue with drunks."

"Do you think maybe it was that Unseelie Court? They could be like a tornado. I'll bet that's what it was. They was over the top of the school house and that's just what they looked like. I think it's another trick that Mab has."

"Well, let's get this suitcase in the car and then we'll head on down to Brimfield."

Lissy hung her head and sighed. Following Janey out the door, she went to stand next to the Rolls, a look of disappointment on her face as Janey loaded the case inside.

26

Nealy Garret trudged up the lane at Headmost House, leaving the patrol car parked outside the gate on Railroad Street. He wanted to sneak up on Janey so she couldn't escape.

The front door at Merlyn's house had been wide open. The place looked ransacked on the inside. Fresh hoof prints showed in the front lawn, but only in a single line of tracks. They had moved around behind the house and headed down toward the river. Nealy started to follow them, but then changed his mind. He had prisoners back at the office and he wasn't supposed to leave them. "Gonna have to let them go," he muttered as he jogged back toward the office.

He returned to the townhall and released the two men he'd taken prisoner, promising that the Gowan police department would get back to them on their lawbreaking. They just left the office, laughing, with

Lawrence asking Jeffery if he wanted to go up to Brenner's for a beer.

Nealy flipped them off when they were out of sight, and grabbing the shotgun shells from the desk, he retrieved the double-barreled coach gun and went down the back staircase to the car. He had questions for Janey Carter and he wasn't leaving until he got some answers.

27

"Hey! You there! Who is that? That you, Janey Carter?"

"Nealy Garret," Janey whispered, "Damn it."

"What would he want?" Lissy whispered back.

"I don't know, but it can't be good."

Nealy stopped at the front of the car, the butt of the coach gun resting on his left hip, his other hand hovering around the revolver holstered on the right.

"Evening, Officer Garret," Janey said, stepping from behind the Rolls.

"Miss Carter. Everything all right up here? Doc inside? Maybe tending to your ma? I seen the car go by down at the belltower."

"No, Doc's not here, I believe he's at the office."

"He let you drive his car? Doc don't let no one drive his car…"

"Well, he let me. So… what can I do for you?"

"Oh, I was just checking on folks. Thought maybe I'd look in on your mother. She home?"

"No, she went on a trip. I don't expect her back anytime soon."

"Oh… relatives?"

"Yes, I suspect she's with relatives."

"Have you seen Chief Cobb around? Can't seem to find him, I…"

Lissy stepped around Janey and stood staring up at Nealy, a look of defiance on her face. "Oh… you're that Potter girl, aren't you? Your pa died. Sorry for you. Got run over by his own car, I'm hearing. What you doing here? You should be home with your ma."

"Lissy's here with me, right now," Janey said, "Helping me."

"We should go inside and talk, get out of this drizzle, you know?"

"We were just leaving. What have we got to talk about, officer? Did we break the law?"

"Got something I want to go over with you. Maybe the girl could stay outside and wait in the car?"

"The girl stays with me while you tell me what it is you are concerned about."

"Let's go inside... please," Nealy said with authority, leaning his head back slightly and cocking it to the right as if to say, 'Don't make me ask again.'

"Very well," Janey said and with Lissy by her side, still glaring, they walked up onto the porch. Janey opened the door, but stopping in the vestibule she turned to face the officer who was just mounting the steps.

Janey was trying to think of an excuse to give Nealy because the moment he saw her mother's corpse lying on the settee, things were going to change. Lissy moved past Janey and stood behind her just off to the right. Nealy stopped outside the door with a look of confusion on his face.

"Well? We going in?"

"I just wanted to tell you..."

Before she could complete her statement, Nealy's eyes moved past Janey to the main stairs and his face grew even more perplexed. "Now, who would that be? You never mentioned you had guests."

There came a commotion from behind her and then words spoken in a language she did not know. Both she and Lissy spun around to see Mab and NicDobhran standing half way up the main staircase. Mab's hand was raised with fingers pointing in their direction.

The air filled with electricity and Janey felt her hair rise. Lissy froze in a stare, a grimace forming her lips as her left hand checked the chain wrapping her waist, the other short length in her right hand, dangling free.

Nealy made a noise, a kind of groan that caused Janey to turn back. His eyes had gone from being attentively curious to acquiring a glazed look. Mab had brought him under her spell. "Kill them," Mab said flatly and then her and NicDobhran transformed into a cloud of mist and tiny leaves that swirled to the top of the stairs as if pushed by a late autumn breeze.

Janey watched Nealy level the shotgun at her throat and the adrenaline coursed in. Before the officer's finger could find one of the two triggers, she was already pushing Lissy out of Nealy's line of sight.

Collapsing to the floor at the same time, she went straight down onto her backside, dropping her chain and the flashlight.

The concussive wave of the gun's discharge raised her hair for a second as the shot passed over her head. The lead pellets took out a chunk of the inner door jamb before burying themselves in the newel post at the bottom of the stairs.

She watched the muzzle of the gun lower toward her as Nealy prepared to unleash the second barrel. Kicking out her foot, she made contact with the officer's knee. He seemed impervious to pain, but the action caused him to lose his balance, and he fell forward pushing the muzzle of the gun against the floor. The ensuing blast made a fist sized hole in the small rug and the waxed boards underneath, the double ought buckshot halted by the hardpacked dirt of the cellar floor.

Janey's ears rang. The smell of nitrate filled the air and splinters of wood peppered her dress. Nealy was fishing in his pocket for a reload, showing some difficulty with the process.

His eyes were still distant and now shone with an unearthly light. There came a semblance of a war cry and the next thing Janey knew, Lissy was barreling past her. Ploughing into Nealy like a linebacker from the Massachusetts State Aggies, she drove him out onto the porch. Nealy went down the steps on his back, Lissy riding him like a sled in winter time.

The coach gun spun away, clattering onto the cobblestones of the drive. Lissy rolled off and scrambled back into the house. Janey got to her feet, watching as Nealy's hand fumbled at his now empty holster. Glancing at Lissy, she saw the old Remington was now in her possession. Nealy, not finding the revolver, moved mechanically toward the shotgun and picking it up, he proceeded to reload.

The air was heavy with electricity. Janey and Lissy moved as if walking under water. A consistent chanting could be heard emanating from the upstairs gallery. Janey closed and locked the front door and then turning to Lissy, she saw her standing, legs spread, the revolver aimed to receive Nealy.

"Give me the gun," Janey said.

Lissy huffed but handed it over. The grip felt familiar in Janey's hand. It was much like the matched pair her father had owned. She had often helped herself to them when Benjamin Carter was away on business. Percy had taught her how to shoot them out in the woods beyond the orchard.

"Come on, we got to get away from the door. Follow me," she said and hurried into the parlor. But Lissy wasn't coming, instead, she was ascending the stairs, swinging her chain.

"Lissy, no! Come with me."

The teen seemed to have lost her hearing, her eyes locked on the two figures that stood at the top. Mab's laughter resonated from the air around them.

The large, frosted oval window in the front door shattered and Nealy stepped through into the vestibule and moved into the entry hall. Stopping, he looked around like he was confused. Lissy seemed impervious to what was going on behind her and continued up the stairs. Mab spoke more unknown words causing Nealy to suddenly regain his purpose and walking to the bottom of the staircase, he pointed the shotgun at Lissy's back.

"Nooo!" Janey screamed, and before Nealy could respond to her exclamation or the discharge of the revolver in her hand, Mab's newest minion felt the force of the forty-four-caliber bullet enter the right side of his chest. The now deformed chunk of lead exploded his heart and not hitting a single bone, passed out of his body to lodge in the spine of *Vol. 1 of Du Chaillu's Land Of The Midnight Sun,* occupying a bookshelf in the drawing room. Nealy spun and dropping the shotgun slammed into the wall and collapsed to the floor with a groan.

The chanting stopped and Mab growled her displeasure. Lissy, so intent on confronting Mab, failed to notice that she had barely escaped death, not even flinching at the discharge of the revolver.

Janey left the parlor at a run and stopping at the bottom of the stairs, she began taking pot shots at Mab and NicDobhran as they moved toward her mother's toilet, staying about two steps ahead of every bullet that flew by. Janey dropped the revolver and snatched up the shotgun before running up the stairs to Lissy, who now stood at the top.

Laughing, Mab and her minion swirled away into a mist to float back to the open door of the cupola stairwell. Once there, they trailed up inside to disappear from view. Lissy yowled at the ceiling and stomped

390

a foot. She glared at Janey and said, "Guns don't do no good!"

"Yeah, well... you're still breathing, aren't you," Janey snarled.

Lissy looked at her like she had no idea what Janey was talking about.

"Snap out of it, we've got to leave while we still can. I just killed Nealy Garret... who almost killed you. There are going to be questions. It's going to be hard to explain."

"No, I'm going up there, and if you go with me, you can just leave that gun right here. You still have your chain, right?"

Janey ejected the shells from the shotgun and leaned it against the balustrade. Then throwing up her hands in frustration, she followed Lissy in a fast walk down the hall to the cupola access.

"Wait, Lissy, let me get a lamp."

Moving to the sideboard that stood against the wall, she took a hurricane lamp with a ceramic font decorated with tiny blue flowers from its top and lit the wick from matches found in a drawer. Holding it in one hand, she took the chain from her waist and held it in the other.

"Okay, let's go get this over with," she said.

Lissy's lips broke into a wicked grin as she turned to the doorway and looked up the stairs. Janey stood behind her feeling it was a bad idea to pursue Mab up under the roof, but she couldn't stop Lissy with her death wish.

A streak of dark smoke shot out of the opening, compelling Lissy to spin out of the way and flatten herself against the wall beside the doorway. Janey ducked as the smoke passed over her head. It took a quick left and moved to the ceiling before speeding down to the end of the gallery. Turning back on itself at the toilet closet, it stopped and roiled for a few seconds before NicDobhran's upper body emerged. Janey knew right off that this was an attempt to divert their attention from Mab.

Lissy stood glaring at the handmaiden, the light from Janey's lamp gleaming in the girl's eyes. Janey could tell Lissy was trying to decide whether to go after NicDobhran or continue up the stairs. Mab's minion couldn't get too close to either of them without losing her power and meeting her end; but she could keep them busy.

NicDobhran laughed in a squeaky voice, and said, "Come, slay me, wee freckled squire. I know it is what you wish."

Janey turned to face NicDobhran and crouching, she let her chain dangle as well. Lissy's heavy shoes sounded on the corridor floor and Janey knew she was heading their way. As soon as the teen came abreast of Janey, NicDobhran withdrew back into her cloud and hurtled toward them. Stopping above their heads she became a fast-spinning smoke ring. Lissy swung her chain high, but with no results. The ten-foot-high ceilings would keep NicDobhran safe from Lissy's wrath.

The smoke ring spun away to the other end of the hallway and hovered above the backstairs. NicDobhran materialized to stand on the top step. Electricity crackled, and sparks played through the handmaiden's hair, her eyes glowing green.

Lissy was already on her way, swinging the chain as she ran. The closer she got, the faster she moved. NicDobhran remained where she was, beckoning the girl with a finger, saying, "Come to me, foolish child. Come to me."

"No, Lissy," Janey shouted, "It's a trick."

Lissy wasn't listening, and within four feet of her intended target, the imp transformed into a ball of electricity and buzzed down the stairwell toward the kitchen. The girl slid on the carpet runner in an attempt to halt her forward action and would have tumbled down the stairs had she not dropped her chain and grabbed the door jamb.

Janey felt the heavy energy in the air. Her neck and arm hair stood at attention. A loud shriek filled her ears and she reacted by ducking and backing into the sideboard. Losing her grip on the lantern, it crashed to the floor, the ceramic font shattering.

NicDobhran had come around through the kitchen and up the main stairwell at the speed of light to screech in Janey's ear. This was followed by a wicked laugh as the cloud streaked again to the toilet closet.

Janey felt heat on her back and turning, she saw that flames now licked the carpet runner and climbed the wall where the kerosene had splashed. She moved to stomp out the flames, but NicDobhran sped over and hovered above her head, shrieking. Janey spun and then jumped, swinging her chain at the handmaiden. She missed, and losing her balance she windmilled toward the nearby stairs. Catching the newel post with her free hand, she found her feet and moved back toward the flames. NicDobhran, now closer to the ceiling with only her head sticking out of the cloud, laughed at Janey and said, "Such a clumsy imbecile."

Janey flung her chain at NicDobhran who dissolved into something that closely resembled windblown sand and moved to hang suspended in the air within the open space of the entry hall. It then formed into a long, brown siliceous snake that wriggled through the air and down into the front parlor.

Retrieving her chain, Janey turned back to the spreading fire. The flames were now at the heavy cornice, turning the white, decorative plaster, black with soot. The smoke began to build and Janey knew the house was lost. Lissy, who had been watching and waiting to jump back into the fray, began to cough along with Janey.

"We have to get out, Lissy, or we won't be able to breathe."

"There's still time. We can still get them."

"Lissy, listen to me, be reasonable. We've got to go."

Lissy grew agitated, her tear-filled eyes moving from Janey to the third-floor stairs and then to NicDobhran slithering over the balustrade as that gritty snake.

Janey, not seeing the handmaiden, moved toward Lissy, her arms reaching. "We have to go, Lissy," she said, and attempted to take the girl by her arm to lead her down the back stairs. Lissy backed away, "Don't! It's not time."

"Lissy, please, we have to get out. We could die."

"Yeah, well... I knew that even before we came into this house. First that policeman, and... lookout!" Lissy pushed Janey to the floor to fall on top of her. A large vase passed over their heads to crash into the wall. NicDobhran's wicked laugh filled the air and transforming into a sparkling ball of motes, she shot their way.

Lissy rolled off of Janey, crouched, and jumped straight up to put herself in the path of the fast-moving specks of light. They hit Lissy full in the chest like birdshot from a scattergun. But unable to penetrate the fabric of Lissy's dress, Mab's imp assumed her solid form. Before she could flee, Lissy wrapped her arms around NicDobhran in a bear hug, bringing the fae in contact with the iron chain that wrapped her waist.

As Lissy's feet hit the floor, NicDobhran burst into a bright, multicolored cloud of mist and rose up out of Lissy's arms. Seconds later it transformed into a ball of ice and fell to the floor where it shattered. At the point of impact, there now stood a large otter shaking ice crystals from its coat. It glared at them, hissed, and fled away down the back staircase.

"Don't think this is over," emanated from the air above their heads.

Lissy turned toward the open door, stumbled, and swooned in the thickening smoke of the burning house. Janey, with some difficulty, scooped up the unconscious girl and made for the main stairs.

"You can flee, princess, but hiding is futile."

With Lissy in her arms, Janey stopped at the open door leading to the third floor to see Mab standing on the first landing of the narrow stairs. "I'm not a princess; I'm just a woman who's sick of your crap!"

Mab laughed and exploded like the puffball mushrooms Janey used to hit with a stick out in the woods behind Carter House. The foul spores spread out into the air, pushing the smoke away. Then reversing direction, they came together to form a swirling greenish-brown cloud that shot straight up to exit a window in the cupola.

The fire was now in the ceiling and the walls. Tendrils of smoke appeared to crawl out from beneath closed doors. Coughing, Janey carried Lissy to the top of the main staircase.

Lissy startled awake and shouted, "What are you doing? Put me down."

Janey obliged her and said, "You passed out, I was trying to get you away from the fire."

"I'm awake now. Where's Mab? Is she upstairs?"

"No, she left. Just like we should do."

They began to cough raucously and Lissy didn't argue this time. She moved down the stairs and Janey followed, staying close incase Lissy should lose her footing.

Pieces of burning debris were falling around them. Passing Nealy, Lissy stumbled out the front door and down the steps. Janey stopped briefly to look at Constance's body and said, "Sorry, mother," before following Lissy outside. Janey would leave her mother there. Headmost House would become her funeral pyre.

Janey found Lissy sitting on the cobblestones, coughing into her hands. She helped the girl to her feet and they lurched to the Rolls where they leaned back against the car to watch the smoke rolling out of the house. The storm clouds dissipated above their heads and stars began to appear.

Losing NicDobhran must have had enough of an effect on Mab to cause her to lose interest in storms and the Unseelie Court, at least for the moment. Janey doubted Mab could come up with new handmaidens all that quickly. That wouldn't stop her, though. Mab would be right back at it very soon. There would always be the other solitary fae.

The inside of Headmost House was fast becoming an inferno and Janey suspected the windows were going to start popping. Gowan didn't have more than a bucket brigade and it would take the Grunewyck department too long to gather and then arrive. They needed to get the hell away from Headmost before anyone showed up.

Lissy's cough was subsiding and other than the soot on her face and the snot dripping from her nose, she was recovering. Janey suspected she, herself, didn't look much better. Pulling a monogramed handkerchief from a pocket in her dress, she offered it to Lissy, who took it, thanked her, and wiped her nose and eyes. Shoving the handkerchief into her pocket, she dropped her chain and surprised Janey with an embrace.

Pushing the side of her face against Janey's chest, she sniffled, "I love you."

Janey hugged her back and said, "We are going to be okay, but we should get out of here. I don't want to answer a slew of questions when those flames start showing on the outside of the house. Come on, let's get in the car and go."

Lissy released her and picking up her chain, moved around to the passenger door and climbed into the front seat. Janey got in, started the car and rolled down the hill, headlamps off. They remained that way until she reached Hill Road. Turning south, the lights popped on and the Rolls picked up speed.

Janey's mind was a whirlwind of thoughts, and emotions soon took over. She began to weep, not for the loss of the house or of the town, but for all the dead. Glancing at Lissy in the dark of the front seat, she saw the girl was just staring through the windshield, lost in thought.

They wouldn't be staying in Brimfield. She would take Hill Road as far as originally intended, but then turn east and zig zag her way to the coast and up to Kingsport. There was a place they could hole up for certain, and for as long as they needed. It would be a while before they ever got to Salem.

28

July 5, 1935
Mysterious Fire

By Cap McKendry
Editor in chief
Gowan Gazette

GOWAN, Mass.—Three people apparently perished after a fire in the early morning hours of July 5 that destroyed the historic Headmost House.

The deceased include residents: Mrs. Benjamin (Constance) Carter and her daughter, Janette "Janey" Carter; as well as Police Officer Nealy Garret. It is presumed Garret had spotted the fire and then succumbed to the smoke while attempting to rescue the occupants.

An investigation was conducted but nothing was determined.

The Italianate style house was constructed in 1870 on the north-facing slope of Prosper Mountain, overlooking the town. It was owned by prominent businessman Bartholomew Carter (deceased 1931). Two generations of Carters had lived in the home.

Residents of the house included: Constance, Janey, and household help, Tabitha and Percy Snoaks.

The structure must have been burning for some time before neighbor Audrey LaVern spotted the flames through the trees from her bedroom window when she rose to start her day. When Mrs. LaVern rushed to the scene, she found the house had collapsed into the cellar.

She told the Gazette the heat was so intense, she had to keep her distance. She had run down the drive to Railroad Street to seek help and found the city police car parked alongside the curb with no one inside.

Mrs. LaVern returned to her residence to call Chief of Police, Merlyn Cobb, but found she couldn't get through. Operator Iris Hazelton reported she couldn't raise anyone at Cobb's home.

After driving to Cobb's residence, Mrs. LaVern found the house empty, the front door standing wide open. A trip to the police office produced the same.

She then raced her car through the treacherous Whip-poor-will Hollow to the village of Grunewyck to awaken the fire chief of the small department there.

Gowan, which has never had a fire, does not maintain a fire department, unlike Grunewyck, which had lost its modern school house to fire two years ago. Gowan had contracted with Grunewyck for fire protection.

By the time the Grunewyck pumper arrived, only the large, metal finial that had graced the peak of the mansion's cupola, was visible from where it protruded from the cellar. The grand old house had become a heaping pile of smoldering ash. "Fire must've been so hot it burned up all but a few bone fragments," said GFD Chief Carwyn Baltz. A partially melted revolver (believed to be Officer Garret's), the barrel and lock mechanism of a ten-gauge coach gun that Garret was fond of carrying, and what had been a molten pile of pot metal, believed to have been the officer's badge, were fished from the rubble.

Gowan librarian, Millie Behnke, reported that she had seen the Carters' hired help, Percy and Tabitha Snoaks, leave in the family's Cadillac the evening before the fire. She said the couple had departed the gate and then turned west on Railroad Street toward Hill Road.

The state police, thinking foul play, traced the Snoakses to Carter's house in Salem, a large Gothic Revival, known as High Gable House. The Snoakses were questioned and released.

Percy Snoaks had told authorities that Miss Carter had requested he and his wife travel to the Salem house and open it up to prepare for their arrival. The Carters, reportedly, were leaving Gowan because of the Tri River Reservoir project.

After being notified that Janey and her mother had perished in the flames, the couple said they would remain in the Salem house to grieve their loss, and await word from the family's attorney, Philp Shannon.

The County Coroner, Bruce Nelson, refused to comment on the incident. He did agree with the Grunewyck fire chief that the Carters and Garret had perished in the intense heat of the fire, and that it was impossible to distinguish the individual remains from one another.

The only solace is that the Gowan landmark would have succumbed to the coming reservoir, regardless. Yet, there is no comfort to be found in the lives lost. They will be sorely missed.

29

An inebriated Prudence Sweeny, dressed all in black with a suitcase in hand, stood looking at the body laid out on the platform of the train station. The expression on her face was one of consternation because the body, lacking its head, left her unsure who it might be. It wore the station agent's style of trousers, but nothing else. The young, partially clothed body would be her clue that it had to be the Billings boy. Prudence's face soon gained a more trepidatious visage and she looked around nervously as if she feared the killer might still be close. The sight of the body wouldn't likely trouble her, though. After so many years as a mortician's wife, it would take more than that to upset Prudence Sweeny. The constant diet of Kentucky bourbon would always play in her favor.

She turned away and took a swig from her freshly filled flask. "Gonna haf to tell shombody," she said aloud to no one. By the time she had tottered her way back to the street, Prudence apparently forgot what she was supposed to do. Heading to her house, she painfully hand cranked the truck to get it started, then climbing inside, she drove away. The Model T would later be found abandon at the Brimfield station and Prudence Sweeny's name on the register for a train traveling west to California.

30

By noon, Vivian Bishop, the young thing that had worked as a clerk for Hector Dent at the Gowan Bank, was given notice that she was no longer needed. No amount of pleading, or offering to expand her repertoire of sexual favors made any difference. The bank was closing and she would have to seek employment elsewhere. Hector was retiring to Boston.

Moping down the boardwalk, Vivian was met by Mayor Wilton who noticed her tears. After a brief conversation, he offered her a temporary position at the telephone house. She grabbed it up in a heartbeat. The mayor said they could do the paper work another time.

Fifteen minutes later, she walked into the small telephone house and informed Iris she was her replacement. The elderly operator couldn't have been happier to hear this news and even more so to teach her the simple procedure of connecting parties.

Vivian, being something of a pretty smart cookie, learned fast and Iris soon found herself happily back in her cottage, seated in her favorite chair, with a hot cup of tea and surrounded by her beloved cats.

३१

When Colin Brenner, Kenny Boyd from the Gazette, and Ross Bailey, arrived at the train station, they were quite horrified at what they found. The Baylor boys, eleven and thirteen, had come across a body on the station platform while practicing walking the steel rails without losing their balance.

Running into the tavern, Blaine Baylor, with terror filled eyes, told Colin of their discovery, while his brother, Gus, puked up his breakfast on the street out front. Colin had muttered, "Glad he didn't do that on the boardwalk."

Ross Baily promptly lost his morning meal of fried potatoes and sausage upon finding Danny and cursed himself for volunteering. Kenny had his pad and pencil out and began taking notes. Colin swallowed back the bile, took a closer look, and then going inside the station, he began to make phone calls with Vivian's help. It was a hopeless attempt.

They tried the mayor's house but Willy was presently standing on the green saying his good byes to Maddie. Gladys Wilton, Willy's wife, was on the townhall porch helping Phil Shannon get set up for the long lines of Gowan residents expected to show up, sign over their property, and collect their money. Colin returned to the other two men to seek suggestions on what they should do with what remained of Danny.

"Did you hear? Nealy Garret died last night?" Colin said.

"Yep," Kenny said, "Cap wrote a piece on it. I'm supposing that you didn't know Headmost House burnt to the ground? Seems ol' Constance Carter, and Janey, got caught in it. Nealy tried to save them, but it got him too. That's how he died, which I suppose is why we can't reach him. No phone lines in heaven, and even if there were, he wouldn't be allowed to come back down here to Gowan and deal with this." Kenny chuckled and looked at the other two, who just stood, staring, their mouths hanging open. Kenny had always been known for his sarcasm and as a young man of callous nature.

Seeing that they might have been put out by his humor, he turned his attention back to his pencil and notebook. Colin returned to the station's interior to look for a canvas tarp. Upon his return, the three of them painstakingly wrapped Danny's body in it, tied it with some rope and

400

lifted it onto a baggage cart so they could trundle it down to the funeral home. They agreed to look, with some reluctance, for Danny's head.

That lasted all of five minutes before Ross said that it couldn't have rolled very far and they were just wasting their time. Pushing the cart down to Sweeny's would only require two men. So, Kenny begged off and returned to the newspaper office to write his story.

When Ross and Collin passed the village green, they saw the mayor and waved for him to come to them. Willy only waved and returned to the townhall porch. Not wanting anyone else to see or question them about Danny's body, they continued on to the funeral home. When they arrived, they searched the whole house, but found no one there. Rolling the body around back, they took it down into the basement through the outside door, and leaving it in the prep room, cart and all, they hurried away with Colin promising to talk with the mayor as soon as he could. Ross just walked away, zombie like, not saying a word.

Returning to the tavern, Colin told Beth that it would be their last day there and to get her clothes packed, they were leaving Gowan for good.

"Did you hear? Janey Carter, her mother, and Nealy Garret, all died last night in a fire that burnt down Headmost House," Beth said, throwing the newspaper down on the bar top so he could see the headlines.

"I heard, Kenny told me," he said, not looking at her or the newspaper as he nervously downed a double shot of whisky.

Beth turned away with tears in her eyes and left the tavern by the back door to go home and start packing. Colin quickly took up the task of doing all he had to do to hand the tavern over. Brown had bought them out and there was no need to stay. The replacement barkeeps were already billeted upstairs and could take over the second he and Beth drove away. He had already met with Shannon and signed over their house. There was nothing keeping them there. Taking the money still in the till, Colin stuffed it in a pocket as he headed upstairs to wake Brown's men.

32

The line outside the townhall was growing longer. Philip Shannon sat at a makeshift table on the front porch, Mayor Wilton standing beside him, a badge pinned to his chest and a shotgun in his hands. It was going to be a long day and Willy was already fuming about Chief Merlyn Cobb flying the coop and leaving him empty handed. He would have to swear in a couple of men to assist him over the next few days until the official unincorporating of the town. Then, he too would be out of a job.

Seeking help to deal with the missing citizens, Willy found acting Sheriff, Jasper Tate, of no help because he was shorthanded and, as he put it, "Up to his ass in alligators!" The state police weren't going to do anything until Willy could prove that the missing hadn't just left because of the reservoir. As for the murders, they let him know that they were on top of that, leaving him with the statement, "None of your concern, anymore, Mayor Wilton."

Willy told his wife, Gladys, "I feel like I'm chasing my tail here." She just smirked and said, "It will all be over soon, and besides, Willy, you don't have a tail." She had laughed at her own joke. Willy didn't think it was funny.

He'd had his fill of smalltown politics. The Wiltons were moving to Worchester and Willy was going to run for governor. The second the bell tower peeled the stroke of midnight on unincorporation day, the Wilton family would be gone. Anyone who remained, would be on their own.

Mab watched the village from the gloom of the belvedere atop the Carter House tower. Janey Carter had won the battle, but the war wasn't over, yet. No mortal could go far enough to escape the Queen of Air and Darkness. The princess of Gowan, Massachusetts, had to die, right along with her freckle-faced squire. Moving down to the second floor, a flock of bogles met her, cackling and squeaking. They gathered around her like a flock of children. As she moved toward her bed, she lay a hand on the heads of the ones she thought capable and sent them on their quest for the last remaining Carter.

Abigail Cunningham stood in front of her cottage, suitcase in hand, just staring at her lifelong home. Memories flooded in of her life there as a young girl. Her mother, father, and husband, were soon to be dug up from the Gowan graveyard and transferred over to Deerfield's Mt. Wray cemetery; along with a few dozen other bodies. She was feeling out of sorts and maybe a little crazy. The night before, she had had guests— and not the human kind.

It was shortly after dark, as she sat in her parlor on her last supposed quiet evening in Gowan, that she heard the screen door at the back open and quietly shut. Rising from her chair, she crept to the kitchen door and looked in. Someone was standing in the shadows, unmoving.

The heavy, cast-iron frying pan that had been sitting on the stove, within arm's reach, was soon in her hand. It was closer than her shotgun. That simple decision would be the thing that would grant Abigail Cunningham a view to morning and the forth coming sunrise.

Whoever was out there, sang her name. Abigail felt a strange kind of disarming lethargy start to take over her eighty-five-year-old body. Gripping the handle of the frying pan with both hands caused that feeling to subside.

The shadow moved toward her and the light from the lantern, perched on the kitchen table, gave away their features. It was Bessy LaVern—or something that resembled Bessy, anyway. Her green dress shimmered and as she moved into the kitchen, small, deer like hooves clacked on the old boards of the floor.

"What do you want? You're supposed to be dead."

The creature sang Abigale's name again, only this time in a whisper. The lethargy increased, almost as if it was fighting to loosen Abigale's grip on the iron in her hands. The Bessie thing grinned, showing its long, sharp teeth, its yellow, snakelike eyes dilating. Abigale gripped the frying pan tighter, raising it higher like she was intent on making a homerun.

The creature charged her, its misshapen fingers with their long, sharp nails, reaching for the old woman's throat. It came fast, but Abigale's reflexes were still pretty keen for a woman her age. Planting a firm blow to the side of the thing's head, a distinctive *clang!* filled the air, followed by an unearthly shriek. So, Abigale hit it again.

The wicked fae croaked something indiscernible and swirled up to the ceiling in a cloud of loam. Once there, it exploded, causing Abigale to duck back around the doorway and become audience to every single grain of dirt erupting into a fleeting spark that made a popping noise, giving the old woman one serious light show.

Abigail straightened up, brushed off one of the many aprons that had protected her clothing over a lifetime and checked the room to make sure the sparkling motes hadn't set anything on fire. Not that it would have mattered since the place was to be flattened anyway and the 'left behinds', sold off.

She walked over to shut and bolt the backdoor but she was a smidgeon too late. Raccoon sized creatures that had no real genus, poured into the kitchen and swarmed her.

Second inning.

Abigale began to bat them with the frying pan like Joe Cronin of the Red Sox working toward the perfect game. The bogles tried to jump on her, but she had backed herself into a corner and met them, tit for tat. Every time she made contact; the little creature would burst into what she would describe later, in her crazy tale to her grandchildren, a brown ball of gas that brought memories of her late husband, Edward.

She was able to stay ahead of them and when the small number of survivors fled, they left the place smelling like an overused privy. Finally making it to the back door, she shut and locked it and then did the same with all the windows. The remainder of the night she crouched on her bed, her back to the wall as the foul smell of her departed visitors occasionally wafted to her nose.

Sleep came in fits and starts. Her legs started to cramp as dawn showed in the east window. It was time to go. Making herself a quick cup of coffee, she nibbled on a piece of toast. Soon she was packing her best dresses, underthings, and a few knick-knacks that had been her mothers. She also grabbed Edward's little, nickel-plated revolver and a box of thirty-two caliber shells, her silverware, and a brand-new pair of shoes that she was yet to break in. Oddly, a pair that Bessy LaVern had sold her several months prior.

It was nearly half an hours' worth of time that she stood in the center of her parlor, lost in reflection. When the bell tower struck six, she began her journey afoot. She would stop to sign over her deed to that shyster Shannon, collect her check, and be on her way. Her daughter had a farm down past Brimfield and that's where she would spend the rest of her days.

The line at the townhall was starting to form and a disheveled, grumpy Shannon was just taking his seat at the table. There were only three ahead of her and she was done with Gowan by six thirty.

Abigail walked south, singing songs, and projecting a thumb at any passing car. Not one person she met, on the way, felt bold enough to question the old woman as to why she had an iron skillet strapped to her suitcase.

CHAPTER FIFTEEN

JANEY & LISSY

~

1

The Rolls Royce cruised eastward past sunny fields and under cotton ball filled skies. Janey's eyes grew heavy with exhaustion. Lissy slept in the passenger seat, sometimes fighting demons in her dreams. They would have to dump Doc's car as soon as they arrived in any town big enough to have a train station. Then they could travel wherever by rail or bus. Janey needed sleep. So, maybe a motel for one night before their train trip. She wondered how much distance she would have to put between them and Carter House to keep Mab at bay. Her preponderance was followed by the realization: there was no true safe distance as long as Mab had Carter House. There were tactics, though, ones that Cora had shared. She just needed to bribe whoever Mab sent. That was one thing she knew for sure. Loyalty among the dark fae was limited. A bowl of milk and a crust of bread was all it would take. Mab would not come herself. Putting too much distance between her and Carter House was seriously risky for the fae queen. She needed to stay close to her castle.

Janey's first stop was a small fuel station where she would fill the tank for their long drive, and for Lissy to slip behind a close-by hedge to relieve herself. When Janey went to pay the grouchy old man sitting behind the tiny counter, it surprised her to see he was reading the Gowan Gazette. The front page showed the still smoking pile that had been Headmost House.

"The Gazette comes all the way over here?" Janey asked.

The old man leveled a stare, and in a loud growly voice, said, "Gowan ain't that far. The misses' has a cousin over there. She picked it up on her way through. Why you asking?"

"Could I have it?"

"I ain't done reading it yet," he said, scowling.

"I'll give you five dollars for it."

"Why you want it so badly you'd pay all that money? Hell, your gasoline's only three dollars. You going to fork out another five for a dime newspaper? Now, that's just crazy."

"It's the last edition, isn't it?"

"Sure is, ain't ever goin' to be another."

"That's why," Janey lied. "The reservoir is going to take my house over there. So, we're going east. I'd like to have it for a souvenir... kind of like... a memoir."

"So, yer from over Gowan way, huh? I see you got yerself a big ol' Rolls Royce. Phantom One, looks like. Bet it was built down in Springfield. Don't see too many of those around these here parts."

"Sure, okay, so...ten bucks for the paper, no more questions," she said and leveled her gaze to convey sincerity.

"Must be loonier than a loon, ten bucks for a newspaper, but I 'spect driving a car like that, you probably weren't hit too hard by the Depression. Some folks just got it all." Rolling up the paper, he held it in his left hand and stuck out his right, palm up. Janey pulled the roll of money from her pocket and watched as the attendant eyes went wide. Shaving off thirteen one-dollar bills, she returned the roll to her pocket before offering the money and her free hand to take the paper.

The old grouch grabbed the cash, but Janey held tight until she had a firm grip on the newspaper, then releasing the money, she stepped back and watched the old guy count it.

"Nice doing business with ya, come back anytime," he said, not looking at her as he rolled up the bills and shoved them in his shirt pocket.

Janey met Lissy returning to the car. "Feel better now?" she asked. Lissy blushed, the red in her cheeks briefly hiding the freckles. "Light as a feather... now," she said. Grinning, she skipped around to the other side of the Rolls and climbed in. It brought Janey relief to see that Lissy may be coming around. But Janey knew Lissy was a fighter; the girl would go down swinging.

They sat briefly in the car as Janey looked over the front page of her expensive newspaper. Lissy did the same, asking, "What's that?"

"Last edition of the Gowan Gazette."

They heard the front door to the fuel stop open. Craning their necks, they watched the attendant flip the sign that read: 'Be Right Back!' and locking up the place, he hurried toward the small tavern next door.

"Let's get out of here," Lissy said.

Janey tossed the newspaper in the backseat and obliged her companion. They drove to Bournemouth and stopped at an inn on the west edge of town, a place Janey knew quite well. Arriving a few days too early to get her reserved room at the boarding house back in 1933, she had to spend three nights at the Brookside Inn until she was allowed to take up her new digs.

Leaving Lissy in the car, Janey went inside and registered as Janice MacLean and daughter, Matilda. Fortunately for them, the girl who checked them in was someone who didn't know Janey. Going to the room, she gave it the once-over and made sure the windows were locked before returning to the car to wake Lissy. The girl reacted violently. Janey cooed her name and kept her distance, giving her a minute to wake up.

"Where are we?"

"Bournemouth. It's safe. We should get inside and get some sleep on a good bed. Car seats can be kind of hard on your back."

"Okay," Lissy said and climbing out of the Rolls, she shut the door. Grabbing their suitcase, she followed Janey inside and up the stairs. When they arrived on the second floor and were out of sight of the clerk, Lissy took Janey's free hand.

Once inside the room, Lissy repeated Janey's check of the windows, looked in the armoire, and under the bed before falling onto the quilt covered mattress. She watched Janey lock the door and pocket the key. Rolling onto her side, she curled up and closed her eyes. Janey moved to one of the two windows at the front and studied the woods across the highway.

"Are you coming to bed?" Lissy said sleepily without opening her eyes.

"Yes," Janey said. Turning to look at Lissy, she saw the girl's hair was a real bird's nest, the iron comb on the verge of falling out.

She unlaced Lissy shoes and pulled them off, setting them on the floor. The girl whispered, "Thank you," and smiled slightly. Janey then pulled the curtains before kicking off her flats and climbing in beside the girl. Lissy rolled over and backed up to her. Taking up a fetal position, she pulled Janey's arm across her waist and held her hand. She was soon asleep with Janey not far behind.

2

Waking that evening, Janey convinced Lissy to remove the chain from her waist and leave it in the room while they were at supper. The comb and the necklace would suffice. Lissy was reluctant but complied. They changed clothes and Janey was surprised to see how well her old dresses fit the girl. She tried to convince Lissy to wear the undergarments she had brought along, but to no avail. Janey suspected it would always be that way while they 'were on the run'.

They cleaned up and used a brush from Janey's suitcase to do their hair. Lissy allowed Janey to brush out her locks and reconfigure the bun before impaling it with the prongs of the comb.

Leaving the room, Janey fondled her necklace and gave Lissy a reassuring smile. With newspaper in hand, she kept it rolled tightly, so as not to allow anyone to see the headlines.

Entering the dining room, she asked for a corner table and was obliged. There was meat loaf and potatoes, along with apple pie and milk; with coffee for Janey. Leaving Lissy to finish her dessert, she assured her she would be right back and would just be out in the entry hall at the telephone table. Lissy just smiled and went back to eating pie.

Janey got through to the Snoaks at High Gable in Salem to inform them that she would not be arriving as soon as she had hoped. Tabby broke down and began to cry knowing that Janey hadn't perished in the fire after all. She heard Percy let out a whoop in the background.

She reminded them that they should just live in the house as if it were their own. She would be in touch at a later time and asked that they tell no one she had called. They promised, and Janey hung up. Helping

409

herself to several different newspapers at the little stand next to the reception desk, she returned to Lissy.

The girl was finishing her milk and after wiping her mouth, she said, "Everything okay?"

"Couldn't be better… for the moment. Want to go outside and sit on the veranda? It's a lot cooler tonight. It might be rather pleasant."

Lissy looked around at the windows and said, "No, it's getting dark," then focusing on the large Ingram wall clock ticking away across the room, she finished with, "It's almost the gloaming, I want to go back to the room, now." Lissy's eyes pled and Janey expected her to start begging.

"We could sit in the parlor across the entry hall? It might be rather pleasant. We'll be safe in there."

"Okay, but I'd rather not go outside until morning."

"Very well, I'm not going to make you, so… just relax." Lissy gave her a forced smile and they left the dining room.

The inn had a large library in the parlor with one wall completely covered in bookshelves, every one of them full from the floor to the ceiling. Janey moved to a settee away from the windows and began to read the newspapers, her eyes perusing for relative news. Lissy looked over the shelves and selecting a book, she moved to sit at the other end of the settee, her eyes glancing up at the uncurtained windows before focusing on her choice. She had chosen *The Adventures Of Tom Sawyer* by Mark Twain.

"Do you like to read?" Janey asked.

"Oh yes, I love to read. I read as much as I can."

Lissy gave her a genuine smile and for a few seconds Janey believed she saw the Melissa Potter that had existed before Mab. A carefree tomboy who liked to read books and roam the woods of Hantescree County.

"I'm glad to hear it. Reading's important. It will take you away."

"Yeah, but that's the only thing I want taking me away," she said and chuckled.

Janey chuckled too and said, "Most certainly."

Lissy smiled and began thumbing through the book as if she had already been reading that particular novel before the darkness came into her life. Finding where she'd left off, she once again immersed herself in life on the Mississippi.

Janey focused on the gazette and smiled to herself. Her old friend Cap had written the article. She was already missing her town. Reading through the piece twice, she then looked up to see if anyone was within listening distance, and whispering to Lissy, she said, "It says they think I'm dead. Gowan thinks I'm dead. I burnt up in the fire."

Lissy looked at her long and hard, then sliding over, she looked at the line of text where Janey's index finger rested. She read for a moment, looked up into Janey's face and said, "That's good, isn't it? Nobody will be looking for you, and maybe Mab will see it and leave us alone."

"Maybe so," Janey said, and Lissy, satisfied, went back to her book. But Janey knew it was just the townspeople and the authorities that, in all probability, wouldn't be looking for her. As for Mab, she didn't need newspapers. She could feel Janey's presence in the world, just as Janey did hers. Maybe not as strong, but she did, nonetheless.

They were soon in the large bed under a sheet. Lissy, in one of Janey's old chemises, lay sleeping on her side with her back against a just as unconscious Janey. It was when the grandfather clock in the hallway chimed three, that the low cackling laughter and scratching at the windows woke Janey. She lay watching the little shadows cast on the curtains by the pole lamp out in the front yard. The little imps were out there, perched on the edge of the veranda's roof.

Janey clutched her necklace. In no time, the noises were in the hallway outside the door, squeaking and scratching. The white china bowl, half full of milk that she had set just outside after Lissy had fallen asleep, clanked against the baseboard. At supper, the girl had questioned why Janey had eaten only half of her cruller. "I'll eat it later, in the room," Janey had said, "Maybe we can share?"

"Naw, but thanks. I don't like them, much. Maybe if they had chocolate frosting."

Neither of them would be the ones to finish it, and when Janey cracked the door at sunrise, she saw that only a few doughnut crumbs remained and the bowl stood empty. Bringing it in, Janey slid it under the bed for the housekeeper to find. She now had all the proof she needed that Mab was on to them, confirming her belief that she and Lissy were fugitives from fairy justice.

They departed the inn early, leaving the door key on the nightstand. Lissy, in a somewhat chipper mood, asked for breakfast. Janey suggested a café in the next town. Lissy accepted, saying, "Beggars can't be choosers, I guess."

They sold the car to an obviously shady auto dealer in Bentonville. The owner wanted it so badly, he practically begged her to let him have it for three thousand dollars. They settled on four and he threw in a 1932 Ford Model B with a dented fender as part of the deal. So much for the train or bus. They would drive all the way to Kingsport.

Taking the key from her outstretched fingers, the dealer drove the Rolls around to the back and draped it with a tarp. Janey and Lissy departed before his return. They agreed he was too devious for their comfort and they didn't want to hang around any longer than necessary.

3

They took up residence in her father's shanty boat in the Kingsport Marina. It was custom built to look just like a small cabin but crafted in a manner to look like the older, cruder looking boats of the migrant workers. After a considerable amount of cleaning, they made it as comfortable as possible.

Janey took a job at the local five and dime and when late August came around, she enrolled Lissy in school. They remained, Janice and Matilda MacLean for the two and a half years they would reside in that port town.

Mab had not forgotten them. She sent her agents every night, but the little imps were easily thwarted. Milk and bread was left nightly just outside the door. The little bogles departed just as quickly as they had arrived, their bellies full and too lazy for shenanigans.

4

It was in the spring of the third year that, by some misunderstanding, Lissy failed to fulfil her responsibility of setting out the bread and milk. Shortly after midnight, the small fae sieged the houseboat in relentless fashion, attempting to breach the doors and windows. The two women took up defensive positions in the forward loft where Janey slept; Lissy with her chain, and Janey, holding an iron made fire poker for a fireplace they didn't have.

The creatures final attack that night was on the roof hatch. But it remained secure and the little bogles departed afterwards screeching and cackling out their frustration. There had been no sleep that night. The two trudged bleary eyed to the school the next morning and after their goodbyes, Janey slogged to the five and dime, rubbing her eyes and yawning the whole way.

She was late, and stepping into the breakroom, she yawned again, punched the time clock and locked her purse in her tiny locker. Moving to the coffee pot for a free cup, two of the older women pushed past her without comment to return to their workstations. Ruby DeNoir remained at the table, doing her nails and sipping from a bottle of RC Cola.

"Hey, hon, how's your daughter?"

"Oh, she's fine, getting better every day. Adjusting, you know? She likes it here in Kingsport."

"Wish I could say the same, but… more power to her."

"Ah, come on, Ruby, it's not that bad," Janey said, bringing her cup of coffee to the table to sit next to her workmate.

"She made any friends, yet?"

"Oh, not really. I mean, she has friends in school, but Matilda's kind of a loner. She prefers her own company." Which was entirely a lie, but Janey didn't dare mention what had driven Lissy to introversion.

The door opened and Mr. Redmond came in. The elderly gentleman smiled politely and stuck a sack lunch in the icebox in the corner. Coming over to the table he dropped the morning edition of the Kingsport Chronicle on its top and said, "Everybody good today?"

They nodded and smiled. "Well, okay, that's great. All set to get to work? Going to be a big day for us. We're taking a delivery of that new Scotch Tape. I think it's going to be a big seller. People can repair things instead of having to use paste or throw them out. Also heard there might be a new stocking coming out. Made of something called nylon. If they work out, I'm going to give each one of you a free pair for every ten you sell. But we'll have to see. Okay, ready to get to it?"

The women nodded again and Mr. Redmond left the room, whistling.

Soon as the door shut, Ruby snidely mimicked her boss's voice and said, "Ready to get to it?" and then sneered at the door.

"Ah, come on, Ruby. Mr. Redmond is a nice man. He's good to us."

"Yeah, but only because you're here. He wants to impress you."

"Well, works out for everyone then, doesn't it?"

Ruby shrugged and said, "I suppose," and returned her focus to her nails.

Janey shared Ruby's lipstick and hand mirror. Her eyes moved past her reflection to fall on the newspaper. As usual, the headline was about the impending war in Europe. It was the article down in the corner that caught her eye. The hair rose on her arms and the back of her neck. It was about Gowan.

May 18th, 1938
The Missing Of Central Massachusetts

By Sylvester Jansen
Staff Writer
Kingsport Chronicle
KINGSPORT, May 18—People are still being reported missing nearly three years after the Tri- River Reservoir Project was completed.

It was believed in 1935 that the missing who resided in towns such as Gowan and Grunewyck, had simply packed up and departed the fated Spry River Valley that was soon to be flooded to create the reservoir that would supply Boston with much needed water.

Yet the disappearances continue in and around towns like Hadley, Scottsburg and Brimfield— places that border the shores of that great body of water. The Massachusetts State Police had no comment other than to say that the case of the missing is ongoing.

A representative of the governor's office reported the investigation was impeded by an increase in rainfall over that period, which caused the waters to rise faster than calculated by the USACE.

Past residents of Gowan, a town that suffered the greatest losses, were questioned about those missing persons.

"Well, of course we left because of the reservoir, but folks was coming up missing long before that, and then there were all those bodies minus their noggins," said Silas McCarthy, who had owned the general store there, and now runs a store in Hadley.

"That all started when old Ben Carter brought that woman over from Scotland, or someplace like that. It's that Carter House over there, still standing up on that bluff. It's full of witches, I tell you, seen'm with my own two eyes."

Prudence Sweeny, wife of the missing Louis Sweeny, the funeral director for the town, told the newspaper by telephone from California, that her husband had been taken up into a passing tornado only a few days after one of their sons had been found murdered in the woods just beyond the local cemetery.

Their youngest son, Duncan, had been reported missing but was later found living in Springfield, married to a one Penelope Southwick. They are expecting their first child. They had no comment.

Village carpenter, Ross Bailey, was located working as a "Woodpecker" for R.J. Brown's Demolition and Lumber Co. When asked about the odd goings on, he said, "All I know is there'd been a lot of talk of witches living up there on Nixie's Bluff in that Carter House. Now, them Carters were good folks, but they's all dead now. Ben, he disappeared like a lot of folk, but his ex-wife, Constance, and their girl, Janey, well, they died in a fire. So, them ain't no Carters that are living there now. I think they're some real bad folk. We tried to tear the place down, but we had no luck with it. The house is cursed and no amount of trying was working out, so, R.J., he say, just forget it, let the water take it. But it ain't gone yet, and I don't think it ever will be. That reservoir just didn't get high enough to do the job."

Other residents were located and most of their comments (if any) eluded to Carter House and its present occupants. Attempts were made to speak with the residents of that once magnificent pile, but it appeared abandoned and dilapidated. No one answered the locked door.

A listing of noted citizens, reported missing to the authorities, follows by town:

Salem: Sally Combs and Thomas Lynn.

Gowan: Louis Sweeny, Cal Loffler, Otis Loffler, Cecil Walker, Sandy Brewster, Charley Bates Jr., Dr. B.T. Bolen, Hannah Bolen, Caroline Moore, Gregory Bly, Helen Blake, Archie Bennet, Beulah McKay, Roy LaVern, Hugh Swinerton, and Benjamin Carter.

Grunewyck: Sheriff Pete Mowery, Stanley Weston, Arliss Balch, Molly Sharp, Melissa Potter, Rev. Aldo Hale, Kenneth Conway, Willow Brackston, Lyle Beasly, Sadie Mills, Blaine Wilson, Sonny Wilson, Fanny Drucker, Robert Bush, Al MacLean, Rodney McAlister, Floyd and Glenda Piper.

Hadley: Ralph Fogg, Daniel Wray, Thomas Graves, Beatrice Plotz, Suki Morris, and Lud Benz.

Brimfield: William Clerke Sr., William Clerke Jr., Dixie Blake, Susan O'Brian, Peter O'Brian, and Philip Black.

Scottsburg: Peter Palfrey, Lester Vaughn, Edward Gyles and Anise Boyd.

These are just a few and do not include the ones who died of unknown causes. For a complete list or if you have any information regarding this matter, contact the Massachusetts State Police. Investigations are ongoing.

The Kingsport Chronicle is dedicated to keeping its readers informed and any new information to arise from the investigation will be reported to you, our faithful readers, as soon as it is received.

Janey shuddered involuntarily and stole a glance at Ruby, hoping she hadn't noticed. Her fellow workmate was still busy with her personal manicure and the emery board rasped relentlessly.

"See you later," Janey said, and left Ruby to her vain pursuit.

At the end of her work day, Janey plucked Mr. Redmond's discarded newspaper from his wastebasket and left the store. Finding Lissy just outside napping on a bench, she woke her and the girl jumped up to stare wild eyed.

"Sorry, sweety."

"I was having a terrible dream. They caught me and I couldn't find my chain."

Janey hugged her and holding hands, they headed back toward the marina. Stopping at the corner grocery, they bought a loaf of bread and two bottles of milk this time. Lissy pretended to ignore the Kingsport Chronicle tucked under Janey's arm even though her eyes had strayed that way many times.

Janey left the newspaper on the sofa before stepping out front to watch the sun go down. She hoped to prompt some kind of reaction from Lissy after deciding there was just no good way to tell her. Better to let her find out on her own. The urge to put an end to Mab's pursuit was strong. She knew what she needed to do but didn't know why she continued to think she could just walk away from the trouble. Almost three years and the fae just kept coming. There had been hope they'd grow tired of it. She felt like a fool. Cora's words echoed in her head,

"Janey, you're a threat for as long as you're breathing. You can't kill her, but you can oust her. As long as Carter House stands, Mab will stay put. Burn down her castle, Janey. Send that woman back to where she came from."

Janey should have heeded Lissy's words when she wanted to burn Carter House to the ground. She thought of Tom, his laughing face and the sound of his voice. The tears came and she rubbed them away, glancing back to make sure Lissy hadn't come up unannounced.

She knew she had the power to do something about Mab. Cowardice was something new to her. This was the first time she had ever run away from a fight. Janey hadn't known what it was like to flee her foe before, but she didn't like how it felt. Now, almost three years had passed, and people were still suffering under the hand of the Winter Queen. She couldn't just hunker down anymore hoping Mab would stop. With Cora and Tom gone, she was now the expert. She had to do something.

Through the window, she saw Lissy sitting on the sofa, reading the newspaper. Janey gave herself a few more minutes before going inside. When she opened the door, Lissy flung the newspaper to the far end of the sofa and moved to the radio as if she had been there all along. She began to adjust the dial in a nervous fashion, passing back and forth over the channel for the Jack Benny Show.

"I'm sorry, sweetheart, but… we have to go back."

Lissy stopped dialing and glared at the floor for a few seconds before standing and running across the room. Flinging herself into Janey's arms, she began to weep, her face against Janey's chest. Through her tears she said defiantly, "I told you we should have burned that place to the ground." Janey couldn't argue. They stood that way for the longest time.

5

Janey sat at the corner table of Aylesbury's most popular cafe. Setting aside a copy of the Aylesbury Press-Courier, she took a sip of her tea. Her eyes rose to meet Lissy's across the table, dressed in dungarees and a checkered, untucked, red flannel shirt. People glowered. Janey had to admit it was odd that this freckled face girl who was dressed like a migrant farmer, also wore her hair like she was ready for the ballroom. She smiled to herself; they just didn't know Lissy.

They had vacated Kingsport the Monday following Lissy's last day in school. Janey didn't give notice; she just didn't show up for work. She felt bad for Mr. Redmond, but it was important she drop out of sight. They were never going back.

Janey and Lissy had spent the last three days at the Sentinel Inn out on the Aylesbury Pike. They were on a mission of discovery. It had been the words spoken by Ross Baily, way back on that night of the reservoir meeting, that had brought them to this place. Yes, there was a demolition shack and that meant dynamite. It had taken them nearly two days to locate their target.

The demolition companies had concluded their work but were slow in dismantling the depots used for storage and supply. There were still shacks full of tools, heavy carts, and dynamite, scattered over the countryside. Janey and Lissy, in their search, had finally discovered the one Ross Bailey had mentioned. It stood about a mile south of the Pike. It was purely happenstance that they had stopped to empty their bladders and stumbled on an overgrown temporary road leading south toward Bibury, the first town to die at the hands of R.J. Brown's Woodpeckers.

A large dog had been tied near the door of the supply shack and occasionally a grizzled old man, acting as watchman, would show up on foot to feed and water the hound before trudging back to his tiny hovel sequestered in a nearby grove of trees.

The two had crept up on the shack from behind, weaving their way through a coppice of pines. Lissy wanted to do all the work, so Janey let her, watching with some amazement as she utilized her plan. Lissy tossed the dog strips of bacon she had saved from breakfast and then she lay a line of them out toward the far side of the clearing. While the animal was eating, Lissy cut its tether, using a paring knife she had stolen from the inns' kitchen. The animal had followed the trail of meat into the trees. It's new found freedom after years of being tied to the shed must have been overwhelming and after consuming every last piece of pork, it bounded away. It could be seen topping a hill in the distance, baying as it ran.

The old man was soon giving chase, shouting "Beezer, you get your ass back here, you worthless mutt!" along with other expletives. They had just enough time to pry the hasp loose that secured the door, get inside, and find one of the fresher boxes of 'Extra' Dynamite. Taking the entire crate and a roll of fuse, they made for the car, taking turns carrying their dangerous booty.

They hadn't been so concerned about the watchman catching them, as getting back to the inn before the gloaming set in. Letting out the clutch of the Ford, Janey said, "We go tomorrow morning," and they sped away.

"Finally," Lissy said and lifting her plaid shirt, she checked the chain she wore as a belt. Touching the iron comb in her hair one time, she nodded and grinned.

The following morning, they were packed with a small suitcase each. Janey removed the ceramic milk bowl and brushed the bread crumbs under the door mat. Other residents commented how nice it was of them to feed the stray cat that had been hanging around the inn. Mrs. Devereux, two doors down, had said, "You should catch it and give it a good home, I'm sure your daughter would love to have it." When Janey gave her an inquisitive look, Devereux responded, "You know? That stray cat you been feeding."

The thought that rolled through her mind, was, "I'd like to catch it, alright, but what I want to do to it afterwards doesn't involve taking it home." After loading the car, she and Lissy went down for breakfast.

6

Stopping at the Aylesbury general store, Janey bought a roll of cotton cord, two road flares, a tin of safety matches, and a box of forty-one caliber ammunition for the two-shot derringer still in her pocket.

They were soon driving south, and arriving at the small town of Scottsburg, Janey turned off the highway to follow Tilson's Furrow to where it ended and Parson's Ridge began.

Janey parked the car in front of the permanent wooden barrier that kept vehicles from crashing head first into the trees. Finding an overgrown lane about fifty feet to the left of it, her and Lissy headed out on foot.

The lane used to be the entrance to the Olney farm, a family Janey had known in her youth. She would sometimes go there and spend the day with Nora Olney, a classmate. The farm failed due to the Depression and Nora's father soon packed them all up and moved away, leaving the place to the bank—and decay.

Janey and Lissy sat for the longest time in a thicket watching the empty farm house. When they decided there was no one around, they took the dynamite, fuse, matches, and cord to the house. The two took turns kicking at the backdoor until the lock gave and the door swung open violently. A family of mice scattered, and a trapped sparrow that had found its way in through a broken windowpane was set free, startling the two as it fluttered past.

Putting everything on the dust covered table in the center of the kitchen, Janey noticed that Lissy had brought the flour sack they usually carried their lunch in. She thought how considerate of the girl, but there would be no time to eat until well after their mission was complete—if they survived.

They began to bind the sticks of dynamite with the cotton cord; six per bundle, leaving the box to sit empty on the tabletop. Cutting and putting varying lengths of fuse in each one, they packed them into an old Boy Scout backpack that someone had left behind in the room they had occupied at the Sentinel.

Janey tied her chain around her waist, touched her necklace through the fabric of her dress and then donning the explosive filled backpack, they left the house.

Finding the path that ran the full length of Parson's Ridge from the Olney's to Mount Ovis, they headed for Nixie's Bluff. Lissy, flour sack swinging from her hand, hummed *Ring Around The Rosie* as she took up the lead.

The day was sunny, but cool. The birds sang and everything appeared as it had back when Janey trudged this way as a girl. When the two came in sight of Carter House, Lissy stopped humming and they slowed their pace. Arriving at the orchard fence, they could clearly see what had once been a magnificent house, now looking like a gargantuan mound of flora.

As they stood watching, the clouds began to form overhead. The two locked eyes and said in unison, "Mab." They both knew they had until the storm blocked the sun, then they could expect the Unseelie Court to make an appearance. They'd be lucky if they could get back to Olney's before being snatched.

"Ready?" Janey said. Lissy nodded, a look of excitement mixed with fear upon her face.

"Go!" Janey said and they broke for the house, both knowing their assigned tasks. One thing they had over R.J. Brown's Woodpeckers was that they knew what they were dealing with long before they arrived. Time was of the essence. None of it could be wasted, standing around, jawing, smoking, and wondering what was happening as unnatural events occurred around them, initiated by Mab.

They placed the first charge at the right rear corner, Janey pulling the bundle from the backpack and handing it to Lissy who quickly pushed it behind the thicker vines just above the foundation. Moving swiftly around the front of the house to the opposite side, they placed the rest as they went, the fuses getting progressively longer to insure they would be well out of danger before the first one went off.

After Lissy placed the last bundle at the left rear corner, Janey whispered, "Okay, head back to the car, I'll meet you there," and making eye contact to be sure the girl understood, Janey watched Lissy turn and run, the flour sack clutched to her chest.

Striking one of the road flares, Janey brought it to a sizzling, bright red, the heat radiating off her face. She began to light fuses as she hurriedly moved back around to the starting point. When she bent to light the fuse of the first one they had placed, movement caught her eye. Turning, she saw Lissy had not returned to the car after all. She now stood next to the stable, the empty flour sack on the ground and a large brown wine bottle in her hand, a burning linen fuse hanging from its mouth.

The teen grinned wickedly and then threw the bottle with its flaming wick through the open stable door. Letting go with a long-drawn-out whoop, Lissy broke and ran in the direction of the car.

Janey had about a minute before the clouds reached the sun or the first sticks of dynamite went off. Pulling the last remaining bundle from the pack, she lit the fuse and kicked open the backdoor. Toddler sized creatures hissed and scattered to evade the light.

"Tough luck, fuckers," she growled and tossed the dynamite, along with the flare, inside. Dropping the empty pack, she sprinted away, picking up speed as she moved toward the back of the property.

The clouds above her began to roil as what seemed like a never-ending swarm of winged creatures shot up out of the well to disappear into the billowing vapor. Crossing her fingers, she forced herself to run faster.

"Please, please, please," she pled to no one.

Lissy suddenly appeared on her left, breaking from a thicket. She grinned at Janey and began twirling her chain above her head as she ran.

"You're supposed to be in the car," Janey huffed out.

"I know," was all Lissy said. Janey recognized that face. The old Lissy was back. The girl had fulfilled her vow.

The wind began to blow, causing the leaves to flutter and debris to lift into the air. Hundreds of Whip-poor-wills began to pipe, and just below the noise of it all, the sound of the Unseelie Court forming up to begin their run.

Janey and Lissy were just out of sight of Carter House when they heard the first bundle detonate. Consecutive blasts followed that were so loud, they were heard by folks clear over in Hadley.

One passenger, waiting at the new train station there, commented to the agent, "I thought them Woodpeckers were done blowing stuff up over Gowan way?"

"Thought so too," the agent said, removing his hat and scratching his head as he gazed eastward.

Fiona Kemp, who had been fishing in her boat along the shore of the reservoir just south of Mount Ovis, heard the thunder, saw the smoke rising in the distance, and assumed the old Carter mansion had been struck by lightning. She later told Henry Witmer at the Boudin general store, "Well, if the storm had lasted long enough to make rain, that ol' Carter place would never have burnt."

Nobody saw the mansion collapse in on itself, nor the bright, baseball sized orb as it streaked from a broken window in the belvedere mere seconds before it crashed down.

The bright little comet, shooting away at tree top height toward the Atlantic Ocean, soon caught the attention of an elderly gentleman walking with his wife on the Quincy Bay beach.

"Looky there, dear, first time I've ever seen St. Elmo's Fire!"

"That makes two of us," she retorted. "Now, let's get home, its lunchtime and I'm starving."

***

The model A raced north and then turned east, nearly taking the corner on two wheels. Smiling bigger than she had in a long time, Lissy said, "You're driving like a maniac." Janey grinned without looking at her, nodded, and responded with a, "Yep!"

Upon reaching the east side of the reservoir, she found the road that used to run into Grunewyck from Princeton. Pulling up to another, newer, bigger wooden barricade with a large sign that read, 'ROAD CLOSED', Janey shut off the car and got out. Lissy followed, her chain still in hand. Moving around the large wooden barrier, they walked to the shore.

Across the vast expanse of water, two pillars of smoke rose to a sky gone back to blue. Carter House burned along with its stable. Only a portion of the belvedere stuck up from what could be construed as the biggest bonfire ever seen in Hantescree County. In another hour, it too would be consumed by fire. As they watched, the wind began to pick up speed, fanning the flames, and bending the columns of smoke toward the north east.

Janey began to cry, her face going into her hands. Lissy wrapped an arm around her waist and whispered, "It's gonna be okay." Lissy's face showed no signs of despair, but it wasn't her house they had just blown up.

They spent the night at Bella's Rest on the outskirts of Concord. The ceramic bowl of milk remained untouched. The hunk of Bella Huel's homemade bread had been gnawed by a mouse or two, but nothing else. They decided to stay one more day before heading for Salem.

Dinner time found them in the dining hall; free of their chains. Lissy wore her hair down and brushed, the iron made comb abandoned to a nightstand up the stairs. After a decent meal, they sat together on the veranda, just rocking and talking until well after the dark of night had veiled the land.

R.C. Davis is the author of several novels, all, of the 5-star variety, along with numerous short stories that can be found in many venerated anthologies throughout the land. His lifelong love is Gothic Horror, and when not rendering his own epic tales, he is avidly reading Stephen King, John Langan, and other greats. R.C. enjoys a good cup of tea and walking in the evening, when the bats are on the wing, Nighthawks soar through the indigo void above, and the Whip-poor-will pipe from the mist filled woods.